The Winter People

The Winter People

REBEKAH L. PURDY

Entangled Publishing, LLC
2614 South Timberline Road
Suite 109
Fort Collins, CO 80525

Visit our website at www.entangledpublishing.com.

Edited by Robin Haseltine and Liz Pelletier
Cover design by Frauke Spanuth & Kelley York

Print ISBN 978-1-62266-368-2
Ebook ISBN 978-1-62266-369-9

Manufactured in the United States of America

First Edition September 2014

10 9 8 7 6 5 4 3 2 1

To my very own Brady Bunch: Tim, Devin, Alyssa, Kris,
Barrett, Erin, and Chase

Winter

I had a dream, which was not all a dream.
The bright sun was extinguish'd, and the stars
Did wander darkling in the eternal space,
Rayless, and pathless, and the icy earth
Swung blind and blackening in the moonless air;
Morn came and went—and came, and brought no day,
And men forgot their passions in the dread
Of this their desolation; and all hearts
Were chill'd into a selfish prayer for light:

—Lord Byron

PROLOGUE

Winter had come again, and *she* lurked in the frozen crevices. Waiting. Hidden amongst the woodland, ready for the next game to begin. This would be the last chance we had to take back our lives.

The frigid air nipped at my skin like tiny razor-sharp teeth. A constant reminder that I was at *her* mercy.

The opening of the backdoor caught my attention, and I watched a blond head poke outside, followed by a bright pink coat.

Voices drifted from the house. "You stay away from that pond, Salome. I mean it," someone hollered. "And put a hat on."

"I'm not a baby, Mom. I'm six now," Salome said, slamming the door shut. She giggled as snowflakes the size of quarters fell from the sky, landing on her outstretched hands.

Salome jumped off the deck into a large snowdrift then raced into the main yard. She giggled again, spinning around in circles until she fell to the ground in a heap.

"Is that her?"

"Yes," I answered. *"Doris's granddaughter—our last hope."*

"I want to see." One of the others clambered up beside me.

The wind picked up, sending tiny tornadoes of snow whipping across the yard and between the trees. The gate at the far edge of the yard groaned open and shut. Salome leaped to her feet. A look of horror washed over her face as she stared at it. She knew as well as we did that no one was to open the gate. Ever.

"Oh no." Salome's boots crunched across the yard as she hurried to latch it. I watched her take off her gloves then fasten the bolt in place. She jumped back as if something had spooked her.

"Unlock it…" her voice called. *"Let me in."*

Salome shook her head and backed away, bumping into a large oak tree.

"Get away from there," I called. Fear gripped me while images of past failures swam through my mind.

At the sound of my voice, Salome spun around, searching for me. But I ducked behind a nearby tree. She moved away from the fence and down the slope of the small hill. Her eyes fixed on the pond.

What did she see?

Her steps took her closer. "Cleo, kitty-kitty, get off the ice." She inched nearer until she stood on the shore.

Shielding my eyes with my hand, I stared out over the pond, but saw nothing except snow and ice.

"Cleo, you're being naughty. Mommy said stay off the ice." Salome pushed forward.

"Yes, that's it," the voice called to her.

"No! Don't listen. Get away from the pond," I yelled.

But it was too late. Salome raced onto the ice, slipping and sliding as she tried to maintain her balance. A loud *crack* reverberated through the woods. The ice broke beneath her, sending her plunging into the dark depths. I heard her gasp before she went under. She struggled to get a hold of the ice and pull herself up, but it kept breaking beneath her flailing arms.

Terror ripped through me as I hurried to her. When I reached the place she'd fallen through, a gaping hole stared back at me.

Without a second thought, I leaped in after her. It was cold. A familiarity I was all too comfortable with. Through the murk and darkness, I saw her small form sinking into the depths. Her pale blond hair fanned around her small body and, for a moment, I thought she was dead, until I saw her eyes open, looking right at me.

The others swam around us, helping me push her back to the surface. We dragged her from the frigid waters and lay her atop the ice.

"*You shouldn't have saved the girl. She'll know you've helped her,*" one of my companions said, his voice like wind chimes.

I brushed the wet hair from Salome's face. "*I couldn't let her die. She's but a child.*"

"Mama." She stared wildly around her.

The wind howled in the background. Snowflakes swirled like someone had ripped open a pillow full of feathers.

"*Quiet child—you need to listen close.*" My other companion grabbed Salome's face in her hands. "*You are not to step foot in these woods again or come near the pond. If you do,* she'll *find you. Do you understand?*"

Her eyes wide, Salome nodded her head, teeth chattering.

In the distance, the girl's parents and grandparents called her name. As the snow's intensity strengthened, we drifted into it, disappearing from sight, but lingering until help came.

"*She will likely grow into a beautiful girl,*" I said, staring at her blue-gray eyes.

"Beautiful and dangerous, Milord."

"Heed our warnings," I whispered to Salome. *"Stay away from here. And stay away from us."* With a wave of my hand, I distorted my features, twisting them with my magic until I knew all she saw was a hideous monster staring back at her.

She screamed, and I knew she wouldn't dare play outside her grandparents' property again. At least, for her sake, I hoped not.

Winter

When coldness wraps this suffering clay,
Ah! whither strays the immortal mind?
It cannot die, it cannot stay,
But leaves its darken'd dust behind.
Then, unembodied, doth it trace
By steps each planet's heavenly way?
Or fill at once the realms of space,
A thing of eyes, that all survey?

—Lord Byron

Chapter One

"Come on in, Salome." Grandma ushered me inside on Friday afternoon. She gave me a warm smile that crinkled the edges of the blue-gray eyes we shared and wrapped me in a tight hug. "Nasty stuff, Michigan in winter and this snow."

"Yeah, tell me about it." My short drive over the icy two-track had been hell, only colder. Even now, I couldn't get into the safety of the house quick enough.

Grandma's intense eyes focused on my face. "I've got a couple of things to finish up. Why don't you go on into the living room with Grandpa?"

She disappeared behind a concealed door into the hidden room. This was the first time I'd seen it unlocked since I was little. The scent of old books drifted from the room, and I took a step forward. When Grandma saw me trying to glimpse inside, she shut the door. I wondered as I always had why they'd never allowed me to go in there.

With a frown, I ambled into the living room. "Hey Gramps. What'cha reading?"

He held up an Arizona travel brochure. "Trying to see what's in this blasted state," he grumbled. "Damn doctors, sending me away from my home."

I flopped on the couch beside him and leaned my head on his shoulder. "Wish you didn't have to go."

"Me too, pumpkin. But winter won't last forever, and then we'll be back. It'll be summer before you know it, and you'll be over here stealing my ice cream."

"I don't steal your ice cream." I laughed. "Grandma gives it to me."

"A bloody conspiracy. That woman is always giving away the good stuff."

"I heard that." Grandma joined us in the living room. She had on a long gray coat, black boots, and carried a knotted walking stick that reminded me of a staff. She gestured for me to follow her toward the door.

"I'm all set now. I'll show you what you need to do."

I stood up, nice and slow, like my legs had forgotten how to work. Worry tightened like a noose around my neck.

So much for therapy.

God, I was such a freak. Most kids loved winter. It meant sledding, ice-skating, snow angels, and snowballs. Even the badass guys enjoyed whipping donuts in the school parking lot. But for me it meant nightmares of icy dark water and skeletal trees heavy with snow.

Chills ran up my spine as I glanced toward the backyard. Eleven long years I'd heeded the warning that whispered around in my head and the hideous face that went with it. I'd stayed out of the woods and away from the pond. Eleven years of avoiding winter, or at least trying to. And now, I had no choice but to face it head on. At seventeen, you'd think I would've outgrown my fear of winter—of the voices I'd heard.

"Salome." Grandma grabbed my mittened hand in hers. With a gentle tug, she led me forward. "I'm sorry we couldn't afford a caretaker. I know how hard this is for you. But with your mom on crutches and your dad on the road driving his truck, we had no one else to ask. No one we could trust to take care of things."

"It's okay," I lied. If Mom hadn't gotten hurt then I wouldn't have to do this. She could've handled it, and I'd just stay inside where it was safe.

Gusts of wind billowed into the house as she threw open the door. Snowdrifts covered the stairs, deck, and path looking like small mountains. In the distance, I saw the gazebo my grandpa had built a couple summers ago. It, too, was coated in white like a frosted cupcake.

My eyes drifted to the pond. No ice yet, but it was only a matter of time. The water rippled, lapping against the shore and dock, the breeze tracing invisible fingers over the surface.

Grandma led me toward the burgundy-colored shed. Producing a key from her pocket, she released my hand and unlocked the door.

"This is where I keep most of the supplies." She gestured to the large bags of seed. Small trinkets and gadgets I'd never seen before littered the shelves. Water jugs, animal food, shovels, rakes, and piles of sticks took up close to every inch of space in the shed.

Turning to Grandma, I slid my hat out of my face. "You've got a ton of stuff in here."

Her gaze became serious as she produced a list for me. "Yes, and it's all needed. You've got the seed to feed the squirrels and birds with. There's some feed to put out for the deer and the other—um, animals." As Grandma peered away from me, I caught a nervous glint in her eyes.

"What's wrong?"

"Nothing child. You just listen closely, okay?"

I shrugged. That's why I was there.

"Every day you need to check the food and water supply for the feeders. After you've finished, you'll take one of these trinkets and place it in the trunk of the oak tree, near the pond." She pointed to the shelves of jewelry, silverware, bits of string, and shoes. There were old watches, scarves, cups, plates, and even picture frames.

Maybe Grandma lost her mind? Who put things in a tree? Seriously?

"Why do we have to leave stuff out here?" The hair on the back of my neck stood on end.

She stared in the distance. "Our family has always done it. Call it superstition or what have you—but we've done it forever and need to continue to do so. Don't forget."

Not quite the answer I was looking for. If anything, it put me more on edge—as if I needed more things to freak out about right now. "Okay, so feed the animals, put things in the tree, what else?"

"Most importantly, you must make sure the back gate stays locked. Once a week, take a couple pieces of this rowan wood and entwine it in the fence." Grandma bent down and picked three twigs from the pile.

My grandparents had several acres of land, all of which were fenced off from the rest of the forest, and they were adamant about keeping the gates secure. Private property signs were posted along the perimeter to ward off any unwanted guests. Like they were scared someone might actually drive all the way out here just to snoop around or steal something. Somehow though, it felt safer on *this* side of the fence, other than the pond, of course, which unfortunately sat right down the path from the house.

"Go ahead and grab a bag of food and come with me."

Picking up a partial sack of seed, I stumbled after her. We came to the first feeder, which was close to the house. I emptied some of the contents into the container, and then on we went. I filled four dishes, until we ventured toward the pond.

My mouth went dry, my grip tightened on the containers. A scream lodged in my throat as I remembered the cold dark depths. How my lungs burned for air. The voices and the glowing beings in the water as I fell deeper and deeper. Beings that I knew now were just a hallucination, but still held power over me as though they were real. I could almost feel the bitter bite of the ice on my back as I lay on top of the frozen pond.

Grandma stopped walking and whirled around. "Salome, it's okay. You're safe." She covered the distance between us and clutched my shoulders.

I let her pull me into her arms. Her hug warmed me and her soothing murmurs calmed me as tears slipped down my face.

"S-sorry. I haven't been out here in the winter since…"

Grandma kissed my forehead. "I know. But you're strong. The sooner you get this part behind you, the sooner you'll be able to move on with your life."

My body trembled, but I continued to follow Grandma to the last feeder.

I see her. She's back. After all this time, she's come back.

I spun around, glancing over the yard. Who said that? My hat fell from my head when a low hanging branch caught hold of it and knocked it from my head. My hair blew about my face, like small snapping whips.

"She's beautiful."

"And a danger to us all."

"The old lady is with her…"

I leaned down to retrieve my hat from the ground, but a current of air blew it across the yard, toward the water's edge. Pushing past my grandma, I raced after it, snagging it right before it went into the pond.

For a moment, I was face to face with my reflection. And just below the surface, a pale hand reached up to touch it. The water rippled as if stroking my image. *No. This isn't happening.* The voices were back. I glanced at Grandma, but she didn't seem to notice them. No one else ever did. It was just me. Crazy. Psychotic. Me.

What was I doing this close to the water? Panic set in, my feet rooted in place.

"Just as I remember her."

"Come away from there." Grandma jerked me back. "You nearly walked right in."

Puzzled and scared, I stared at the pond but I didn't see any hands or strange people coming out. God, I was losing it. The psychiatrist said I might have relapses from time to time, but it'd been a while since I'd heard the voices. And what about the hand I'd seen in the water, had I made that up or had it really been there? Was I losing touch with reality, again?

"Salome, are you listening to me?" Her forehead creased with more wrinkles.

"Yes, I'm fine. And I didn't *nearly* walk into the water. Not even close." I shuddered because this was the second time something had led me toward the pond. This time, I didn't feel any sinister presence, though.

"Just be more careful next time."

When we got back to the house, Grandpa had suitcases and

boxes sitting in the living room. His coat hung over the back of the chair, and he was locking the windows.

Everything had been picked up. No magazines on the coffee tables; remotes were on top of the television. The dishes were washed and put away, no dust clung to the pictures and knick-knacks that lined the large shelves.

Suddenly, it hit me. They were really leaving. And they entrusted me to keep an eye on their house.

Grandma changed out of her yard clothes, then came back wearing a jogging suit and heavy winter coat.

"Well, I think that about does it. Make sure you come over to clean out the fridge and freezer. I don't want any food going to waste." Grandpa's keys jingled in his hand. Grabbing two suitcases, he headed into the garage.

I picked up some of their things and followed him. I hated good-byes. It was only for a few months, but their house was my second home. At least during summer months, when I stayed nestled inside with Grandpa on the couch, eating ice cream in front of a fan.

"Don't look so forlorn, Salome. We'll be back before you know it." Grandma tucked me into her arms, wrapping me up like a blanket.

I took a deep breath, filling it with her peppermint and floral scent. "I'll miss you."

"I'll miss you too, sweetie." She pulled back then handed me the ring of keys. "Take good care of things. If anything comes up, call."

A nervous edge had entered her voice, making me question what she was worried about. I waited for her to elaborate, but instead she turned away.

Grandpa jerked me into a tight hug, making my ribs feel like they might pop through my back. "Be good, kiddo. And try to stay warm." He released me and climbed into the car. I locked the side door then went onto the porch to watch them pull away.

I wondered if their leaving meant bad things to come. Things that could change my life. And I was scared.

Tomorrow I'd be on my own. Alone in the woods.

*O*nce they disappeared from view, I drove over to my friend, Kadie's. She'd understand.

I explained about my grandparents dropping the bomb after school today. That I'd have to watch their house all winter. Be in their backyard alone.

"You've got a little time before your date tonight, and I know just what you need: Perky Joe's," she said when I showed up at her door. The local coffee shop, home to all the high school degenerates. She liked the disturbed guys she met there, most of whom had various piercings and tattoos. Me, I tended to veer more toward the light.

She grabbed some cash from her purse and steered me toward her car. It wasn't long before we'd pulled into a spot near the coffee shop.

The bell above the door jingled as we pushed inside. Coffee and hot chocolate overwhelmed my senses as I stared around the room. Maybe this would help.

The small tables had glass mosaics on top of them and chairs that looked more like bar stools. Dark cherry wood lined the walls, gothic figures carved into the wooden molding. The floor-to-ceiling scarlet curtains, swaying beneath the forced air blowing from vents, looked like waves of blood. Or maybe not.

"I think I know why people might be perky after coming here. Check out the new baristas." Kadie nudged me in the ribs, pointing to the two guys behind the counter.

The first one didn't look much older than us with his shaggy golden hair and skin that seemed to have a natural bronze glow. His brown eyes would make a cup of coffee jealous. I gasped and my stomach took a tumble, like I was falling off a mountain. A smile tugged at his lips when he saw us staring. As if he'd expected us to notice him.

Next to him stood a guy with curly dark hair and eyes the color of topaz. His gaze did a head-to-toe sweep of Kadie then he gave her a smile that lured her right up to the counter.

"Afternoon. What can I get you?"

"I'll have a mocha-latte." Kadie sounded sultry. "With a cherry on top."

She was a complete seductress. Poor guy, he didn't have a chance. But he nodded, unfazed by her in the least, and went to work preparing her drink.

"And for you?" The blond guy's voice sounded like warm, rich chocolate. He stepped closer and turned his deep brown eyes on me. For a moment it felt like he knew my every secret; the way he watched me made me think he recognized me. My insides twisted and churned, and I shifted my gaze to his tattoos, following the strange looping design up his arm. The intricate green and gold strands changed into vines around his bicep, like a cuff.

Vines? Since when did tats change shape in front of my eyes?

Oh no, not now. Not again. I really was crazy.

I reached for the counter as my legs grew weak.

"Salome, hey, are you okay?" Kadie gripped my arm, urging me to sit down.

I buried my head in my hands for a few seconds, attempting to push the images away. I had to get it together or Mom would send me to the shrink if she found out I had had another episode. She'd been on the verge this morning.

I forced myself to clear my mind. Keep calm.

"S—sorry, I'll have a caramel cappuccino," I said, as the blond guy leaned toward me.

"Coming right up." He stood, his nametag catching my eye.

"Gareth?" I said aloud.

"Yeah?"

"That's an interesting name." I shot Kadie a glance in an attempt to shift their attention from me.

"Well, this here is Simeon." She grinned, gesturing to the dark haired guy. Kadie took a sip of her latte then said, "Gareth and Simeon, your names sound like they belong to medieval knights."

"And doth the damsel need rescuing?" Simeon leaned against the counter, his arms folded at his chest.

"Always." She batted her eyes at him.

"How does Saturday work for you?"

"Perfect," Kadie said.

I watched the two exchange numbers and turned to see Gareth peering at me, his long golden lashes making me envious. He closed the lid on my cup, but kept staring. Did he know something?

Shit. If I kept this up, I'd be questioning everyone's motives for even glancing at me. This guy was just a barista, although he looked more like someone who ought to be a bodyguard or a bouncer.

Gareth handed me a napkin. "Try and take care of yourself." His fingertips brushed mine, and I was filled with sudden warmth, like sunshine hitting you on a summer day.

I stared at the tattoos once more—the shapes looked different now. Instead of the spiraling loops, they seemed more gothic, almost pointy. Had I imagined the vines?

Chills raced up my back, making my scalp itch. I managed a shaky smile. "Um, thanks."

"I'll see you around," he said as we headed to the door.

"Yeah, maybe." I glanced at him one last time as we walked out of the café. Would I see him again? Better question, did I want to? Yet another person who'd learn how crazy I really was. And of all people, I didn't want him to know. That sounded insane, right? I shouldn't care what this virtual stranger thought of me. But I did; I deeply wanted him to accept me, befriend me, and love me even.

"Get over yourself, Salome," I muttered to myself, shaking my head, "He's just a barista."

CHAPTER TWO

*A*t six o'clock, Kadie was back at my front door. "Um, I thought we decided on the sexy blue sweater?" She quirked an eyebrow at me. "You haven't even changed out of your school clothes." She tugged me down the hall toward my room. "C'mon, let's get you dressed. Otherwise we'll be late."

I squirmed from her grasp. "I—I'm not going."

I was supposed to have my very first date tonight with Colton. Colton. Freaking. Myers. Captain of the basketball team. My lifelong crush. My dress for the date that night sat on my bed like a guilty reminder of the promise I was about to break.

Kadie's face fell. "Salome, you have to go. You told him you'd be at his game tonight."

Taking a deep breath, I said, "Will you please tell him I can't make it?"

I hated the disappointment in her eyes. "Okay, spill, what brought this on? You were so excited earlier."

I didn't want to tell her how the swirling tats on Gareth's arm freaked me out. Instead I told her how I'd seen the forecasts and knew snow was on the way. I definitely didn't want Colton to witness my crazy-pants routine when I had a meltdown over an icy lake or snow or the cold.

Kadie gave me a sympathetic glance. "I'm sorry. This totally blows. So what do you want me to tell Colton?"

"Just tell him I'm sick. Mental illness counts, right?" I forced a laugh and crumpled onto my bed, my knees tucked under my chin.

"That's not funny." She leaned down to give me a hug. "We'll get through the winter. I promise. I'll call you later, okay?"

She shut the door, leaving me alone.

I was missing life. Why couldn't I just forget everything? Be normal for one flipping minute, without worrying that winter was going to kill me. It'd been years since the incident in the pond. I should be over it by now.

I left my bedroom and made my way onto the porch to watch Kadie pull away.

She didn't fight me on this—she never did. She made sure no one threw snowballs at me and pulled up to the school sidewalk so I wouldn't have to walk through the snow. In fourth grade, she beat up Tyler Stein when he tried to whitewash me.

All winter long Kadie made me feel comfortable, staying in when I couldn't, or wouldn't, go out. She kept me sane, not letting me fall into that cold, dark place in my mind.

I stared at the trees as they waved in the wind. Piles of leaves were stuck between the iron fence posts—our lack of raking evident as they blew across the yard. Debris littered the birdbath, the fountain long since turned off. Brown burlap covered Mom's roses, protecting them from winter. Everything seemed dead.

Dead.

The word stuck to the roof of my mouth like a sandwich

with too much peanut butter. Clutching the railing, I squeezed my eyes shut. *Focus. Breathe. Forget.*

When Kadie's car disappeared, I went back inside. Mom met me at the door, propped up on her crutches, worry creasing her forehead.

"I thought you had a date?"

"Changed my mind." My voice cracked as a sob escaped. "I hate being like this."

My shoulders shook as I buried my face in my hands.

Mom brushed my hair away from my face. "Oh, sweetie."

She let me cry until my tears dried up. By then I was hiccupping, and my nose ran like a leaky drainpipe. If anyone could've made me venture out, it would've been Colton. But here I sat, curled up on the couch with Mom, watching chick flicks and eating double chocolate fudge ice cream. My cure-all.

We'd just finished our first movie when the doorbell rang. "I'll get it." I raced for the door.

"Okay, I hope you're not going to be pissed at me, but I couldn't let you miss tonight." Kadie pushed the door wide open, pointing to the two vehicles sitting in the drive. One was hers. The other belonged to Colton Myers.

"Hey." Colton waved, coming up the sidewalk. His green eyes twinkling, he handed me a single rose then ran a hand through his shaggy dark hair. "Hope you don't mind us barging in."

Good God, I covered my shirt with my arms, wishing I'd changed.

"Salome, who's there?" Mom called from the living room.

"Kadie. She brought Colton with her," I said.

"Well, let them in."

I stood back, ushering them into the kitchen. Kadie caught my arm, dragging me toward my room. "We'll be back in a second. Salome just has to change."

When we got into my room, I turned on her. "What are you doing? Are you crazy?"

She rolled her eyes. "I'm not letting you regret your senior year. Colton really likes you. You don't think he'd be here if he didn't, do you?"

I covered my face. "But I thought you were going to tell him I'm sick?"

"Um, I never told him. Trust me. You'll be glad I did this for you."

I swallowed hard. "Please tell me you're coming with us."

"Actually, Duane Clark asked me out tonight. I kind of told him yes. But, if you need me, I can cancel," she said in a rush.

"No. I can do this." She'd already missed a lot because of me. I knew I couldn't back out of the date. Besides, Colton was in my kitchen, waiting.

"Of course you can." She tossed the black dress at me. "Tonight has been in the making for seven years, Salome. Ever since he traded his Twinkie for your cupcakes." She smiled then left me to get cleaned up.

What if Colton and I didn't have anything to talk about? My palms grew clammy with sweat. I wiped them on my dress. Or worse yet, what if he found out what a freak I really was?

I changed in record time and stood staring in the mirror, styling my straight hair to frame my heart-shaped face. I took a deep breath to calm the nervous flutters in my stomach.

He wouldn't have driven all the way over here if he didn't want me to go with him.

Heart pounding in my ears, I left the room, my shoes clicking on the floor. I spotted Kadie talking to Colton in the living room. I'd never been on a date. Almost every Friday night was spent at either my house or hers. Now, I was being forced out into the cold. Away from home, when it was supposed to snow. Why the hell did Kadie do this to me? Did she want him to see me freak out?

I pushed the panicked thoughts aside and took a deep breath. I had to do this.

After Mom called out a curfew time, Colton reached for my hand and we stepped from the security of my house. His skin was warm against mine. I caught the faint scent of soap wafting between us, his hair still damp from a shower. I cast a sideways glance to find him staring at me. He smiled, a dazzling, perfect teeth kind of smile. The kind that would make toothpaste models jealous. A prickle ran down the back of my neck, and I rubbed at it.

"I can't believe we're finally going on a date," he said. "I've wanted to ask you for a long time."

"So why didn't you?" I noticed a pair of eyes glowing in the woods. I shivered, hoping it was only a wild animal. What if it was *them*? I went still. Maybe going out wasn't such a good idea after all. My stomach sank, twisting until I thought I might throw up. I hadn't thought of *them* much in recent years, so I didn't know why I was thinking of them now. But there it was. Niggling at the back of my mind like a splinter.

He chuckled, which snapped me out of my stupor. "Because I was a chickenshit and you've never gone out with anyone at school."

Great, he noticed I didn't usually date. He probably thought I was a social pariah. I ignored the woods, turning my focus instead on him. If I didn't stare into the dark, then nothing bad would happen—or at least that's what I told myself as I tried to think of something clever to say. "Maybe I was waiting for the right guy to ask."

He smiled, and I thought maybe this dating thing wouldn't

be as hard as I thought.

When we got to his truck, he opened the door for me then went around to the other side. Colton started the vehicle and cranked up the heat.

"Why do girls always make the guys ask?" The porch light illuminated the interior as he grinned at me. "How are we supposed to know if you like us?"

"Well, I did trade you my cupcakes—"

"For my Twinkie, yeah, I remember," he said. "Three cupcakes for one Twinkie, you must've really liked me," he added, laughing.

I must've looked surprised because he chuckled again.

"I didn't think you'd remember that." The heat blasted from the vents, and I held my palms out to warm them. Daring a quick glance, I spied Colton staring at his hands.

"You'd be surprised at what I recall." He offered me his gloves, which I declined. "Like the time you fell in gym class and bumped your head on the floor. Then there was the year I had a locker across from yours. You had so many posters hanging up in it I couldn't figure out how you got the thing closed."

My face warmed as I fidgeted with the zipper on my coat. Had I been so scared all these years I'd missed noticing a boy liked me this much?

"You know, last year on Valentine's Day, I sent you carnations—" I admitted. My heart raced out of control.

"I can't believe it was you that sent them. You've got to tell Bill Decker. He accused me of sending them to myself." Colton pulled the truck onto the road, driving toward town. "If I'd known, I'd have asked you out sooner."

Relief flooded through me. "I'm glad you finally did."

After a few minutes, we parked in front of Bailey's. The place was busy, but Colton managed to find us a booth near the back. The scent of pizza clung to the air, while people talked loud to hear one another over the music. Posters of bands hung on the walls. White and red-checkered tablecloths covered each table.

The waitress stopped at the table to take our drink order, and Colton let her know he'd called ahead.

"With the crowd that's in here tonight, it'll probably be at least twenty minutes before your order's up. I hope that's okay." She set ice tea down in front of us.

When the waitress left, Colton gestured for me to follow him. We walked over to the pinball machine, which blinked with pulsating lights and played eighties music my parents would like.

"Here, you go first." He dropped quarters into the machine.

Three balls rolled down, and I pulled the trigger back, shooting off the first one. It banged and bumped against the fake space ships, wormholes, and rubber bumpers. The ball rolled toward the bottom.

I squeezed the buttons at the side to hit the ball, but missed. "Ah, I just lost the ball." I laughed, feeling Colton come stand behind me. He reached around me, his breath warm on my cheek as he leaned down, and tingles inched down my spine.

"If you don't mind, I can help you."

Was he kidding? Of course I didn't mind. My pulse raced as his chest rested against my back.

"You've got to keep your fingers on the buttons," he said. "Like this."

He let me fling up the next ball. His hands covered mine on the buttons. Colton pushed my fingers down when the ball got close, sending the paddles flipping it back up.

"We did it." I squealed as the ball zoomed across the game, triggering more points.

God, he was gorgeous and sweet. His proximity made me think of anything but pinball. And for tonight, he was all mine.

After losing again, we sat down and waited for our pizza.

"That was fun." I took a sip of tea. "I've never played pinball before."

"Now you know what you were missing." He grinned, crossing his arms over his chest. "So how come I never see you in town?"

I grimaced, twisting a straw wrapper around my fingers. "I don't leave my house much."

"We'll have to change that, won't we?"

I raised an eyebrow at him. Did he want to see me again? From across the room, I spotted Bill Decker and Trina Gulvante. They waved, and I could tell they were surprised to see us together. We didn't run with the same crowds. Colton hung out with the jocks and preps. Me? I just had Kadie. The only friend who'd survived my weirdness and freak outs growing up.

"Hey, what's happening?" Bill sauntered over to our table.

"Not a whole lot," Colton answered. "Bill, you remember Salome."

Bill smirked. "Yeah, we've gone to the same school since kindergarten. And you haven't shut up about her since like fifth grade."

"Hey, Bill," I said.

"I'm glad you said yes to this dill weed. If I had to spend one more year listening to him talk about asking you out and not doing it, I might've choked him."

Colton's face turned red. "Don't start," he warned.

I decided to save Colton from his friend. "Did Colton tell you I'm the one who sent him the flowers?"

Bill chuckled. "No way, that was you? Damn it! I owe him ten bucks now."

Colton grinned. "That's right buddy, pay up."

"I'll catch ya next week." Bill hurried off, leading Trina to another booth.

"Thanks." He turned to me. "He doesn't know when to shut up sometimes."

I stifled a giggle. "I didn't mind, really." And I didn't because now I knew my fantasies weren't one-sided.

My mouth watered as the waitress came over with our pizza. She cut us each a slice and put it on our plates. The cheese was stringy, and I had a hard time keeping it off my chin. And the sauce definitely had garlic in it. Great, my breath was probably rancid. To my relief the waitress dropped some after-dinner mints on the table.

Colton and I spent the remainder of the meal talking about school and our families. We chatted for a couple of hours, until I glanced down at my watch. It was after eleven.

He saw me checking the time and clutched my hand. "Sorry, I forgot your curfew is coming up."

"Yeah, Mom wanted me home by midnight," I said.

He smiled then he stood and grabbed the bill. "Then let's get you home. I don't want to make a bad impression. Otherwise your parents won't let me take you out again."

Colton paid for our meal, then took my hand as we headed toward the door. As soon as we stepped outside I stopped in my tracks. Large white flakes fluttered from the sky. The ground was already covered under more than an inch of snow. Frigid gusts tugged at my loose hair. Flakes stuck to my skin like heavy masking tape. *It* was happening. Winter. My knees locked. Crap. Not now. I sucked in deep breaths of air.

"Salome." He clutched me to his chest. "Are you okay?"

"I'm sorry." I managed a shaky smile. "Maybe, I should wait inside and have Kadie come get me."

He stared at me, then seemed to have an "aha" moment. "Why don't you wait in Bailey's while I clean off the truck? I'll pull around to get you when I'm done."

Colton touched my face, then ushered me back inside. I sat on a bench in the lobby until he parked his truck in front of the entrance. He rushed from the vehicle to open my door, shutting it only after I had my seat belt on.

I clenched my hands together. After tonight, I doubted he'd want to see me again. "I'm sorry if I ruined our date."

He stopped at a red light. "You didn't ruin anything. Kadie gave me a heads up about the snow thing."

"Wh-what?"

He pulled the truck into a nearby parking lot then turned to me. "She explained how you fell through the ice when you were six and that winter scares you."

I gave a bitter laugh. "Did she tell you I don't like to leave my house when it gets cold out?"

Tears painted streaks down my cheeks and I stared at my dress. I sounded insane.

Colton stunned me when he reached over and threaded his fingers through mine. "I don't care what issues you have with winter. I like you. And I'm not going anywhere unless you tell me you don't want to see me." Squeezing my hand, he whispered, "We're all scared of something, Salome. It's human nature."

I turned my head and smiled at the sincerity in his eyes. "I've tried so hard to forget that night, but it haunts me."

"We'll get through it. I'll come to your house after basketball games. We don't have to go into town. We can stay in. Just give me a chance, okay?"

I tilted my face upward, studying him. He looked serious. Maybe he was as crazy as me. How else could I explain his willingness to date me? The truth was, I'd always been drawn to him. "You might need serious therapy after me."

He slid back behind the steering wheel, chuckling. "You're worth it. Any girl who'd send a guy flowers for Valentine's Day is a keeper."

Even though he'd made me feel somewhat better, nothing he did or said would chase away the terror of facing my nightmares. Tomorrow I'd have to walk the woods.

Goose bumps prickled across my skin. I'd never feel warm again.

Chapter Three

The next day I stumbled from bed, having tossed and turned all night. The visions of icicles falling from the eaves of my grandparents' house and piercing my chest made me shiver. All I pictured was my body sprawled on the ground, the sound of tinkling voices standing over me telling me I should've heeded their warning.

I cringed.

When I walked into our dining room, ice and snow covered the floor-to-ceiling windows. The patterns looked like squashed flakes and leaves. Killer veins of cold—waiting for me.

Mom looked up from her coffee when I plopped down across from her at the kitchen table. "You okay?"

Shrugging, I grabbed two pancakes from the platter; their steaming scent made my stomach growl. "I'm fine."

I slathered butter onto my pancakes then drizzled the hot maple syrup on top. After snatching a couple sausage links, I concentrated on my food. I didn't want to think about what I had to do next.

"So I thought, if you wanted, I could sit on Grandma and Grandpa's deck while you check the feeders. That way you won't be alone." Mom glanced at me over her mug.

God, I wanted her to come so bad, but staring at her crutches, the last thing I needed her to do was slip and fall. No. I had to suck it up. I had to do it. Shit, what was I saying? I didn't want to do this. Not by myself.

"I'll be fine." The words left a bitter taste in my mouth. My stomach knotted, fear settling over me.

I loaded my plate into the dishwasher then traipsed back to my room. Eyeing my clothes, I wondered if anything could keep me warm. I hurried to dress then sat on my bed, staring at the movie posters on the wall. They seemed to taunt me, calling me a wuss. My cat, Cleo, pushed into my room, her tail slinking back and forth as she attacked my feet.

"Hey, knock it off fur ball." I laughed when she swatted at my toes. "If you don't quit, I'll use you as a scarf."

She answered by rolling onto her back for a belly rub.

"Thought you'd see it my way." With a final pat on her head, I took a deep breath and slid into my fur-lined boots and heavy down coat. I headed to the hall closet and grabbed one of Dad's Elmer Fudd-looking hats, and pulled it down over my ears.

"You look like you're going hunting for grizzly bears." Mom grinned. "You want me to get your dad's rifle, too?"

With a snort, I tossed a glove at her. "Funny." But maybe it wasn't such a bad idea.

"Be careful, okay?" Her tone turned serious. "Make sure you have your cell on you."

I gnawed at my dry lips. Her worry made me more insecure about going over there.

"It's in my pocket." I squeezed my keys so tight they left markings on my palm.

Mom handed me back my glove and I stepped into the bitter winter air. Smoky tendrils of breath snaked in front of me. Standing on the porch, I gripped the railing. Too much white, too much ice. Tree branches bent beneath the weight of the snow. Birds twittered their disdain from their perches.

I was behind the fence. I'd be fine. I just had to stay out of the woods. One foot in front of the other. My boot sank into the powdery snow as I headed toward the garage and climbed into my vehicle. I sat in the Jeep, letting it warm up. Not that it mattered; the drive wasn't exactly a thousand miles away or anything. In fact, it'd probably take me five minutes to walk next door—but I wasn't ready to slog down the wooded path. The vehicle seemed safer.

Staring at the sparkling landscape, I remembered a time when I used to think winter was magical. Back when I believed in snowmen, Santa, even Jack Frost. Now, they represented the macabre.

"Come on, just put it in drive and go," I muttered. And yet, I made no attempt to shift into gear.

The dining room curtains moved back. I spotted Mom peering out at me. Ugh! Okay. Deep breath. My hand shook as I put the vehicle into drive. It inched forward and I gave a wave, proving to her that I was going to do this.

Shadows penetrated the trees, casting dismal shapes on the surface of the ivory surroundings. Each dark silhouette seemed to reach for my Jeep, urging me to turn around. I slammed on the brakes in the middle of the drive, skidding several feet before coming to a stop. My seat belt jerked me against the seat.

Great. Add whiplash to my list of problems. Reaching for the shifter, I contemplated putting it in reverse, then took my foot off the brake and moved forward.

When I got to my grandparents' house, I turned off the

engine, and went in through the garage. Beams of sunlight captured dust particles in the quiet house. Opening the slider door, I stepped onto the snow-covered deck and slipped on the wood.

"Keep it together. Just a little bit further." One. Two. Three. Four. I counted the steps to the storage shed. Eleven. Twelve. Thirteen. Fourteen. Fifteen.

Wind howled through the trees. The hair on the back of my neck stood on end. My eyes darted across the wintry landscape, watching flakes swirl down from the treetops. Nothing here.

I took the keys from my pocket and trudged farther through the deep drifts until I stood in front of the shed. Twenty steps.

See? Not so bad, you survived.

It took several tugs to get the door to slide open. The scent of spices hung in the air. It smelled like Grandma. For a moment, I felt safe. That everything really would be all right.

I filled a bucket with seeds then moved to pick a trinket from the shelf. A beaded bracelet of varying shades of blue caught my eye, and I shoved it in my pocket. Next, I filled up the water jug and set out to fill the feeders.

After I'd taken care of the first three feeders I headed to the oak tree. I slid the bracelet into the hole in the trunk and stood there staring. What did I think would happen? With a shake of my head I backed away, rubbing my nape.

The sky darkened with ominous storm clouds. Giant flakes fell onto my face, sticking to my eyelashes and cheeks. Snow blew unhindered across the yard in what looked like small tornadoes.

Oh God. It was happening again. The frigid air. The creaking of the treetops beneath the wind. Even the way the snow blew across the yard. My mouth went dry, my pulse thundered like a spring time storm.

"Everything's okay. Just keep it together. You can't lose it now," I said aloud, hoping to calm myself before I had an anxiety attack. I didn't want to have to go back on the meds again or start seeing Dr. Bosworth, who had breath that smelled like rotten mangos.

One more feeder. Toss the seeds in then I could leave.

The pond water rippled while the trees bent beneath the strong gusts. Soon, everything became so white I couldn't see the house. In the distance a strange tinkling sounded, like dozens of wind chimes. *Not the chimes. Not the chimes. Not the chimes,* I repeated over and over in my mind.

What had the shrink told me to do?

Ten, nine, eight. Breathe. Seven, six, five. Shit! I held my head in my hands for a long moment. Get it together.

Panic stole my thoughts and I raised my head, backing away from the pond as the flurries swirled toward me. Chasing me.

I bumped into something—something that felt quite human. A firm chest, arms, hands. Not something, *someone.* A shriek tumbled from my lips and I spun around to face my captor.

"It's okay. I won't hurt you," a soft masculine voice said, pale hands clinging to my arms as he kept me from falling.

My gaze followed those long fingers, then up black leather sleeves, to the most gorgeous face I'd ever seen. My breath caught in my throat. I was gawking. But I couldn't help it. His raven hair was shot with strands of blue, his face was pale and perfect, like an ice sculptor had chiseled it into existence. His eyes—oh God, his eyes. They were the palest blue I'd ever seen. Glacial. He had to be over six feet tall, muscles evident through the tight shirt he wore beneath his unzipped leather jacket.

His mouth turned up at the corners as if enjoying my scrutiny. A cocky grin that made my cheeks warm and my whole body buzz.

"You're trespassing." I tried to keep the tremble from my voice. "This is private property, or can't you read the signs?" Bravo. I'd scare him off with my bitchiness.

He chuckled. And it sounded like the low song of chimes. "Doris doesn't mind me coming around. In fact, I've met you before, Salome."

My name on his lips made my knees go buttery. I groaned inwardly.

"You know my grandma?" I fidgeted with the bucket still in hand.

He gave a nod. "Yeah, I've known her for years. But I haven't seen you since you were a child."

Years? He looked around the same age as me. Warning bells went off in my mind, but something made me push them aside. Like when I tried to focus on what bothered me, it blurred. I relaxed. If he knew my grandma, then he must be okay. "Funny, I don't remember you at all."

"Don't you, Salome?" Strands of my hair blew about my face. He reached a hand out as if to touch them then stopped, dropping his arms back to his side.

"No. Grandma's never mentioned you."

He gave me another cocky grin. "Well then, maybe we should be reacquainted."

"Or maybe not." I snorted. "I'm not sure how you got on the property, Grandma keeps all the gates locked."

He produced an antique-looking skeleton key. "She gave me this. Like I said, Doris has known me for a long time."

"I'm sorry. I'm not trying to be a jerk or anything, it's just my grandma never mentioned I'd have visitors." In fact, I wondered why she didn't ask this guy to watch her house instead of me.

The arrogance left his face and he stared at me. "Perhaps,

we can try this again." He held his hand out to me. "I'm Nevin."

I stretched my free hand until our fingers touched. The chiming intensified and a jolt went through me. My heart pounded in my ears. My stomach rolled over with butterflies. His touch was cold, but familiar. We stood gazing at one another for long minutes, my hand cupped in his.

"She's back and Nevin's found her." A voice drifted across the yard.

I turned toward the tinkling words. Maybe I was going mad. Who left plates in trees and crazy crap like that? When I didn't see anything, I glanced back up at him. He peered off into the distance like he'd heard them, too.

"She's as beautiful as he said she was."

This time, I had no doubt he heard them too because his lips turned up into a dazzling smile. I wanted to ask him about the voices, but couldn't work up the courage. For now.

"So, will you be coming around a lot?" I held my breath waiting for him to answer. If he noticed the things in the woods, maybe he knew what they were. And maybe he could help me, be someone I could to talk to. Someone who wouldn't chalk the voices up to my insanity.

The prickles intensified, probably because I might have a new friend.

"That depends." His eyes melted me from the feet up.

"On what?"

"You," he whispered, his cool breath tickling my ear.

"Me?" Heat crept up the back of my neck.

Chuckling, he caught a loose strand of my hair between his fingers. "As long as you're here, I'll find reasons to come around."

I smiled. "I'll be here every day."

"Then so will I." He let my hair drift from his fingers. "The winter is ours."

The wind picked up, as if his words had been captured, locking this single moment in time. My cell rang, bringing me back to reality. I jerked the phone from my pocket and pressed talk.

"Hello?" I answered, noticing Nevin's eyes never left me.

"Is everything going okay?" Mom's voice cracked.

"Yeah, I'm just finishing up."

"I've put some hot chocolate on for you for when you get home."

"Okay, I'll be there soon." I hung up. "Overprotective mother." I shoved the cell back into my coat.

Nevin frowned. "With good reason."

"What do you mean?" I stiffened.

"Doris told me what happened when you were a child—falling through the ice." Concern shadowed his eyes.

"Oh, that." The wind suddenly became too cold. Memories spilled over me, the voices, the murky depths, and the darkness on the other side of the gate. Why would Grandma tell him something so personal about me, when she'd never mentioned Nevin at all to me?

He clasped my hand. "I'm here. I promise I won't let anything happen to you."

I frowned. His concern seemed kind of sudden. I mean, I barely knew the guy. But I wanted to know him. His ice-touched features made me curious. And for some reason, I felt the need to keep him close. How could I crave friendship from someone I'd just met?

"Thank you," I said with a sigh. "I should probably head home or Mom will send the National Guard to find me."

"Can I walk you home?"

"Actually, I drove over." Damn it, why did I drive? I

could've spent more time with him. Why did I suddenly care so much about someone I hardly knew?

He smiled, looking disappointed. "Well then, I'll have to settle on your promise of coming back tomorrow."

"Tomorrow." It couldn't come soon enough. "It was nice meeting you," I called over my shoulder as I made my way to the shed.

"Nice seeing you again, too." Nevin stepped back as the snow swirled, making it impossible to see him. I shook my head and everything suddenly seemed clearer, but when the breeze died down, he was gone.

Chapter Four

Red brick buildings, reminiscent of days gone by, sat on the main street of Starlynn Village. Old-fashioned lamps lined each side of the road. Their buttery yellow glow washed away the dreary grayness of dawn.

At last, Kadie pulled her rusty Volkswagen Rabbit into the school lot, parking next to a dark green mustang. The color made me think of Colton's eyes. I let my hair fall over my cheeks, hoping to hide the blush from her.

"Salome, are you even listening to me?"

"Hmmm…" I stared out the dirty windows.

"Your bra's on fire."

Fire. Now that registered. "What's on fire?" I whipped my head around to face a smiling Kadie.

She tapped her fingers on the dashboard, then reached toward her cup holder. "I knew you weren't listening. You've barely heard a word I said the whole car ride."

"Sorry, I can't concentrate."

"You always get like this during the winter." She shrugged,

sipping cappuccino from her travel mug. She was a total caffeine addict. Coffee, pop, chocolate, none of it stood a chance with her around.

I closed my eyes. "It's not that."

Slurp. Kadie set her cup in the duct-taped holder. "Oh?" I heard the curiosity in her tone.

"I feel like a, like—" I glanced at her.

Her cherry lips fell open and she grinned. "Oh. My. God. You and Colton did it in his truck, didn't you?"

"Wait, what? No." I slapped her arm. "I wouldn't have sex in someone's car."

She giggled. "Well, he doesn't drive a car, he drives a truck."

"Seriously, I didn't sleep with him."

"Okay—but if it's not the deed," she made a circle with one hand, stuck out her pointer finger with the other, and proceeded to show me how it was done, "then what's got you acting so weird?"

"Thanks, smart ass. I know what sex is."

Maybe I should tell her about Nevin. Not that I planned on going out with him or whatever, but I hadn't been able to get thoughts of him out of my head. I didn't have a lot of friends and hanging around someone who didn't know me from school or know about my major freak outs and breakdowns sounded nice. But he was something I wanted to keep to myself.

"I met someone this weekend."

Her eyes got big. "You mean someone other than Colton? But where? You never leave your house."

"This is going to sound crazy, but I met this guy in my grandma's woods."

She looked wary. "What was he doing out there?"

"Taking a walk."

"In the snow?" She took out a tube of lipstick and adjusted the rearview mirror so she could see herself.

"Some people like the winter, you know."

"How do you know he isn't an axe murderer or something?"

"He wasn't carrying an axe," I teased. "Besides, he knows my grandma *and* he had a key to the property."

Kadie capped her pink lipstick, shoved it in her pocket, and then turned to me with a shrug. "So what about Colton?" She snatched her book bag from the floor by my feet, tossing her keys into the front pocket.

"Our first date was amazing and I like him a lot."

"I need details, like did he try to kiss you or hold your hand? Maybe a little making out in his truck? You know I live for this stuff." She waggled her eyebrows at me.

My face flushed. "No. He was a gentleman."

"Your dates definitely aren't in the same league as mine, that's for sure."

"Does that mean there's something wrong with me?"

"No. I'm sure the hotness will be trying to lay one on you soon enough. Sooo…now, what about this other guy?"

"Not sure yet. I just met him. I—I thought it might be nice to sort of get to know him." I wished I was better at disguising my emotions, because even I heard the hope drenching that statement.

"I think it'd be sexy to have two guys fighting over me." She grinned.

I shook my head and pulled the door handle. "Your idea of trying to get to know someone and mine are not the same thing," I said over my shoulder as I climbed out of the car. Frigid air took my breath away. Crap.

Now that I'd left the safety of the vehicle, it hit me full force. The bitter chill snaked down the nape of my neck; blinding whiteness blanketed every tree, bush, and rock. People stomped the snow off their boots, heading toward the school as if they could beat away winter.

Kadie hurried to my side. "It's okay. We're only a couple of feet from the entrance."

I let her lead me through the throngs of students. When we came to the senior hall, she let go of me.

"Don't look now but tall, dark, and yummy is waiting for you." Kadie nudged me.

Glancing down the hall, I spotted Colton leaning against my locker. For a second, he blurred in my vision. I wiped my eyes with the back of my hand. Strange. It must've been the going from the bright outdoors to the dreary interior of the school.

Colton raised his eyes to mine, a smile touching his lips. He peeled himself off my locker and headed toward me. I didn't realize I'd stopped walking until Kadie gave me a push.

"Go get him, tiger," she said, before deserting me.

Several heads swiveled when Colton took my bag from me. "Morning." He handed me a single white rose.

"Thank you. But you didn't have to get me this." We came to my locker and I fumbled to get it open. He leaned close and tiny shivers chased down my back.

He smiled. "I wanted to."

When my door finally sprang open, I saw Colton glancing at the small posters hanging on my door. Good God, why couldn't I have had pictures of my friends up?

"So you like pirates, vampires, and werewolves, eh?"

"And basketball players," I blurted. Kill me now. Had I just said that out loud?

His chest rumbled against my back as he leaned forward to slide my geometry book from the top shelf for me. "Count me glad I chose basketball and not hockey then."

I chewed my fingernail and turned around to look at him. His gaze pierced me, like he saw every thought in my head, which was kind of unnerving. Inhaling deeply, I caught the scent of honey and soap clinging to his shirt. He was so hot. And he was standing here with me. I couldn't count how many times I'd willed him to glance at me, like he was now. Which forced the question, why now?

But I pushed the uncertainty aside. Who was I to argue with fate?

"So, how did the three-on-three basketball tournament go on Saturday?" I asked as we headed toward first hour.

"Wow, I'm impressed. I didn't realize you followed basketball so closely." Colton caught my hand, his skin warm against mine. "We won, of course. Not that I'm bragging."

"Right, because jocks don't brag."

"Hey now." He pretended to be insulted. "I thought maybe we could sit together for lunch today." He led me into our classroom.

"My table or yours?"

"We could find a private table."

This made me laugh. "A private table, in our cafeteria?"

"Yeah, I bet I can find us one."

I quirked an eyebrow. "You really want to bet?"

He smirked. "Name your wager."

Was he kidding? If I were Kadie, I'd have said something suggestive or told him I'd bet him a kiss or a backrub. But since I was me, I stared at him. "Why don't you decide?"

"Are you sure you trust me?" He slid into the desk behind mine. "Letting someone else decide the stakes can be costly."

His moss-colored eyes grew darker, challenging me to name the wager.

"I trust you." My voice fell to a whisper. "I'm sure you're far more creative than me."

"Here's a game lesson, Salome. Never trust anybody to

make your decisions for you." He glanced out the windows. "Not everyone will have your best interest in mind."

"It's just a bet." I shrugged, but his warning creeped me out.

"Is it?" He gave me a lazy smile.

Sucking in a deep breath, I decided to take things into my own hands. My fingers trembled as I ripped a piece of paper from my notebook and scribbled one simple word across the front of it.

Kiss.

Wadding it up, I dropped it onto Colton's desk behind me. The blush crept up the back of my neck and spread across my face. For a moment, I wished I could take it back. What if he thought I was too forward? All these years I'd known him, and I wondered again why everything about our relationship seemed different.

His breath brushed my cheek as he leaned to whisper in my ear. "Sounds good, but I'd like to add a date of my choosing to the pot if I win."

I turned my head ever so slightly, my lips a breath away from his. "Okay. But you do realize I'm going to win, right?"

"Ms. Montgomery and Mr. Myers, I'd appreciate it if you two could leave your date plans for the end of class," Mr. Klecken said.

The class erupted in laughter and I slumped in my chair. Mr. Klecken was an ass. But I wouldn't let him ruin this moment. I'd just bet Colton Myers a kiss. And not just any kiss. My first kiss.

*W*hen the bell sounded for lunch, I rushed toward my locker.

Kadie waved at me. "Hey, Craig Cedars asked if I wanted to

run into town to grab a burger with him."

"Go. I'm having lunch with Colton," I said, wanting to tell her about the bet.

"You sure?"

"Yeah, but only if you can give me some gum."

Her mouth turned up into a devilish grin. "My little Salome is growing up. Make sure you watch out for Ms. Perez. If she catches you locking lips, she'll have you in the office."

"I never said we're gonna, you know, kiss." I took the piece of gum she pulled out.

"Didn't have to. It's written all over your face." She gave me a sly wink and hurried down the hall.

Colton met me at my locker, his eyes intent on my every movement. "You ready to lose that bet?" He entwined his fingers with mine.

I snorted. "Right. Have you actually ever eaten in the cafeteria? There are never extra seats, let alone private eating areas."

With my brown bag in one hand and Colton's hand in the other, we went into the lunchroom. There were kids everywhere. Most of the tables were full. The scent of meatloaf and pizza ushered us in, idle chatter growing louder the farther we went.

Colton pushed toward the back of the room, until there were no tables left. He tugged me toward an old curtain used to partition off part of the cafeteria. We slipped behind it, where a small, antique table was set up. There were only two chairs. It looked out of place.

Silence surrounded us. I didn't hear the clanking of trays or kids shouting and talking. It was like we'd stepped into another dimension or something. Colton pulled out my chair for me and gestured for me to sit. How was this possible? For a second I felt off balance, like I was on a carousel spinning faster and faster, but then I looked at him and suddenly the weird feeling drifted away.

"Wow, if I didn't know any better, I'd think you're having an affair with the lunch lady." I laughed. "No way could you pull this off on your own."

"What can I say? She likes my smile." He grinned.

God, who doesn't like his smile? My heart thumped against my rib cage.

"So, I guess this means I lost the bet." I tried to hide the disappointment in my voice. Guess my first kiss would have to wait. But on the other hand, I'd get to go on another date with him, which totally made my day.

"I don't need to lose a bet to kiss you." He caught my hand across the table. "Besides, I want our first one to be special."

I raised my eyebrows. "Now you're assuming I wanted one. Maybe I didn't have anything else to bet."

"Oh, is that how it is?" He released my hands and leaned back in his chair, staring at me.

His gaze swept over me. My skin tingled as if he'd rubbed his fingers along my arms. I wet my lips with my tongue. No one had ever looked at me the way he did. Nervous flutters tickled my belly. From somewhere behind him came the sound of tinkling music. The kind you'd hear if you opened a children's jewelry box. I glanced around for its source, but soon found my focus drawn back to him. More than anything, I wanted him to lean forward and press his lips to mine. Ah, what was I thinking? I so didn't want my first kiss to be in the school cafeteria. And what if I screwed it up?

Why was I all of a sudden feeling such a pull to him?

I cleared my throat and shifted my eyes to the table. "Aren't you going to eat?"

"Yeah, I've got to go get it."

He stood, eyeing our private spot. For a second, I thought he muttered something under his breath—something about someone staying away from me. Colton was only gone a few seconds. When he reappeared he had a plate full of fruits and vegetables. Most too exotic to be lunchroom food.

"Want some?" he offered.

"No, I'm good," I said, too nervous to eat too much.

"Are you sure?" He pressed again, a strange gleam in his eyes.

Digging through my brown paper lunch sack, I smiled. "I think I've got enough food right here."

He pushed the tray aside, his head propped up on his hands. "Well played."

Well played, what the hell did that mean? I shrugged off his crazy behavior and forced myself to eat, which was hard to do with him watching me.

"*U*gh! Guys suck." Kadie dropped her books onto our lab table during fifth hour.

"Since when?" My chair scraped across the tile floor as I sat.

She closed her eyes, massaging her temples. "Since lunch. Craig asked me to go out to eat with him. But when I showed up, he swore he never invited me."

My mouth dropped open. I lowered my voice. "He what?"

"He said he never even talked to me today. I don't know, it was weird, Salome. He looked serious when he said he didn't invite me." She ran a hand through her dark hair then reached into her purse to check her make-up.

"What a dick." Stuff like this never happened to Kadie. The

girl was a legend. I mean, guys lined up to ask her out.

She tapped her purple polished fingernails on the table. "So where did you go during lunch?" Kadie's eyebrows raised.

"We were in the lunchroom, toward the back."

She shot me a baffled look. "Impossible. I searched the whole place for you. Trust me, if you were there I would've found you."

I narrowed my eyes. "Um—I was in there. Behind the curtain."

"What curtain? At least if you're going to lie to me, make it believable."

What was going on? How had she *not* seen the curtain? Had I imagined it?

For the rest of the day, I couldn't concentrate. My mind wandered until the last bell rang. After I went to my locker, I decided to stop off in the cafeteria. I went toward the back of the lunchroom, but this time there was no partition or curtain. Instead I found the wooden stage they used to do the school plays on before they built the auditorium. There was no private table or area to eat in.

Disbelief overwhelmed me. This didn't make sense. Was anything that had happened with me and Colton real? Fear coiled in my stomach. Oh, God. Maybe I really was crazy.

CHAPTER FIVE

$\mathcal{T}$he car ride home was quiet. Kadie's attention was elsewhere, while I pretended to stare at the scenery, clutching my rose to my chest. This was insane. We never fought.

When she parked in my driveway, I jerked the door open. "I'll see you tomorrow."

"Listen, I'm sorry about freaking out earlier. I shouldn't have accused you of lying."

"S'okay." I crawled back through the car and gave her a quick hug. "Remember your motto, hoes before bros." I wanted to tell her about Colton's strange behavior and about the missing curtain—if it ever existed at all. But today had been weird enough and I didn't want to get into it again.

Kadie giggled. "You know it."

"So I'll see you tomorrow?"

"Of course. You've got to help me get back at Craig for ditching me today."

And Kadie was herself once more.

Relief flooded me while I watched her pull away. What

would I do without her? I hurried into the house, where I found Mom sitting at the kitchen table phone cradled in her hand, smiling.

"She just walked in, do you want to talk to her?" Mom said. "Okay, I'll chat with you again when she's done." She handed me the phone. "It's Dad."

"Dad, hey, where are you?"

"In Texas. And let me tell you it's hotter than a frying pan down here."

"When are you coming home?" My school bag slipped down my shoulder.

"I've got a couple more loads to do, so I'm hoping it'll only be a couple more weeks."

My dad was a truck driver and only got about five days off a month. Which sucked. At least he'd be home for Christmas.

"I miss you," I said.

"Miss you too, sweetheart. So, your mom said you went on your first date?"

My lips twitched. "Yes. It was perfect. He took me out for pizza and we played pinball."

"Do I need to sit down and have a chat with this boy?" he teased.

"Um—no. I'd prefer not to die of embarrassment, thank you very much."

"Well, if you change your mind, I can always bring some rattlesnake skins back from Texas with me and tell this boy I wrestled them with my bare hands. Make him real scared of me." Dad laughed.

"Funny."

"Listen, I have to pull out in a few minutes. Why don't you put your mom back on real quick."

"Okay. I love you. Be safe."

"Love you, too."

"I'm heading back to Grandma's," I said as I handed the phone back to Mom and walked to the bathroom. I ran a brush through my hair and double-checked my make-up. I felt foolish for primping to go fill the bird feeders. However, I didn't want to chance a run-in with Nevin while looking like something my cat spit up.

With a sigh, I pulled my coat around my shoulders.

From the kitchen I heard Mom lower her voice. "She's doing okay so far. But I've seen the panic in her eyes again. My mother told me she had a small episode near the pond before they left. I almost called Dr. Bosworth to see if we could get her in."

Crap. No. I couldn't go back to the shrink again. Explain what happened that winter. Like the stupid psychiatrist didn't already know that. Plus, I was scared I might blurt out something about the weirdness with Colton and then she'd really know I'd flipped.

"Okay, I'll hold off. Maybe you're right. She might just need time to adjust being back on my parents' property again."

Not wanting to get caught eavesdropping, I hurried across the room to the counter. I eyed my Jeep keys. Okay, if I left them here maybe I could spend more time with Nevin.

But that meant having to walk down the wooded two-track. Alone. In the snow.

My hand hovered above the dish, where my keys were. I shifted my gaze to the window. Two hundred and fifty steps. That's all I'd have to go. I left my keys in the bowl and took hesitant steps toward the front door.

When I moved onto the porch, the frigid air surrounded me and panic clutched my chest. In one swift motion, I rushed back inside. No way in hell could I walk over.

"Salome? What in the world are you doing?" Mom glanced at me as I ran into the kitchen.

"Um—nothing. I, uh, forgot my hat." Crap, if I let her see how freaked out I was she'd probably set that appointment. I stared at my key ring on the other side of her. My legs trembled, but I gave her a forced smile.

"Are you going to drive over? If so, I can ride with you."

She'd given me an opening to grab my keys. "No. I thought I'd try to walk today."

She maneuvered closer to me. "Honey, are you sure about this?"

"Yeah. I have my phone. And you and Gram said I needed to overcome this." I gave her a quick wave before I changed my mind and made my way outside once more.

Taking a deep breath, I stepped into a drift wishing I'd worn two pairs of socks.

The pine and oak trees waved back and forth, dropping snow from their branches. I tried to keep my eyes forward, but the deep shadows of the forest beckoned my attention.

Snap. The sound of breaking twigs shattered the silence.

My pace quickened and I glanced over my shoulder. Beyond the fence surrounding our properties I heard a low growl, then a high-pitched scream. I covered my ears with my hands and took off in a sprint.

"*That's right, run, Salome. Fear me. Your time is coming. They cannot keep you safe forever. Remember eighteen.*"

My lungs burned as I crashed into my grandparents' front door. I fumbled to get the lock open. Once inside, I slammed the door and sank to the floor. God, that voice. I recognized it. *She* was back. And s*he* knew I was here.

My thoughts got the best of me as I put my head in my hands. A sob escaped my lips. I didn't want to go back outside. I didn't want to feel the cold air on my skin, or see the treachery winter brought with it.

I needed to get a grip and quit being so stupid—my imagination was running wild.

Grandma counted on me to take care of things. Sitting on her foyer floor crying wasn't getting the chores done.

Nevin. Maybe I'd drum up enough courage today to ask him about the voices.

His name brought me to my feet. Wiping tears away, I forced myself to the slider door.

My gaze swept the yard. Disappointment overwhelmed me when I didn't see him. Stepping onto the deck, I trudged toward the shed.

One. Two. Three. Only seventeen more steps.

I stared at the wrought iron gate and a shiver raked through my body. Evil lurked somewhere, on the other side of that fence. Or maybe it was all in my head like the shrink said. Damn, I should've let Mom come with me.

I got through the first couple of feeders then stopped at the oak. When I peered at the ground I noticed tiny footprints in the snow. Bending closer, I gasped. They were like small human footprints. Impossible. People weren't *that* tiny.

"I'm definitely losing my mind." I stood back up. Out of sheer curiosity, I reached inside the hollowed area in the oak to find yesterday's trinket gone.

Frowning, I dropped a gold watch in then delivered food to the last two containers, all the while counting my steps. Once finished, I headed back to the shed and locked it. I sighed. Looked like I'd been stood up.

Then I saw him. Leaning against the gazebo. Nevin's dark hair touched the collar of his black leather jacket, his wintry eyes focused on me. A slow smile spread across his face.

"I thought you might not show." I fought to keep the surprise from my voice. Geez, was I so desperate for a friend that I put all my hope in a complete stranger? No, I told myself, he was the key to my sanity…or maybe insanity.

He straightened to his full height, sauntering gracefully to my side. "There isn't anything that could've kept me away."

Holy God, he needed to turn down the charm. I moved closer to the gazebo steps and reached for one of the poles, twirling around it as flakes peppered my cheeks.

"So, what've you been up to all day?"

Nevin watched me and chuckled. "I hope you're not deciding on that profession."

"What?"

He pointed at the pole I'd been swinging on. "Your parents really ought to encourage you to try other things."

In my surprise, I released the pole and went flying down the stairs. Nevin moved quick, catching me in his arms before I hit the ground. He held me suspended, like he'd dipped me back in an elegant dance move.

His face was inches from mine, his honey-scented breath cool against my face. Needle-like prickles shot threw me and my pulse quickened as we seemed frozen in position. I got that dazed feeling, and everything blurred a little.

He pulled me up until I stood on my own two feet. "Sorry." I took a step back. "My routine obviously needs work."

Grinning, he reached into his coat pocket. "Here, I made something for you."

"What is it?" I held out a gloved hand.

"Look and see."

He handed over a beautiful rose carved out of ice. It looked like glass, the way each petal and thorny detail was etched into the frozen art. For a moment, I smelled the sweet nectar of a rose wafting in the air. Then it disappeared.

"Wow, I've never seen anything like this."

"I have many talents." Nevin's voice took on an air of conceit.

I rolled my eyes and set the ice rose on the gazebo. "Has anyone ever told you arrogance is not a virtue?"

His gaze darkened. "Once. And that was one time too many."

Whoa! Where had that come from? Talk about brooding male.

"I, for one, find arrogance unattractive." I lowered my voice. I knew enough guys like him at school. The ones who'd tormented and picked on me when I'd had my last "winter" episode my sophomore year. Which was why I was so surprised Colton had asked me out.

Nevin sighed, tracing his finger along the snow covered railing. "Is that so? Then why are you here?"

Why *was* I there? But my pulse pounded so hard in my ears I couldn't think. "I'm taking care of my grandma's house while she's gone."

He took hold of my arm, tugging me closer to him. "Then why did you wait for me?"

So he had been watching me. "Because I told you I would. If nothing else, I stand by my word."

"Does my arrogance really bother you?" His lips twitched, his hand stroking my arm.

In a way it did, but I wanted him to be different and I was certain that deep down he could be. "Not really, with hot guys you kind of expect it." Shit! Not again. I had to think before I talked.

His head fell back and he laughed. "I like a girl who speaks her mind, especially when she says nice things about me."

"Moving on." I averted my gaze.

He tugged on my sleeve until I glanced back up at him. "Sometimes it's easier to be an ass than it is to be kind. You never know who you can trust."

Déjà vu. Colton had lectured me about trust earlier. And also gave me a rose. My hair stood up on end. Okay. Now was not the time to freak out. So they'd both done similar things. Who cared?

Refocusing back on him, I said, "You can trust me."

He took a seat on the gazebo steps. "That's yet to be seen."

"I don't like being called a liar." I squeezed into the spot next to him. "Besides, you don't even know me."

"You're all the same." Nevin stared at the pond. A strand of dark hair brushed his forehead.

"Okay, I think you lost me here. All of who?"

"Huma—women."

Asshole. The muscles in my jaw tightened.

"Glad to see you've got such a high opinion of me. We've known each other for what? A day and you know every nuance of me." I shot to my feet, glaring. "I can't believe I actually looked forward to seeing you today. That I thought we could be friends."

I spun on my heel and marched through the snowdrifts toward the house.

"Salome, wait." Nevin bounded after me, catching my hand before I got to the deck. "I'm sorry. I'm not much of a people person." His tone softened, his face lost the hostility that had been there moments before. "I—I have trust issues. It's not you—I'm just bad at this."

"Then I don't understand why you suggested we hang out. I'm a person, or at least I was the last time I checked." I jerked my hand away from his.

He closed his eyes as if collecting his thoughts. When his

lids flipped open again, I saw the pain reflected back at me.

"I've wanted to talk to you, to see you up close. I have waited a long time for this moment—for you to come back."

The breeze picked up. The need to get inside crept up the back of my neck and I folded my arms across my chest to conserve body heat.

"I don't know what you mean. I never went anywhere," I whispered.

"Then where were you every winter?" He shoved his hands in his pockets. "I searched for you every time I came around."

"Every time you came around? You act as if we've met before. Like I should know you."

He pulled a dead leaf from my hair, then stared into my eyes. "So tell me, why are you so afraid of the snow?"

Embarrassment washed over me. How could I explain my fear to him? My courage fled and I doubted he'd understand the voices or the warnings.

"I don't like to go out in the winter, not after—" I swallowed hard.

"You fell in the pond," he finished, closing the distance between us. He cupped my chin in his hands, forcing me to look at him.

Icy blue eyes stared through me, eyes that seemed so familiar. "How do you know about that?"

A soft laugh pursed his lips. Tinkling, like wind chimes. "I have a good memory. Remember, I told you the other day that Doris spoke of your fall."

Nevin's hands dropped to his sides. Had I met him before?

We made our way back to the gazebo and sat down again. I didn't want to think about the cold or the pond. I'd had enough psychotherapy over the years that made me reminisce about things I'd much rather forget.

"So where do you live?" I leaned against the steps.

"Around."

"Can you be more evasive?"

He shrugged, shoving his hands in his pockets again. A nervous habit it seemed. "I live nearby."

"Okay, I get it. You're trying to play up the whole man of mystery thing."

"Something like that," he muttered. "So, how was school today?"

School. Was he serious? "Boring. I'd much rather be home."

"This is your last year, isn't it?"

"Yeah. But I have no idea what I'm going to do with myself. Thought about going south, to get away from the weather and all." At least that's what I'd planned to do until Grandpa had gotten sick.

Nevin stood abruptly and turned to face me. He shoved his hand into his hair and sighed. "You'd leave?"

I gave a bitter laugh. "Probably not. Colleges aren't jumping to admit kids like me."

After a moment, he sat back down next to me and his leg brushed against mine. He looked like he wanted to say something important, but stopped himself. "I'll be glad if you stay."

"Then it's decided," I teased. "I'll stay!"

"It didn't take much to convince you. I thought I'd have to get down on my knees and beg." He gave a strand of my hair a playful tug.

"And here I believed begging was beneath you."

"Drastic times call for drastic measures." He winked, and I shifted, wondering what he really wanted from me.

Daylight faded and my legs felt like frozen blocks of wood. "I should probably head home. It'll be dark soon."

Nevin stood, reaching down to help me up. "Can I walk

with you?"

Leaving the Jeep home totally paid off, even if I nearly had a heart attack getting here. Maybe we'd both hear *them* on the way back and I could ask him about them.

"Sure." I hurried to the deck to lock the slider and then gestured for Nevin to follow me around the side of the garage. He held my hand as we trudged down the driveway. I glanced at the woods, its sinister presence making me feel small. My heart hammered and I fought to keep the panic at bay.

"So, does this mean we're friends?" Nevin asked.

"Maybe."

"I take that as a yes," Nevin answered, his thumb caressing my palm.

"I don't think that was the word I used." I glanced down at our entwined fingers. It should feel wrong, it did in a way, but I also felt safe.

"You don't have to say anything. I see it in your eyes."

"And again with the arrogance. Just for that, I should take the key my grandma gave you back."

Chuckling, he picked me up and swung me around until I squealed. "Ah, but you won't. You find me too interesting."

When the warm glow of the porch light came into view, we stopped walking, "Do you want to come in?"

He stared longingly at my house, then back at me. "I wish I could, but I've got to get back home."

"Maybe next time." From within the darkened woodland, an eerie shriek sounded. Like the cross between a wild animal and a child in pain. My blood ran cold as I hurried toward the house.

"Stay inside tonight," Nevin said.

I called over my shoulder, "Are you sure you want to walk back to your house in the dark? I can drive you." What was I saying? I didn't want to drive. I wanted to rush inside and bar the door behind me.

He held out his arms and said, "Do I seem like the type of guy who's scared of the dark?" He grinned. "I'll be fine, just get in the house."

I launched myself onto the porch, throwing open the door. I stopped on the threshold and spun around. "Will I see you tomorrow?"

"Yes."

CHAPTER SIX

"Cleo, here kitty-kitty." I shielded my eyes against the porch light, searching the early morning gloom. "Cleo, c'mon, I need to brush my teeth."

Near the back gate I caught a glimpse of my cat. Ugh. Sometimes she was a pain in the ass. I called, "If I'm late for school because of you, I'm gonna be pissed."

I stalked back into the house, where I slipped on my boots then trudged out the door. As I got closer, I realized Cleo wasn't moving.

"Hey girl, are you okay?" I softened my voice. Normally, this would be the moment she'd dash away and I'd have to chase her. But today, she didn't budge. I had a sudden urge to turn around as the shadows splayed before me.

My footsteps crunched across the frozen ground.

Oh God. I stopped walking, and fell to my knees. The cold seeped through the fabric of my clothes.

"Cleo." My mouth went dry. Vines were wrapped around her neck and legs—they'd come from the other side of the fence.

From the woods. Like an infestation of snakes, they coiled around her lifeless body.

Dead.

She was dead.

The darkness was coming. The harsh iciness I'd dreaded. I screamed, my voice echoing around me.

Gusts of wind ripped over me as if trying to tear me limb from limb—and then I heard the tinkling voices.

"We've got to do something. She's too close to the gate."

"Why won't she get up?"

"Nevin, we've got to find Nevin."

"Salome, you have to move."

Covering my ears with my hands, I continued to scream. I needed to drown out the noise.

"Salome." Mom's frantic voice broke down my terror.

"Make them stop. I can't take it. Why won't they leave me alone?" I twisted to look at her. She stumbled in an effort to get across the yard on her crutches. At last, she sank to her knees next to me, gripping my shoulders.

"Shh…it's okay. Just tell me what hap—" Her face crumpled when she spotted Cleo. "Salome, get up to the house now."

"Mom?"

Her cheeks paled. Heavy dark circles practically made her eyes pop off her face. "Go. Now. I'll ask Mr. Graham across the street to bury her. You need to get ready for school."

Mom somehow dragged me to my feet and pushed me toward the house, while balancing on her crutches.

Sobs shook my entire body. Someone or something had killed Cleo. I wondered if I might be next. I never wanted to go outside again. But I couldn't hide forever.

Once inside, Mom wiped my face with a warm washcloth, brushing away the tears. She knew more about what was happening than she let on.

She watched me for long moments. "Salome, when I first got out there, you said "they" wouldn't leave you alone? Who's *they*?"

"Y—you didn't hear the voices?" My gaze met hers.

"No." She stroked my hair. "Maybe I should see if Dr. Bosworth can fit you in this week."

I gripped the side of the kitchen counter. Not again. I couldn't meet with that woman. She didn't understand. She'd put me on meds that'd take the edge off and give me sleeping pills. I didn't want to fall into a deep slumber. Because you never knew what might happen.

Mom clearly knew more than she was telling me, so how could she justify this? What was her excuse for sending me away all of these years to be drugged, without even telling me what was wrong? I wanted to bring it up, to scream and rage and fight, but I knew that she would only shut me down. She must have had a reason for making me feel crazy all these years, but as the days went on I was beginning to realize more and more that she might be the misguided one.

"I—I'll be fine, Mom. It was probably just the shock." I gave her a forced smile and brushed past her to wait on the porch for Kadie.

"I'm sorry about Cleo." Kadie drove past the post office.

Tears burned my eyes and I blinked them away. I was sick of being weak, sick of being afraid.

"Thanks." I sniffled, wiping my nose with a soggy tissue.

Kadie chewed her bottom lip, giving me the same look

Mom had. "Are you sure about the vines?"

I leaned my head against the window, tearing my tissues into small pieces. "Yes. The vines strangled her. I mean, it was like a boa constrictor got a hold of her or something."

"And the voices?"

"They were the same ones, I know they were. Man, I sound like a fucking Fruit Loop."

"Okay, I know what will make you feel better." Kadie pulled into an empty spot in front of Perky Joe's.

"I can't believe Simeon asked me out again. He didn't seem that interested after our last date." Kadie gushed as we climbed from her car an hour later.

For some reason, I was disappointed the blond barista… Gareth…was on his way out as we entered. He'd given me a nod and told me to take care of myself, which sent a surprising shiver down my spine, then left. Before I could answer, not that I knew what I'd say anyway when all I could do was think about Cleo, Kadie had hurried over to the counter and hung over it, teasing and chatting with Simeon.

"How can you be surprised? You were practically humping his leg."

She snickered. "I did lay it on thick, huh? But the end result was fabulous, although, I did notice his friend checking you out, too, when he walked past." She toyed with her purse. "You're not interested in him, are you?"

"Do I look like his type?" I replied, not answering her question.

"Not really. But who knows, you could really fall for this

guy. God, I bet he's a good kisser…" She winked.

"In case you forgot, I have Colton." I sipped the last of my cappuccino and dumped it in the trash can near the school entrance. My tummy felt warm, but it didn't do anything for the rest of my body.

Kadie leaned over to whisper in my ear. "Incoming."

Colton sauntered across the parking lot. He smiled when he saw me.

"Morning."

"Take good care of my girl, she's had a rough morning," Kadie said before rushing off.

He studied my face. "What's going on?"

I gave him a rundown of the nightmarish start to my day, leaving out the bit about the vines. Last thing I wanted to do was make him think I was a freak. When I finished talking, I noticed the muscles in Colton's face clenching.

He gripped my elbow then wrapped his arms around me. His warmth radiated around me like an electric blanket and I let him comfort me. It felt safe standing here with him. Kids pushed past us, reminding me we were still outside.

"We should head in." My gaze flickered to his face as I left the security of his embrace. If I had it my way, I would've stayed there. Unfortunately, Colton wasn't a school subject. And I needed all my credits to graduate.

"How about this weekend I take you someplace to forget everything?" He guided me into the crowded school. "Nothing fancy or anything, but somewhere out of the way."

"I don't need fancy." I smiled.

"We still have to fit in that kiss you've been looking forward to."

"Now you're being presumptuous. I never said I *wanted* to kiss you." I stopped in the middle of the hall. I didn't know how

I felt about that kiss now. Everything surrounding that lunch had been strange. "All I did was wager one."

His fingers traced the back of my neck. He leaned down, until our mouths were only a couple of inches apart. "Does this change your mind?"

Colton's ivy-colored eyes gazed into mine. In the distance, I swore I heard the same tinkling music as I had yesterday. My heart sped up. Why couldn't I get enough of him? It was like he'd cast a spell over me.

"I might have to reconsider your offer," I whispered as I pushed even closer to him.

He chuckled, backing away right as a teacher rounded the corner. "I thought you'd see it my way."

"I said, might." But there was no *might* about it; both he and I knew it. "I think you're reading far too much into it." Dazed, I shook my head and put more space between us.

"You're a terrible liar."

Mom had been right—I needed to be at school. But I wasn't sure Colton was the distraction I needed to stay sane.

CHAPTER SEVEN

"Are you okay?" Nevin asked as soon as I emerged from my grandparents' house.

"You heard about Cleo?"

"Bad news travels fast in the woods."

Okay, what'd he mean by that? I waited for him to elaborate further, but he didn't—just like always. So instead, I hurried to get my job done. He fell into step beside me. He watched as I dumped seed into the feeders then took the bag from me.

"Thanks. You know you don't have to help, right?" I shot at him, coldly. Maybe my frigidity was a bit unwarranted, but I had had bad day, and he wasn't helping anything with his vague answers.

He shrugged. "Yes, but the quicker you finish, the sooner we can spend time together."

"You missed me today." I smirked, satisfied to think of him waiting around for me. Taking off my glove, I yanked a lacy doily from my pocket, one of Grandma's trinkets I'd grabbed for today's offering, then tossed it into the tree.

Nevin glanced at the pond, a faraway look on his face. "Yes. I don't have many friends out here."

I felt bad, then, for my attitude. I knew how he felt. I found his hand and I gave it a squeeze. "Well you've got me around now. Hopefully I'll be good enough company after the horrible day I've had."

"Maybe we should do something to take your mind off everything." Nevin grinned, tugging me toward Grandpa's hammock.

He climbed in first. The hammock swung back and forth like a playground ride. Once settled, Nevin pulled me in next to him, so we sat side-by-side. His fingers traced mine, skin as cold as the weather around us.

"Here, let me warm you up." I covered his hands with mine.

"If only you could," he whispered.

What in the hell did that mean?

"You know, your cryptic answers are not endearing." I glared. "Do you want me to go make us some hot cocoa?" I added, to soften the blow. It was hard to turn and look at him without sending us rocking. However, I managed to shift enough to see his face.

"I'm fine. I'd much rather sit here and talk about you."

"Seriously, do these lines work for you?"

"I'm being sincere. I want to get to know you. Last time, you told me very little about yourself."

I traced the pattern of the hammock strings, looping my fingers through them. Very few people wanted to know me. And to be honest, I didn't want them to. They'd think I was a freak. Except, Nevin already knew about my phobia and he was still here.

I sighed. "Okay, what do you want to know?"

"Everything."

"Everything?"

"Tell me, Salome, what is your favorite color? And your favorite foods and music?"

Snatches of the tinkling music floated by on a chill breeze, and his gaze sent my heart into overdrive. He was so familiar, so beautiful.

"Let's see, my favorite color is blue, favorite food is a toss-up between pizza and lasagna. I love pretty much any kind of music."

He went on to ask me about books, clothes, places I've been, amongst other things. The surprising part was how interested he acted. Like he absorbed every word I spoke.

"Humans are competitive by nature," Nevin said. "Are there any sports you participate in?"

God, he sounded so old-fashioned and weird. "Yes, we mere mortals like to compete — I've done dance."

Nevin's cheeks turned pink. "I didn't mean anything by that."

Sensing his embarrassment, I decided to change the subject. "So, you've never told me how old you are."

He hesitated, turning to stare at the pond. "Nineteen."

"How come I never saw you at school then? I mean you're only two years older than me."

"My mother schooled me before she got sick."

"Oh, sorry, I didn't mean to pry."

He shifted, swinging his legs further over the edge of the hammock. "She's the reason I don't get out much. I take care of her."

"Nevin." I touched his shoulder.

"I should head home." He stood so abruptly I came close to falling out of the hammock. But then he caught me, holding me against his chest.

"You don't have to go." I swallowed, losing myself in his gaze. "We could go into my grandma's and warm up." Actually, I'd prefer to be inside. Not that I'd admit that to him. The only reason I could be brave right now was because he was there with me.

"I really can't."

"Why?" I pressured. "Every time I invite you in, you say no. Is there something wrong with me?"

Nevin smiled, caressing my face. "There's nothing wrong with you. It's just that Doris trusts me. I don't want to be in there when she's not here."

"Does this mean you'll never go anywhere with me outside this property?" I chewed on my lip.

"How about Friday?"

"Really?"

He laughed. "Yes. But you'll have to dress warm. I plan on breaking you of your fear of winter."

If only it was that easy. But this wasn't something that could be cured overnight. No matter how nice he was.

"This isn't a date is it?"

This time he blushed. "Um, no. I didn't mean it like that."

"Okay, that's good. Because I'm kind of seeing someone and—"

"Salome. It's all right. I'm fine just being around you."

"So, I'll see you tomorrow." I leaned toward him, without really thinking about it.

Nevin bent down, his thumb catching my chin. For a brief moment, I thought he might kiss me, but at the last second he backed away. "I'll be here waiting."

I couldn't deny the disappointment. Not that I thought kissing him was a good idea, but because I was beginning to believe I wasn't kissable. First, Colton didn't kiss me after our first date. Although, he acted like he wanted to. Now Nevin jumped back. Maybe he thought I was a nut case like all the others did.

Embarrassed, I turned to go, giving Nevin a wave. I glanced back ready to ask what he thought was wrong with me, only to find him gone. He'd disappeared. Again. Somehow, I was going to figure out where he lived.

"Why haven't you returned my calls?" Grandma asked as soon as I picked up the phone.

"I've been busy." I tried to catch my breath.

Mom poked her head around the corner and gave a wave. "Tell her I need to talk to her when you're done."

I nodded, sat down, and cradled the phone against my ear.

"Since when are you too busy for your grandparents?"

"Don't put it like that. It makes me sound like a jerk."

"Your mom told us about Cleo. Are you doing okay?"

My throat constricted at the mention of my cat's name. "It wasn't normal, Gram. The way she died, I mean."

"That's why I'm calling, dear. You need to stay away from those woods. Probably got wild animals running loose."

Wild animals? Nice try. I'd never heard of animals that strangled things with vines. This wasn't a comic book villain.

"Trust me, I'm not venturing into the woods anytime soon."

"Your mom also told me you've been spending a lot of time back at our house," Grandma said. Her intake of breath streamed through the phone as she waited for my answer.

"I'm only spending like an hour a day back there. It gives me some alone time."

Okay, so I lied. Shoot me.

Grandma remained silent for a moment as if digesting my lie. "Well, you be careful and don't talk to strangers."

Don't talk to strangers? What was I, nine? Besides, it wasn't like anyone lived close by. I started to ask about Nevin then changed my mind. I wanted him to be my secret.

"If you need me, Salome, just call."

I did need her. Dad was on the road driving the truck and I didn't want to burden Mom with everything, especially when she already had enough to deal with on account of her ankle. Not to mention, I worried she might schedule me a trip to go see Dr. Bosworth. A lump welled up in my throat making it hard to speak. "Miss you."

"Miss you, too. Oh and Grandpa says hi."

My laugh came out forced. "Tell him hi and that I finished off his chocolate fudge ice cream for him."

She chuckled. "I will. I'll let you go for now."

I handed the phone to Mom and headed to my room for my pajamas. All I wanted to do was get warm. I eyed Cleo's cat bed in the corner. My eyes welled. Visions of her tiny body flipped through my mind. The vines. The snow.

Not wanting to spend the night remembering the nightmarish scene, I walked back toward the kitchen. I stopped when I heard Mom's voice.

"I wish I could take Salome away from here, Mom. Find somewhere safe for her. Yes, I'm well aware that we're responsible for the gates. It's something you've never let me forget, although I wish you'd tell me why that's so important. Lord knows if we weren't responsible, I'd have left Michigan years ago."

Somewhere safe? Gates? What the heck were they talking about? I'd thought we couldn't *afford* to move south. That's what Mom and Dad had argued about more than once. I inched toward the second phone and picked up the receiver, covering the mouthpiece with my hand.

"You know she's safer there than she is anywhere else," Grandma said. "As long as the gates remain closed and she stays away from *them*. If she gets too far away from the safe zones, she could be in real danger."

"That's what I'm worried about. Those vines came across the fence. That could've been Salome. And she's having episodes again, hearing voices. Mom, I was right there with her. I didn't hear anything."

"Don't send her back to the psychiatrist. I already told you before they can't do anything to help her."

"You say that, but at least with the pills she can sleep at night without nightmares—she can forget some of what's going on. Of the trauma she went through."

"I've explained to you that it isn't the trauma that's causing this. Just because you can't hear things doesn't mean they're not happening. The last thing she needs to do right now is live in a drug-induced fog. We need her alert—so she can be safe." Grandma sighed on the other end. "I'd have you send her out to me, but you're in no condition to keep the gates secured, not with you unable to get around. And I can't leave your father. Besides, you know she'll be in more danger the further away from the property she gets."

"I hate this. We didn't ask to do this. You keep telling me that we have no choice, but I don't believe that. We have to find a way, Mom. Salome can't keep going through this. *We* can't keep going through this."

Grandma snorted. "Well, we don't have a choice. We can't change what our ancestors did. Besides, there are things even you don't know. Things I can't tell you. You have to trust me and do what I say where Salome's concerned."

My fingers tightened on the phone. What *was* so important about keeping the gates shut? Obviously, something more serious than keeping animals off the property. And who was this *them* they spoke about? Somehow they knew way more than they'd ever told me. A part of me wanted to let them know I listened on the other line. But I remained quiet, hoping they'd let something else slip.

"Listen, I need to go for now. I have to get dinner going." Mom sighed.

"Call me if anything else comes up."

"Let's hope it doesn't."

After they hung up, I clicked off the phone and rushed to the fridge, where I pretended to look for something to eat.

"Hey, do you want me to throw on some spaghetti?" I asked as Mom came into the kitchen behind me.

"Sure." She smiled as if nothing was wrong.

One way or another I was going to get to the bottom of this.

CHAPTER EIGHT

*H*omework. Lots and lots of homework. My backpack was weighed down with textbooks, tearing my shoulder out of its socket. It seemed only natural the day would end like this. School had been shitty. Both Kadie and Colton were absent and a jackass sophomore decided it'd be funny to put snow down my shirt, which landed me in the counselor's office for all of first hour. *Asshole.*

As if things couldn't get any better, I was running late and found myself rushing across the slushy parking lot toward bus number sixty-six. Otherwise known as the "banana boat from hell."

The smell of sweaty teen boys, the bus driver's lilac perfume, and nacho cheese Doritos hit me as I ascended the stairs. Brown seats lined either side of the mint green interior walls.

I just hoped I'd find an empty seat.

About midway back, I found a place to sit and slid in next to the window. I tossed my bag next to me, hoping to deter any idiots from thinking the seat was open.

Thick clouds loomed outside; large flakes already sputtered down like someone was hocking spit wads from the sky.

"I so hope we get a snow day tomorrow." A girl climbed into the seat in front of me.

"Yeah, because you haven't finished your biology project." Her hyper friend snickered.

I rolled my eyes, slipping my earbuds into place. Rock music blasted, drowning them out. One hour. I just had to get through the bus ride then I could see Nevin. Maybe he knew something about the *gates*, since he'd lived near us for years.

Today, I determined I'd also find out if he knew about the voices in the woods and discover where he lived. Even if it meant following him. Not that I liked the idea of trudging through the snow, but I needed to know that I wasn't a mental case.

The bus flopped around as we pulled out of the parking lot. As we drove into town, we got stuck at the main stoplight. Wiping the fog from the window, I noticed Kadie coming out of Perky Joe's. What the hell? She'd called this morning telling me she was too sick to go to school. Too sick to pick me up.

Flipping liar, she'd totally skipped. My jaw clenched as I ripped out my earbuds and fished out my cell. Kadie's phone rang twice before she picked it up.

"Hello," she answered.

"So how are you feeling?"

"A little better."

"Where are you?"

"At home, on the couch."

The light turned green and the bus jerked forward.

My stomach knotted. I didn't like confrontation, but I couldn't let this go. Best friends weren't supposed to keep secrets. Why was she lying to me?

"Strange. The bus just passed Perky Joe's. I thought I saw you coming out."

"Salome, I can explain." I heard the catch in her voice.

"You lied to me."

"I—I'm sorry. It's just Simeon's gorgeous and he mentioned this band that was playing today. So I kind of invited myself along. I would've told you but you get on me when I miss school…"

"You should've told me." I wanted to throw my phone across the bus, maybe punch the girl in front of me in the face for her stupid laugh.

"I'll make it up to you. There's just something about Simeon. Something indescribable. It's almost like I hear bells when he smiles at me." She giggled. "Wow, that sounds nuts. Anyway, he said there's another great band playing this Friday. We could double. Or better yet, if you're not too into Colton, I think Gareth might be there. Remember him from the other day? Tall, blond, kind of gorgeous."

Of course I remembered Gareth. It was kind of hard to forget him and the strange reaction I'd had to him at the coffee shop. There was something about him. Almost like Colton… and Nevin…but different. With a sigh, I rubbed the bridge of my nose. What was wrong with me? A week ago I hadn't thought about a guy, and now I had three of them on my mind. Maybe it was just my fear of winter, of the snow, of what happened to Cleo, and I desperately needed someone to lean on. Someone who understood me and made me feel safe.

"Salome? You there?"

A part of me wanted to hang up on her, but I didn't. "I'll think about it, Kadie. I mean the going with you thing, not sure I need you trying to hook me up with some guy who looks like a bouncer. And, by the way, this doesn't mean you're forgiven.

There is such a thing as a best friend code, you know." Static buzzed in my ear. "Listen, I'm about to lose my signal. I'll talk to you later."

I clicked the phone shut and threw it in my bag. Yep, another bad day.

Frost crept across the windows as if someone had splattered them with ice. When the bus stopped, kids jostled to the front to get off. Scraping the window, I peered out to see how fast the snow was falling. The roads were covered, while dusk loomed, ready to chase away the light.

The driver turned onto the dirt road, jarring and bumping us around, sending my bag to the floor with a *thud*. At the next stop, I noticed how close the trees were to the side of the bus. My heart hammered in my ears, an eerie tune meant for only me.

Scraaaatch.

A hand reached up on the other side of the window, touching the glass. Long, thorn-like nails trailed across it. Taking several deep breaths, I scooted away from the window until a pair of glowing, angry eyes stared back at me.

With a screech, I lunged backward, toppling from my seat.

"Hey, you okay?" A guy I recognized from my English class helped me up.

"Y-yeah, thought I saw something." I didn't move back to my seat right away, not until the bus driver yelled that I get back in my seat. And when I did, bile burned the back of my throat. Traced across my window in long looping letters was the word DEAD and the number eighteen.

Dizziness washed over me. Crap. I couldn't faint on the bus. Squeezing my eyes shut, I gripped the seat until my hands hurt, half-tempted to jump off at the next stop and call Kadie to come get me. But I couldn't move, not until we pulled up in front of my gated driveway. With my bag in hand I rushed down the aisle, not caring who I knocked in the head. I slid the wrought iron gate open and ran like hellish fiends tailed me. Of course, when I turned to look there was nothing but snow. Always the damn snow.

No one was home when I sprinted into the kitchen. A note from Mom fell from the table saying Ms. Watson from across the street had driven her into town for her doctor's appointment.

Whatever. I needed to find Nevin.

I dropped my bag in my room and stood against the wall, head in my hands. After consoling myself, I decided to drive to Grandma's. No way in hell did I want to walk.

"Please let him be here," I pleaded on the verge of a breakdown. The Jeep pushed through the snow with no trouble. Once there, I parked and hopped out.

Instead of heading inside, I cut through the walkway between the house and garage. Almost slipping, I grabbed a hold of a shrub, staggering into the backyard.

And there he was, standing by the oak tree. Relief flooded through me when Nevin turned toward me. His smile faded when he saw me.

Within a few strides, he stood over me. "What's wrong?"

My lip quivered. I tried to compose myself but the tears won out. "It's been an awful day."

He wrapped me in his arms, nestling my head against his chest. His hands stroked my hair as I fought to quit crying.

"Everything's okay now. I'm here," he said.

Between hiccups and sobs, I told him about Kadie lying to me and the strange thing I saw from the bus.

His brows furrowed at the mention of the hand, making me wish I'd kept my mouth shut. But somehow, I knew he believed me.

"I sound like I belong in an insane asylum." I clutched his

waist.

"No, you sound like someone who's been through a tragic experience. Promise me, you won't venture anywhere alone."

Was he kidding? I didn't need a vow to keep me from doing something so stupid. "I promise."

He gave me a sympathetic smile, leading me to the gazebo. "Why don't you sit here and relax, while I take care of the feeders for you."

I met his gaze. There was a yearning there so strong it almost knocked me from my feet.

"You don't have to."

"I want to help." His fingers touched my face for the briefest of seconds, but that was enough. He took care of the chores, then came back and sat next to me.

"I—I have to ask you something," I said.

"Anything."

My mouth went dry and I took a deep breath. "Do you hear voices in the woods?"

His eyes widened as he stared at me. "Sometimes."

"What's out there?" I scooted closer to him.

"I don't know. Maybe just the wind. Maybe something else."

"You've got to give me more than that. Please."

He sighed. "I don't know. Sometimes I think I hear soft words being spoken."

"But I've heard them call you by name." I frowned.

"I wish I had a better answer for you, but I don't." He stared off into the distance again.

"What's beyond the gates no one will tell me about?"

Nevin shrugged, but I could tell he knew what I was talking about.

In the end I conceded, and we talked about school and the painting he was working on. The two of us huddled together, even as the snow piled up. Cold nipped at my bones, making my skin tingle. My teeth chattered and I glanced up at Nevin.

"I know you don't like the idea of going into my grandma's house when she's gone and you don't want to impose on my mother, but what if we went back to your house?" I tried to sound innocent.

He stood, bringing me up with him. "I can't bring you home, Salome."

I shifted my gaze, biting my lip to keep from crying. "Okay." The hurt was evident in my voice and I cursed, wishing I sounded like I didn't care.

He squeezed me tight, his chin resting on my head. "It's not like that. I would invite you if I could."

"Maybe another time then." I pushed my hands against his chest to free myself from his comforting hold. Peering into his eyes, I wished I could read his thoughts and figure out what he wouldn't tell me. I turned and walked inside. Hiding behind the drapes, I watched him head back into the woods. Then I slipped back outside, hurrying to follow him.

Maybe this wasn't such a great idea.

I took several gulps of air to calm my nerves. I wanted so badly to know where he lived. What he was keeping from me. A branch snapped somewhere in front of me and I screeched and raced back into the house. I stood against the slider, heart pounding against my chest.

My cell rang and I jumped. Kadie.

"Hey," I said, out of breath.

"Okay, so I'm calling to apologize for earlier. I'm a seriously shitty friend. Trust me, even though I was with Simeon, I spent most of the day telling his friend Gareth all about you."

"Um—doesn't sound like much of a date then." I gave a forced laugh.

"So, what are you doing?"

"Well, I was going to try following the guy I told you about to find out where he lived, but I chickened out."

Kadie giggled. "Oh. My. God. My little Salome is turning into a stalker. Do you want help?"

"I can't believe I'm gonna say this, but yeah, if you want to become an accessory to stalking, I'm at my grandparents."

Ten minutes later, Kadie knocked on the front door. She smiled when I let her in.

"So, where do we start?"

I put on my mittens, eyeing the darkening sky. "The woods."

"Okay. Let's do this." She followed me onto the deck. "Do you want to wait here while I go in?" She gestured toward the tree line.

I swallowed hard. This was my idea. Was I really gonna make her go by herself? "I—I can try…"

She offered me her arm. "So does this guy have a name?"

"Nevin," I whispered.

"Well then, Project Stalk Nevin now underway."

Our footsteps crunched through the drifts as we walked into the woods. Already shadows splayed across the white backdrop and my hands trembled. Just keep it together, I told myself. Kadie wouldn't let anything happen.

"These are his footprints." I moved closer to Kadie as the wind howled, whipping through the canopy above.

We followed them through the brambles and thicket. The deeper into the forest we got, the more uneasy I became.

Soon the branches and greenery became a hindrance. But we had to be getting close, since we'd been walking forever. After a few more minutes, we burst into a clearing and stood on the shore at the back of the pond. I glanced down. His footprints had disappeared.

"This is crazy." Kadie bent down and stared at his footprints. "Either your boy is part frog and lives in the pond or he knew you trailed him and decided to sweep his real tracks away."

"Right, because everyone thinks like James Bond." What the hell was going on?

She laughed. "Well, I say we head back to your house, my ass and toes are about frozen."

I glanced around one last time. "Yeah, I think it's time to go." I would figure this out, because Nevin seemed to be the key to what was in the woods.

CHAPTER NINE

Kadie poked her head around my locker door. "Okay, so I know I already helped you last night with Operation Nevin, but I brought you a second peace offering." She handed me a king-size candy bar. "You know, for ditching you."

"You think you can buy my forgiveness with chocolate?" My fingers toyed with the shiny wrapper.

With a grin, she tore it open for me. "Um—yeah, hello, chocolate is like the world's best Band-Aid."

Truth was I'd forgive her and she knew it. It didn't mean I had to like the BS she pulled. But she'd totally helped me out last night and I kind of owed her one. "Fine, you're back in my good graces."

"So, have you decided anything about Friday?" She held onto my bag while I fumbled with my books.

"I thought you guys were going out Saturday."

"We are. It seems I've won Simeon over with my charm and he can't get enough of me." Her eyebrows waggled up and down.

With a groan, I pretended to plug my ears. "I don't want to hear what type of *charm* you used."

"Ha-ha. No, seriously you should come. Simeon and Gareth know this out-of-the-way place where a bunch of bands play. Besides, they invited us."

"Us?"

"Sure, I mean they didn't say you couldn't come. Besides the guys will be helping backstage with sound equipment and stuff. And I don't want to spend half the night alone. Not to mention, I think you kind of made an impression on Gareth at Perky Joe's when you nearly fainted."

My cheeks flamed as I toyed with the zipper on my sweater. "Actually, Nevin asked me to hang out Friday."

Her mouth dropped open. "What about Colton?" Kadie nodded toward him.

Suddenly I felt like I had betrayed him. God, he was so hot, and nice. But things were strange with him, too.

I bent closer to Kadie. "It's not a date. Nevin and I are just friends."

With a wink, she started walking away. "Sure you are. But let me just say for the record that most girls don't stalk 'friends' into the woods."

As Colton drew closer, I noticed the serious look on his face like his mind was somewhere else. But when he saw me watching, he smiled.

"Hey, missed you yesterday." I shut my locker door.

He backed me up against the line of lockers, one arm on either side of me. A faint bruise painted his cheek and I muffled a gasp. My fingers trembled when I lifted them to touch his face. But he caught my hand midair, sending my heart pulsing.

"I missed you, too."

"Wha—what happened?"

His gaze darkened. "I got jumped in the parking lot the other night. But don't worry, I took care of it. That's why I was gone yesterday."

Took care of it? What did he mean by that? Chills raced down my spine.

The shadows left his eyes and he grinned, stroking my hair.

Closing my eyes, I took a ragged breath. "Promise me you won't do anything stupid." My lids fluttered open to find him staring at me.

Colton leaned closer, his warm breath tickling my ear. "I promise not to fight unless it's to protect you."

Blood pounded in my ears like waves slamming into shore. He was so close—his face mere inches from mine. Heat radiated off him. A low humming started in my ears, the familiar tinkling sound I'd heard the last several times Colton had been around me.

"And what would I need protecting from?" Concentration wasn't possible when he was this close.

"Everything."

"Ms. Montgomery and Mr. Myers, I hate to interrupt this touching moment, but I'd advise you to save your make-out sessions for when you're off school grounds," Mrs. Stanford said, her heels clicking on the tiles.

"We weren't doing anything." I peered around Colton. The music sounded muffled, but it wasn't gone.

She sneered, pushing her glasses back up her nose. "Only because you got caught. Now, I suggest you both get to class."

Colton chuckled as she walked away. "She's just mad because she's not getting any."

"Well, I'm not either," I said, then groaned. "I didn't mean it like that."

"Are you sure?" Colton's gaze burned right through me. He

slid his hand down my back, guiding me toward class. "All in good time," he said with a sly wink.

"Um—you know that's not what I meant. We've only been on one date."

Colton stopped walking and scrutinized me. "I know. That's what I like about you. You're so sweet and innocent. Everything about you is perfect, your smile, your eyes." He chuckled softly. "Even your quirks."

I suddenly felt really warm and looked away. "If you think compliments will get you in my pants, you're wrong."

Did I have a mute button?

After the initial shock of what I said wore off, Colton laughed. "That wasn't quite the angle I was going for. I'm not like that."

"Then what's your angle?"

"I want to know you." His words sounded so sure, like he dared someone to try and prove him wrong. "And I'll be there when you need me."

"You know you shouldn't make promises you can't keep."

"I always keep my word. In fact, I promise to take you out tomorrow night."

"Oh?"

"You did lose a bet, remember? I get to take you on a date of my choosing," Colton said as we stepped into class.

I had a strange sense of drowning. But the feeling didn't frighten me like it should. Instead, I just felt safe.

When I jerked open the door the next night, there stood Colton, brown leather jacket with the collar high up around his neck, green eyes twinkling. He was so hot in a pair of faded blue jeans, brown leather boots, and a navy sweater.

"Hey, you ready?" He handed me a bouquet of wildflowers, the wind tousling his shaggy dark hair.

"Well, I thought about taking another shower, vacuuming the floor, and shoveling the driveway first." I smelled the flowers. "Do you mind if I throw these in a vase before we leave?"

He followed me into the kitchen. "I take it your parents like lighthouses and ships?" He stared at the walls, shelves, and décor.

"Lucky guess. You should see the upstairs playroom. It has a ship's wheel and tiny windows. My bedroom looks like the inside of a captain's cabin. My dad even got me some of the old lanterns."

"Is that an invitation to have a look around?"

"Sure." I took him upstairs first, showing him the ship's wheel, the bell, even the nautical brass spyglass that rested in one of the windows. My dad had built me a catwalk too, which led up to a little nook hidden behind drapes that looked like sails.

"Wow, this is amazing. I bet you had a lot of fun up here."

Closing my eyes, I thought back to all the times I'd spent in the playroom. It was my refuge, especially in the winter. I'd go up there and imagine I was at sea, someplace warm.

"I played here a lot more than I should of." I forced a smile. "Why don't I show you the rest of the house?"

Colton caught my hand, giving it a squeeze. I gave him a tour of the different rooms, saving my bedroom for last. When I came to my door, I hesitated. I'd never let a boy in before. You could tell a lot from someone's bedroom, like what kind of person they were.

I chewed my lip as Colton stepped over the threshold. His eyes scanned every wall. His glance lingered on my bed with the blue lighthouse quilt. My gaze drifted to the overstuffed mattress and back to him. Prickles crept up and down my neck, and then *thud-thud, thud-thud.* God, my heart was so loud. My face felt like I'd shoved it in the oven it was so warm. I cast a glance at Colton only to find him watching me.

"That's a big bed," he said.

"Yeah, you can fit a couple people in it."

I might as well just toss myself onto the mattress and change my name to Cleopatra.

Sparks practically sizzled in the air between us and he took a step forward. I wiped my sweaty hands on my pants, half hoping he'd sweep me up off my feet and carry me to my bed. Then the reasonable part of my brain kicked in, reminding me I definitely wasn't ready for that. Man, I was glad Mom wasn't home.

"I suppose we should…" He pointed at the door. "Head out now." His voice deepened and for a moment, he blurred in my vision.

With a sigh, I wiped my eyes and nodded. God, I hoped I wasn't having hallucinations again. "Right, um, let's go."

Before I dashed down the hall, Colton's arm wrapped around my waist. "Just so you know, I'm a gentleman, I'd never do anything you didn't want to."

A nervous chuckle found its way from my lips. "Good thing you can't read minds then."

"You deserve the best." His lips grazed my ear.

The very sound of his voice gave me chills, but in a good way. My fingers traced his cheek.

"And are you the best?"

He grinned. "I don't know, am I?"

Giving me a tug, Colton broke the moment and led me out of the house, to his truck. But all I could think about was his smoldering eyes.

Geez, what was wrong with me? I never acted like this. It was like he had some magnetized cologne or something that made me forget myself when I was with him. Or at least forget my inhibitions. I mean, I'd had a crush on him for years, but somehow this was more.

"So, where are we going?"

"You'll see."

We pulled from the driveway, heading west, away from town. The surroundings grew more somber the deeper into the woods we drove. There was no light, other than from our headlights. No houses. No signs of life.

I bit back the fear that bubbled inside me to enjoy the moment. At last, Colton turned onto a dirt road, which looked more like a two-track. I caught sight of tiny glowing orbs weaving in and out of the trees.

I must be seeing things. I rubbed my eyes, willing the craziness away. So not the time for a breakdown. My stomach clenched with fear. This couldn't happen now. It couldn't. I'd never live it down if I had an episode in front of him. I took several deep breaths, visualizing palm trees and sunshine. I had to stay focused.

Soon we came into a clearing I realized was a parking lot. An ancient-looking cabin loomed ahead of us with a sign welcoming us to the WOODEN NYMPH.

After finding a parking spot, Colton shut off the engine then turned to me. "Wait here a second. I've got to run in and talk to someone." He opened the door, sliding his long legs out first. "Keep the doors locked until I come back."

What the heck was he worried about? I swallowed hard, trying not to freak out. Suddenly, I became too warm, too aware of the out-of-the-way place.

"Okay," I said before he shut his door behind him. Oh, hell. What'd I gotten myself into? The Wooden Nymph was a pub and, well, I wasn't old enough to drink and neither was Colton. Maybe this wasn't such a great idea.

As I scanned the forest I heard eerie music. Like flutes calling to me from the darkness. My blood sang in tune. I reached for the door, ready to let myself out and follow it.

No. Colton said wait here.

A pair of glowing eyes pierced the shadowy tree line and stared at me. I undid my seat belt and shrunk away from the windows. Oh God, no. My hands trembled as I scooted across the seat. As I did, my foot bumped something under the seat.

I bent down to see what I'd kicked. With a gasp, I stared at the long silver blade etched with strange symbols. A sword. Why would Colton have a sword?

Something in my head whispered to just put it back and pretend I'd never seen it.

A tap on the window made me scream until I saw Colton gesturing for me to get out.

"Holy crap, you scared me." I placed my hand against my chest.

"Sorry, I thought you heard me."

He helped me from the truck, clutching my hand in his. We walked toward the entrance where a big beefy guy stood at the door. He nodded at Colton, giving him a salute of sorts.

The interior of the Wooden Nymph was dimly lit, flickering candles centered on the tables, and rustic-looking chandeliers hung from the high ceiling. I inched closer to Colton. Several guys with long dark hair and leather pants regarded us. Some congregated around a pool table, while others threw back beer at the bar. They had tattoos, knives, and menacing smiles. Bikers, I assumed. But when they saw Colton they took a step back. Why the heck would guys like them be wary of him?

I could almost smell the danger in the room as couples danced to the rhythmic beats of drums and flutes. Each movement was enticing and made me dizzy. The air smelled like honey and sweetness, not at all what I thought a bar should smell like.

"So this is what all the fuss is about," a woman with golden blond hair approached us and purred. She reached out a long red fingernail, as if to trace my cheek. "Hardly seems worth it."

"Might want to watch your tongue, Caralina. Hate for word to get back to the woods." Colton's lip curled.

Her face paled and she stepped out of our way.

Okay, this date was getting stranger by the second. This so wasn't my scene. Nervous, I cast him a quick look. "What was that about?"

"Nothing. She just likes to cause trouble."

And apparently my date had a side to him I never knew about. Something told me I might not want to know that side.

We went to the back of the room, where Colton pushed open a door that led outside. An older man with gray hair waited for us. He gave me the first friendly smile I'd seen since getting there.

"You must be Salome?" He offered me a wrinkled hand. His grip was stronger than I expected, making me wince.

"Yes."

"I'm Ferdinand, an old friend of Colton's." He ushered us toward a log fence. "You must be something special for him to bring you all the way out here."

Colton's arm dropped to my shoulders, pulling me close. "She is. I suggest you remind the others of that."

The two exchanged knowing glances, then Ferdinand flipped on an outdoor light. A sleigh waited for us with Clydesdales hooked to the front of it.

"Are you for real?" I gasped. "I've never—"

"I told you this night would be memorable." Colton grinned, brushing strands of hair from my face. "Not everything about the winter is bad—I wanted to show you."

Geez, this must've cost a fortune. How the heck had he paid for it? Not that I didn't think it was flipping awesome, but still.

Ferdinand helped me into the sleigh, then Colton. He draped blankets and furs across our laps, and then slipped into the front. He gave the reins a snap, sending the horses trotting into the night.

"What are those blinking lights?" I pointed to the tiny balls of illumination between the trees.

"The trail is set up with motion sensing equipment. It makes the Christmas lights blink." Colton wrapped another blanket around my shoulders.

Giant flakes drifted from the sky and landed in soft, cool kisses on my cheek and nose. Bells from the harnesses jingled. We went deeper into the woods where ancient oaks and maples waved in the wind as if welcoming us home. We finally came to a clearing with a bonfire roaring. Bright orange, blue, and yellow flames danced in the night.

"Here you are. There's a thermos of hot chocolate next to the bench. And we've got some stuff for you to roast, hotdogs and s'mores over the fire." Ferdinand helped me from the sleigh. "Enjoy your time. I'll be back in a couple of hours."

Oh my gosh, Colton had done all this for me. There was a chair swing perched between two trees that faced the fire, along with a hollowed-out log. A pile of blankets and furs sat neatly folded on the swing.

"So, do you like it?" Colton whispered.

"It's awesome. No one has ever gone to so much trouble

for me."

He took a hold of my hand and led me over to the swing, where he bundled me up beneath the blankets.

"You sit here, while I get our food ready."

I watched Colton, his dark hair tumbling over his forehead, as the wind picked up.

When the hotdogs blackened, he put them on buns and we sat down to eat. It was surreal the way the snow glistened against the backdrop, sparkling like a diamond ring. Heat radiated from the fire and from where his leg pressed against mine.

Once we finished dinner we grabbed the bag of marshmallows. I charred mine until it was flaming like a torch.

"I think it might be overdone." He laughed, handing me a graham cracker and a bar of chocolate.

"Nope, you've got to burn 'em. It makes the inside nice and gooey." I licked, or rather chewed, the sticky white marshmallow off my fingers. "I think I'm going to make a mess."

And I couldn't imagine how to not look like an idiot in front of him. Where was a sink and mirror when I needed them?

Colton chomped his down in two bites, leaving a marshmallowy residue on his lips. Giggling, I covered my mouth.

"Um—you've got something, right here." I wiped at my own lips.

He chuckled, raising a hand to his mouth. "Did I get it?"

"Nope."

He did another swipe, but it still didn't come off.

"Since I can't see what I'm doing, you want to help?" He waved me over.

I tossed the rest of my s'more in the fire and scooted nearer to him on the log. My hands trembled when I moved my thumb across his lips. He ran his hand through my hair, eyes blazing like the bonfire behind us.

Colton pulled me closer, until his forehead touched mine. Music swirled in the air, he smelled like chocolate, and I did all I could not to take a bite out of him.

"I thought you wanted me to help you get the marshmallow off?" I murmured. My first kiss. Oh God, it was going to happen. Finally.

"I do." He moved closer yet.

His lips grazed mine sending shock waves through my body. My lids drifted shut as I wound my arms around his neck. Our bodies pressed together and he deepened the kiss, his mouth warm against mine.

He tasted so good and his tongue. Oh my God, I couldn't think straight. I'd never been drunk before, but I felt kind of lightheaded—almost like my body was going through these motions without me.

He leaned me back, propping himself above me. My fingers traced the chiseled contours of his face as he eased away and stared down at me.

Then all at once, a strange look came over him like he'd just been caught doing something he wasn't supposed to. Colton stood, bringing me with him.

"What's wrong?" I touched my lips where his had just been.

He grinned, clutching me against his chest. "Nothing. I just don't want you to think I'm moving too fast."

I rested my head against him. "I wouldn't think that. And, if I'm being honest, you're kind of my first kiss."

"Kind of?"

My face burned with embarrassment. "I mean, you are my first kiss."

He held me at arm's length. "I was your first?" he said again. For a moment, I saw a look of arrogance take over his features.

"Yes."

He bent down again, lips capturing mine. I thought I might explode, my body screamed for so much more. Each touch sent me spiraling out of control.

Breathless, he pulled away again. "And now I'm your second, too."

"If you keep this up you're going to be my third, fourth, and fifth."

Seconds later, the jingling of bells sounded and Ferdinand led the sleigh into the clearing.

"Hope you two had a good time." His mouth twitched at the corners.

Great. I hoped he hadn't been watching the make-out session.

"Yeah, it was fun."

"And here I was, shooting for romantic." Colton leaned over to whisper in my ear.

Nuzzling against him, I smiled. "That too."

After we parked back at the cabin, Colton lifted me from the sleigh and I followed him back into the club. My eyes immediately came to rest on a guy sitting in the back corner with a black hoodie pulled up over his head. Shaggy blond hair peeked out from the edges.

I don't know how I knew, but he was staring right at us. There was something very familiar about him. I felt drawn in his direction, but Colton tensed.

"We need to get out of here, now." He dragged me through the crowd and I thought for a moment he might jerk my arm out of its socket.

He unlocked the truck and threw it into gear before my door even shut. The tires squealed and I fought to get my seat belt on.

We whipped onto the road and I gripped the armrest for

dear life.

"Colton!" I screamed, wondering if I would live through the car ride home.

He seemed to snap out of whatever daze he'd been and glanced over at me. The vehicle slowed.

"Sorry. That guy back there is trouble. I didn't want to have any run-ins with him. Not tonight." He reached across the seat and laced his fingers through mine. "Forgive me?"

"What the hell is going on? You're acting like a flipping maniac." I tore my hand from his. Was his temper always this bad? I mean, the other day in the library he'd mentioned a fight. Was it with this same guy?

He focused back on the road. "I was trying to do the right thing. If we'd stayed, there'd have been a fight. Trust me, I don't get along with that guy back there. The last thing I wanted to do is have you in the middle of a bar brawl."

Was that all there was to it? I chewed my bottom lip and sighed. "Who was he?"

"Please, can we not talk about him? I really don't want our date to end with us arguing over some asshole who doesn't even matter." He turned to gaze at me, his eyes swirled with darkness.

An unsettling feeling gnawed at my belly. I'd never seen him like this and I never wanted to again. What'd happened to the Colton from our first date? Who'd seemed clumsy and fun and easily embarrassed?

"Fine, let's just get back to my house." I gave him a shaky smile and spent the rest of the car ride dissecting every last detail of our date, both good and bad.

CHAPTER TEN

All day, Kadie analyzed my first kiss. I don't know how many times she made me tell her about the date. I left out the parts about him tasting like chocolate; I mean I had some dignity. And for a few minutes I'd forgotten it was winter.

When I told her about his angry outburst, she seemed kind of concerned. And if I was being honest, so was I. She said if something like that happened again, to call her and she'd come get me.

With a sigh, I attempted to erase last night from my mind, because tonight I'd be able to spend time with Nevin. There were so many questions I planned on asking him and I wouldn't take no as an answer. Pushing into the house, I stopped mid-stride when I heard Mom's loud voice.

"Don't do this, Rich… Me? I'm the one here, taking care of everything. You're never around." Mom sounded choked up.

Whoa. What was going on? I clutched tight to my backpack.

"And how would you have me deal with her… Oh, don't criticize me for how she's being raised. Not when you can't be a father. When was the last time you were even home? I can't do this by myself."

I needed them to please stop fighting. My stomach grew queasy, the knots twisting tighter. They were arguing about me. I had no idea what had happened. Dad had sounded so happy last time we talked.

"Maybe you could find another job so you're home more. I have to go, I can't deal with this right now." She slammed down the phone. Muffled sobs sounded from the living room. My heart broke. She didn't deserve that.

What in the hell had gotten into him? Dad never yelled at Mom. Matter of fact, he used to call me and Mom all the time from the road. But I noticed in the last couple of weeks he'd barely gotten a hold of us. It was like he was a completely different person.

Slipping into the room, I tossed my bag on the floor. "You okay?" I pretended I hadn't heard anything.

Mom gave me a forced smile. "Yeah." She sniffled, then wiped the tears away with her hands. "How was school?"

Why didn't she talk to me? I was old enough to understand. "Fine. So, I'm going to head over to feed the animals real quick. And I'm gonna hang out with a friend after that."

She perked up. "With Colton?"

"No, someone else." I smiled. "Don't worry, he's a complete gentleman."

"Shouldn't I meet him first?" Mom called after me.

"Everything's fine. It's not a date, I promise. We're just friends. I've gotta go or I'll be late."

"Wait. Maybe I can drive over with you." She smiled.

Guilt nagged me. She was probably just lonely. It wouldn't kill me to have her sit in the house and wait for me to finish my chores. But then she'd want to meet Nevin and I'd never get out of there on time. With a sigh, I stared at the clock. I could just have Nevin meet me after I got Mom back to the house. "Okay, c'mon."

She grabbed her coat from the back of the chair and followed me outside on her crutches.

"Wait here while I pull the Jeep around," I said, thankful our neighbor had plowed a path to our garage.

When I got to Grandma's, I helped Mom get situated at the breakfast nook in the kitchen.

"I shouldn't be too long." I tugged my hat over my ears.

"Are you sure you don't want me to sit out on the deck or even at the gazebo?"

"I-it's okay."

She patted my arm. "Can you hand me Gram's phone? Since you're going out tonight, I'm going to give Nancy a quick call and see if she wants to go see a movie or something. No sense staying home alone."

I moved across the kitchen, picked up the cordless phone from the receiver, and handed it to her.

"Thanks honey—and be careful out there."

"I will."

When I finally stepped onto the deck, I noticed Nevin was nowhere to be seen. Which was probably a good thing. At least then he could avoid my mom, who would want to play twenty questions with him.

Taking a deep breath, I left the safety of the porch and headed to the shed, where I grabbed everything I needed to get my chores done. With two rowan twigs in hand, I hesitated near the gate. Wind pushed through the trees, howling like rabid animals on the loose.

I told myself to just put the damn things in the fence and leave.

But I stood motionless, staring into the sinister fortress of timbers. Inky silhouettes slunk through the overgrowth like they marched toward me.

Hiss.

The twigs trembled in my hands and I forced myself forward. Trying not to look in the woods, I wove the sticks into the gate then staggered backward, landing on my ass in a snowdrift.

"Brilliant." Damn, I was jumpy. I climbed back to my feet and wiped off my pants, then trudged to the feeders.

When I got back to the deck, there was still no sign of Nevin, but I found a note inside the door. Disappointment flooded me when I saw it was from him. He simply wrote something had come up and he couldn't make it. But if he'd been here, why hadn't he told me himself?

Maybe he'd reconsidered my confession about my mental state and changed his mind?

No. He'd said he liked me. Yet, deep down I knew he hid stuff from me and I didn't like secrets. In fact, the more mysterious Nevin was the more I felt inclined to unravel the puzzle.

As I stood on the deck, goose bumps broke out over my skin. Then I heard the scream. My stomach clenched, my eyes darted over the landscape. No. I had to ignore it. I was just hearing things like I always did.

"Salome!" Mom's frantic cry came from the woods. "Help me. I've fallen."

"Mom?" I called. What the hell was she doing out there? I'd told her to stay inside.

"Hurry," she shrieked, sounding more desperate. "I'm bleeding."

"I'm coming, just hold on." Holy shit. If something happened to her… My fingers touched the cell phone in my pocket, making sure it was still there if I needed it. Terror set in as I rushed into the trees. My footsteps crunched in the snow, feet sinking in as I ran. The air was brisk, the surroundings dead silent. There were no birds singing, or crickets chirping, no frogs serenading the pond. Everything was drab—branches bare of leaves, fruit vines withered and brown beneath the heavy ice. The only things that seemed to survive were the thornbushes gripping at my coat and jeans like the teeth of a shark.

"Mom, where are you?" I glanced around, not seeing any footprints. My body tensed. I had to keep it together. She needed me.

"I'm farther back." A sob bounced off the pines and oaks.

How did she get in so far? I stayed close enough to the fence inside Gram's property to keep my bearings. A rotted log blocked my path and I hopped over it, nearly falling into the snow. I grabbed hold of the nearest cluster of foliage and screeched when thorns bit my skin. With a tug, I got my glove free and took it off to examine my hand. Tiny beads of blood bubbled to the surface then fell to the ground. The crimson color spread across the snow like red ink on white paper. I sucked my fingertips; the metallic copper taste made me nauseous.

Once again I searched for Mom's footprints. But there weren't any. Uneasiness gripped hold when I realized my tracks were covered as well.

"Salome, hurry. My leg, it hurts so bad."

"I—I don't know where you are." My chest tightened. What if I couldn't find her? What if she froze to death because I wasn't fast enough?

My eyes welled, blurring my vision as I pressed further in. I couldn't freak out now.

Silence settled over the woodland. The deeper in I went, the brisker the air became. Wisps of fog trailed like ghostly soldiers trudging off to battle.

I cupped my hands together and screamed, "Mom?"

This time there wasn't an answer. I swallowed hard and tried again.

"Mom? Answer me." My voice cracked. Then, I saw it. A corroded cement archway, surrounded by wrought iron spires, barred the entrance to an ancient looking cemetery.

My cell phone blared and I jumped. "Holy frick." I tore off my glove and grabbed it from my pocket.

Grandma's number.

"H-hello?"

"Where in the world are you?" Mom said from the other end.

"Mom, you're okay. H-how did you get back to the house?"

"Back to the house? I never left it."

"Wait, you're not in the woods?"

"No. What's going on?"

"But you called to me from the woods. You said you were hurt, you said—"

"Oh God. Salome, you get back here, now. You understand me?"

Fear coiled inside. If Mom hadn't called for me, then who the hell had? I needed to get out of here. Now. But as my gaze shifted to the cemetery, I felt drawn to it. Like I couldn't stop my boots from moving in that direction.

I took a step closer to it. Fuck. What was I doing?

"I'll be there soon. I need to check something first."

This was stupid. I didn't have to go any closer to the flipping cemetery. I needed to get the hell home. I swallowed hard and took another step toward it.

"For the love of all that's holy, you don't need to check anything. Salome, you're having one of your episodes. You shouldn't be alone." Mom sounded freaked out.

"Did you know there's a graveyard back here?"

"Yes, it's a family one," she whispered. "And it's really far from the house. So worry about it later, okay?"

"All right. Be there soon." I hung up the phone. Why hadn't Grandma ever mentioned a cemetery on the property? I wondered if this had something to do with what they'd talked about on the phone the other day. A loud crash sounded beside me and, against my better judgment, I raced toward the entrance.

Right, great idea—spooky woods, fog, graveyard. Might as well just put a *dumb ass* stamp on my forehead. How many scary movies had I seen over the years where I yelled at the stupid actresses for going into places they shouldn't? And here I was, playing the stupid actress.

A gust of wind sent snow whipping through the woods, the cemetery gate groaned like a savage beast as it swung back and forth on rusty hinges.

My lungs froze. I took a deep breath, pushing into the gravesite. Erosion made some of the writing on the headstones hard to read, but I could tell they went back to at least the 1700s.

Starting in the back, I began to read the names. *Sarah Jane Smythe, Born September 14, 1775, Died December 21, 1793. Martha Arianna Brown, Born January 17, 1799, Died January 21, 1817. Anna Mae Brown-Fredericks, Born October 4, 1829, Died December 27, 1847.* And on they went. I read each headstone, until I came to the most recent one. *Maude Felice Hanover, Born December 11, 1940, Died January 29, 1958.*

My stomach rolled. Maude was Grandma's sister. I'd seen pictures of her in Grandma's house. I backed away from the headstones. God, this was unreal. Every grave belonged to a female. They had all passed away at the age of eighteen. *Eighteen.* What I'd seen scratched on the bus window. The number I'd heard carried on the wind.

And they were related to me.

That wasn't the worst of it. Every last one of them had died in the *winter*. Snow. Ice. Darkness. The scenery spun in circles and I gripped tight to a cold cement slab. The stone seemed to vibrate under my hand. I screamed and toppled to the ground. Scared shitless, I scooted back, running into another grave marker.

"She's out here by herself."

"We have to get Master. She shouldn't have come this far."

A sinister cackle echoed through the woodland, the air humming with the malice.

"Foolish beings, do you think any of you can save her from this fate? I will get to her. She'll soon be eighteen, too. Look how easily she was led out here."

I had to get out of here. The light that streamed through treetops above grew dimmer. Night would soon set in. I'd come here to find my mom and instead found death.

Winter always meant death. How could I be so stupid to think anything good could come of winter?

"He's coming," a tinkling voice whispered on the breeze.

Oh. My. God. Who was coming? Who?

I peered up to see Nevin burst through the trees like a chivalrous knight. His pale eyes were wild with terror. When his gaze finally landed on me, he rushed into the graveyard, lifting me to my feet.

"Are you okay?" His hands stroked my face while he examined me.

"I—um, yeah," I stammered.

He let out a sigh of relief. "What kind of madness made you come out here by yourself?" He gave me a shake.

My body quaked with fear. "I—I thought I heard my mom calling for me."

"Damn it." Anger flared in his eyes. "Don't come out here

by yourself. It's not safe." His tone softened. He wrapped his arms around me, hand smoothing my hair.

"How did you know where to find me?"

He didn't answer right away. "I had to gather wood and happened to hear you scream."

Liar. Why didn't he ever give me a straight answer? Had he heard the voices, too?

"I'm glad you're here," I said.

"Yeah, well, as I hear it, this isn't the first time you've gone wandering in the woods lately."

"Um—I'm not sure I know what you're talking about?"

"A couple days ago, you tried following me."

Heat scorched my skin beneath his scrutiny. "I—I just wanted to know where you live."

He chuckled. "Is that what it was about?"

I shifted away from him. "You're so secretive. You never answer any of my questions. About the voices. About the gates. I thought if I found you at home—"

"I didn't think where I lived mattered. Besides, the place is kind of run down." He ran a hand through his raven colored hair.

Suddenly, I felt like a jerk. I never thought he'd be embarrassed by his house. But it made sense why he never asked me over.

"Sorry." My fingers clasped his, and I noticed how cold his skin was to my touch.

"Just trust me, Salome. I care about you. You've become such a good friend." He gave me a sad smile. "We'll do something fun together soon, but there are a few things I have to take care of first. Until then, promise me you'll stay away from here. And out of the blasted woods."

Tossing my head back, I stared up at him. "I promise. But first, can you answer one thing for me?" My teeth grazed my bottom lip. I was about to admit my craziness to someone outside my tight circle. Nervous flutters ate at my gut like leeches sucking blood.

"And what's that?"

My eyes focused on the ground. "What's going on with the voices in the woods? They knew you were coming to help me. How do you know them?" What I really wanted to know, though, was if they belonged to the beings that'd pulled me to safety as a child. The people, if you could call them that, who'd warned me to stay away from here.

I fidgeted with the zipper on my coat as I waited for him to answer. The silence seemed to swallow us up.

"I didn't hear any voices tonight," he said. "You probably just got scared and imagined it. I think it's time to walk you to Doris's. It's getting dark."

Great, he did think I was nuts. Why couldn't I have just left things alone? Because I didn't want to be crazy. I wanted to know someone else could hear and see what I did.

When I didn't move, Nevin touched my sleeve. "Listen, there are things I can't speak of. But there is a certain danger that lurks nearby. One I'd advise you to stay away from."

That didn't exactly clear things up. If anything, it raised more questions. "What's beyond the gate?"

Nevin's brow furrowed and he tugged me away from the cemetery. His darkened gaze let me know that the subject was dropped.

Our hike back was fast. And soon I found myself standing in the tree line.

"Is someone in the house?" He glanced down at me.

"Yeah, my mom came with me today."

"I'll say good-bye here." He touched my cheek, then disappeared back into the woods.

When he was gone, I hurried to the deck, where Mom met me at the door.

"Thank God, you're okay." She hugged me tight.

"I'm fine." I gave her a forced smile.

I needed to know what led me into the woods. Not to mention she and Grandma had some major explaining to do.

CHAPTER ELEVEN

"*M*aybe I should cancel my plans with Nancy tonight and stay with you until your friend comes," Mom said when we got back to our house.

I rolled my eyes. "No. You need a break from this place. Go on, I'll be fine. Besides, Kadie wanted me to hang out with her tonight."

"Wait, what happened to the guy you told me about?"

I tossed my coat on the back of the dining room chair. "Something came up."

Her fingers rubbed the rungs of her crutches as she stared out the window. "Are you sure Kadie will be with you?"

Okay, so I didn't know for sure whether or not she still wanted me hanging with Simeon, Gareth, and her. But I dang sure wasn't going to tell Mom that. We'd spent the car ride back home arguing over my going off into the woods after voices no one else heard. If I had any more episodes, I knew I'd be shipped off to see Dr. Bosworth.

"Yes. Geesh, what's gotten into you?"

She gave me a tight smile. "I just worry about you, honey."

"I know. But I pinky-swear that I'll be fine. So go get your hot mama clothes on before Nancy gets here."

Thirty minutes later, she went with Nancy and left me alone in the house.

My stomach churned. Now at least I could get a hold of Grandma. She'd be easier to get answers from than Mom. I found our address book next to the phone and flipped it open, searching for Gram's new number. My hands shook as I dialed, whether from fear or anger, I wasn't sure.

"Hello?" Grandma's familiar voice buzzed.

"It's me. I need to talk to you."

I heard the television in the background turned down, then a door shutting.

"What is it, dear?"

"Why didn't you tell me about the cemetery at the back of the property?"

Silence followed. At first, I thought she'd hung up, until she cleared her throat.

"I didn't see the point. Besides, you never go into the woods."

"All those people, they were our family?"

"Yes."

I squeezed the phone and sat in a chair. "They all died in the winter, Grandma. And they were all eighteen."

"Accidents happen, honey," she said, her tone hushed.

Accidents? Did she really think I'd believe that?

"You can't tell me every one of those girls had an accident. I don't buy it." I could almost taste the acid in my response. I counted to ten to keep my temper in check.

"Stay out of those woods," she snapped.

Grandma never snapped. But the seriousness lacing her

words made me even more curious about what she hid from me. And what part did Mom play in all this, if any?

"Why doesn't anyone think I can understand what's going on? First, Mom with Dad. Now you."

Grandma sighed. "Please, just do as I say. We can talk more about this when I come home in the spring. Until then, don't speak to any strangers and keep out of the woods. They're no place for you."

I wondered if I'd be alive come spring.

*A*lone in the house, my mind went into overdrive. Maybe having Mom leave wasn't such a good idea. Each shadow reminded me of some horror movie monster. Each thud of my heart, too loud in my ears. I jumped when the chime of the clock struck six.

Wind whipped against the outside shutters, howling and yipping like something tried to get in. Lights flickered and I shot off the couch. No way in hell could I stay home alone. No matter how loud I turned up the television I still heard the gusts and the eerie creaking of boards as the house settled.

I grabbed my cell and dialed. Please pick up, I thought.

"Hey, Kadie," I said when she answered. "Is that invitation still open for tonight?" My teeth grazed my bottom lip, praying she'd say yes.

"Um—well..." She hesitated. "About that."

My heart sank. "If you'd rather be alone with Simeon, I totally understand."

"No. It's not that. It's just, remember how I said the guys wanted us to come? Well they didn't exactly invite us."

"What do you mean?"

"Let's just say Simeon mentioned helping out at the club in passing and I figured we could tag along."

"Kadie, we can't invite ourselves. Maybe they had other plans. You know, with other girls."

She laughed. "Trust me, if he didn't want me to chase after him, then he wouldn't have brought it up. Besides, even if he doesn't want to hang out with us, there will be tons of people there. It's not like Simeon owns the place."

"Are you sure about this?"

"Yeah. Now go put on that little black dress I got you for your birthday."

Her voice calmed me.

"Um—in case you didn't notice it's, like, twenty-nine degrees out." I tromped into my room, flipping on my bedside lamp.

"Didn't your mama ever teach you beauty is pain?"

I dug through my closet, tossing possible outfits onto my bed. "If you want frostbitten boobs then fine, but I like *all* my lady parts."

"You so exaggerate—just wear what you want." She laughed. "I'll be there in thirty minutes."

After hanging up the phone I decided to wear the black dress she'd suggested, along with some tights and black boots. Once dressed, I went back into the living room to wait.

"I'm here." She entered without knocking.

I pulled on my coat. "I didn't notice."

"So, what happened with Nevin?"

I frowned, toying with my purse. "Something came up."

"And, of course, your other boy wonder has a game tonight. But no worries. I promise to introduce you to every hot guy at the club." She grinned, linking her arm through mine.

When we got to Kadie's old beater she handed me a slip of paper. "What's this?"

"Directions to the club. I think I remembered all the turns and stuff."

"You think? Did you try to pull it up on your phone?"

"It's not listed anywhere online, which is odd, because this place is freaking awesome."

The more we talked about this, the more I believed it was a bad idea. "Maybe we should just stay in tonight. I don't want to chance getting lost or pissing off Simeon and Gareth." More than that, I wasn't sure I wanted to see Gareth at all, although I wasn't sure why.

"Relax. Everything will be fine. Besides, have you ever known a guy to turn me down?"

I was envious of Kadie's don't-give-a-damn attitude when it came to guys. If only I could be like that.

Our car bumped down the back roads, snowflakes peppering the windshield. What was the deal with out of the way clubs? Hello. Didn't they want people to find them?

The road narrowed, curving like the coils of a snake. Soon we came to a covered bridge and my thoughts drifted to several children's stories I read about monsters under structures just like this. Time to turn the mind off.

"Shit, could the road get any smaller?" Kadie maneuvered us onto the bridge.

The tires *cu-clunked* over the wooden planks. The motion jarred the vehicle and I grasped the armrest, praying we wouldn't topple into the creek below.

My grip on the armrest didn't loosen even after we were back on solid ground. We came to an eerie line of trees that bent inward like the opening of a tunnel. Each branch-like skeletal finger tracing the car windows. We lost sight of the road as we rounded the bend. The shadows thickened, plunging us into darkness.

"Where the hell is this place?" I inched away from my door.

"Right there." She nodded toward the large building that seemed to come out of nowhere.

The structure was made of black bricks. Purple neon signs flickered eerily against the CLUB BLADE sign.

"Are you sure this place is safe?" Good god, the guy standing by the door looked like a cross between a wrestler and Tyrannosaurus rex.

Kadie eased into a parking spot then flipped her mirror open to apply more lip-gloss. "Yes, it's safe. Quit worrying."

Large shadowed mounds surrounded the building. I didn't realize what they were until I stepped from the security of the car. I wondered why the hell there was a rock formation around the club.

Music throbbed in the air, conjuring pictures of hellish fiends, yet enticing me closer. I no longer felt like myself. My blood tingled. My feet urged me forward while my mind screamed to stay away. This place felt otherworldly. Like we didn't belong.

"Who are you here for?" The guy at the door stopped us.

"Simeon and Gareth," Kadie said.

"Names?"

"Kadie Byler and Salome Montgomery."

A slow smile spread across his lips as he glanced at us. I had the sudden urge to vomit.

"Go on in."

If it wasn't for Kadie jerking on my arm, I don't think I would've made it past the front door. Rock music pulsated and strobe lights flashed like a cop car, making me dizzy. She led me toward a booth where the strobes weren't so bad; in fact, the dim candlelight made it almost bearable.

"What the hell are you two doing here?" Gareth tapped Kadie's arm, seeming to appear out of thin air. His eyes darkened, and I almost stopped breathing. "I thought Simeon told you he was busy tonight?"

Kadie shrugged. "It's a free country. Besides, I figured he could visit with me after you guys finished setting stuff up backstage."

As if hearing his name, Simeon stalked through the crowd. "Kadie, what's going on?"

"Apparently, she's here to see you." Gareth frowned. "Thought we decided we'd be too busy to entertain people tonight."

"Come on." Kadie practically pouted. "We won't bug you. In fact, we'll just be dancing."

Simeon sighed, but his eyes traveled over her skimpy outfit and his finger traced her chin. "What do you say, Gareth, can they stay?"

Gareth's gaze flickered to me then darted around the crowd as if searching for someone. "Fine, but you two need to be out of here before midnight, got it?"

My throat went dry. I just wanted to grab Kadie and go.

Kadie glanced at me with a "see, I told you so" kind of look. "Okay," she said, then ran her hand across Simeon's chest, "I guess, I'll see you in a few."

"Yeah, I'll try to take a break when we're done setting stuff up." Simeon bent down and gave her a quick kiss then pulled back and sauntered into the crowd.

Gareth gave me a wary smile. "Try to stay out of trouble."

My hand smoothed down my hair and I fidgeted with the edge of my sweater. "Yeah, no problem."

He disappeared into the crowd as well, leaving Kadie and me alone.

I looked around the room, staring at the packed dance

floor. Most of the people were beautiful, surreal. They dripped danger from every pore. A tall girl with long sleek black hair made her way over to a guy at the bar. She merely pointed at him and he followed her onto the floor.

His eyes glazed when she leaned over to whisper in his ear. Goose bumps crawled across my skin like tiny spiders. Tearing my gaze from them, I focused on the rest of the crowd. Some wore bizarre masks like we were at a masquerade ball while others hid behind filmy curtains.

We sat in the booth for about twenty minutes, sipping pop while eyeing the crowd and the strange décor. The more time we spent in this place the more uneasy I got.

"C'mon, let's go dance," Kadie yelled over the music. "Simeon can find us when he's done."

We threaded through the thrashing bodies, finding a place in the middle of the chaos. We had our hands up in the air, swinging our hips back and forth to the beat. I closed my eyes, letting myself get lost in the music. Spinning around, I felt someone crash into me. I looked up to see the blond-haired woman from the Wooden Nymph glaring at me.

"You're out of your element here," she sneered, red nails scraping the side of my face. "And Colton isn't here to protect you."

My hand flew to my cheek and I stumbled back. "Who says I need his protection?"

"Me." She flipped open a blade; the metal flashed beneath the strobes.

What the hell was going on? We needed to get out of there now. I took another step back. My body quaked. I knew we shouldn't have come here. Bad things always happened in the woods. I grabbed hold of Kadie's hand.

"Let's just go," I said.

"I don't think so," the blond moved closer.

Kadie glanced at the knife, her eyes narrowed as she stepped between us.

What the hell was she doing? This wasn't some kid from school.

"Kadie," I said, fear coiling in my belly.

She shook my hand off then stared down the blonde. "Why don't you back the fuck off?"

Oh shit! Not good. We were going to die. Why wouldn't Kadie just back down?

"What's wrong? Can't fight your own battles?" the blond said.

"Is there a problem, Caralina?" Gareth clamped a hand on her shoulder.

Where in the heck had he come from?

Her eyes widened. "N—no. I was just going."

"I thought as much." Gareth's voice was colder than a tray of ice cubes. He watched her walk away then turned to me. "You should be more careful about the company you keep."

Kadie gave me a forced smile. "What'd you do to piss her off?"

Good question. "I have no idea."

"Hey listen, why don't you go back to the booth, while I get us more drinks," Kadie called as she moved into the crowd, leaving me alone with Gareth. God, she acted like this whole thing was no big deal.

Gareth leaned in closer. "Colton is bad news."

"Excuse me?" I hugged my arms to my chest.

He bent his head until his mouth was by my ear and I shivered when his breath tickled my neck. "I'd stay away from him if I were you. I'd hate to see you get hurt. You're a nice girl, Salome."

"And, h—how would you know that? You've only met me once."

"Word gets around."

My tongue suddenly felt swollen, making it hard to swallow. My eyes trailed up his gothic tattoo until they focused on his face.

"Thanks for the warning but I—I can take care of myself. Besides, Colton's a nice guy."

"And sometimes people aren't what they seem." He stared down at me. "Maybe you and Kadie should leave now. This isn't the type of place you want to be."

"What are you? My mother?" I asked, standing straighter. All I wanted to do was get the hell out of here, but I wasn't about to tell him that.

He ran a hand through his hair while he stared at me. "Look, I'm not trying to be a dick. It's just, you don't really belong here."

"Well, we're here now, so we might as well stay."

"Don't say I didn't warn you. You might also want to tell your friend not to show up places she's not invited." With that, he left me standing alone in the middle of the dance floor. People moved out of his way like they were afraid of him.

Maybe I should be, too. And that's when I realized why I hadn't wanted to see him again. I knew I'd disappoint him, and somehow I had.

The club suddenly felt too small, the air heavy, music too enchanting. I had to get out of there. Now. Gareth was right about one thing, we didn't belong here. Freaked out, I scanned the crowd for Kadie. My legs trembled beneath me as I sucked in a deep breath. I needed fresh air.

"Come on, hurry up," I whispered.

When Kadie came back, she glanced at her watch.

"You okay?"

"No, I'm lightheaded and want to get out of here."

The strobes pulsated above, each drumbeat calling to me, urging me to get lost in the maze of thrashing bodies.

"Fine, we can go if you want." Kadie glanced around the room. People were all over each other, kissing, dancing, sharing food in a way I imagined only happened in porn movies.

I frowned. "You're not mad at me are you? I know we haven't been here that long… And you didn't really get to hang out with Simeon."

"No, I'm not mad. Let's just go." She stared at some guy pinning a waitress against the wall. "Simeon and Gareth wanted us to leave before midnight. And well, it's close enough."

A sigh of relief parted my lips. We grabbed our coats and rushed toward the door, the urgency to get out of there overwhelming. My hair stood up on the back of my neck and my mind screamed for me to run.

When we got to the parking lot, the lights were dim, plunging the building and grounds into darkness. Kadie fumbled to get the doors unlocked. When I heard the audible click, I leaped in, slammed my door shut, and snapped my seat belt in place. I buried my head in my hands. Shit. I'd almost been stabbed tonight. I should've just stayed home.

I turned to Kadie, who threw the car into drive. For an instant as we drove away, I thought I heard screaming. Then I glanced at the dashboard clock. *Midnight.* We hadn't been in the club that long, had we?

"That was weird." She let out a nervous laugh.

"We're never coming back here again. I don't care how hot a guy is." I curled my fists in my lap to steady my shaking hands. Something was definitely wrong with that place. No wonder Gareth hadn't wanted us there. "And next time, don't step in front of someone with a knife. God. You could've been killed."

"I can take care of myself."

"Do you hear yourself right now? That chick had a knife. You're not invincible."

"Well, I wasn't about to let her attack you. You're my best friend."

She was so nonchalant about it, like we'd taken a walk in a park or something. But when I glanced at her again, I noticed her furrowed brow and her white knuckles.

Kadie turned onto Bench Road, but her bright lights barely pierced the gloom. Gauzy shapes wove in and out of the trees. I wanted to dismiss it as animals, but knew better. Then I saw it.

There, standing in the middle of the road, was the figure I'd seen from the bus.

"Look out!" I shrieked, jerking the steering wheel.

The tires squealed as we hit a patch of ice. Round and round the car spun, until it hit the ditch and rolled over. Pain shot through my head and arm as I struck the passenger side window. Glass shattered, spraying the side of my face. The horn blared. The airbag jammed against me, shoving me back against the seat, where I hung upside down.

A scream sounded, jarring me. My scream.

"Kadie!" I tried to reach my seat belt.

She cried out, but said nothing. Her sobs quieted to a soft whimper.

Footsteps crunched nearby and I cupped a hand over my mouth to hush my cries as they neared. In terror, I peered out the glassless window and saw the figure moving toward me. A woman covered in woodland debris, her hair snarled, twigs sticking out every which way. With eyes that glowed like two fiery coals.

Her mouth twisted into a hungry smile. Then she laughed, sending me into hysterics.

My hand fell from my mouth and I shrieked. Frantic, I fought to release myself from the seat. "Kadie, you've got to move! Shit, answer me." Why wouldn't my fucking seat belt come undone? I needed to get out. She was coming for me. I tugged on the belt once more, pushing the button on the buckle multiple times. It wouldn't release. No. This isn't happening. The thing in the woods was here. It was going to kill me. And I couldn't get out.

"Please, help me!" I kicked my feet against the floor of the car trying to give myself leverage.

Long bony fingers reached through the broken window, clawing at my face. A screech tumbled from my mouth.

Headlights came into view, sending the creature scurrying into the woodland. I heard a door open and there was Gareth, blade in hand, looking every bit a warrior. Oh God, what was he doing? Why did he have a sword?

"Salome." He rushed to my side. He jerked the door open with more power than I'd ever seen anyone use. In one swift motion, he cut the seat belt, catching me before I hit the ground.

Tears streamed down my cheeks, pain making me nauseous.

"Gareth," I whispered. My savior held me in his arms, his worried eyes the last thing I saw before the pain swept me away.

CHAPTER TWELVE

*O*verwhelmed by a sterile scent, I fought to open my eyes. I blinked, trying to overcome golden blurred spots. I focused on the fluorescent lights overhead, their brightness giving me a headache.

What the hell? What happened? Then it came back to me. The crash. The figure in the road. Gareth wielding a glowing knife. Fear gripped me tight, squeezing until I thought I might explode. The figure. It had been so close to me.

I attempted to stay calm by sucking in several deep breaths. My body throbbed and I shifted on the firm bed. While a heart monitor beeped faster, I glanced around the room. Right, I was in the hospital.

"Salome." Mom clutched my hand. "Are you okay?"

"Yeah, I'm fine." My voice sounded shaky. Unconvincing. I squinted beyond my mom to find her friend Nancy sitting in a chair.

"You scared me to death." Mom blinked away the tears trickling down her cheeks.

Patting her hand, I forced a smile, which hurt my cheeks. "Mom, I'm okay. How's Kadie?"

"They released her already. She had a couple of scrapes, but nothing more. You on the other hand, have a concussion and several abrasions on your arm that required stitching. If it wasn't for this nice young man here, it might've been worse." She pointed at Gareth, who stood leaning against the doorjamb, as if on guard.

I turned back to my mom. Dark rings circled her red, puffy eyes. I glanced at the clock. Four in the morning. "You should go home and get some sleep." I gave a fake yawn. "There's nothing else you can do for me that the doctors aren't already doing."

Nancy stood, stretching. "She's right. You need your rest, too. I can drop you off at home then pick you up later in the morning when Salome's ready to be released."

Mom looked uncertain. "Are you sure? I can stay."

Gareth peeled himself from the wall, appearing less tired than the other two. "I'll stay with her Mrs. Montgomery. My family isn't expecting me home tonight anyway."

My vision blurred hot with tears as I stared at him. He'd saved my life. And right now, I had so many things I needed to ask him. Like, what the heck did he save me from on the side of the road and why was he here with me now? I barely knew the guy. But there was something so bright and shiny and warm about him I couldn't catch my breath.

With a sigh, Mom put on her coat, positioning her crutches beneath her arms. "I called your dad to let him know what happened, and he's heading home after his last run tomorrow. He should be here sometime mid-week." Mom touched my face. "Try and get some rest, okay? I love you." She followed Nancy to the door.

"Love you, too." I lifted my head off the pillow and tried

my best to reassure her with a smile, then collapsed as soon as she was out of sight.

Gareth came over and sat beside me on the bed.

"Thank you." I squeezed his palm.

He glanced to where my hand held his. "You scared the shit out of me tonight. When I came up on the crash, I thought you—you were…"

I cringed with discomfort when I scooted into a sitting position. Gareth helped to prop the pillows behind me.

Biting my bottom lip, I traced the pattern on the thin hospital blanket. "What was in the road tonight?"

A look of bewilderment crossed his face and he shook his head. "I didn't see anything there."

"But you carried a sword or a knife or something."

He smiled. "I didn't have a sword. I came from the club, maybe five minutes behind you and Kadie. The only thing I had was my flashlight."

Maybe I was going mad.

His phone buzzed and he glanced at it. "Listen, I've got to take this. I'll be back in a few."

I really wondered if I had imagined it until I heard Gareth's voice from the hall.

"Yes, she's safe…I know…I'll keep an eye on her."

Keep an eye on me?

After a minute, he came back into the room.

"Who was that?"

"Just a friend. Now, why don't you lay down and get some rest."

"I—I don't think I can sleep after what I saw tonight." My voice cracked.

He grabbed a chair and moved it closer to my bed. He tossed his jacket aside and sat down.

"Just close your eyes." He clutched my hand and I couldn't help but sigh. "I'll be here all night. I won't let anything happen to you."

"Why are you so worried about me? You don't really know me, other than the fact your friend's dating my friend."

"Because you seem like a nice girl. And for the record, I'm not sure Simeon is actually dating Kadie."

"That's not what she said."

"He told her maybe they could hang out some time and now, she seems to show up everywhere he goes. She's persistent, I'll give her that."

That sounded like Kadie. She didn't take no for an answer. If she would've, then we never would've found ourselves at Club Blade. But that didn't explain Gareth's sudden interest in me.

"Listen, why don't you close your eyes. We can talk about this in the morning," he said.

My gaze met his. Could I trust him? Well, he did just save my life, so he kind of had one up on me now. My fingers warmed where he held them and I gave him a shaky smile.

With that, I drifted off.

Mom and Nancy wheeled me down to the parking lot. I argued that I didn't need a wheelchair, but the nurse insisted it was protocol. At least I didn't have the hospital gown on any longer so my ass was covered.

"How are you feeling?" Mom asked as we pulled away from the hospital.

"Fine, a little sore is all." Although, the mirror made me

wince when I saw the huge black and blue mark on the right side of my head and face. I looked like I'd gone ten rounds in a boxing match.

"I want you to take it easy today," she said, over the soft music playing on the radio.

Problem was, I *needed* to see Nevin. If anyone would believe me, it would be him. Yet, terror made me shiver, wondering if I wanted to step foot into the winter landscape. Images of the bus, the crash, my strangled cat, and my near drowning experience flipped in my head like a bad slideshow.

Nancy helped Mom and me into the house, making us promise we'd call if we needed anything. When she left I kept my coat on, grabbing a pair of mittens from the closet.

"Where are you going?" Mom's lips tightened with worry.

"To Grandma's. I've got chores."

She moved to block my way. "Absolutely not. You're in no condition to be over there by yourself. The chores can wait a day or two."

"I have to. I promised Grandma."

"And I'm sure she'll understand. For God's sake, you just got out of the hospital."

This wasn't going well. "Okay, how about I call a friend to come over and help with the chores? All I'll have to do is sit there and watch to make sure they get done."

With a look of defeat, she threw her arms up in the air. "Fine. You're not going to let this drop until you get your way. But I'm telling you right now, you better be careful or I'll ground you. And you better call me as soon as you get there."

Not giving her the chance to change her mind, I scooted out the door. Of course, I moved a lot slower today with my body aching. A headache pounded behind my eyes, but I tried to ignore it.

Nevin sat waiting for me when I got to the house. He pulled me into his arms carefully. "What happened?"

Taking a deep breath, I told him about the accident. My voice faltered as I described the creature in the road and I dabbed my face where its fingers had scratched my cheek.

"Maybe I imagined it—"

"You're not crazy," he whispered and anger hardened his jaw.

"Sometimes I'm not so sure." I rested my head against his chest. But even as I said the words, I knew this couldn't all be in my head.

"You said some guy named Gareth saved you?"

"Yeah. He's the one who found me."

"I'm glad he happened along when he did." He took my hand. "I'll take care of your chores for you. You can sit and relax."

"I'd like to walk with you." I clung to him.

His face softened, the fiery gaze melting away into cool pools of blue as he studied me. "Okay, but if you start feeling bad, I want you to sit down."

"Sure, Mom."

With a grin, he sighed. "I worry about you. I want you to be more careful."

"Sometimes it doesn't seem to matter how careful I am. Danger just finds me."

Which was the truth. I couldn't go anywhere without feeling a sense of impending doom or someone watching me. Life was becoming scarier by the minute and I wasn't sure how much more I'd be able to take before breaking.

My cell rang, displaying our home phone number. "Hello, Mom," I said.

"I'm just checking on you."

"My friend is here helping me." I covered the mouthpiece with my hand. "Will you please tell my mom that you're here doing the chores?"

Nevin took the phone from me, giving me a wink. "Hello, Mrs. Montgomery—I've taken over Salome's chores." He paused for a moment and traced his finger gently across the scratches on my cheek. "Yes she's taking it easy." He nodded absently. "You're welcome." He hung up the phone.

"Sorry, she's a little protective."

"I can't blame her."

Once he finished with the last feeder, we made our way back to the gazebo. I stood against the railing and stared out over the pond, the breeze brushing at my cheeks.

Nevin came up behind me, his arm encircling my shoulder.

"I feel so secure when I'm with you." I inhaled his wonderful scent of honey and pine.

He gave a bitter chuckle. "And yet, I can't be there when you need me most."

"That's not true," I whispered. "I needed you today and here you are."

He was the only person who believed me. Around him, I felt a little less crazy.

"Will you meet me here tomorrow?" Nevin turned me slowly to face him.

That familiar, dizzy feeling returned with the sound of wind chimes carried on the breeze and I grinned. "Well, I kind of have to be here anyway."

His fingers played with strands of my hair, eyes intent on mine.

"I didn't have chores in mind." His voice deepened. "I want to take you someplace."

"Okay," I said.

"Wear something warm." He released me.

"Are you going to give me a hint?"

He started to walk away. "Nope. It's a surprise."

I soon lost sight of him in the woods then headed for home. Maybe things weren't so bad after all. But the dull ache in my head warned me not to be too sure about that.

Chapter Thirteen

The phone rang the next morning and I stumbled out of bed to grab it. Who called at eight thirty on the weekend? Hadn't they heard of sleeping in?

Yawning, I pressed the talk button. "Hello?"

"Are you okay?" Grandma's frantic voice erupted on the other end. "Your mom said you were in an accident."

"I'm fine." I sat down, rubbing my fist across my eyes until the blurriness went away.

Grandma let out a sigh. "Was there anything unusual about the crash?"

I went still. How did she know? Unless… Visions of the graveyard flashed in my mind.

"There was a figure in the road." I stared at the frosty windows.

"What kind of figure?"

"I don't know. It looked like a lady, but she didn't seem human." I shivered as the memories came spilling back. Her long stick-like fingers, the sinister voice. My chest tightened, constricting each breath. Geez, I sounded like a mad woman.

In the distance, I heard Grandma calling my name. "Salome, are you still there?"

"Y-yeah."

"Listen to me and listen close. You need to stay inside whenever possible. If you must go out, take a piece of rowan wood with you. It will offer you more protection." She muttered to herself, "I knew it was only a matter of time."

"What do you mean 'a matter of time'?"

"I don't mean anything dear, just a crazy lady rambling on. Just heed my words. And stay away from anyone you meet in the woods, you hear?"

Did she mean Nevin? God, he couldn't be a part of all this, could he?

"You know what's going on, don't you?" My fingers clenched. "The last time I talked to you, I asked you what happened to the girls in the family and you said accidents. But it's more than that, isn't it?"

"Trust me, the less you know the better off you'll be."

I snorted. "Right, because not knowing almost got me killed the other night. If Gareth hadn't come along when he did..." I fought back the tears. We'd always been so close, why wouldn't she talk to me now? I needed to know what I was up against.

"Gareth?" Grandma whispered.

"Yes, he's a guy I met at Perky Joe's."

The line went silent for a long moment. "Are there any other boys? Anyone else who might have approached you?"

I wanted to be honest, but so far she hadn't been upfront with me. A part of me knew I should mention Nevin and meeting him in the woods. But he was my secret—someone I didn't want to share with anyone.

"No, there's no one else." The lie fell easily from my lips.

"I hope you're telling the truth because this is more serious than you think."

"But not serious enough for you to tell me what's going on. Listen, I've got to get over to your house and get the animals fed. I'll talk to you later."

"If you're going to ignore my warnings, at least carry the rowan like I asked." She sounded so tired as she hung up.

Should I trust Nevin? He hadn't given me any reason not to. I mean, who cared if he had secrets or if I didn't know where he lived? But how could I explain him never wanting to come into my house or my grandparents'? In fact, I'd never seen him anywhere but our property.

Great. Just what I needed—to doubt the one person in the world who possibly didn't think I needed psychiatric help. Someone who'd become a close friend in a short span of time.

"Who was on the phone?" Mom said as she came out of the bathroom, a towel wrapped around her wet hair.

"Grandma."

"I forgot to tell you that Colton and Kadie called yesterday while you were out doing chores." Mom sat down on the edge of the couch, her crutches propped next to her.

"Yeah, I got a text from Colton asking if I was okay."

"Salome, there's something I need to talk to you about before you head out." She wrung her hands together in her lap.

"What's wrong?"

"Kadie and I had a long conversation about the crash."

I watched her. "What did she say?"

"Kadie told me that the crash was your fault. She said you screamed and then grabbed the steering wheel from her, telling her there was something in the road."

My mouth went dry. Oh God, she hadn't seen it. "But I saw it…"

"Salome, just stop and listen to me. She said there was nothing there. I—I think maybe it's time we scheduled an appointment with Dr. Bosworth. Your episodes are coming on more frequently. We need some way to help you."

My pulse pounded in my ears. "No. You promised I wouldn't have to go back."

"What choice do I have? You could've been killed the other night. You and Kadie both. We need to figure out what's wrong with you. To be able to control your episodes better. At least when you're medicated you're not seeing things."

"Mom, please. Give me another chance. I—I'll be better. You'll see." This was why I didn't like to tell people about things. Didn't want them to know what I heard and saw. Because it always led down this path. Everyone thought I was crazy and maybe they were right.

A bird twittered on a low hanging branch as I sat on the deck waiting for Nevin. I smiled, watching it fly upward then glide toward the roof of the house, where it perched staring at me, cocking its head back and forth. At least Mom still let me come out today. I needed to see Nevin. To know someone was on my side.

The bird whistled a long song, rocking his head back and forth as if trying to get me to follow. I stood, feeling foolish as I tramped after the blue bird. But when it landed on the wrought iron gate, I stopped. It sang one last high-pitched note then fell to the ground dead.

Holy crap. This wasn't happening. Not again. Backing away, I stumbled into a pair of strong arms.

Nevin caught me before I hit the ground. "Whoa, are you

okay?"

"Did you just see that?" I pointed at the ground where the bird was.

"You need to stay away from the gate."

Obviously. "Why do I need to stay away?" I gave him an innocent look. Thing was, if Grandma wasn't going to give me answers I had no problem going somewhere else to get them.

Nevin's eyes grew dark. "The woods can be dangerous. Wild animals and such."

Wow, would it kill someone to give me a straight answer?

"This is bullshit. You know what's going on around us. You hear the voices. And why don't you ever question my sanity when I bring up the creature I keep seeing?" My chest heaved with anger as I fisted my hands at my sides. "It's because you know this is all real. So tell me something. Give me some piece of information—you keep saying you're my friend, but if you truly were, you'd look out for me and help me."

"I am looking out for you—maybe not in ways you notice—"

"Seriously? That's your answer. You know what, just forget this whole hanging out thing. I—I can't do it anymore. Not unless you can be honest with me."

Nevin's gaze darted over the woodland. He reached for my arm, frantic-like. "Fine. I promise to tell you more, but can we at least wait until we get to where I planned on taking you?"

I inhaled deeply, then let my breath out slow to calm down. "Okay, but you better keep your word." My boot scuffed at the snow and I glanced at him. "So where are we going?"

"Some place special. Come on." He held out his hand, leading me toward the path that went around the pond.

I took bigger steps to keep pace with him, taking in the scenery as we passed. Where the heck was he taking me?

The deeper in we went, the more overgrown everything

was, like it had never been touched by man.

"Okay, close your eyes," he whispered in my ear.

My lids fluttered shut as he scooped me up in his arms. Geez, why the heck had he picked me up? I rested my head against his chest, his heart beating as fast as a hummingbird's wings. I shouldn't be so close to him. Not like this.

"Can I open them yet?"

He chuckled. "In a minute. Hasn't anyone taught you patience?"

"It's not my best virtue."

At last, he set me on my feet. "Go ahead and look," he said, a hint of nervousness entering his words.

Before me stood the ruins of what looked like a large estate. The house seemed like something I'd find in the English countryside. I never heard a gate open so that must mean it was inside my grandma's property line. How did I not know about all this stuff on her land?

I gasped, moving toward the remnants of a door. I ran my fingers over the detailed carvings of roses, crowns, birds, and dancing couples in the amazing stonework.

Half of the roof had collapsed and trees branched up through it while dead vines and moss clung to the stone. The sagging part, which was still tiled, looked as if a strong gust of wind could topple it. Remains of a grand staircase wound upward to a large balcony. Old chimneys lay crumbled on the floor.

I imagined grand balls and gatherings held there when the estate was in its prime. Sadness washed over me, making me wonder who had left such a fantastic house to rot. It was as if the occupants had disappeared.

"This is beautiful." I spun around to find Nevin staring at me.

His grin made my knees weak. "I'm glad you like it. Now, you have to come this way for the surprise."

He draped an arm around my shoulders, guiding me through a rotting doorway into what remained of the ballroom. The marble tile looked unaffected by time and neglect. It had been cleared off and cleaned. Though the roof was missing, the room was magical. A surreal feeling washed over me, like I'd stepped onto the set of a Disney princess movie.

My gaze settled on a woolen blanket laid out in the center of the room, covered with a wicker picnic basket, bottles of juice, and plates of food. There were sandwiches, vegetables, and various types of cookies spread out.

I wondered how he'd gotten all this stuff out here. He could've carried it, but the basket alone was enormous. I mean, I never saw any vehicle tracks or anything.

"How did you get all this out here?"

He chuckled. "Magic."

"Funny." I hugged him. "I can't believe you did all this for me. This place—I never knew it was here."

"I told you I wanted to make today special for you." He released me from our embrace then led me to the blanket where he motioned for me to sit.

After devouring two sandwiches, a helping of vegetables, and three cookies, I noticed Nevin hadn't eaten. He sat watching my every move.

"Aren't you going to have something?" I asked, deciding against another cookie.

"I'm not hungry. But it looks like you were."

I shifted my eyes away. "Sorry."

"No, I'm glad to see you have an appetite." His fingers brushed mine across the blanket, his thumb swirling across my palm and prickles slithered along my spine.

Wanting nothing more than to change the subject from my eating habits, I glanced around the room. It kind of surprised me how similar this outing was to Colton's. Outdoors. In winter. Food.

"So how did you find this house?"

Sadness swept over his features. "This estate belonged to my family. From what my mom told me, they lost it in some game or something. And now it sits decaying year after year."

"Then your family has been around here as long as mine then."

"Longer."

"I don't understand though, it's on my grandparents' property."

"The person who won it sold it off to your family. But Doris still lets me come by and visit it."

I wondered if he was angry about it. If so, he didn't say.

In the distance, faint music played. Soft alluring music. It sounded so familiar. A memory begged to be opened, but my mind refused to conjure it.

Nevin closed his eyes, his head swaying to the sound of the music.

"Would you like to dance?" He stood, coming around to my side.

I draped my coat on the floor, but decided to leave my hat and scarf on, hoping I didn't look foolish.

Feeling almost intoxicated by the tune, I whispered, "Yes, I love to dance."

The music grew louder, mimicking the tinkling of wind chimes and flutes. I glanced over my shoulder, searching for the source. He'd probably planted a radio or an iPod somewhere. Or, at least, that's what I told myself.

Nevin spun me around, my body pressed tight against his.

The hardness of his chest flexed beneath my hands and his sure and steady movements were elegant. Glacial eyes stared at me, intense, feeling. The melody swirled about us, and this was what I wanted—him, forever.

"She's beautiful."

"And look at Nevin. He looks so happy. It's been years since he's smiled."

"Perhaps she's the one."

"Do we dare hope?"

I scanned the surroundings searching for the voices.

"D-did you hear that?"

"Hear what?"

I swallowed hard. I couldn't go through this again. To have another person question my sanity. "Nothing."

"Salome, you can talk to me." He stared at me.

"The voices, I—I hear them again."

"So do I. There's nothing to be scared of. I'm here, okay?"

"You promised you'd tell me something when we got out here."

"And ruin our perfect moment?"

The music started to crescendo and my heart sped. Suddenly, I couldn't remember what we were talking about. It was just him and me. Like I was in this fairytale-type haze. Holding my hand, Nevin glided me across the floor, our strides matching perfectly like we'd danced a million waltzes together.

"Where did you learn to waltz?" he asked.

"I'll tell you, but first you have to agree not to laugh."

He leaned in, his promise tickling my ear, leaving me breathless.

"I used to do ballroom dancing and swing dancing competitions. My grandparents got me into it."

"Well, it paid off."

"What about you? I don't know many guys who can dance. At least not like this."

"We're taught very early on," he said, before getting lost in his own thoughts.

I was about to ask who "we" was, but he snapped out of his daze and started to question me about my week at school. So I gave him a dull run down of my class assignments, trying to figure out why he wanted to discuss something so lame.

The music changed to something softer—slower. Fluffy flakes sputtered through the hole in the roof, the room dimmed. As if nature set *the mood*. My heart slammed into my chest like it wanted out.

God, I ached for him to kiss me. What was wrong with me? Why was I so drawn to him? My body smoldered like an out-of-control fire needing him to control the burn. The sweet scent of honey filled the air. Dizziness washed over me. His fingers traced my jawline, tipping my head upward.

Our eyes clashed, igniting an even more powerful spark. Nevin bent his head slightly then came up short as though a barrier was erected between us.

Maybe he just didn't want to make the first move. Right. Pucker, lean in, and kiss.

I tightened my arms around his neck, standing on my tiptoes, until our lips were a breath apart.

Nevin threw his hands up between us and shoved me backward with such force I stumbled and fell on my butt.

"No," he said, out of breath. His chest heaved and his face reddened. The warmth in his eyes disappeared, replaced with something hostile. "Damn it, stop the music. Stop this nonsense." His hands covered his face for a second and I watched him take several deep breaths.

My head cleared and my vision seemed sharper, I pushed

myself from the floor then backed away, bumping into the stone wall. I was such an idiot. Why the hell had I tried to kiss him? I mean, I thought he was hot, but he was my friend. And then we'd danced, and I'd wanted more. I'd wanted him. My stomach knotted like a ball of yarn wound too tight.

"I—I'm sorry…" Tears burned my eyes, my throat so thick I couldn't swallow. I grabbed my coat, searching for the path out of there.

Nevin's voice stopped me. "Please don't leave." He caught my waist.

I wiped my eyes with the back of my hand, not wanting to cry in front of him. "I—I'm sorry, I don't know what came over me."

"I do. And I promise, I won't let it happen again. You don't know how badly I wanted to kiss you." His words laced with a heat I'd never heard before. "But sometimes things we think are real, really aren't."

I twisted around to face him. Was this a sick joke? "What's that supposed to mean? And why did you push me away?"

He stared beyond me, seeming lost. "Because I *can't* kiss you, Salome."

Okay, and I'd thought I'd heard it all. Was he serious? The overwhelming urge I'd had to kiss him was gone, but I wasn't so horrible he'd reject me. Or was I? "This makes no sense. As usual, you're talking in riddles."

Nevin tilted my head up. He wiped away my tears with such tenderness my knees turned to Jell-O.

"I'm sorry." He shook his head. "I wish I could explain this and spare you the pain, but I can't."

"Why? Damn it, quit playing games with me, Nevin!"

"Can't you just let it go?"

He released me, a different kind of fire blazing in his eyes.

I stared as he stormed across the ruins, picked up one of the plates from our meal, and hurled it at the wall.

In one quick motion, he kicked everything from the blanket across floor and slammed his fist into the wall. I grimaced as the stone split down the middle, breaking in two.

"Nevin," I called, frightened by the change, and humiliated by his rejection. What I needed to do was run and get the hell out of there. But I didn't know the way back. I'd get lost in the snow. And I didn't want to be alone out here.

He stopped, his back to me. "I'm not a good person to keep as a friend. I always hurt the people I care for. I don't mean to, but it always happens that way."

Misery filled his words, a misery I didn't understand, but wanted to ease. My chest ached like he had stabbed one of the forks into my heart. I closed the distance between us, my gaze focused on him.

"Just settle down, okay. I don't know what this is about, let's just go back to my grandma's." I was certainly not ready to forgive him, but if he stayed out here, he could hurt himself. And I would never find my way back.

Nevin reached for me, and cradled me against him, stroking my head. "Please forgive my temper. None of this," he gestured to the mess on the floor. "None of this was directed at you. It's just…"

"It's just what?"

"I've ruined the whole day."

"No you didn't," I whispered, but I wasn't sure that I was telling the truth. The night had been amazing, but his outburst had scared me, and his rejection hurt. "Let's go home," I whispered.

But there was more to his temper than he let on and every moment spent with him spurred more questions I was determined to answer. Why wouldn't he kiss me? He'd seemed frightened by the gesture. And why had he chosen here, of all places, to bring me?

Still, hanging out with him brought me a contentment I didn't understand. Something I'd never felt with anyone else. We had things in common. The stuff in the woods, the crazy outbursts. It's like he understood me. We both knew what it was like to be different. Something about Nevin made me more normal. Or perhaps it was because he was just as messed up as I was.

Time with Nevin was like stepping into a forbidden place. A plane of existence separate from everyone else. Which, with our lunacy, was kind of scary.

CHAPTER FOURTEEN

Monday morning, Mom woke me with a shake.

"Time to get up."

"Ugh, can't I sleep just a few minutes longer?" My lids opened and I glanced at my alarm clock. Eight o'clock. Crap. I was late. "Mom, first hour has already started."

I leaped out of bed, racing for my closet.

"I thought you could use a day off." She smiled.

"Wait, what?" Okay, this was so not like her. Mom never let me skip before.

"Come on, get dressed. Nancy will be here in a few minutes to bring us out to breakfast." She cast me a strange look.

Who was I to argue with food and no school? I hurried to get dressed, tossing on a sweater and pair of jeans. I tied my hair up in a ponytail then rushed downstairs to find Nancy sitting at the kitchen table with Mom.

"Ready?"

"Yeah."

We piled into Nancy's vehicle. She headed into town, taking

the winding back roads. Snowflakes melted as they hit the front windshield. Things didn't look as scary as they had the other night. But I knew better than to think I was safe. When we neared Main Street, Nancy turned down Apple Avenue. Familiar buildings sprung up on either side. My stomach clenched as I gripped the armrest. I knew now where we were going.

"Mom?" My voice cracked when we turned into the parking lot of Dr. Bosworth's brick office building. "You lied to me."

"Salome. It's for your own good. You've had way too many episodes lately. You almost got yourself and Kadie killed the other night. I just want you to talk to her, okay?"

This wasn't fair. How could she do this to me? She knew how much I hated coming here, how I hated telling Dr. Bosworth things. The woman pried and pried until I was reliving every nightmare I'd locked away in my head. Things I didn't want to remember. If Kadie would've kept her mouth shut, I wouldn't be here.

"I'm better now," I said. "It was just a mini freak out."

"Please, don't make this harder than it already is. Do you think I like bringing you here?"

"Then don't. We can still have breakfast and then you can drop me off at school."

"I'm sorry, not today. Just listen to what Dr. Bosworth has to say."

When we parked, Mom and Nancy led me inside the brownstone. The lobby was decked out in drab gray paint and matching carpet. The only colors on the walls were paintings of circus scenes. Creepy clowns, tents, elephants, and lions. There were magazines on the waiting room tables, along with a box of toys for kids to play with.

My palms grew sweaty. How many times had I sat out here waiting to go in for my appointments? Forced to tell Bosworth about my plummet into the pond and the voices that warned me away? I couldn't freak out now. I had to show a good face. Let the doctor ask questions and act like everything was perfectly fine.

Mom checked in at the front desk while I had a seat next to Nancy. I grabbed a magazine from the pile and thumbed through it. The perfect families inside it gave me mocking smiles. Parents pushed their kids on swings, while others swam in pools. I bet their moms wouldn't have forced them to see a shrink.

"Salome Montgomery, come on in." Dr. Bosworth poked her red head out the door and waved me in.

I glanced at Mom who gave me a forced smile. "I'll wait out here. When you're done we can go out to breakfast, okay?"

Like eating out was going to make up for this. With a sigh, I stood and followed the doctor down a long hall to her office. When I stepped inside, the scent of coffee filled the air. A neat desk sat at the back of the room. Bookshelves wound around the left hand side of it. To the right was her large aquarium filled with several fish of varying colors that reminded me of rainbows.

Dr. Bosworth closed the door behind us and pointed to the overstuffed chairs in front of her desk. A desk that was void of everything but a thick, blue file. My file.

"Have a seat, Salome." She settled into her chair and waited for me to sit.

Once seated, she slid a pair of cat-eye glasses on her nose and peered at me. Her brown eyes swept over me and she smiled.

"You've certainly grown up since the last time I saw you. How long has it been?" She took a pen out of her drawer along with a pad of paper.

"Three years," I whispered. My fingers wrapped around the arms of the chair as I chewed my bottom lip. Although, right now it felt like it was only yesterday that I had last slouched in this very same spot, crying, trying to explain away the fear I had of winter. To make her understand that bad things happened when the snow came.

"Your mother explained to me that you had another hallucination. Do you want to tell me about it?"

No. Because she'd look at me with that knowing gaze and think I was crazy. Just like everyone else.

"I'm not sure what it was. Most likely it was just a deer that ran out in front of us." I shrugged.

"Salome, I can only help you if you tell me the truth."

"Yeah, well I remember what happened the last time I told you the truth." I gave her a hard smile. She'd had me sedated with so many pills it was like living in a constant fog.

She set her pen down, took off her glasses and leaned back in her chair. "Okay, why don't we start from the beginning— when you first fell through the pond. We can work our way forward."

And there it was. I squeezed my lids closed. My breathing staggered. I didn't want to do this. Not again. I couldn't. She didn't get it. Every time I relived those moments, I lost another piece of myself. The more I thought of it, the more fragile I felt.

"Salome. Open your eyes," Dr. Bosworth said. "We need to face this head on. I promise, I'll be here every step of the way. You won't be alone."

But I already was. The doctor probably thought I was just some experiment. A new clinical study for her to dig her fingers into.

"You already know what happened when I was child. I've told you several times."

"Yes. But perhaps this time, something new will stick out. We can get to the root of your problem. I know how traumatic that day was for you. You almost drowned."

My pulse thundered in my ears. My skin prickled as if I was beneath the frozen water again. I sucked in deep breaths as panic settled over me. *Please. Make it stop. Make it go away.*

"I—I was going outside to play in the back yard. But someone left the gate open. It never should've been open. After I shut it, there was this voice. I…"

I fisted my hands in my lap. Damn it. I didn't want to relive this. I couldn't. Not if I wanted to stay sane.

"What happened next, Salome?"

Not wanting to continue, my gaze shifted to the aquarium, where the fish swam around as if they didn't have a care in the world. Bubbles floated on top of the water where the pump filtered it through.

"Salome, are you listening to me?"

Frost crackled across the glass. The air suddenly became colder and my arms broke out in goose bumps. There, looking back at me was the gnarled face of the creature I'd seen the other night.

"No," I shouted, leaping up out of my chair. Panic stole my thoughts as I backed away.

"You can't hide from me…not here. Not anywhere…"

The face pressed closer to the glass, distorting it.

"Make it stop."

"Salome, what is it?" The doctor followed my glance.

"It's here. She's found me," I screeched as I raced for the door.

But Dr. Bosworth caught my arm. "There's nothing there. Salome. You need to calm down. Face your fear."

A high-pitched laugh echoed around me and I covered

my ears and screamed. Why couldn't Dr. Bosworth hear it? I needed to get out of here. I had to go back home, where I'd be safe. I sank to the floor, rocking back and forth.

Moments later, two men busted into the room, followed by my mother.

"What going on?" Mom sounded panicked.

"I think your daughter needs to go somewhere safe for a while. Maybe we should talk in private about some type of placement where she can get help."

"No. I don't want her sent away." She dropped down beside me, letting her crutches fall to the floor. "Sweetie. Shh…it's okay. I'm here. We can go back home."

"If you won't consider having her placed, then at least take this prescription." She took a slip of paper from her desk and signed it. "It should help with the hallucinations. But if it gets worse, you'll have to bring her in. She could become a danger to herself or others."

Mom brushed hair from my face. "Come on honey, let's go now. We'll have Nancy drop us off then see if she'll pick up the pills for you."

Pills. God, I didn't want to be on those again. They'd make me sleep. And if I was asleep then I wouldn't know if something was after me. I always felt off when I took the medicine.

When we got back to the house, Nancy helped me into my room and got me settled into my bed. She left the door cracked open and I heard her and Mom talking.

"You should've seen her, Nancy, I've never seen her like that before."

"What are you going to do?"

"Try to keep things as normal as possible. I don't want her to go into an institution. She needs normal. It's just winter. If we can get her through it, she'll be fine."

"I'll run out and get her medicine."

When Nancy left, Mom came down and sat on the edge of my bed. "I'm really sorry. I never should've made you go. I thought it would help."

"It never does."

She stayed in my room with me until Nancy got back. At which point, her friend got me a cup of water and put a pill in my hand. Mom watched me carefully as I slid the medicine in my mouth and took a drink.

I handed the glass back to her. "Why don't you lie down and get some rest? I'll check on you later."

"Okay." I gave her a hug and, when she left the room, I spit the medicine back into my hand. No way was I going to be drugged up. I needed to stay focused and know what was going on around me. It was time for me to figure out what the heck was stalking me. And why. But I couldn't do it today.

I spent the day pretending to be asleep, while I lay in bed replaying what'd happened in the doctor's office. Another nightmare to add to the dozens I already had.

Texts came in all day from Colton wondering where I was, and saying that he wanted to see me, but I didn't feel like answering. He confused me as much as Nevin. When I was near him, I really wanted to be with him. But then he'd do something strange, acting so different from the guy I'd grown up with, and I didn't know what I wanted.

Around dinner time, my cell rang. Sitting up, I kicked my blankets off and climbed from bed to answer it.

"Hello?"

"Hey, are you okay?" Kadie asked. "I tried texting you earlier, but you never answered."

Anger swelled inside. A part of me wanted to yell at her for talking to my mom behind my back. "Sorry, I had to go see Dr.

Bosworth."

"Wait, that's where you were today?"

"Yes, thanks to you telling my mom everything."

"Please don't be mad. I—I didn't know what to do. You scared the shit out of me the other night when you jerked the steering wheel like that."

"Just forget about it, okay? Because I really don't want to get into it right now."

"I'll make it up to you, I promise," Kadie said.

"I've got to go."

"No, wait. I thought maybe I could swing by. Maybe bring a few chick flicks and some chocolate."

With a sigh, I rubbed my temples. No matter how pissed off she made me, I always forgave her. "Fine. I could use some company."

Kadie showed up about ten minutes later and we spent the next couple of hours losing ourselves in movies and food, a definite distraction from the real world and just what I needed.

CHAPTER FIFTEEN

*G*oing back to school sucked. My head continued to throb, and Mr. Calvin's monotone voice made me sleepy. Five more minutes—I just had to keep my eyes open.

The day started off wonderful: me, the big yellow banana boat from hell, winter, and, final destination, Mr. Calvin's psych class, otherwise known as the torture chamber.

With Kadie's car out of commission and my fear of driving my vehicle to school in the winter, I'd have a lot more of *these* kinds of days.

After class, I made my way to the library, where I found Colton leaning back in a chair at one of the tables.

"Hey." He stood when I approached.

"Hey, yourself." I let him pull a chair out for me.

Colton quirked an eyebrow, studying me. "You okay?"

Hell no.

"Yeah, it's just been a long day—the bus ride, class, the horrible start to my weekend." I left out the part about how the winter was closing in on me. As I spoke, I traced the carved names in the table with my finger. *Jack loves Mindy. Fuck off. Amy + Sam.* I pasted on that perfect smile everyone expected to see.

But Colton was no fool.

"Come here." He tugged me from my chair and down the aisle marked Sci-Fi. His hand rubbed my arm, in soft, reassuring motions. "Would a kiss make you feel better?" he teased, then pulled me closer.

Yes. No. Maybe. Heck, I didn't know anymore.

"Just listen close. I'll make you forget everything," he whispered. The faint trill of tinkling bells echoed softly. Or did they? He glanced around then backed me into the bookshelf. Colton's lips captured mine, soft, demanding, the flavor of mint lingering from his gum. His tongue stroked mine and I pressed myself closer, wanting more. My mind swirled and the music grew louder.

What's wrong with me? We were in the library. God, I had one guy who wouldn't kiss me, and another who had no qualms about public make-out sessions. Colton broke away. "Sorry, I can't seem to keep myself in check when you're around."

But it was just the distraction I needed. My hands trailed up his chest, tracing each hardened muscle beneath his shirt.

Shyness made my fingers quiver. "Kiss me again."

He ensnared me in his arms. Fire licked through my veins. And I was all too aware of how far this was going. I felt shaky, kind of off. "We should cool it before I lose control." Colton nibbled my ear. "Would hate for the librarian to kick us out."

"You're right, we need to stop," I said in a hushed voice, shaking my head to clear it.

He grinned, guiding me back to our table. "Do you feel better now?"

"Um—yeah. So, how about that weather." My face burned.

"You're adorable when you blush." He held my hand as we sat down

For the rest of the lunch hour we huddled together, thumbing through magazines and casting occasional sideways glances at one another. The sun beamed through the windows, spotlighting Colton's handsome face. Like I needed a reminder of his perfection. And yet, he wanted to be with me—flawed, crazy, me.

*T*he halls filled with people as the last bell rang. Since I had to take the bus home, I rushed to get my homework thrown into my backpack. I managed to tug my jacket on without dropping my bag.

"Hey, do you need me to walk you out?" Kadie said coming up beside me, her bag already in hand.

"No, I'm fine. You better hurry or you'll miss your bus," I said.

"Okay, I'll call you tonight." She sprinted down the hall while I finished gathering my things.

Pushing past the crowd, I emerged into the parking lot. A snowball whizzed by my head when a group of guys bombarded everyone coming out of the building. I clutched my bag tighter, trying to duck down out of their way. Kevin Freeman led the assault with Connor Whelpman following his lead. Two others joined in.

I moved fast, wanting nothing more than to board the bus and leave the immature jerk-offs behind. But Kevin Freeman spotted me and grinned.

I hated Kevin Freeman.

"Salome, guess what I've got for you." Kevin rushed toward me and caught a hold of my jacket, jerking me to a stop.

"Let go," I shrieked, trying to tug loose.

"Nobody gets by without a whitewash." Next thing I knew, he had my face pressed into the frigid white snow. Ice scraped at my face like tiny fingers trying to claw my skin away. I couldn't breathe.

"Stop." I gasped for air and got a mouth full of snow instead.

"Get the fuck off my girlfriend." Colton's voice cut like a knife and everyone went silent.

He shoved Kevin off me and helped me up. Tears streamed down my face. Then Colton did something I never expected. He drew his fist back and punched Kevin in the nose. Blood spurted out, spraying the ivory ground like a water balloon popping.

And he didn't stop. I watched in horror as he slammed Kevin into the ground and proceeded to beat the crap out of him. Scared, I backed away from him. Kids gathered around yelling, cheering, and egging them on.

"Colton," I hollered, seeing some teachers rushing into the lot. I shoved my way into the crowd, tugging on his coat. "Colton, stop. The teachers."

It took several seconds for him to register what I said, but at last he hopped up, pulling me aside.

"Get on your bus." Rage flickered in his dark eyes.

"But—"

"Salome, I can handle this. Please get on the bus." He kissed my forehead.

"You could get suspended. What about basketball?"

"Kevin won't narc me out or he'll be off the team too. Now go, so you don't get dragged into this."

Some of the buses were already pulling away and if I missed mine, I wouldn't have a ride home.

"Call me tonight," I said over my shoulder before bolting.

Okay, I'd never seen him like that before. It was like he was a totally different person back there. And I didn't like it. I sunk into a seat, wiping frost from the window so I could see Colton. He blew me a kiss, before going over to talk to the group of teachers.

What if he got kicked out of school because of me? Shit, could this day get any worse?

I pressed my face against my hands, trying to ignore the chatter around me.

"Oh my gosh, I can't believe Colton totally got into a fight over you." Sasha Jenkins twisted around in her seat. "That's totally hot."

"So have you two kissed yet?" another girl asked.

Like I wanted to tell them anything about my love life. Lucky for me, two of their friends came bounding up the aisle. I took the opportunity to move back several seats, hoping to go unnoticed.

I ducked down and tugged my jacket tighter around my shoulders. God, it was freezing. Usually the bus was hotter than the bowels of hell, but today I saw my breath like smoky tendrils lacing the air.

I glanced around and saw that the window in front of me and the window behind me were opened.

"Hey, can you shut your window?" I leaned forward over the seat. But no one was sitting there. Instead, I saw icy footprints dotting the brown pleather upholstery.

Uneasiness danced across the back of my neck, my hair prickling until it stood on end. I had to get a grip. I couldn't afford to have another breakdown. Dr. Bosworth wanted to send me to the nut house. I had to just put my earbuds in and ignore everything.

"You can't hide from me, Salome. It's almost your time."

Oh shit, that voice. It belonged to *her*. I sucked in several deep breaths, trying to remain calm. Where had the voice come from? The bus thumped around, headed toward Ellis Road. Wiping the window clean of frost and steam, I peered out. But nothing was there. I sank deeper into my seat, pretending everything was okay. My fingers slipped around my iPod, and I changed it to a louder rock song. I just had to drown everything out.

The air brakes hissed to a stop as the bus let off its first passengers. Within the shadows of the trees, I saw *her*, gliding toward the side of the vehicle. Her dark clothes appeared gauzy, nature clinging to their every fiber. Her bony fingers pointed at me, her lips curling up into a hideous smile.

"I see you," she said.

I rubbed my eyes, but the woman had disappeared. Fear coiled around me, I broke out in a sweat. Why did I keep seeing this thing? Why wouldn't it leave me alone? Unless it really was my imagination. I jerked my earbuds out and sat up, tapping my foot on the floor to distract myself.

When we stopped again, my eyes fell to a gnarled maple tree. It looked like a demonic creature, its bony branches like daggers piercing the sky. The bark started to separate at the trunk and I gazed in horror as a face started to form. *Her* face.

"I'm everywhere. Can't you feel me watching you?"

A scream lodged in my throat. Tearing my eyes from the window, I glanced up the aisle when the driver came to another stop. Kids clambered off the bus at the same time *she* got on.

She drifted down the aisle like a cloud of poison gas. No one else saw her. No one but me. A screech I couldn't stop fell from my lips.

The guy behind me leaped up and grabbed me by the shoulders. I saw his lips moving, but I couldn't hear him. My body numbed and for a moment, I couldn't move. People turned around to stare at me, then shifted back to their conversations, conversations I couldn't hear. It was like I was suspended in time. The monster was here and no one else noticed.

The need to get off the bus overwhelmed me. I wasn't safe. Not here. Not anywhere.

I shook my head, trying to get back to reality. The creature laughed at me, the sound like rusty wind chimes, then she sashayed toward the front of the bus, stopping near the driver.

"Aren't we having fun? Say good-bye, Salome. Nothing can save you now."

She jerked the steering wheel, sending the bus skidding sideways, right toward the Rumblederry Bridge. Kids were thrown from their seats. Screams erupted around me. At last, I could hear and move again. But it was too late.

"No!" I covered my head. The bus crashed, its metal twisting as it hit the bridge. My worst fear was coming true. It was winter and I was going to drown in the freezing watery depths.

Everything moved in slow motion: the flailing bodies, the smashing windows, the metal sides of the bus caving in. The scent of smoke filtered in.

I was going to die. Vomit burned the back of my throat as pain seared up and down my arms and legs. I gripped the seat, wondering if we could get out the emergency exit once we hit the water.

Then we stopped. The bus teetered on the edge of the bridge and the road. For a long moment, no one moved, fearing any shift of weight might send us spiraling downward.

"The emergency exit," I called to the boy sprawled in the aisle next to me.

Holding onto one of the seats, he climbed up slowly, rubbing his left arm. Cries for help echoed around us.

"Everybody needs to get off the bus," he yelled through cupped hands. "But take it slow."

He shoved the emergency door open and passersby helped kids off the bus. Frantic sobs and shouting filled the air. Someone smashed open my window and I found Gareth standing there, his hand bloody from the glass.

"Climb out, now." He held his arms open for me.

I nodded, tossing my backpack out first. As Gareth gripped my arms, the big yellow banana started to shift.

I cleared the window right when the metal groaned, spiraling into the river like a spear. Gareth's strong arms held me tight, burying my head, guarding me from the devastation. He smelled so good. Like fresh, sharp pine and coffee. I felt warm and safe.

I shut my eyes, too afraid to see the injured people or the remnants of the crash. A sob raked through me, and I shuddered with relief. When was this going to end? I wasn't safe anywhere. This was the second accident in a week's time. I was beginning to fear vehicles as much as the winter.

"It's okay. I've got you." Gareth carried me away.

"Did everyone get out?" I hiccupped, holding onto my rescuer with an iron grip.

"Yes. But if I hadn't come along *you* wouldn't have." His angry undertone made my lids fly open. "From now on, I think you would be better off bumming a ride from me." He stared at the highway as sirens sounded in the distance.

"Thank you," I whispered. "This is the second time you saved me." A wave of pain washed over me. I glanced down to see blood had soaked through the arm of my coat. Great, the stitches must've busted open. But, the stitches were the least of my worries. Winter was going to kill me. My mind flipped back to the gauzy monster who'd floated down the aisle. The eerie sound of her voice. How close she'd come to ending me. Again. Maybe I should let Mom put me away; it had to be safer, right?

"We need everyone over here for a head count," the bus driver commanded, her voice wobbling.

Flashing lights blocked off the road and Gareth carried me over to my classmates. He set me on my unsteady feet.

"I'll check in on you later, but until then, keep this with you at all times." He handed me a carved piece of wood. Not just any wood. Rowan wood.

Staring at it, I turned to ask him what in the hell was going on, but he'd disappeared.

CHAPTER SIXTEEN

My eyes fluttered open, focused on the screaming bright lights overhead. This was the second time I'd woken up. The first had been in the recovery unit after surgery, before they moved me to my room.

Throat dry, I tried to swallow, then fumbled for the button to bring myself into a sitting position. The bed whined as it slowly moved up. My arm felt confined and I glanced down to see a white sling and bandages. Great, pins in my broken arm.

"Knock—knock." A familiar voice called out. Kadie pushed in, holding a bouquet of flowers as Mom shot into a sitting position.

"You're awake." Mom reached for her crutches. "How do you feel?"

"I'm fine."

Mom turned to me and said, "Listen, since you're awake, I think I'm going to head down to the cafeteria for a quick bite to eat—give you girls a chance to visit."

She kissed my forehead before hobbling out the door.

Kadie put my flowers on the table then unrolled a poster of a shirtless guy, beach sand stuck to his tanned abs.

"Thought you could use some cheering up." She grinned and taped it to the makeshift closet door.

"Um—I don't think I'll be in here that long."

"Colton wanted me to tell you that he'll try to drop by later, too. Seriously, the hotness has got it bad for you. You should see what he did to Kevin Freeman. Totally kicked the shit out of him."

I frowned. That, I did remember. And I wasn't sure if that was the type of person I wanted to be dating. I mean, who's to say he wouldn't flip out on me? His mood swings were getting kind of crazy. "Did he get suspended?"

"Nope. Everyone told the principal Kevin started it. Besides they don't want to lose their star basketball player. Although, by the sounds of it on the phone, his parents grounded him, so hopefully they'll let him out long enough to come up and visit you." She rolled her eyes. "So what the hell happened to the bus?"

My hand clenched the hospital blanket. "I don't know," I lied. "Everything happened so fast."

"From what I heard, you barely made it off—shit, Salome, you almost fucking died." Kadie's gaze met mine. There was a catch in her voice and she turned away trying to hide the tears from me.

"I'm okay, see." I held up my non-injured arm.

She came over to the bed and sat down next to me, hugging me close. "Mitch said that right before the crash you started screaming, like you saw something no one else did."

Great, now everyone would think I was crazy or on drugs. I wanted to tell her everything, but what if that put her in danger? Or what if she told Mom again? Hell, I didn't know what was going on, only that I seemed to have a giant target painted on me.

Sighing, I let my head rest on her shoulder. "It was a mini snow freak out. Kevin scared me when he shoved snow in my face."

She gave me a look of disbelief, but let it go. Instead, she changed the subject to the hot orderly making his rounds.

"What about Simeon? I thought you were *madly* in love with him."

"*Love* is such as strong word. Besides, the guy won't even take my bait."

"Take the bait?"

"We haven't gotten beyond second base and, believe me, I've tried. I've thrown myself at him every available moment and nothing."

I stifled a giggle. "And this is a bad thing?"

"A woman has needs." Her wicked grin made me laugh.

"There are support groups for this kind of thing. Nymphos' Anonymous or something."

"Funny. But seriously, I don't think he's all that into me and, if I'm being honest, I'm not sure I'm that into him either."

"Um, okay. But his friend did save my life twice so he at least keeps good company."

She glanced at me with a smile. "Gareth. Now there's an idea. Maybe *you* should date him. Forget about Colton and this Nevin guy."

I picked at my sling with my good hand, ignoring the blush that fanned across my skin. "No. That's not why I brought him up."

"Seriously though, you should keep him in mind. You know he used to ask about you when Simeon and I hung out. And now he's saving your life and stuff. I think it's fate."

I snorted. "You sound like the back of a romance novel."

"Go ahead, laugh at me, but you'll see." She winked.

We both went quiet as Mom made her way back into the room. Her eyes drifted to the poster then back to us.

"Well the scenery has certainly improved." She smiled. "And look who I found in the lobby."

Colton stepped into the room holding some flowers. His gaze met mine and I saw the worry. "Hey, my parents are waiting outside for me. They said I could come up real quick to see you."

"I think I'm going to head out now," Kadie said. "I promised my parents I'd watch the twins tonight." She bent down and gave me a quick hug.

"See you," I said.

"Do you want me to leave you two alone?" Mom glanced at Colton and me.

"No, I can't stay long," Colton said.

When Mom sat back down, I clutched his hand. "Did you really get grounded?"

"Yeah, but don't worry about it. Kevin had it coming. Trust me, he won't ever pull a stunt like that again." His eyes darkened, his jaw clenched.

"You shouldn't have jumped in like that." This was exactly what I was talking about. Not that I didn't appreciate his coming to my rescue, but he seemed so aggressive.

"I'd do it again. He had no right scaring you like that. Speaking of which, how are you feeling?"

"Sore. But I'm fine. Just a broken arm." I tried to ignore the savageness in his tone.

"I was freaking out when I found out about the crash. Kids were texting and posting pictures of the scene. Kadie called me and told me you were in the hospital... I-I thought the worst."

"You have nothing to worry about. I'll be home in the next day or so."

He bent down until his lips brushed my face. "Just don't scare me like that again."

My mouth twitched. "Trust me, I don't plan on it."

"Listen, I better get downstairs, my dad is pretty pissed off about the fight at school. But I wanted to check on you to make sure you were all right."

"Thanks for stopping by."

"I'll talk to you tomorrow, okay?"

Colton left shortly after, but Mom stayed until Nancy picked her up at nine. She didn't want to leave, but I convinced her I'd be sleeping anyway. When she was gone, I sat in the silence of the room, contemplating how I'd ever be able to have a normal life. I didn't feel safe anymore. Cars, buses, winter, the woods—the creature was everywhere.

The only place I felt like I could escape it was in Grandma's and my houses, nestled safely behind the gate.

A shrill ring next to my bed startled me. I answered, trying not to drop the phone on the floor.

"Salome," Grandma said on the other end. "We've been worried sick."

"I'm fine. Just a broken arm."

"Two accidents in one week isn't fine." The acidic tone in her voice was raw.

I couldn't agree more, but it wasn't like I had any control over it. "I hope you haven't called to lecture me."

"No, I wish I was. Did you see anything during the crash or after it that seemed out of place?"

Why would she ask something like that unless she already knew the answer? Same as the last time we'd talked. How could I explain what I saw?

"I—no."

"Salome."

So I told her about the shadowy figure in the road, then described the hallucination I had on the bus and again in Dr. Bosworth's office. I quivered with each memory.

"Dear God, it's happening again. Why you? Why can't she just leave our family alone?" Grandma's breath hissed through the phone.

"Who?"

"I can't explain."

"Great. You're going to give me this same lame excuse? What part of 'I almost died' don't you understand? How can you keep whatever this is from me?" I snarled, but she silenced me with a loud *shush*.

"We can't speak of the curse or bad things can happen."

Curse? Now that got my undivided attention.

"Don't you think this might've been good to mention prior to now?"

"Just listen," she said.

"Grandma?"

"In my closet, there's an old trunk. In the bottom of it you'll find a compartment and a key," she whispered. "The key is for the hidden room."

"You mean the office?"

Grandma remained silent.

"What am I looking for?" I asked.

Static buzzed on the line. "Answers. But be careful."

My palms grew clammy. "And you can't give me any clues?"

Grandma's sad laugh worried me. "No child. We can't talk about it. *She's* made sure of it. But you have everything you need to figure things out. Look through books you loved as a child. The fairytales. Read the notes and ledgers in that room."

"Does this have to do with the cemetery?" The pit in my stomach grew into a deep chasm. Accidents, they'd all had accidents.

"Yes."

"I'm going to die, aren't I? I only have until I'm eighteen."

I didn't really want to know the answer.

"No, not if I can help it." Her protective tone was as sharp as daggers. "There's one more thing I need to ask."

I hesitated, afraid of what might come next. "Yeah?"

"Have you met any strangers in the woods?"

My heart pounded in my ears like a snare drum. I sucked in a deep breath. Please don't let him have anything to do with this, please.

"Yes." The hushed words came out like I'd never even spoken.

"And what is this person's name?"

"Nevin." His name fell from my lips like raindrops on a window.

The click of her tongue sounded on the other end of the line, followed by a soft groan. "Well, when you decide to do things, you do them big, don't you? And how many times have you met with him?"

"Um—several."

"I think it might be best if you stayed away from him."

The ache started in my chest, winding its way up to my throat. She asked too much.

I clutched the phone tighter. "I can't. I need him. He gets me."

"You're begging for trouble. He can't love you."

"I'm not asking him to love me. You don't understand, he's always there for me. He's the only one who knows what I'm going through and doesn't think I've lost my flipping mind."

Grandma fumbled with something. It sounded like paper crinkling. "He can't always be there for you. I like him, Salome.

He's kind, handsome, and he did something wonderful for our family eleven years ago. But he can't be with you, child. Not as a friend. Not as a companion. Not as a lover. He simply cannot be a part of our world."

A sob shook me. She was mistaken. She had to be.

"I care about him. Besides Kadie, he's the best friend I have." I wiped my eyes on the sleeve of my hospital gown. "And you said you like him."

"I do. But I love you more, sweetie. I want you to be safe and you can't be if he's around."

Pain ripped through me. "You don't know anything."

"Please, just trust me. Look through the room before making your decision." I'd never heard her sound so broken, so worried.

"I—I have to go." I hung up the phone then buried my face in my pillow. No more Nevin? Impossible.

Then I realized something I'd said to Grandma. *I cared for Nevin.* I didn't know him that well and yet I felt as if I'd known him for several lifetimes.

The next night I sat on my bed, the lamp casting eerie silhouettes on my wall. I'd wanted to go to Grandma's when I got home from the hospital, but Mom and Nancy shooed me into my room to lie down.

I hadn't been over there in two days—two days, which felt like a million. What if Mom refused to let me go over there tomorrow? And the next day?

I flipped on my radio to drown myself in classical music.

When that didn't work I readjusted my arm, propping it on my pillow, and stared at the ceiling. God, I couldn't get comfortable. So I sat up, leaning against my headboard with my eyes shut.

Tap-tap-tap.

The noise came from my window. I stared at it for long moments, wondering if I dared to check it out.

Tap-tap-tap.

It came again. This time I swung my legs over my bed, clutching my injured arm to my chest. After counting to three and taking a deep breath, I threw open the curtains to find Nevin standing outside my bedroom window.

I unlocked it, struggling to slide it up with one arm. A cold breeze tickled my cheek as it swirled inside around me, whipping my nightgown around my legs.

"Nevin, what are you doing here?"

Pale eyes met mine and he stared like he hadn't seen me in an eternity. "I had to come and see if you were okay."

My knees wobbled and I clutched the sill for support. "Do you want to come in?" I asked.

Regret washed over his face as he shook his head. "I can't."

"Because of the curse," I whispered.

He looked startled, taking a step back. "What do you know of the curse?"

Ah, so he *did* know about it. Maybe getting answers would be easier than I thought.

"Wait here." I rushed toward my closet to put on my boots. I grabbed a jacket, too, and when I came back to the window, Nevin still stood there.

"I'm climbing out." I slipped out, first one leg, then an arm. Then my nightgown caught on a nail on the sill and with my arm in a sling, I wasn't sure if I'd be able to make it. But Nevin's strong hands wrapped around my waist and he helped me to the ground.

I clung to him with my one good arm, staring up into his face.

"What do you know of the curse?" His hands tilted my face upward.

I couldn't look away. He seemed so haunted. So sad. "Nothing, yet," I admitted. He looked disappointed. Angry, even.

"Did it ever occur to you that maybe you should leave things well enough alone?" He touched my cheek, his thumb tracing the contours.

"Yes, but I can't. So, please don't ask me to. More than that, I seem to be involved whether I want to be or not."

His face darkened. "It's selfish of me *not* to ask—but I'm a selfish person. It's been so long since I've had someone to talk to. Someone who didn't want something from me. We have a kinship I can't explain and I want you in my life, Salome."

More than ever, I knew I'd have to figure everything out, the sooner the better.

"You're not selfish. Arrogant maybe, but not selfish."

A smile tugged at his lips. "You've had me worried sick. I thought you…"

"Died," I supplied for him.

"Don't utter that word again." His grin vanished and his mouth twisted in anger. "Things will be different this time. *She* will not win."

Whoa? *This* time? A clue, my dear Watson. And yet a knot squeezed my stomach telling me to be careful—to tread lightly.

"Why did you come to me that first day in the woods?" I asked in a soft voice.

He smiled, hand catching mine. "Because I've been waiting for you. You're the one person who could change everything."

With that he ushered me back toward the window. "Get some rest."

"Grandma said I should stay away from you," I said when he boosted me onto my sill. "That we shouldn't be friends."

He patted my leg. "She's probably right, but what do you want?"

That was simple.

"To still see you."

"Then prove it." All traces of humor were gone.

My heart leaped into my throat and I almost choked. "How?"

"Solve it." He touched my hand to his face before walking away.

I planned to. My silent promise was made.

CHAPTER SEVENTEEN

After two days of Mom saying no to my going to Grandma's, I was about to burst. She didn't understand that I *needed* to get over there, and if she said no one more time I was going to have to sneak out—at night, in the dark and cold. I had a mystery to unlock.

"It's supposed to be fifty degrees today," Nancy said, driving toward town. Since my school was on her way into work, she'd swung by the house to get me. I owed her one.

"Thank God." I toyed with my sling.

"Try and have a good day." She pulled up to the main entrance of the school.

I snorted. "Yeah, I'll see what I can do."

Snow dripped from the roof, causing puddles to form on the sidewalk. A small break from *winter,* which wouldn't last. It was December after all. Inhaling the warmer air, I longed for spring, enjoying the sun as it peeked out from behind puffy white clouds.

I hated to go inside on such a nice day. However, I forced

myself through the doors. Staring down the hallway, I gasped when I saw Kevin Freeman. The whole side of his face was bruised and his bottom lip was split and swollen.

He looked as if someone had dropped a semi-truck on his face. For a moment, I couldn't believe Colton caused so much damage. He'd hurt someone, for me.

Kevin glanced up and walked toward me. "Hey listen, I…" He looked around at the kids passing by. "I wanted to apologize for the other day. I didn't mean to knock you down." He sounded freaked out.

"It's okay. I'm fine."

He nodded then backed away.

"Okay, that was weird," I muttered and continued down the hall. Did Colton put him up to that? Was that the reason he seemed scared? Okay, I had a huge decision to make. And I had to make it soon. Because it was becoming more apparent that Colton wasn't the person I originally thought he was.

Up ahead, Kadie stood at her locker holding onto her newest boy toy's hand.

She needed a serious talking to. This guy was the biggest stoner in the school. I wondered what'd happened between her and Simeon. Not that I should be surprised, it's not like she stuck with any one guy for any length of time. But still, this was Lon Pinder, in other words, trouble. At least Simeon had seemed like a decent guy.

Kadie spotted me and waved. She whispered something in Lon's ear and he smiled, kissing her neck before she left him to come see me.

"What the hell are you doing with that guy?" I dropped my psych book on the floor.

"Wow, wake up on the wrong side of the bed this morning?" She rolled her eyes, "Lon's a good time."

"And the biggest dope dealer in school. Shit, what happened to Simeon?"

"I told you in the hospital we're seeing other people."

"No, you didn't say that. You said he wouldn't take your bait. That's a huge difference."

"Well, then it must've slipped my mind."

I sighed. Talking to her was like talking to a brick wall. "Just be careful okay?"

"Always am." She picked my book up and handed it to me. "You don't need to worry about me so much. I'm a big girl, Salome. Besides, you know I like to date. I'm not looking to tie myself down to anyone."

"I know, I just don't want to see you get hurt."

She held up her hand and linked her pinky through mine. "I promise to be careful, okay."

I nodded. "All right."

"By the way, I'm glad you're back, I've missed you." She gave me a quick hug then hurried down the hall.

I needed a vacation. Everybody around me had lost their minds. Me included. When I got to my first hour, Colton wasn't there. I hadn't seen him since he had visited me in the hospital and I had a lot to say to him, mostly about the fight and Kevin Freeman's face.

I plopped down in my usual seat and waited for the bell to ring. The teacher took roll from his desk and, right when he rose, the door to our classroom opened and, standing there, in all his bad ass glory, was Gareth. My eyes widened and my heart skipped and thudded. He wore a black t-shirt over a pair of faded jeans and black biker boots. Holy crap he looked good. He handed the teacher some paperwork and he glanced over it.

"Gareth Summer." The teacher went over to his shelf and grabbed a textbook then said, "Why don't you have seat behind

Ms. Montgomery for today. Salome, raise your hand so he knows where to go."

"It's fine, I already know her."

Well *know* was kind of an overstatement. He grinned at me when he walked by my desk and my face grew hot.

"Hey," he said as he slid into his chair.

I spun to face him. "Hi. Um—what are you doing here?"

He chuckled. "I thought that was obvious." His fingers tapped his textbook.

"I thought you were in college."

"No. I just transferred in from West View."

"But you were working at Perky Joe's in the morning," I said.

He leaned closer to me. "Didn't realize you were keeping such close tabs on me."

"I—I…" Suddenly my cuticles became real interesting.

"I'm teasing, Salome. I actually did the work release program for my first couple of hours of school. But they don't offer that here."

"Oh. Sorry. I wasn't trying to be nosy."

"Well, it's nice to have a friendly face in here." His brown eyes held mine and I wanted to lean forward.

"Here, let me see your schedule." I held out my hand.

His fingers brushed mine as he slid the piece of paper to me. A jolt went through me, my skin tingled at his touch. I read through his classes and exhaled. Whoa.

"Do we have any other classes together?" he said.

"Actually, we have all the same classes."

He smiled. "Then at least one thing has gone right today. I won't be completely friendless."

"No. You won't," I said, turning back to face the front of the room. Maybe it was just me, but it seemed strange that the guy who'd saved my life twice was now going to my school. And just happened to have the exact same schedule as me. I wanted to believe it was a coincidence, but I had a feeling it wasn't.

*D*uring lunch hour, I sat in the back of the library, a paperback in hand.

"So you like to read?"

I glanced up to see Gareth standing over me. "Yeah. And you do, too?" It was hard to keep the surprise from my voice.

He shot me an amused look. "You seem shocked that I like books. Should I be offended?"

"No. I—I." Why did I always turn into a stammering fool in front of him?

"You can tell when I'm teasing, can't you?"

"Sometimes. You got that kind of wicked-dry humor. But I'll catch on to it."

He watched me for a moment, then reached into his pocket. "I was gonna bring this up to the hospital, but I never got a chance to visit before you were released." He held out a wooden beaded bracelet to me.

Not just any kind. But one made of rowan wood.

I knew my face had turned red. "Oh, you didn't have to get me anything."

He reached for my non-injured wrist, his fingers gently fastening the jewelry to it. I held my breath as his thumb swept against my skin. Could he feel my pulse soar? God, I hoped not.

"It was meant as a get well gift. And you should keep it on you at all times." His eyes seemed more intent. "It's made of rowan."

"I know," I said. "But why—"

Right then, I looked up to see Colton saunter into the library, eyes scanning the tables. His smile faltered when he saw Gareth. His jaw clenched as he made his way over to where we were.

"What the hell are you doing here?" Colton glared at him.

"Didn't realize I answered to you." Gareth was rigid, his fist clenched at his side.

Colton moved closer to him. "You're not welcome here."

Gareth snorted. "Worried I might interfere with something?"

Okay. Did I miss something here? I stared between them. The air sizzled with animosity. At last, Colton moved around him and stood next to me, his hand resting on my shoulder.

"Salome, let's go eat in the cafeteria," Colton said.

"Actually, I just want to hang out in here today."

He cast me a strange look as if I'd said something wrong. "But I thought we could eat together."

"I'm not really that hungry right now."

"Why isn't it working?" he muttered under his breath.

"Excuse me?" I said in confusion.

Gareth grinned. "Not so easy to manipulate her now, is it?"

"What'd you do?" Colton snarled.

"What I should've done to begin with. Protected her."

"Stay away from her, Gareth."

"Or what?"

But before either of them could answer, the librarian came over. "Is there a problem here gentleman?"

"Nope, I was just leaving." Gareth waved. "I'll see you around, Salome."

"Bye."

When he'd left, Colton spun to face me. "Why the hell are you hanging out with him? Don't you realize how dangerous he is?"

I glowered at him. "What was that about?"

"Nothing. Just try and stay away from that guy. He's bad news."

Funny thing was, Gareth had told me the same thing about him.

"So, how are you?" he asked, changing the subject.

I noticed the small bruise on his cheek. He'd definitely fared better in the fight.

"I'm doing okay."

He slid his chair closer to me and sat down, then reached across the way, tugging me against him. But I pulled back.

"I think we should cool it, the librarian's watching our table," I said.

His lips turned down at the corners. "You seem different today."

"I'm just over winter, I guess."

He watched me for long moments then said, "I'm sorry I couldn't stay at the hospital longer. When I saw you lying there, I didn't want to leave. I was just glad my parents let me stop in. They're still ticked off about the fight."

"Speaking of the fight, you kicked the crap out of Kevin. You could've been expelled." I played with my new bracelet. "I don't like what you did to him. He didn't deserve that."

"You're right, he deserved more for what he did to you. I don't regret anything," he said, matter-of-factly. "He won't hurt you again, I'll make sure of it."

"You can't go around beating people up all the time." I rested my head on the back of my chair. The sun streaked through the windows and warmed me. "I don't want you to."

"Sometimes you need to knock people down a couple pegs. It's the only way they learn." He glanced at my sling. "How's the arm?"

"Sore, but okay."

"I should've taken you home that day. After the fight and all, I should've just left with you and ditched basketball practice."

"You're not a superhero; you can't fight all my battles for me." In fact, I wished he'd stayed out of it. This Colton, the one who sat with me now, wasn't who I had wanted to be with. He was too volatile. Too controlling. Too dangerous.

"So, I wondered if I could stop by after practice tonight and bring pizza and a movie."

Guilt sank in. I needed to be honest with him. But I didn't really want to have this conversation with him now. Not at school.

"Sure. I can use the company," I said at last.

"Cool. I'll see you after practice." He gave me a peck on the forehead right as the lunch bell rang.

It was the right thing to do, I told myself as he walked away.

After school, I stood in the parking lot, staring at our new bus. There was no way I wanted to get on. It wasn't safe. Hell, nothing was safe anymore. Gulping in several lungfuls of air, I took a hesitant step forward.

I could do this. Just pretend nothing had happened. Right— easier said than done. On second thought, maybe I should call Nancy and wait in the library until she could come get me.

"Hey, there you are. I stopped at your locker to find you," Kadie said, hanging onto Lon's hand. "Lon said he could give you a lift home if you want."

He smirked at me as he grabbed Kadie's butt. "Yeah, there's

plenty of room."

My cheeks warmed as she nuzzled his neck. "You know what, I think I'm good. I—I'll just catch the bus." *Or walk.* I didn't really want to sit in the backseat of Lon's car and watch him grope my best friend. The guy was an idiot. Too bad Kadie wouldn't open her eyes and see that. But I guess the good thing was, he had a car and she didn't.

"Are you sure?" She glanced at me.

"I'm fine. Go on."

I watched her follow Lon into the parking lot then eyed the buses. With a sigh, I jerked my cell from my pocket and scrolled through my contact list for Nancy's number.

The roar of a motorcycle made me jump and I glanced up to see a sleek black Harley coasting across the lot. And it stopped right in front of me.

"Hop on." Gareth slid his helmet off, shaking his golden hair out.

My mouth dropped open. I stared at him, hesitating. I mean, I barely knew the guy. Although he did save my life. Twice. But the question remained what had he been doing there both times?

Gareth put down the kickstand, throwing his leg up and over. He took my backpack from me and put it in one of the large leather pouches on the sides.

"Are you sure about this?" I asked, wondering how safe the bike was.

"Yes, now hop on."

"But I've never ridden on a motorcycle before."

"Hold on tight and lean when I lean." Gareth handed me the extra helmet and I tugged it on, letting him tighten the chinstrap. I slid onto the seat right as Colton came out the side door. Even from far away, I saw him glare. I turned just in time to see the smirk on Gareth's face.

Wonderful. Was that testosterone I tasted in the air?

I held on with my one good arm, pressing my knees tight around Gareth's hips, hoping I wouldn't fall off. I squirmed. I wasn't sure I liked being this close to him. It seemed kind of intimate.

He shifted the Harley into gear and we tore out of the parking lot.

Beams of sun splayed over the road and the trees billowed in the breeze. There was a chill in the air, but I didn't mind. We sped through town and onto one of the back roads, racing through the turns. I closed my eyes, smiling. It felt like we were flying and the exhilaration made me crave more. I wanted to keep driving. Never come back.

My hair blew behind me and I tucked my helmeted head against Gareth's leather jacket, his muscles flexing as we leaned into the turn.

And then it was over. We stopped in my drive and he turned off the engine. Gareth climbed off first then helped me down.

He chuckled, staring at me as I struggled to get the helmet off. "Are you glad you accepted the ride?"

"Yeah," I said out of breath. "I felt so free, like I could just go on forever."

He unsnapped the chinstrap for me. "That's why I like my bike."

"So, what's really up with Kadie and Simeon?"

He handed me my backpack.

"They're not dating. Your friend wanted a good time—he wasn't into it. End of story."

What happened to romance, love, flowers, and just being *with* someone? Okay, so maybe I was like the only seventeen-year-old romantic left.

"So why did you give me a ride home?"

He smirked. "Because you can't keep your ass out of danger. And your choice of company leaves a lot to be desired."

"I didn't realize it was any of your business—my safety I mean."

"You'd be surprised." He revved the cycle. "I'll be here in the morning to get you."

With my one good hand resting on my hip, I glared. "Won't it be kind of cold?" I gestured to the bike. "You're not picking me up on that, are you?"

"Then what would you like me to pick you up with, milady?" The husky edge in his voice made me shiver.

Maybe letting him drive me wasn't such a good idea.

Staring at the woods and melting snow banks, I wondered if I'd feel safe in anything.

"A Hummer." I flashed him a smile.

"Your wish is my command." He raced out of my drive, spraying up gravel.

*T*wo hours later, Colton knocked on the door.

"Hi." I threw it open. Mom had taken off to go grocery shopping with Nancy, giving me a chance to talk to him alone.

He grinned, holding up a pizza box in one hand and a movie in the other. "Hey, where do you want me to set this?"

"Pizza can go on the table and just put the movie on the counter for now." A stack of paper plates sat on the shelf and I grabbed a couple. "Do you want some pop?"

"Yeah, I'll get my own." He came up behind me and caught my good arm. His fingers swept across my new bracelet. He jerked back as if stung by a bee. "Where'd you get that?" His eyes narrowed, no longer smiling.

"Gareth gave it to me as a get well gift."

"Why you were with him today?" Colton's voice was too calm. "I don't want you hanging around him."

"You don't get a say in who I decide to be friends with." My brow furrowed.

"He's got a bad rep when it comes to girls. I'm just trying to watch out for you."

"Well, I don't need you to." I stepped away from him, to put some distance between us. "Colton, I—I can't do this anymore," I whispered.

"Do what?" He stared at me.

"This. Us. You're not the guy I fell for. I don't like this version of you."

"This is about Gareth, isn't it?" He knocked the pizza box off the counter.

Scared, I took a step back. "No. This has nothing to do with him. Please, just go."

"You'll regret this." His eyes took on an eerie glow.

Shit. What was wrong with him? "Get out, now!"

Colton cringed and let out a gasp as he held his head. "It doesn't have to be this way." He choked.

"Go," I yelled at him, refusing to back down this time. He bounded from the house and never looked back. A loud exhale sounded from my lips. I slid to the floor in relief and cradled my head in my good hand. The bracelet on my wrist felt much colder against my skin now, while red marks appeared where the wood had touched my skin. Had it been the rowan wood that'd protected me? If so, what did that mean, and how did Gareth know I'd need it against Colton?

Everywhere I turned, I ran into more walls. More questions.

Chapter Eighteen

 hadn't seen Nevin for three days, not since the weather warmed. And it worried me. It was odd for him to be missing for so long. Even Colton was out sick this week and I wondered if it had anything to do with our fight. But on a happier note, it gave me a lot more Kadie time, which was a good thing. She was full of best friend advice, especially on the Colton breakup front. She even suggested I ask Nevin or Gareth to go see a movie with me or something. But I didn't want to be "that" kind of girl, stringing guys along. Heck, I had a hard enough time trying to figure things out as it was. With a sigh, I glared at the clock in seventh hour.

At last, the bell rang. Christmas break here I come.

"I'll see you in a few minutes," Gareth said from beside me. "I'll pull the car up to the sidewalk to get you."

"You don't have to, you know." I tucked a strand of hair behind my ear.

"It's no problem." He smiled and glanced down the hall. "Colton hasn't bothered you since that day in the library, has he?"

I shot him a startled look. "No. Why?"

"Just making sure."

From down the hall, Kadie waved. "Hey, wait up. I want to give you a hug before you leave," she said.

Gareth slipped away before she reached me, which I assumed he did on purpose to avoid Kadie asking about Simeon. Again.

"So, want to tell me anything?" She waggled her brows at me. "Like, where the heck is Colton and why are you and Gareth so chummy lately?"

"I told you, Colton and I are done. He just got too intense for me."

"And Gareth?"

"Is a friend."

"A friend-friend, or a friend with benefits kind of friend?" Her cherry-colored lips turned up at the corners.

"Oh. My. Gosh. I can't believe we're having this conversation." My face suddenly felt hot.

"Admit it, you think he's hot."

"Fine. He's cute. But that doesn't mean anything."

"But it could." She laughed then gave me a hug. "We'll have to get together over break. I don't think I can go two weeks without seeing you."

"I should be home. Just give me a call and maybe we can watch some movies or something." I squeezed her back, then let her go as she hurried down the hall.

With bag in hand, I trudged outside to wait for my ride. I stifled a laugh as Gareth parked next to me with the black Hummer. I didn't think he'd take me literally, when I suggested it. But two days ago he had showed up to give me a ride in it.

He flipped on the wipers, cleaning the giant flakes from the windshield as I climbed in.

"Winter's back." I shut the door behind me. "Thought maybe I'd have more of a break from it."

Gareth turned on the radio. "Not a chance. It's December you know, Christmas, snowmen, frolicking in a winter wonderland."

"Right, don't remind me." My fingers traced the fabric of my sling. "So, I was wondering if you might have time to swing by the library on our way home?"

He glanced at me, his dark brown eyes reminding me of a cup of steaming hot chocolate. "Sure. I don't have any plans. Are you trying to get a jump start on your homework so you don't have to do it during vacation?"

I turned my head and stared out the window. "Not exactly. T—there's something I need to look into."

Something that had to do with the curse. I hadn't gotten the chance to spend much time back at Grandma's since the accident. My mom was watching me like a super spy. So I figured I'd start at the local library, see if there was anything there about either the deaths of my family members or about any other strange accidents. Not that I thought I'd find anything, but I had to try.

"So this is a trip for fun then?"

"No. Definitely not."

This time he grinned. "I get it now, you wanted to spend more time with me since you won't see me for two weeks."

My neck grew hot and I felt the blush creep up my skin until it painted my cheeks. "I—I, no. I'm just researching my family history—"

He chuckled. "You're blushing, Salome."

Suddenly the window became very interesting. "I always blush. Horrible family trait."

It didn't take us long to get across town. We pulled into the parking lot in front of the old two story, brick library. The sign above the doors indicated it had been established in 1842.

As I climbed from the vehicle, I noticed the heavy dark clouds looming overhead. The trees surrounding the library bent beneath the gusts of wind. A chill snaked up my back and I hurried to Gareth's side.

"You okay?" he asked.

"Yeah, sorry, just a little spooked." I glanced at the trees once more. It'd be so easy for something to hide in them. I had to shut my mind off. I was safe. Just needed to get inside and get this over with.

Gareth wrapped a protective arm around my shoulders, his eyes scanning the area. "Don't worry. I won't let anything happen to you."

He was the third guy to tell me that in the last few weeks. Why now? Why had he enrolled at my school? Why had he been at both accident scenes? Not to mention, Colton and he had some kind of past. There was so much more going on here, but I couldn't wrap my head around it all.

When we got indoors, I inhaled the familiar scent of books. We headed past the main desk, where the librarian had her head buried in a book, and toward the back of the building. Hard wood floors were well worn from traffic, while various tables sat empty about the room. Aside from a couple studying and the librarian, we appeared to be the only ones here. With a sigh, I led us to the small research room off the non-fiction section. The dim light did little to light the space up, even the floor to ceiling windows let in miniscule amounts of light.

As I logged on the computer, Gareth sat across from me. His eyes were intent. "So what are you really looking up?"

"Old newspaper articles."

"On what?"

I swallowed hard, unsure of how much I wanted to tell him. My gaze met his and my legs trembled. "I'm checking into accidents around here. And maybe some disappearances and deaths."

"That's kind of a morbid subject." He crossed his arms, but didn't seem quite as surprised as I thought he would.

"The thing is, I found a cemetery on my grandma's property. It holds the graves of some of my family members. I know this sounds crazy, but all the headstones belonged to women and they all died the winter they were eighteen."

His gaze softened and he reached over the table, catching my good arm. "I get it. What can I do to help?"

"Could you ask the librarian for books on local history while I scan some of these papers?"

"Yeah, I'll be right back." He stood and I watched his tall figure saunter away.

The newspaper archives on the computer only went back to the late eighteen hundreds. But I soon found what I was looking for. Missing persons.

December 28, 1889

Two young men, Isaac Masterson, age seventeen, and Clyde Donhide, age eighteen, have gone missing after going into the forest to fetch firewood. Searchers found tracks in the woods, but nothing more. They went missing on December 21st and have not been seen since. There will be another search party going out on December 29th for those interested in joining the search.

December 23, 1893

The town of Starlynn is grieving this day as a group of young men and women have gone missing. They were last seen at the winter festival on December 21, 1893.

Seventeen-year-olds John Bartell, Cornelia Hunter, Maxwell Fisher, and Deborah Clover were said to have been driving to the Bartell's manor house. The Bartell's sleigh was found a few miles from town, but the children were not with it. Authorities are asking anyone with any information to please come forward. The Bartell family is offering a reward to anyone with information that will lead to the discovery of their son.

There were several more articles on missing teens and children. And the one thing that stuck out in each of them was the date they'd gone missing.

"Holy crap," I said aloud.

"What's wrong?" Gareth asked as he slid into the seat next to me.

"All these people went missing on the same day. December twenty-first. I mean, they're in different years, but this seems like too big of a coincidence."

Gareth read through the ones I had. His brow furrowed. "The Winter Solstice."

"Wait, what does that even mean?"

"Some people see the solstices as magical times. Some look at it as a way to travel between the worlds, human and otherwise, because that is when the veils are thinnest. Others look at it as a time of sacrifice…"

"What do you mean, human or otherwise?"

"People believe that there is a world that exists next to ours. A place called faerie. I'm sure you've read enough fairytales to know what I'm talking about."

I nodded and he continued.

"During the solstices, the Fair Folk, as people like to call them, can travel freely between their world and ours."

"Do you believe in them?"

He hesitated a moment, his eyes searching mine. "Yes. Do you?"

Goose bumps broke out over my skin. "Sounds like a fairytale. People don't disappear into a fairy tale."

"But you've seen things, haven't you?" He touched my cheek, not letting me turn away from him. "Lots of things that don't seem normal. You know, you're not the only one to see things. Why do you think there are so many books on faeries? I mean, take this book for instance." He held up a large, leather-bound book with a fairy on the front of it. "It talks about people leaving gifts in the trunks of trees for faeries. Like a peace offering. A lot of people believe it'll keep fair folk from getting mad at them. Some people leave items in other places, like in shoes or on porches or in the woods."

"Wait, what?" Holy crap was that what my grandma was doing all these years? Leaving gifts to appease the faeries or whatever?

I opened my mouth to say more when the lights flickered overhead. We both looked up. Everything in the room became quiet and unsettling. Somewhere outside our door I thought I heard the shuffling of footsteps.

"Gareth, please tell me you're hearing that, too?"

He stiffened beside me. "Whatever happens, stay close to me."

"What?" Just then the lights went out sending us into complete darkness. No. Not again. Why did stuff keep happening to me? A whimper fell from my lips.

Gareth grabbed my arm. "Stay calm and do as I say. I want you to get on the floor and crawl under the table."

"Please don't leave me," I cried.

"Shh...I won't. Now come on." He tugged me gently to the

floor and pulled me beneath table.

I sat cowered against him. Sweat beaded my brow, my body quaked with fear. The shuffling of footsteps seemed to draw closer, sounding like something was being dragged across the wooden floor.

The stench of rotten fruit almost made me gag. A flash of lightning pierced the darkened sky outside. What the hell? It was snowing. How could lightning just appear like that? Frantic, I backed up farther away from the window. Then I saw the shadows splay across the glass. Tall, bulbous figures, covered in woodland debris.

A scream bubbled in my throat, but before I could let it out, Gareth covered my mouth, drawing me into his lap. "I've got you. Just stay quiet. They won't find us if we stay still."

A light cold wind blew through the library, sending papers to the floor. The air around us chilled and I shivered.

"Come out, come out wherever you are. I know you're here, Salome," she said.

I squeezed my eyes shut. Please. Make it stop. Make it leave me alone.

Gareth's thumb swept across my cheek. "I will not let her harm you. But I need to leave you for just a second." He uncovered my mouth and eased me to the floor.

"Please don't go. I—I can't face this alone."

"Salome, I'll only be gone for a moment. I have to find us a way out of here." He climbed to his knees then pulled something out of his pocket. "I will be back."

My eyes darted about the darkness, my stomach twisted until I thought I might be sick. What if she came to get me when he was gone? What if he left me here?

I leaned my back against the wall, heart pounding so loud I could barely hear anything else. A few seconds later, a high-pitched shriek echoed around me.

I attempted to cover my ears, but with my arm in a sling I could only manage one. What was going on? Where was Gareth?

The lights flickered back on and the shrieking stopped. I went still. Waiting. After long minutes, I saw Gareth's black boots enter the room. He knelt down and offered me his hand.

"It's safe now. Come on, let's get you home." He pulled me up and I melted against his chest and sobbed. This was safety. This was comfort. Right here in his arms. He let me cry, then brushed away my tears and led me through the maze of tables.

When we got to the main area of the library, I saw wood shavings on the floor. My gaze flicked to Gareth, who reached for my hand and pulled me around it.

When we were back in the Hummer, I turned to him. "You heard the creature in the library, too?"

"Yes."

"Thank God." I flopped against the seat. "Then maybe I'm not as crazy as I thought." That was two people who believed me.

"Why would you think you're crazy?" he asked.

"Because no one else ever sees or hears it. It can attack me in broad daylight without anyone knowing. My parents forced me to see a shrink due to my 'hallucinations,'" I said.

"There's nothing wrong with you."

"H—how come you can see it too?" So far, he and Nevin were the only other people I knew who could.

"That's kind of a long story. One we don't have time for today."

"But—"

"Salome, please let it go for now."

"I—I need your help." My throat went dry.

"And you'll have it. You have my word."

We rode in silence for a bit before Gareth shot me a look. "Be careful while you're on vacation from school."

Playing with my scarf, I nodded. "I will. I don't plan on being out much."

"Good. You're much safer behind your gates." He put the Hummer in park when we got to my house.

Whoa. He was echoing exactly what Grandma and Mom had said. How was I the only one not in the know?

"Thanks for the ride. And looking out for me at the library," I said, turning to him.

"You're welcome. Hey, before I forget, hand me your phone a second."

I dug it out of the side of my book bag and gave it to him. "What are you doing?"

"Programming in my number. In case you need or want to get a hold of me."

"Thank you," I said.

In the distance, I spotted a truck in my drive. Dad was home. My fear subsided and excitement had me scrambling to get my seat belt off. I hadn't seen him in weeks.

Gareth seemed on edge, eyes scanning the surroundings. "You still have that rowan bracelet, don't you?"

"Yeah."

"Good. Keep it on you at all times."

I hesitated, on the verge of asking him again what was going on, but he shifted the Hummer in reverse, which was all the indication I needed that he wanted to go. So I threw my door open, clutching my backpack in my arms.

"See you." I waved, before making a mad dash toward the house. Blustery winds tore across the yard, while sleet pinged the side of my face until it stung.

When I reached the porch, I stopped in place. Raised voices

echoed from inside. But a glance toward the woods made me jerk the door open. I didn't want to barge in, but I didn't want to sit on the porch either. Sure I was behind the gate, but I'd seen what had happened to Cleo.

As soon as I stepped indoors, my parents stopped arguing. Dad gave me a glassy-eyed glance then came over to hug me. He reeked like beer, his hug more of a pat on the back. Several empty cans sat on the counter.

Mom looked as if she'd been crying. It took all I had not to rush to her and comfort her. This couldn't be my family. We didn't act like this.

"I'm going to go look for something for dinner." She headed toward the pantry.

Dad gave a pissed-off grunt then turned his attention to me. "I missed you on the road." He glared as Mom dug through cupboards, clanking things together, then headed toward their bedroom. "I'll visit with you later, I'm going to lie down. It was a long trip home."

When he trudged out of earshot, I turned to my mom. "What's going on?"

"Nothing. Everything's fine. Why don't you go clean your room?" Her lips pursed into a too tight smile.

"Mom."

"Salome, not tonight."

So I sat in my room until dinner, wondering why everything was falling apart. Dad never drank or, at least he never used to. Maybe he was a closet alcoholic and I never knew. And Mom used to get so excited when he came home. They'd practically be jumping each other's bones in front of me. But not tonight.

Mom called me to the table a while later, where she had spaghetti and meatballs piled on our plates. Garlic bread steamed from the bowl. I inhaled the scents. Man, I was starving.

I twirled some noodles around my fork, slurping it into my mouth. We were all quiet—any attempt at conversation felt forced and uncomfortable, like we were a bunch of strangers. Dad asked about school. Mom talked about sewing. Dad burped a rancid beer burp.

And that was it. I played with my food, pretending to be engrossed in each long, stringy noodle. Then the weather report came on in the other room, indicating we were in for a heavy snow this weekend. Lake effect. Seven to ten inches of fresh powdery stuff.

"I suppose that means you'll be staying inside all Christmas break." Dad slammed his can of beer on the table. It sloshed over the edges, spilling.

I noticed the odd silver ring on his finger. Gothic markings surrounded by what looked like snowflakes. Where'd he get that?

Mom dropped her fork to her plate with a *clang*. "Rich, don't start. Not right now."

"Then when is a good time? Never?"

My appetite lost, I pushed my plate away. My eyes flickered to Mom who stood to clear the table.

"I think I'll just do these dishes real quick then head for bed," she said and I jumped up to help her.

Where was the Dad I remembered? The guy who gave me piggyback rides and bear hugs? He got up, jerked the fridge open, and pulled out another beer. He staggered into the living room where he turned the channel to the sports station.

"Don't forget to make me a Christmas list." Mom wiped down the counters.

"I'll do it later." I gave her a quick hug before going to my room. I grabbed a pen and some paper and started my list, feeling about as festive as the Grinch.

CHAPTER NINETEEN

*A*t about ten, I switched off the light, staring at my ceiling. Dad's shouting carried from the next room over. "She's never going to learn if you baby her."

"She's getting better."

Something crashed into the wall, then more arguing.

With my head buried beneath my pillow, I tried to shut them out. But each word they said to one another, each bad thing that Dad said about me, penetrated the thin walls.

Thirty minutes later, I'd heard enough and tossed back my covers.

I scribbled a quick note and left it on my bed, telling Mom I'd gone over to Grandma's. I needed to just get outside and run.

I could do this. I'd made a lot of progress this winter. I just needed to forget the bad things that had been happening. Like the accidents and the stuff at the library. My mind made up, I grabbed my coat and boots. With my parents' fighting, they never heard me sneak out the back door.

The twilight-shrouded yard looked menacing, but I had to get out of there. Keeping my eyes straight ahead, I ran like a banshee trailed me. On occasion I lost my footing and slipped, but I never stopped. Once I got to my grandparents' place I'd be safe.

My breathing came in loud gasps. My pulse pounded an eerie chorus in my ears; with each cold nip at my skin I visualized a frozen death. Then there it was. Grandma's house. My sanctuary.

Key in hand, I rushed to unlock the door then slipped into the kitchen. I bolted the lock tight behind me and flipped on several lights. In a matter of seconds, I stood hunched over the kitchen counter. If it wasn't so late, I'd call Kadie.

A teakettle caught my eye and I gave a sad smile. Grandma would've made me tea if she were here. And it would soothe me, chase away the chill that saturated my bones. I calmed at the thought, pushed away from the counter, and kicked off my boots by the door. Dropping my coat over the back of a chair, I headed toward "my" room. A room designed for me long before I fell in the pond.

I hadn't slept over in ages, and the familiarity of Grandma and Grandpa's house comforted me.

All I wanted to do was curl up in a ball and forget life for a while. I turned the handle, giving a slight push. The scent of cedar and flowers welcomed me. I flicked the light switch on, which brought the overhead fixture alive, bathing the room in dim light.

I stared at the whimsical walls painted for a young girl obsessed with fairytales. There were trees and woodland creatures, fairies and princes taking up every square inch of the murals. The large four-poster bed was hand carved, with roses and fairies decorating each of the poles. Lacy curtains with garlands of fake red roses hung down like the bed belonged to a princess. There were lamps with wooden fairies etched on them and several framed photos of my grandparents and me scattered about the room.

Bookshelves lined either side of the bed, filled with stories about magic kingdoms. With a sigh, I stood glancing at each memory I'd lost. Why had it taken me so long to come back in here?

The antique armoire caught my eye. I grinned. In a few short steps, I stood in front of the massive mahogany cabinet, jerking the doors open.

"You kept them," I murmured and reached in to pull out the costumes Grandma had made me for dress up. Princess gowns, fairy wings, and dresses for gardening. I set the clothes aside to search the back of the cabinet. My fingers touched a lacy material and I tugged the hanger out.

This one looked bigger, like it had been made recently, and I held it up to me, spinning around in circles. I saw a few others the same size. Feeling like a child, I stripped out of my pajamas, which was hard to do in the sling. But I managed to slide the long white gown over my head. *A perfect fit*, the way the lace clung to my curves, falling away in waves at my feet. Small red roses were sewn into the bottom of the fabric, the long sleeves see-through. I glided across the room, pretending to dance in the arms of a secret lover.

After I stopped, I collapsed on my bed, noticing my old music box. A wooden chest, carved with tiny footprints and trees. My hands trembled as I reached for it. I flipped open the top and watched the boy and girl figurines dancing around in the woods. The tinkling of music sounded haunting and familiar. Similar to the music I'd heard when I was with Nevin. That was odd.

Focused on the boy and girl spinning together, my eyelids became heavy. So tired, I yawned.

I step into the backyard, the wind swirling my gown. All around tiny lights blink, weaving between trees and snowflakes. Nevin stands near the big maple staring at me, dressed in white pants, and a dark tunic. His blue eyes glow, a smile tugs at his lips.

"You've come at last. We've been waiting." He points to the others. Faeries enter the clearing, followed by satyrs and fauns. Willowy figures encircle us, watching our every move.

I twirl around, staring as small men carry wooden chairs to sit on and lift silver flutes to their lips. Nevin offers me his arm in time with the enchanting song. He pulls me close, dancing me across the snow covered landscape, twirling and spinning me around. Each movement precise and elegant like the figures in my music box. Unlike them, however, he dips me back and my hair grazes the ground.

His fingers trail along my back, making me want more from him. But still we just dance; each note sends us gliding and moving as one.

"I wish we could always be together." My head touches his shoulder.

"We can, right here, right now." He presses me closer to him. "You're mine, Salome. You always have been."

The woodland creatures applaud our dancing then begin to dance as well, moving as if we are in a giant outdoor ballroom.

And I'm dizzy with happiness. This is where I belong. With Nevin.

I shivered, sitting up in bed the next morning. With the blankets clutched around my shoulders, I staggered into the hallway to check the thermostat. When I'd gone to bed last night it had been set at sixty-five. But the inside temperature indicated fifty-four. A brisk breeze carried down the hallway and caught strands of my hair.

I wandered out into the living room to find the slider-door ajar and footprints covering the deck and yard.

"What in the?" I jerked my boots and coat on over the lace gown.

I examined the prints. Some looked like hooves, others like tiny footprints. Oh my gosh. Last night *had* to have been a dream. Maybe I was still asleep.

I rushed into the yard, spinning around, staring at even more footprints. There were some of my own, and some that belonged to someone else. I tilted my head upward, staring at the pond and the gazebo. And there he was. Watching me.

"Nevin."

Within seconds, he joined me. "You look so beautiful."

I blushed, meeting his gaze. "Thank you, but—"

"I've missed you." He smoothed my hair. "Not a day has gone by that I haven't thought of you." A ghost of the music from my dream flitted past.

"Where were you?" I asked, wondering if I imagined him holding me. Embarrassment sank in as I remembered the dream I'd had of him last night.

"Away, but I'm here now."

"Were you here last night, I mean out here, dancing?" God, I sounded like a lunatic. Why didn't I just ask him if he had wings?

But he only smiled. A secret, sexy grin. Then he hugged me tight.

I would not have the answers I sought today—but no matter, I knew where the hidden key was. For the first time in days, I felt like I could finally handle going into the secret room. And I vowed to discover everyone's secrets.

CHAPTER TWENTY

*G*randma's phone rang. I picked it up to find my mom on the other end.

"You need to come back home now. We're putting the Christmas tree up today."

"Tell her to hurry up," Dad grumbled in the background.

"Has he settled down?"

A deep sigh sounded. "For the most part. I'm s—"

"Be there in a minute." I hung up the phone to avoid hearing how it wasn't my fault they were fighting. I cast a longing glance at the door to the hidden room. It'd have to wait. A part of me was relieved to put it off, but, on the other hand, I was anxious for answers. Either way, I didn't have a choice.

By the time I got home, Dad already had the tree in the stand and Mom was untangling lights. Our red and green storage boxes sat in the middle of the floor with their tops off, revealing an array of ornaments. An angel collection, blue and silver glass bulbs, and tiny red-and-white candy canes glittered in their cases. Along with several homemade beaded ones I'd made when I was younger.

"Hey, why don't you throw on a Christmas CD?" Mom handed a line of lights to Dad, who stood on a ladder.

"Sure." I attempted a smile for her sake and thumbed through several CDs before finding one.

With musical bells tinkling through the speakers and the decorations going up, I thought things would start to go back to normal. But it didn't. Granted, there was no fighting, but the awkward attempts at conversation were almost worse.

Where the hell was the holly jolly, ho-ho-ho shit?

Once everything was put strategically on the tree with Dad making *his* adjustments, he plugged in the lights. We hovered there watching the rainbow of blinking colors move in time with the music. It was calming and beautiful. And it reminded me of when I was a kid, the whole magical feeling about Christmas.

"I'm going to go into town to do some shopping." Dad pulled on his heavy Carhart jacket. "I've got some last minute gifts to buy and I'm out of beer." He tucked his wallet into his back pocket and left.

Mom looked disappointed as she watched him get ready to leave, but when she saw me staring, she clapped her hands together like I was eight years old again.

"I've got everything out so we can make cookies," she said.

Sure enough, there were various Christmas-themed shades of frosting, colored sugars, sprinkles, nuts, chocolate chips, and our circa-1940 cookie cutters laid out in the kitchen. Next to those sat several bowls of dough ready to be rolled out and cut.

So I grabbed a festive holiday apron that read, RUDOLPH ISN'T THE ONLY ONE WITH A RACK. And Mom sported her, I'M SANTA'S HO-HO-HO apron, a gift from Dad when he used to be home more. She set to rolling out the dough, her mouth drawn into a frown.

"What's wrong with Dad?" I placed a doughy wreath on

the cookie sheet.

Her eyes shifted away. "He's stressed."

"It's because of me, isn't it?"

The rolling pin slammed down with a little more force than necessary. "Some of it."

"He never used to be like this."

"No, he wasn't, not until after—"

"Until after I fell in the pond."

Not meeting my gaze, she slid the first pan of cookies into the oven, adjusting the dial to the correct temp.

"It didn't bother him right away, but after a few years and the therapy, he realized things might be more complicated." She wiped her hands on a towel. "He just wanted you to be normal again."

Biting back tears, I pretended to be interested in stirring a dish of frosting. "He stopped coming home."

"He doesn't know what he's missing. You're such a smart, beautiful girl."

"Who has lost her mind," I snapped. "It's okay to say it out loud, Mom—Salome's crazy—she's off her fucking rocker."

Her face turned a bright shade of burgundy. "Don't you ever use that type of language again, you hear?" She swung the spatula around in the air.

"Yep. Loud and clear." I chopped the cookie snowman's head off with the cutter.

"I've got enough to deal with, without fighting you, too." Her voice sounded tired. "Let's just pretend to have a Merry Damn Christmas."

For some reason, hearing her curse made me laugh— uptight Mom cussing. Soon we were both giggling like maniacs, and it felt good.

And we kept smiling until Dad came thumping through the door, bags in one hand and a twelve pack of beer in the other.

Once again, the strange ring caught my eye. His gaze met mine. For a moment, his eyes seemed to change color. But I chalked it up to the lighting.

Mom tossed the leftover decorations into storage bags.

"Head into your room so I can get the gifts brought in," Dad said.

"Rich, you smell like alcohol. You can't be out driving like that."

He didn't answer. Instead he pushed around her and trudged outside.

After setting the apron on the counter, I went into my room, flipping on my radio to hear the traffic reporter warning people to stay off the roads. There had already been several slide-offs due to the ice and snow. I switched it off and lay on my bed, staring at the ceiling.

A few minutes later, Dad barged into my room, eyes dark.

"Go shovel off the porch," he said.

"Rich, she's in a sling." Mom came up behind him.

"Sh—shut the hell up." His voice slurred. "She's fine. Getting some winter air will do her good."

I stared at him. "Are—are you serious? It's dark out there."

"Serious as a heart attack. Get off your ass and get it done. You need to get outside more. Face the winter. In fact, it'd be a good idea for you to leave the property every now and again."

Terror enveloped me, twisting my stomach like it was in a blender. This was insane. I couldn't go out there. Not tonight. Something felt wrong.

"Honey, just scrape it right off the porch onto the ground, no lifting," Mom murmured. "And if you need to come in, just do so."

"No. She has to get used to this. You can't baby her forever."

And they broke off into another argument about me. With my coat and mittens on, I went onto the porch. Streams of snow blew in from the trees, creating a blanket of white in the air.

"Just get it done and get back in," I said aloud as if that would make me work faster. Holding the shovel with my good hand, I scraped it across the wooden planks, jarring myself every time I hit one of the cracks between floorboards.

My hair prickled on my neck and I glanced toward the woods. For a moment, I swore I saw a pair of fiery red eyes following my every move. My knees trembled. I reached for the railing to keep from falling.

"Can't avoid me forever, Salome. I'll come when you least expect it."

"No." I backed up until I bumped into the porch swing. It swung back and forth, chains creaking like the damned had come back to haunt me.

"Oh, yes. I can almost smell your blood. See your terror as I watch you die."

Dropping the shovel, I skidded across the slippery surface and barged into the house. Eyes closed, I leaned against the door and slid to the floor.

"You done?" Dad peered up from his magazine.

"N-no." My body quivered. "I um—I can't do it."

His chair crashed to the floor as he bolted up. "You're going to deal with winter one way or another." He stormed over and gripped my arm.

"No—please, don't! Please." Panic embraced me as I tried to jerk free. Not outside, I couldn't go back out there. "There's something in the woods."

He shoved me outdoors, knocking me from the porch onto the ground. Then he slammed the door shut. The deadbolt clicked into place.

Oh God, he was out of his mind.

My arm throbbed as I pushed myself to my feet and rushed

to the porch. I twisted the handle, pounding on the door.

"Please, don't leave me out here." Tears traced my cheeks. I punched the door then ran around to try the windows, but none of them budged.

From inside, I heard Mom shouting at my dad to let me in, then came the sound of breaking glass and more yelling.

The shadows in the yard became longer, creeping closer to me. I pressed my back against the house, crying and screaming.

"Poor—poor Salome. Nowhere to hide."

With horror, I watched a tree on the other side of the gate tip downward. Its bare branches reached toward me. Vines shot through the wrought iron, slithering like snakes.

Oh my God, I was going to die.

"Mom!" I kicked and clawed at the door. Taking a running start, I rammed into the wood, but I bounced off, falling to the ground.

I scrambled away, crawling on my knees, trying to grip the railing. Something latched onto my leg, dragging me backward. Snow seeped into my clothing.

"No," I shouted until I thought my veins would explode.

Strong hands gripped my shoulders, tugged me free, and pulled me to my feet.

Though my vision blurred, I recognized that face. Nevin. He'd come for me.

"Shhh…it's okay, I'm here." His powerful hands became soft like velvet when he caressed my face and hair. "I won't let anything happen to you."

Sobs wracked me, relief making my legs weak. "My dad," I said.

"I know. I'll deal with it. Come on, let's get you to your Grandma's now." The vines shriveled back beneath the gate. The trees straightened like nothing had happened.

"Nevin."

"Just run."

We scrambled down the path, until we reached Grandma's house. "Go on inside," he said again. "I'll check on you soon."

With a nod, I rushed inside. After long minutes I watched out the window as a strange light encompassed the woods. I didn't dare go outside to see what had caused it.

CHAPTER TWENTY-ONE

With all the pacing I did, I half expected to find a chunk of my grandparents' carpet missing. It had only been fifteen minutes since Nevin had left me, but if felt like a billion years. The loud tick-tock of the rooster-shaped clock made it all the more apparent that he wasn't there yet.

I didn't want to believe in magic or wicked fairytales, but even I couldn't ignore the insane crap that had happened lately. Now that I knew Gareth believed me, and Nevin heard things, too, it was becoming more obvious that maybe it wasn't just me. That there was this whole other world that people didn't know about.

I wrung my hands together, staring at the door. Please be okay, I thought.

Just then, a knock sounded. I glanced up to see Nevin standing there, pale fingers pressed against the glass.

With a deep sigh of relief, I answered the door.

"Are you all right?" My eyes studied every inch of him for wounds.

"I'm fine. Listen, you need to stay the night here. Your father will be gone in the morning."

My teeth scraped over my dried lips, my lashes still wet. "I don't know what got into him tonight. He acted like a man possessed."

Nevin stared beyond me, rocking back and forth on his heels. "He very well could've been."

"What do you mean?"

"Salome, try and get some sleep. This will look much better in the morning." He flashed me a faint smile.

I didn't want to be alone, not after what my dad had done and what I saw in the woods. Just when I thought I might be able to get my fear of winter in check, tonight happened.

"Will you stay with me?" I stepped onto the deck so we stood toe to toe.

"If only I could." Regret filled his eyes. Instead, his arms enfolded me, his breath tickled my cheek and ear. "I want to protect you, but I can't do that if you're out here. And I can't come in."

I nestled closer, his body hard with muscles, yet his touch gentle.

"Are you a vampire or something? I mean you won't come into my house. Are you scared you might lose control and take a bite out of me?"

His chest rumbled against my hands as he laughed. He drew back his lips in a perfect smile. "See, no fangs. When I say I can't come in, I mean I can't come in. Vampirism would be a blessing compared to what I've got going on." He sounded bitter. "You have to trust me on this. You're one of my best friends, Salome. And those are hard to come by."

"Okay." I clung tight to him.

"Now go inside." He released me and leaped down the stairs

of the deck. "And whatever you do, keep the doors locked."

Like he had to tell me twice. As soon as the door shut, I clicked the bolts in place then circled the room making sure the shades were drawn and windows locked. No way in hell was I taking any chances.

Now it was time to do what I should've done days ago. The closet door groaned when I tugged it open, revealing layers of old sweaters, suit coats, and dresses hanging like racks of meat in a warehouse. Hangers clanged together, tinkling like tinny bells when I shoved clothing out of the way.

Everything smelled like floral fabric softener and Grandpa's leather boots. I rubbed the sleeve of one of his sweaters against my cheek, inhaling deeply. I dropped the sweater then knelt, clearing the shoes from in front of the trunk.

"Geez." I eyed the ancient mahogany trunk. "What'd they do, bring it over on the Mayflower?"

With shaking hands, I lifted the lid and wrinkled my nose at the scent of mothballs and old wood. Several quilts and dresses were folded neatly inside. I took them out so I could get to the false bottom. It took me a few tries before finding the hidden latch, which lifted the thin shelf away. And there, taped to the bottom of the trunk, was the key.

My stomach churned. In a way, I felt like I was doing something forbidden even though Grandma gave her permission.

"Time to solve this mystery," I said, feeling like I'd just stepped onto the set of a Scooby-Doo cartoon. *Jinkies, Fred, do you think the monster in the woods is real?*

I wedged the key into the lock of the office door and twisted it. The odor of ancient books, spices, and scented candles overwhelmed me as I flicked on a light switch.

A cobweb brushed my cheek. I swatted at it hoping no creepy-crawlies were attached.

The décor of the room left a lot to be desired. Ancient books lined the shelves with titles such as *Reading the Stones: A Book on Runes; Herbs: The Art of Healing; Complete Book of Faeries; Witches, Warlocks, and other Magical Creatures.* There were books on arcane magic, wards, and rocks. Small jars and pouches of herbs, stones, and seeds, cluttered several shelves and tables. There I stood for long seconds, half expecting to see jars labeled eye of newt or puppy dog tails.

An antique cherry rollaway desk sat against the back wall, an wrought iron sconce on either side. The candles in them were nothing but small, blackened nubs. Seriously, it was like stepping into a museum of the supernatural and weird.

I had no idea where to start, but the desk looked promising, so I sat down in the high-backed cherry chair.

Giving the desktop a tug, it rolled into itself, revealing shelves with more books, maps, pens, and notes. One of the old maps caught my eye and I studied it.

It showed the location and lay of our property, both my parents and my grandparents. An outline of the fence was marked on the map. The land within its confines was labeled "safe-zone" with a side note about possible areas of breeching.

There were several other maps of outlying areas and some of town and the school property. Someone had jotted down almost illegible markings. Circles labeled "travel rings" and a few more safe-zones, one of which looked a lot like Perky Joe's. The woods outside our gates had the word "danger" in bright red.

"Shit, tell me something I don't know." I set the maps back down.

I bent down and picked up a large, leather-bound ledger. Inside were the names of the women who had died, their dates of birth, death, and how they perished, as well as who survived them.

Dead in the woods.
Strangled near the wood line.
Horse and buggy accident.
Drowned.

I gasped. The *being* in the woods had gotten to them all. The creature was a pro and rehashed some of her creative methods of killing. Cleo had been strangled near the wood line, I'd almost died in a crash and a drowning, and there was definitely something in the woods that had tried coming after me last night.

This room wasn't helping me solve any mysteries. If anything, it made me more terrified. I slammed the ledger shut and set it on the floor, away from view.

I rested my head against the desk until my breathing returned to normal. Then I opened one of the drawers and rummaged through it. More books, scraps, and notes. As I shoved to the bottom, my fingers brushed a stack of letters tied with a faded red ribbon.

The paper looked yellowed, brittle with age, and the looped writing had faded. Yet someone had taken great care to preserve them. Untying the bundle, I saw some were addressed simply to *N*, while the rest had been to an Aidrianna.

"Your first clue, Scooby-Doo." And so I opened the first letter.

June 14, 1789

My Dearest N,

I enjoyed your company last night and hope you will be in the woods again this evening. I do not appreciate being neglected for HER. You should be more mindful of me because I could have anyone. I do not like that you are meeting with that peasant, Kassandra, too. She is beneath us, remember that. If you continue to see her, it will encourage the servants to talk and that will make me look foolish.

  Aidrianna

  Dear Aidrianna,

  Are you jealous? You speak as if you fear I will desire her more. Remember it is you who should feel grateful for my attentions—my kind does not often seek favor from mere mortal women. You are a delicious morsel, but you can be replaced. If it makes you feel better, love, Kassandra is merely a tool in my game.

  Yours for tonight,

  Nevin

Nevin? No way, that couldn't be possible. The letters were too old. Maybe it was one of his ancestors; he'd said his family had been around forever. I picked up more letters.

  N,

  You make a fool of me and yet I cannot stay away. Do you not worry about Kassandra finding us out? I fear the peasant could pose as a problem, one I am not certain is worth either of our risk. One word from her will make my father suspicious. Not to mention the danger she might cause you. Still, I will meet you in the woods near your estate. Another night with you may corrupt me forever.

   Always,

   Aidrianna

   Aidrianna,

   You worry far too much. Kassandra's abilities are not strong enough to overtake my kind. You shall have no more worries, for after today I will not see her anymore. I have gleaned what information I needed from her. She is of no threat to either of us. With my charm alone I will make her believe my rejection is her fault. Tonight you will find us in the woods dancing in merriment over our victory. If you are particularly good, I will give you that which you desire most.

   Nevin

The letters left a bitter taste in my mouth, like I'd chewed on a rusty nail. I didn't like this Aidrianna—and Nevin sounded so cruel. I refused to believe it could be the same person. I dropped the letters to the desk. This Nevin was horrible and a womanizer. Someone who reeked of arrogance.

Like my Nevin.

I didn't want to read anymore because deep down, I had a feeling I knew the author personally. And if these letters were his, that made him over two hundred and fifty years old. This wasn't possible. It couldn't be. My head throbbed and my stomach grew queasier the more I thought about it.

Before sliding from the chair, I put things back as they were before my visit, taking the letters with me. I locked the door and crawled into the large four-poster bed. And there I lay, staring at the ceiling. God, how did I know he wasn't using me, or leading me on?

And what had happened to Kassandra?

A creature in the woods wanted me dead and I wasn't sure if I could trust the one person who I'd come to consider one of my closest friends. And why the hell did Colton act so strange, and Gareth always show up out of nowhere when I needed to be rescued?

For an added bonus, I now had to deal with the letters, a curse, and my grandma who wouldn't tell me a damn thing.

"Can one thing go right?" I pounded my fist into my pillow.

*T*he next morning I went onto the deck with the letters, knowing Nevin would be along soon. Bitterness seeped through my bloodstream, burning at my skin and throat.

And like clockwork he sauntered up the path, that familiar arrogant smile pasted on his face.

In an even voice I asked, "Who's Kassandra?"

His jaw tightened. "Don't ever say that name in my presence." Venom laced every word, making me shiver.

"Who was she?"

"A peasant."

I didn't want him to be the man in the letters. A sourness settled in my gut, making me want to throw up.

"And Aidrianna?" I held my breath. Let me be wrong.

Nevin stared through me as if I'd thrown a bucket of frigid water over his head. "A woman I once knew."

Oh God. How was this possible? That meant he was over two hundred and fifty years old. Stuff like this didn't happen in real life. Only in books and fairytales. I bent my head, my body trembled, but not from the cold. Anger and confusion swirled through me.

"T—that means you're a couple centuries old—and you were with that woman in the letters? This is crazy. Please tell me this is a joke?"

Nevin glowered, pacing the deck. "She and I were lovers."

My heart seemed to detach itself from the rest of my body, breaking into a million pieces. "Then why did you lead Kassandra on? Why?" My voice broke.

He gripped my shoulders. "I said, don't speak her name."

"How could you be so heartless?" This was not the Nevin I'd come to know. The friend who'd helped me stay sane this winter.

"You know nothing of what went on."

"I know more than you think. You and Aidrianna played some fucked up game with Kassandra. You broke her heart." I jerked the letters out of my pocket and tossed them at him.

"She was a peasant," he spat, like that explained everything.

"No, she was a person, you asshole. I—I thought you were different. But it was all an act, wasn't it? Our friendship, your concern? Tell me, was any of it real?"

"Let it go, Salome." His face darkened, and his eyes took on a menacing glow.

"No, I won't. Just because you're good looking doesn't mean you can act so superior."

"But I am superior, whether I want to be or not."

If I had a knife I could've cut the arrogance-frosted air between us.

"Can you be any more of a prick? Don't you understand what you did to her? I mean she had to have figured it out."

Nevin's gaze flickered away. "I told her that her inferiority kept me from being with her—then I made sure she caught Aidrianna and I together in the woods," he said as if it was no big deal.

How could I have been such an idiot? My eyes burned like acid had been tossed into them.

"You're heartless and cocky."

"And yet these qualities didn't deter you."

"And I'm just one of many fools who has fallen for your act." I backed away. "Bravo, Nevin, great show. You win."

God, I couldn't breathe. I didn't want to feel the pain. This was why I always stayed inside my safe little bubble. Why I didn't let people in. They always let me down. And hurt me. First the people at school. Then my dad. And Kadie when she went to my mom. Colton. Now, Nevin.

"Salome—"

"Have you ever cared about anyone or anything besides yourself?"

Everything was silent. The trees on the other side of the gate bent as if listening to our conversation.

Nevin glanced at the fence then back to me. He closed his eyes as if trying to compose himself. "No, I don't have time or patience to care."

A piece of me died. Numbness took over my body. Nevin had become a better part of my world over the past month, the one constant I had. But it had been a lie. "You don't deserve happiness. You use people like they're dispensable."

"Please." Nevin tried to catch my arm.

"Leave me the hell alone." Tears brimmed my eyes. "I can't believe I thought you might actually care about me. That I cared about you."

I spun around in a wave of fury and dashed back into the house, slamming the door shut behind me. Through the glass, I saw a look of anguish wash over his face.

Oh God, maybe I was wrong. But the letters flashed in

my mind. He was over two hundred and fifty years old. He'd admitted as much. So either he was crazy or he was telling the truth. And if it was the truth, how many of those years had he spent cursed? How was it even possible to begin with? Nothing in my world made sense. The voices. The strange beings. The near deaths. Nevin, a stranger in my woods who I should've left well enough alone. Grandma had warned me of as much. The Nevin who wrote those letters was someone I didn't want to know. Not now. Not ever.

Chapter Twenty-Two

When I got back home my dad was gone, just like Nevin said he'd be.

"I'm sorry your dad did that to you last night," Mom said, in a low voice. "I—I don't know what came over him. It was like he was someone else." Her eyes welled. "But we don't have to worry about him anymore. He left and I won't ever let him step foot back in this house again."

"When did he leave?"

"Not long after he tossed you out. It was strange. One second he was shouting like a mad man, and the next he just stopped. His eyes glazed over, he grabbed his coat and keys, then drove off."

"So what's all this?" I gestured to the boxes in the living room all addressed to a Grisselle Morris.

"Your father's things." Mom's tone could've curdled milk.

I fought to keep from crying. Unreal, my whole life, unraveling before my eyes.

"W—who's Grisselle?"

She frowned, tossing a pile of his hunting pictures into a box. She taped it up. I glanced around, seeing all of his pictures were missing, as were his magazines, and his blankets. There were no traces left of him.

"Grisselle is your father's new love interest." Her words were laced with ice.

"His what?"

"Don't worry. Monday morning, Nancy's taking me to the courthouse to file divorce papers. Grisselle can have that sorry piece of shit."

She hobbled across the floor in her cast, her crutches nowhere to be seen.

"I need an aspirin." She headed into the kitchen.

Me too.

I followed after her. She stopped at the cupboard and tugged out the medicine bottle.

"Mom, are you going to be okay?"

She eyed the bottle, then me, then the bottle again. "Yeah, I'll be fine. I think I might go out with Nancy and the girls tonight." She glanced at me, then frowned. "On second thought, maybe I should stay in with you. Rent some movies."

"No. You go on. I'll be fine." Mom looked like a wreck and I knew there wasn't anything I could say or do that would make her feel better.

"Are you sure you want to be home alone?" Mom said later that night as she put in her diamond earrings. Her wedding band had disappeared, probably down the toilet.

"Seriously, Mom, everything is fine. I'll probably just read a book. I've got like a million of them in my to-be-read pile."

Her sad smile told me she was reconsidering this whole idea. But the thing was, I knew she needed people to talk to. Someone who knew the right things to say, and I wasn't sure I was that person. At least not tonight. "Promise you'll call me if you need me. I'll have Nancy bring me right back home." Her voice softened.

"Go. Have fun."

A horn honked from the driveway and Mom gave me a peck on the cheek. "I'll try not to be too late."

When she left, the house was quiet. But it was a sad kind of quiet. The kind that reminded me of how alone I was. I considered calling Kadie, but she wasn't the kind of comforting I wanted tonight.

Colton was out of the picture. And, well, I didn't really have any other friends. I grabbed my cell from my room. On second thought, I could get a hold of Gareth. He'd programmed his number into my phone. Right. I was sure he'd want to drop everything and come over and hang out with me. However, he could always help me with some research.

Before I could talk myself out of it, I pulled up his contact info. With trembling fingers, I dialed his number.

"Please pick up." But it went to voicemail. So I left a lame, stammering message asking if he could come over.

When I hung up, I triggered the security latch for the gate to unlock, just in case he actually got my voicemail and decided to drop in.

Twenty minutes later the doorbell rang. Oh God, had he actually come? Taking a deep breath, I hurried to the door. Gareth stood there like a blazing knight in shining armor, holding a box of chocolates.

"You sounded upset on the phone, so I thought I'd bring

you something to cheer you up." He grinned, holding out the candy to me.

"You didn't have to do that."

"I know. But I wanted to." He shrugged. "So what's going on?"

I ushered him inside, nervousness tickling my belly. For a moment, I just stood there, staring at him.

"Salome?"

"Everything is so screwed up," I said, staring at the boxes of my dad's stuff in the living room.

"Do you want to talk about it?" Gareth took off his coat, shut the door, and put my box of chocolate on the counter.

I nodded my head, then led him into the living room. We sat on the couch, my leg pressed against his. At last, I glanced at him and gave him the grim details of my dad's odd behavior and ended on the high point of my parents pending divorce. I spared him the details of my fight with Nevin, thinking he wouldn't want to hear that, since he had no idea who he was.

"I just want to forget it all," I said.

He wiped away my tears with his thumb, his callused hand caressing my cheek. "Things will get better." Gareth's warm breath fanned across my neck as he leaned closer, pulling me into his arms for a hug.

My blood thrummed in my ears when he rubbed my back in soothing circles. My fingers trembled and I slid my good arm around his shoulders, resting the side of my face against him. Even through the fabric of his sweater, I could feel his muscles. And his cologne smelled so good. It was strange being so close to him. Not that he hadn't held me before, it's just those times had been when he'd rescued me. But I guess, in a sense, that's what he was doing again.

"Did you want to go to your grandma's still?" His voice

sounded deeper.

I swallowed hard. "Yeah, sorry. I didn't mean to go all damsel on you." I started to pull back and he stopped me.

He cupped my chin, tilting my head so I stared into his eyes. "Does it look like I mind?"

My palms slid down his chest and I heard a deep exhale. "I—I don't know." I shifted my gaze to his tattoos. Without thinking about it, I traced a finger over the gothic designs.

"Do you know what you're doing?" Gareth said, his eyes darkening. Not with anger, but something else.

My face sizzled with heat and I dropped my hand. "Sorry. I mean, I wasn't trying to seduce you or anything."

"Well, that's too bad." He chuckled.

My eyes widened and I glanced at him. "What?"

"Teasing."

"Right." I probably wasn't his type, which, for some reason, made me feel kind of disappointed. "So, I wondered if you might be willing to help me do some more research."

"I think the library's closed." He smiled. "Wait, did you lure me over here under false pretenses? Did you actually miss me?"

I laughed. "For your information, there are some things at my grandparents' house I wanted to show you. Maybe some of it will make more sense to you. And yes, I admit, I kind of missed you. But only kind of. Don't let it go to your head."

He chuckled and it warmed me from my head to toes. "I think you and I are going to be hanging out a lot more."

A knock sounded on the door to the deck. My brow furrowed. Who the heck could that be?

"I'll be right back," I said.

When I opened the door, I was surprised to find Colton there.

"What are you doing here?" I asked, my fingers clenched tight to the handle.

"I came by to see you. And to apologize. You're right. I've been a dick. I'm sorry." He leaned against the side of the house, his dark hair sweeping his forehead. "But do we have to not be friends now?"

"I think it's best if you stayed away." I went to shut the door and he caught it with his hand, stopping it.

"So that's it?"

"Colton, please."

Behind him, Nevin climbed the deck stairs, his eyes the color of ice and just as cold, gazing right through me.

"W—what are you doing here?" I stared beyond Colton to Nevin.

"I need to talk to you," he said. His face hardened as he glanced at Colton

"What brings you here, cousin?" Colton spun to face him, voice filled with amusement. "We're kind of busy."

Whoa? Cousin? No way. No fucking way.

If Nevin was put off or upset, he didn't show it. Instead he grinned with his infamous arrogance.

"Didn't think she was your type, *cousin*," Nevin answered. "I thought you would've moved on by now. In fact, last I heard, you were told to stay the hell away from her."

Colton glowered. "Yeah, well, I don't answer to you here. In fact, things were going great until you sent your friend my way."

I stepped onto the deck, away from both of them.

"You guys are cousins?" My throat tightened. Did that mean Colton was over two hundred years old too? Was he in on all the crap with Kassandra? Shit. What was wrong with these two? And why were they both so interested in me?

Nevin nodded. "Yes."

"And you both knew about each other?"

"I knew as soon as you mentioned his name," Nevin said.

"But I guess I didn't think he'd be any competition or that he'd try to take things this far."

I scowled at him. "Wait, what?"

"Because you prefer my company over his. You chose me, Salome," Nevin whispered, ignoring his cousin. "You chose to spend time with me, to share all your secrets with me. Did you ever once tell him about the voices or the creature that stalks you in the woods? Did he know about all the grisly details of your fall into the pond and the people who saved you?"

I swallowed hard. No, I hadn't told him any of those things. The question was why? Because I wanted one person to think I was normal.

"You guessed wrong." Colton sneered. "I *am* competition or at least I was until you pulled a fast one on me."

"She needed to be kept safe." Nevin's gaze never left mine.

Suddenly I wasn't feeling so good. Damn, they pissed me off. Here they'd lied to me this whole time and I was just supposed to be okay with it all? Nausea churned in my belly. They were both a couple hundred years old. Older than my parents and grandparents. Maybe older than the town. And they didn't give a crap about me. "Just stop, okay? Is this some kind of messed up game you two play with women? I don't know what's going on, but I think one or both of you owe me some answers."

"Why don't I come inside, then *we* can talk," Colton said.

When I moved toward the door, Nevin caught my arm. "No, I need to speak to her. And she's already told you that you're not welcome here."

"You've had your chance, cousin, and it sounds like you blew it. Or so a little birdie told me." Colton seemed almost bigger, his eyes darker, his body tenser.

Nevin sighed. "She might be the *one*."

The one what? My heart thundered in my ears like stampeding cattle.

"Is everything, okay?" Gareth came to the door and peered outside. His wide shoulders seemed to fill the small space.

Colton backed away with a glare and headed toward the driveway. Over his shoulder he gave Nevin a look I didn't understand, but they both nodded like some silent agreement had been made.

Nevin waited for Colton's truck to pull away before turning to Gareth.

"We're fine," Nevin answered.

"If you need me, I'll be right here."

I wasn't sure if Gareth was saying that to Nevin or me, but I watched him go back into the house. Why had he just left me here with someone he didn't know? Or did he?

"Why are you here, Nevin?" I whispered, my energy tapped. I didn't want any more bullshit stories.

"Because you left before I explained myself to you." He closed the distance between us, his arms encircling me.

I attempted to jerk free, but he held me tight. "Just leave me alone. You made it perfectly clear how you feel. That our friendship was a fluke."

"No, I didn't," he whispered in my ear. "*She* could hear us earlier today. If she found out how much I care about you, she would've killed you on the spot."

My eyes widened as I stared at the tree line behind him. I lowered my voice. "How do I know you're not just saying that? You could be playing me like you did that other girl." Already, I inched closer to the house. I didn't want to be outside.

"Trust me."

"I don't know if I can trust you. You're not the person I thought you were."

Nevin brushed my hair from my face, forcing me to look at him. "I messed up in the past, but I promise you, I'm not that man anymore. You mean everything to me. How can I prove that to you?"

Cold air assaulted us, the winds battering the side of the house. My teeth chattered.

"I can't do this tonight," I said. "Give me a few days." After what he'd put me through earlier, I wanted him to suffer a little. To understand the pain I'd felt when he'd rejected me—telling me he didn't care. Friendship was something that I didn't offer very often, for this very reason.

Was it worth the risk to let Nevin stay in my life? Especially now that I knew whoever wanted me dead, might be connected to him as well? It would be so much easier to turn around and never look back.

He released me and stepped back. "Find me when you're ready."

What was I doing? Weren't the letters convincing enough? He'd brought Kassandra to her knees. He'd probably showered her with fancy gifts and words of love and to what end?

I rushed back into the house and slammed the door. Damn him! He couldn't just show up when he wanted. I was tired of being hurt and of being scared. I needed to stand up for myself. To be strong for once.

"Are you all right?" Gareth watched as I stalked across the kitchen and leaned against the counter.

"I hardly know anymore."

"I heard Colton out there, but it sounded like you handled him and I didn't want to interfere. Was he giving you trouble?"

"Kind of, but don't worry about it. I don't think he's going to be coming around much anymore." I wondered why he didn't mention Nevin, and it hit me. I shuddered and caught his eye. "You're like them aren't you?"

He shrugged. "Are you sure you want the answer to that?"

He was right. I decided that was the last thing I wanted to talk about right this second. Instead I said, "You ready to go to my grandma's now?"

"Are you still up for it?" He grabbed his coat from the back of the chair.

"Yeah. Definitely. I—I need to concentrate on something else."

"Do you want me to drive?"

"No, it's not far."

Gareth walked beside me as we trudged through the snow and down the path. He kept his pace even with mine, reaching out to steady me when I lost my footing and nearly face planted in a snow bank.

"Geesh, you'd think I forgot how to walk."

"I thought you might've done it on purpose so I'd catch you." He chuckled.

"You seriously enjoy the fact that I've been a damsel in distress lately."

"Well, it hasn't been all bad."

I shifted my gaze to the snow. He was right. It'd been nice being able to talk to him. And if he hadn't been there, then I'd be dead. Several times over. I shivered at the thought.

"You cold? If you want, you can have my jacket, too."

"I'm good." Finally, we stepped into my grandparents' driveway and I led him into the house. I flipped on the switch and light flooded the kitchen. With a sigh, I reached into my pocket and pulled out the key to the hidden room.

When I opened the door, I heard Gareth let out slow breath. For a moment, I thought he said the word "magic."

"What's wrong?" I peered back at him.

"Nothing." He grinned. "Man, your grandparents have a lot of antiques in here."

We both stepped the rest of the way in. "And a ton of a dust and cobwebs." I waved a web away from my face.

I grabbed some of the ledgers and maps to show him, hoping something would stick out to him.

He ran his hand along a stone tablet type thing on one of the shelves. "Do you know where your grandma got this?"

"No. This is only the second time I've been in here. Why, do you recognize it?"

"It looks like a faerie artifact I saw in some fantasy book a while back."

I moved next to him and studied the carvings of suns, flowers, leaves, and snowflakes. Why would Grandma have an item like that? Not to mention, how did I even know that it was real? Maybe she just liked to collect fairytale stuff.

"So what do you make of these?" I handed the ledger over so he could see the deaths of the women in my family.

"Well, I think you need to focus on the fact that they all passed away during the winter."

I swallowed past the lump in my throat. "Everything always leads back to winter."

He stood straight, his hand touching my shoulder. "And that's your starting point."

We searched through more documents and books, but nothing more stuck out at us. After a couple of hours, Gareth walked me back home and headed out.

Alone, I stared out the window. Winter. That was my only clue. Frustrated, I let the curtains fall back in place. When did life get so screwed up?

After I fell through the ice.

I stormed into the living room.

Picking up the TV remote, I whipped it across the room. Confused was the understatement of the century. Who could

I trust? Both Nevin and Colton had lied to me, not just about their age, but about everything. Which also begged the question, were they human? If not, what the hell were they and what did they want with me? Did they have anything to do with the disappearances I'd read about, the ones that happened in the nineteenth century? And what about the tiny footprints I'd seen around the trees on Grandma's property, and the frickin' crazy creature lady who'd tried to kill me? I wasn't losing my mind. I knew what I'd seen. But what did it all mean? My head throbbed, confusion taking over.

I went to my playroom, where the glow-in-the-dark star stickers welcomed me. I collapsed on my old beanbag chair and flipped on my reading lamp. I had to figure it out. I needed normality again—to be that six-year-old girl who used to love winter, who had two parents who loved me and each other.

Against my better judgment, I grabbed a stack of fairytale books from the shelf. Hmmm…how to break a curse. Like I should help Nevin.

But I knew I would, if only to win back my life.

CHAPTER TWENTY-THREE

I stifled a yawn, questioning why in the hell I was going to so much trouble for Nevin. Okay, so he'd apologized and admitted to caring about me. And this meant the witch would have all the more reason to want to kill me, or so he said. But since when did an apology and caring constitute putting my life on the line?

And what was up with Colton and him? When I remembered seeing the two of them—the conceit and challenge in both their eyes, each daring the other to make a move—I shivered. There had been some major testosterone in the air. Although, Colton seemed to have backed down.

My pen fell from my ink-splotched hand and I rubbed my temples.

I couldn't trust either of them. I needed to just suck it up and walk away. But it wouldn't be that easy. I mean, I'd still see Colton at school, and Nevin would probably still show up in Grandma's backyard.

Recalling them side-by-side triggered a thought: *"Something wicked this way comes."*

"Yeah, one too many fairytales." I flipped open another book.

Several jotted notes later, I realized fairytale writers were full of shit. Or so it seemed. Let's see, pretty girl eating poisoned apple. Cured by a kiss. Girl pricks finger, falls into deep sleep. Cured by hot guy kissing her. Sexy guy acts like an ass, turned into a beast. And you guessed it. Cured by true love, then a kiss.

So why wouldn't Nevin let me kiss him the day of our picnic? Did he know something I didn't? Or maybe he was afraid of what would happen once the spell broke. With a sigh, I continued on.

Battling dragons…learning true names…yada, yada, yada.

The authors were either on drugs or horny as hell. Seriously, every curse could be cured by a little making out and true love. But, Nevin didn't kiss me when he'd had the chance, and love wasn't on the radar for either of us. So why did he think I had a chance of breaking the curse?

Mom was just getting in when I came down for breakfast the next morning. My brows raised when I noticed the pink splotches painting her cheeks.

"I take it you had fun?" I snorted.

"Don't talk so loud." She moved to the kitchen, pulled out a bottle of aspirin, and then poured a cup of water. "I never should've stayed out so late. I'm sorry."

My smart-ass remark was lost on my lips as the phone rang.

Mom cringed. "Make it stop."

"Mom, not to sound like a parent or whatever, but maybe you shouldn't have drunk so much."

She muttered something like, "In hindsight, you're probably

right…" And collapsed on the couch, her coat still on.

"Hey." I picked the receiver up.

"Good, you're up." Kadie's voice was way too chipper this early in the morning.

"So it would appear."

"Okay, so my parents are taking us up to that indoor water park, Waterfall Lodge, for the weekend. They said I can invite someone. You *have* to go with me. Otherwise I'll be stuck with the dweeb twins."

Aw crap. I didn't want to go anywhere, not after everything that had happened. "Well, I'd love to, but I can't get my sling and stitches wet." Thank God for broken arms.

Kadie harrumphed. "Come on, that's a shitty excuse and you know it. There will be arcades, pools, scantily clad men in wet swim trunks. Besides, we barely hang out."

Great, she was pulling out the big friendship guns.

"But I'll be a total bummer."

"No you won't. You can slink around in your bikini and soak your feet in the pool. Or just watch all the eye candy swim by. Come on, an indoor water park, in the winter. It'll be fun."

Defeated, I exhaled with a hiss. "Hold on, let me ask my mom."

"Yes, to whatever you want." She held up her hand before I could even speak. "No talking. Just do whatever."

"Great, then you won't mind that I just got invited to a huge orgy in California."

She glared through narrowed slits. "Ha-ha. Tell Kadie I said you can go with her."

Right, she chose to not be a good parent, when I needed her the most. A big fat "no" would've been okay.

"What about my arm? Not sure if it'll hold up at the Waterfall Lodge."

Mom raised her finger to her lips and gave me a loud *shush.*

"Go, have fun."

"She said I can go." I sounded about as excited as kid getting a shot.

"Sweet, we'll be there in about two hours. Bring your blue bikini."

After she hung up, I trudged past the traitorous woman I called mother and went to pack. My duffle bag filled up fast and my stomach knotted as I thought about the long car ride. What if something attacked us?

Maybe going wasn't such a good idea. I didn't want to be responsible for anyone else getting hurt.

But I'd be far away from here—away from *her*.

And so with that logic I finished packing then went to wait in the kitchen for Kadie. Mom had gone to bed, so I left her a note saying I loved her and would see her in a couple of days.

*T*hree hours later, Kadie's dad parked in front of a humongous rustic lodge with aged logs, a high beamed entrance, and curving stone walkways. A huge sign indicated we'd reached the Waterfall Lodge, home to the Twisting Toilet Bowl water slide.

And if that didn't make me want to jump in, I didn't know what would. I mean come on, giant toilet—probably had turd brown tubes, too.

"We got adjoining rooms so you girls can have some privacy." Mrs. Byler handed us our room keys. "Make sure you check in with us every few hours so we know you're okay."

A very happy Kadie said, "We are so going to have a blast. There are so many guys here. Maybe we can find you a replacement for Colton."

Yeah, like I needed any more help in that arena. I already

had too many.

I dropped my bag onto the bed, which was covered with purple and blue spotted comforters and giant, black suede pillows. "I'm not sure I need one."

"Whoa, what's going on?"

I chewed absently at my fingernails, not sure I wanted to say anything. But I needed to talk to someone. So I went on to explain Nevin and Colton being cousins and them both showing up at my house.

"Oh my gosh, seriously? And neither one bothered to tell you?" Kadie shook her head, tossing her dark hair over her shoulder. "So who are you going to choose?"

I groaned. "Neither of them."

She nodded her approval, whipping her clothes off and tossing them on top of the dresser. The girl had no qualms about undressing in front of people, that was for sure. But with a body like hers, she had no reason to worry. All legs, tanned skin, perfect boobs.

Several minutes later, I had on my electric blue bikini, complete with a big ass white sling. I readjusted my top, the amount of cleavage visible made me blush.

"The guys are going to drool." Kadie winked, handing me my towel.

We headed down to the indoor water park and arcade. The scent of chlorine and coconut hit me as soon as the doors opened. Not sure why people were wearing suntan lotion; there was no flipping sun.

Kids rushed around in floaties and life jackets, splashing into pools, while parents screamed for them to slow down. Lifeguards stood like stoic statues with whistles pressed to their lips. The male ones wore tight white shirts with big red crosses on them and red swim trunks, while the females donned red one-piece bathing suits.

It seemed like bleached blond hair and tanned skin was a part of their uniforms. Their eyes were on a constant scan of the sloshing blue water.

I opted for the snack bar while Katie swam with two guys. Ice tea in hand, I stood under the fake palm trees scanning the twisting water slides. There, standing across the way, was one of the last people I thought I'd *ever* see at a water park.

Gareth.

His golden hair was pulled back into a ponytail, strands stuck to his damp face. Let me just say that he was holy-helluh ripped, standing there in his Hawaiian board shorts, with a six-pack worthy of a photo shoot. Not to mention the tattoos that spiraled up his arms. And he stared right at me.

I gave him a non-committal wave and he sauntered toward me.

"Okay, are you like stalking me now?" I glanced back at Kadie, who did a perfect dive off the board.

He chuckled. "My family comes up here every year for Christmas. We stay the whole week."

"Oh, sorry." I dragged my bare foot over the wet cement, where small puddles had formed from kids' constant splashing.

"I thought you were supposed to stay home—out of trouble." Gareth gave me a meaningful glance.

"Her family invited me along." With a sigh, I nodded to Kadie, who was coming our way, the two guys she'd been hanging out with, trailing after her. "And my mom practically shoved me out the door."

Kadie grinned, looking back and forth between Gareth and me. "Anything I should know about?"

Good God, the football-player-type guys she'd brought over acted like they were watching porn or something, the way they eyed the two of us.

Gareth shrugged. "Nope, we're just talking."

"Good, then you won't mind if I steal her away." Kadie turned to him, batting her eyelashes. "Zac and Jeremy invited us to play pool with them."

"Maybe I'll tag along." Gareth's arms crossed at his chest.

Kadie pouted. "Then we'll have an uneven number."

Oh crap, she was trying to play matchmaker again. And these boys seemed a bit too eager. Zac grinned, scooting closer to Kadie. Frowning, I raised my good arm to cover my chest as Jeremy's eyes zoomed in on my boobs. Kadie sure knew how to pick 'em.

Gareth suddenly had a towel in hand that he draped over my shoulders. I fought to keep from laughing when Jeremy's face and ears went red.

"It's fine if he comes along," I said. "He can play for me." I held up my arm as a reminder that I wouldn't be playing pool.

"Okay, more for me then." Kadie giggled, dragging me after her. As they racked up the balls, she leaned in to whisper, "Okay, spill. Are you and Gareth hooking up?"

I gaped. "What? No." I glanced over to see him leaning against the wall, a smile tugging at his lips.

He seemed to be enjoying this too much. My face burned. I wondered what he was *really* doing here. His showing up was a bit too coincidental. I swallowed hard. Shit. Did he think something might happen up here at the water park? I mean, normally when he showed up it was because something bad happened or was about to. My gaze fanned out over the park. I watched the water sloshing back and forth in the pool, searching for any signs of the creature's face. What if it tried to drown me or Kadie or one of her brothers?

She interrupted my thoughts. "I say go for it." Kadie

waggled her eyebrows up and down.

"It's not like that."

"But it could be. Live a little Salome, you might actually like it."

With a groan, I watched her sandwich herself between Zac and Jeremy. "And now you see why Simeon didn't hook up with her." Gareth slid into a chair beside mine. "She's too casual with herself."

That was putting it mildly. I snorted. "I didn't think guys were picky."

He grinned. "You'd be surprised."

"Really and what do you, Gareth Summer, want in a girl?" I turned my hooded eyes in his direction.

He leaned closer, until his lips were next to my ear. "Someone sweet. Sincere. Beautiful. A girl who isn't afraid to be herself. Someone who will love me unconditionally."

The warmth from his breath sent chills across my skin. "Does this girl exist?"

"Maybe." We stared at one another for long moments, making me all too aware of his closeness.

My heart catapulted against my rib cage, when he shifted away, his hand grazing my arm. "So, how would you like to watch me kick some ass in pool?"

I laughed. "Sure. But only if you win a game for me."

"For you?"

"Yeah—I mean you are taking my place at the table."

"How about I win all of them for you?" He smiled.

"Now you're being cocky."

"Watch and see."

For the next couple of hours I witnessed far too much PDA from the "Kadie Sandwich." I also learned Gareth never lost a game of pool. If I didn't know any better, I'd swear he was a pool shark the way he swindled unsuspecting kids out of their money.

"Dad says it's time to go up to our rooms." Kadie's brother Casey came into the arcade, goggles hanging around his neck.

"Be right there." She turned to her newest victims. "Until later." She raised a finger, touching them each on the cheek.

I shook my head in disbelief, grabbing my towel as I came up from the chair.

"I'll see you tomorrow," Gareth called over his shoulder.

"Yeah, see ya." I could hardly believe he wanted to hang out with me, with all the beautiful girls here.

After room service pizza and pops, we plopped down on our beds, surfing through the cable channels for anything not news or sport related.

"Jeremy and Zac invited me down to the arcade tonight." She flipped off the bedside lamp.

"You barely know them. Are you really going to go?"

"Yes, it's the whole not knowing them that makes it more fun. I'll be some hot girl they tell their buddies back home about."

"Kadie, you can't be serious. I mean don't you want to—you know wait for the right guy?"

She laughed her sexy, husky laugh. "We're only young once. We gotta flaunt it while we got it. Besides, it'll be fun."

Sometimes it was hard to believe she and I were best friends.

"It's just the arcade though, right?"

"Yes, I promise."

But before she could go anywhere, there was a knock on our door. "Hey Kadie," her dad poked his head in. "Listen, we need you to watch the twins for a little bit. Your mom and I wanted to head down for the adult swim."

Under the warm glow of the television, I saw her roll her

eyes. "C'mon Dad, seriously?"

"Your mom and I hardly get time to ourselves. Besides, you'll have all day tomorrow to hang out at the pool."

She sighed. "Fine. But you owe me."

"Thank you. I promise, we won't be gone too long. The boys are already in bed so you can watch a movie or something."

After he walked out of the room, Kadie groaned. "I swear, they ruin everything. What am I supposed to tell the guys tomorrow?"

"The truth. That your parents stuck you with your brothers." And if I was being honest, I was glad they had. "Do you want me to come over with you?"

"No. It's fine." She grabbed a magazine from the table and went over to her parents' room.

When she was gone I turned off the TV. For a while, I just laid there staring off into the dark. My gaze focused on the balcony doors, right as a shadow sifted past. I went still. Holding my breath, I noticed other silhouettes dancing behind my curtains.

Scrape—scratch. Something sounded against the glass slider. Like claws trying to tear their way in. Sweat beaded on my brow. My heartbeat deafened me. With my head buried beneath my blankets, I gulped in a deep breath and squeezed my eyes shut.

None of this was real. I was on the fourth floor of a hotel— nothing was going to get me.

Then came a loud knock against the window. Through a crack in the blankets, I peeked out. My mouth went dry; I couldn't swallow, or breathe.

The glass door slid open. Curtains billowed when a gust of wind tore at them as if to rip them from the rod. Something slithered across the floor, moving toward my bed. Long finger-like digits tugged my blanket. A screech lodged in my throat.

My room door crashed open and light from the hallway poured in. Gareth rushed forward, blade in hand.

He slashed at the root fingers and a fearsome shriek filled the room, like he'd injured whatever was in the shadows.

When I kicked off my blankets to dive across the room Gareth shouted, "Get down." He landed on top of me, his body covering mine like a shield. The glass door and windows shattered, blowing inward like someone had set off a bomb.

This time I screeched, good hand clutching tight to Gareth's waist.

"It's okay," he whispered. "Just stay still."

Then the door between our room and Kadie's parents' suite burst open, lights flicking on.

Oh shit!

Mr. Byler took one look at Gareth on top of me and his face went red with fury.

"Wait, it's not what you think."

Right. Gareth on top of me, nightie shoved up to my waist, blankets on the floor. Yeah, this couldn't look good.

"We're calling your—" Then Kadie waltzed into the room, Zac on her arm. Where the hell had she snuck off to?

And I'll take a double scoop of oh shit.

"What in God's name is going on here?" he demanded

And the shit was hitting the fan.

"I—I don't know," I said. Which was true.

"Just stay quiet," Gareth whispered, climbing off me. He helped me sit up then stared at the broken window. "Watch out for the glass." He acted oblivious to Kadie's dad.

"So was this your plan all along. To invite your friend along so you could both sneak boys into the room?"

I spotted Kadie's mom coming to stand in the doorway. "What's going on?"

"Nothing Rose, just go back to bed. And you" —he pointed at Zac whose eyes had widened to the size of saucers— "are going to get the hell out of this room, do you hear?" Mr. Byler grabbed Kadie's arm and marched her into his room, but before he got all the way out he turned back to me. "Don't you dare move. You and Kadie have got some explaining to do."

When he left the room, I spun around to face Gareth. "Okay, how in the heck did you know that thing was coming after me?"

"I saw it from outside." He glanced at me then sat back down.

"Are you like my bodyguard or something?"

He chuckled and I followed his gaze to the tree limb and puddle of blood soaking into the carpet. How in the world did a tree bleed?

"You could say that. It makes four times I've saved your life. You owe me."

"I didn't ask you to."

Gareth picked a piece of glass from my hair. "I have my orders."

Okay, what did that mean?

"H—how did that thing get all the way out here? I mean, I'm nowhere near my house."

"It can use travel circles to get from one place to another. It's not confined. You have a safe zone where she can't touch you."

"My grandma's?"

He nodded, but didn't say anything else.

I covered my face with my hand and groaned. "You do realize I'm in deep shit here, right? I'm going to be grounded for the rest of my life."

"That's the least of your worries. Why is it every time you

almost die you worry about the silliest things? After the bus accident you worried about your stitches, now you're worrying about your mom finding out there was a boy in your room."

I swallowed hard. "Because, I don't want to think about what's really happening. You know how long I've seen crazy things like this and everyone has chalked it up as me going nuts? Sometimes thinking about real things makes me feel more grounded."

"You're not crazy, Salome. You've got to know that by now." He touched my arm.

"Yeah, it's becoming a little more obvious."

Cold wind snaked through the broken window, the curtains whipped back and forth like angry ghosts. Without another word, he shook the blanket off and covered me up. His fingers rubbed my shoulders as if to warm me. We sat down right as Kadie and her dad came stomping back into the room.

When she saw Gareth on the bed with me, she gave me a lopsided grin that said, *go get him tiger, I don't care if my dad is standing right here and I just got my butt chewed.*

"You two are in serious trouble," Mr. Byler said. "And you." He pointed at Gareth. "Shouldn't be taking advantage of young girls."

"I never do anything they don't want." Gareth smirked.

My eyes went wide. "You're not helping things," I muttered.

"You're a punk kid." Kadie's dad rushed forward, but Gareth was too quick and caught him by the neck.

Gareth's eyes gave off an eerie glow. "You will forget I was here. You'll go back to bed and not wake up until Kadie screams for you. When you awaken you will find a branch that broke their window."

What the hell. It was like I'd stepped into some weird dimension or something. This stuff wasn't supposed to be real.

I mean, there were sci-fi flicks with storylines like this. I rubbed my temples. More than anything, I wanted to believe this was nothing more than a bad dream. And, like Gareth said, I wasn't crazy.

Mr. Byler nodded mutely and went back to his room, shutting the door behind him.

"What the heck did you do?" I caught his arm.

"Kept you from getting grounded and me from being noticed," he said.

Kadie crawled into bed like nothing had happened and shut her eyes.

"Who are you?" The blanket dropped from my shoulders as I stood between him and the door.

His tattoos glimmered beneath the light and he flashed me a smile.

"Don't ask questions you don't want the answers to."

"That's where you're wrong. I do want answers. I need them. Don't treat me like I won't understand. Like I'm just some dumb, brainless girl."

"I've never thought you were dumb or brainless. Bullheaded, maybe. But let's just say someone wants me to keep an eye on you. And to answer your earlier question, yes, I'm your bodyguard." Gareth's fingers pried mine open and he shoved something hard into my palm. "You seem to have forgotten yours."

I glanced down to see another hunk of rowan wood in my hand. When I peered back up, he was gone. As if on cue Kadie screamed and her dad rushed in. Everyone stared at the broken window.

Kadie's parents called the front desk and we were moved into another room, no questions asked.

The next day was nuts. Especially when Kadie waved Zac and Jeremy over. They seemed shocked to see her.

Zac treaded water near the edge of the pool where we sat, soaking our feet.

"I hope your dad didn't bust your ass after last night," he said.

Kadie appeared confused. "No, he's cool."

As if to reiterate the fact, her dad gave us a wave from the lounge chairs then went back to reading his crime novel.

Oh great. Gareth had screwed with Kadie's and her dad's memories but not the guys'.

"Damn, wish my parents were like that. If my dad would've caught us sneaking out like that, my car would've been gone."

Kadie slipped into the water next to him, splashing as she swam around him. "Why don't you go get Jeremy? We can all hang out again." She blew bubbles in the water.

He grinned. "Sure, be right back."

"God, he's hot. A little dumb, but who needs brains." She smirked at me. "And speaking of hot, you want to fill me in on a certain blond-haired guy in your bed last night."

I groaned inwardly. Of course he'd leave that memory intact. My eyes scanned the indoor water park until coming to rest on Gareth. He stood at the edge of the wave pool, arms across his chest, with a smug look on his face. He gave me a wink and my face blazed.

Piece of advice, never trust a guy who says he wants to protect you—because sooner or later it comes back to bite you in the ass.

CHAPTER TWENTY-FOUR

*B*etter than half of winter break was behind me and, until now, I'd managed to distance myself from Nevin and Colton. In the end though, here I was, sitting and waiting for Nevin to show.

A sigh escaped my lips as I fingered the locket that dangled around my neck, one of the deciding factors in my decision to visit him. He'd left the small piece of jewelry on my back porch, probably his form of an apology, and I'd struggled to keep him out of my thoughts.

I'd run up against a wall in my research and hoped he'd be able to give me a few more clues. Waterfall Lodge, and learning the tree woman could follow me no matter where I was, drove me to solve the curse before I wound up in the family graveyard with all the others.

My gaze flickered to the trees, which swayed like Latin dancers beneath the strong gusts of wind. I tugged my hat down. Heavy flakes cascaded across the yard, the downy-looking piles drifting against the house.

Everything was silent except the sound of my breathing. I kept checking over my shoulder. I don't know what I expected to find, but there was only snow.

I sat and waited, hoping he'd turn up. I wandered around filling up the feeders, knocking snow off the stairs, and staring off into space. After more than an hour, I knew he wasn't coming. Could I blame him? I mean, I hadn't been to visit him in over a week. I stopped in at odd hours in order to try and avoid him and so far I'd managed not to see him.

My eyes drifted to the woods surrounding our property. I'd have to suck it up and find him. And there was only one place he might be. The ruins.

"This is a really shitty idea," I said, trying to force myself to walk forward. The stuff in Grandma's office said as long as I stayed on our side of the fence and kept the gate shut, whatever was on the other side couldn't get me. But now I knew better.

I had to solve the mystery before it killed me. Today, tomorrow, in the woods, on a bus, it was going to find me.

Right. I took a deep breath. If I wanted to see Nevin I'd have make myself find him. It was only a couple of trees and snow. Sure it was dumb-ass, and Jason from *Friday the 13th* was only a hockey player. But this was what breaking curses was all about. Wasn't it?

Before I talked myself out of it, I trudged into the gloom, heart clunking like a car with its muffler dragging on the ground.

I could do this. One. Two. Three. I counted each step. If I focused on my steps everything would be okay.

"She's come back."

"But what is she doing in the woods?"

"Should we tell Master?"

"She's heading to the estate."

I quit walking and searched the woods.

"Hello? I can hear you, but I can't see you." I cupped my hands around my mouth. "You don't have to be scared of me. I won't hurt you." But that didn't mean they wouldn't hurt me.

So maybe calling to them wasn't such a good idea. I thought I heard something scurrying away, knocking a chunk of snow from the treetops. Shielding my eyes with my hand, I glanced upward, but still didn't find anything.

In an effort not to get lost, I stuck close to the fence line, struggling to push my way through the mounds of deep snow, downed branches, and brambles. The farther away I ventured the more my thighs burned.

The snow came down harder, almost blinding me, but I didn't turn around. Instead, I bumped into the wrought iron spires of the fence. Movement on the other side caught my eye.

Wiping the flakes from my eyelashes, I leaned closer to get a better look. Then I saw Colton, bent over a large rock structure.

What was he doing? I wanted to shout to him, tell him he was in danger. *She* would get him. Then he glanced up, his eyes glowing eerily against the white backdrop. He raised his hand as if to examine it and I saw the dagger clutched in his fist, cutting his other palm. Blood dripped onto the stone. His face twisted in an evil smile.

"I command you to show yourself. To give me what I've asked for. What you promised me," he said.

Oh God, what the hell was he doing? Spooked, I backed up, stepping on a dead branch that snapped under my weight. The noise sounded as loud as a firecracker in the quiet. Colton shot to his feet and looked around.

I spun away, racing through the maples, oaks, and pines. Branches snagged my clothes; limbs scratched at my face and grabbed my coat like an angry mob. Behind me, Colton called my name. But I didn't stop.

Panic overcame me as I scanned my surroundings. The trail and the fence had disappeared and I couldn't see anything. The snow whirled about, creating a white out.

The sky grew darker, each cloud taking a bit of daylight with it. Every tree looked the same. I was lost. Tears streamed down my cheeks and I started to sob.

"Nevin! Please. I don't know where I am." I tripped over a stump. Too much white, the air too cold.

The last remnants of light faded, pitching me into blackness. Like the shadows had opened their mouths and swallowed me up. I leaned against a tree while the air howled through the naked branches like monsters on the hunt.

"Salome," a familiar voice called. Oh God, he'd found me.

"Nevin?" I croaked.

Then he was there, clutching me to his chest. He carried a lantern, which illuminated his icy features.

"You scared the hell out of me. What in the world are you doing out here this late?"

"I needed to find you," I said. "But then I saw Colton and he had a dagger—"

"What?"

I explained what I'd seen while he led me to a clearing. The gusts had increased and the raw air stung my skin.

Nevin ripped off his jacket. "I have no way to keep you warm." He seemed distraught.

My teeth chattered. "M—maybe we can find shelter."

He draped his coat over my shoulders; flurries clung to his dark sweater like stars in the night sky.

"Keep this on."

"You'll freeze to death."

"If only it were that easy." His mouth drew into a sneer. He sat the lantern on the ground near my feet.

"What do you mean?"

"Just stay put while I go find someone to stay with you."

"But I need to go home."

"Not in this you won't. You'll get lost. That's what she wants," he said. "Please trust me. I'll bring back someone who can keep you warm and get a fire going."

I swallowed hard. "I don't want someone else to stay with me. I want you to be here for me."

For the first time, Nevin looked torn. "I—I'll be right back. I promise."

He disappeared behind a knotted oak tree, leaving me alone in the clearing. The lantern dimmed against the blizzard's fury.

I gripped his coat tighter to my shoulders. Long minutes ticked by, my feet numbed. I did some one-armed jumping-jacks to keep the blood pumping.

At last, Nevin reappeared, his arms loaded with furs.

"Follow me."

With the lantern in hand, I trudged after him until we came to the ruins. I'd been so close to them and didn't even realize it. We found a corner with the roof intact out of the wind.

"Where did you get all this?"

He spread a bed sized white fur on the floor. "An old trunk." He shifted his gaze away. "Take your boots off and lay down."

Sitting on the edge of the fur, I fought to tug them from my feet. Once I had the boots off, Nevin covered me with several furs, tucking me in like he'd woven a cocoon.

Slowly, my body warmed. "Where did you find a trunk out here?"

"Let's just worry about keeping you safe, okay?" Nevin sprawled beside me without a coat or blankets.

"You never answer any of my questions. That's why I

came looking for you. How can I help you if you won't tell me anything?" I propped myself on my elbow to see him better.

"Because I *can't* tell you."

I sighed, offering him some of the blankets, but he shook his head no. I slipped off my mittens. "What are you?"

"Your curse," he said bitterly. He turned to face me. His fingers entwined with mine, thumb tracing my palm like it was a precious artifact.

"Nevin, don't say that."

"It's true. If it wasn't for me you'd be safe."

I inched closer, hovering over him. An overwhelming ache encompassed me. I wanted to make everything okay. As if sensing my intentions, Nevin cupped my head, easing it down to his chest and far away from his lips.

"Thank you for rescuing me." I listened to his heartbeat.

He snorted. "Some rescue. You're stuck outside in a blizzard, no fire, no heat—just me."

"Maybe that's enough."

"Get some sleep," he said in a hushed voice. He stroked my hair and pulled the fur over my shoulders.

"He saved her."

"She has to be the one."

"And she likes him. Did you see how she looked at him?"

"Go to sleep my friends. You can debate over Salome in the morning. She needs her rest," a more familiar voice said.

And the woodland fell silent.

*T*he next morning Nevin and I left the ruins behind, walking toward my grandma's.

"You're certain you saw Colton last night?" He cast me a sideways glance.

"Yeah, I'm sure. I don't understand what he was doing out there."

"That makes two of us." He caught my hand in his as we came to Grandma's deck.

Nevin traced my lips with his thumb, his free arm pressing me against him. "I will never harm you." He released me. "Time passes quickly for some and for others it feels like an eternity. Remember that." He sauntered off leaving me with yet another riddle.

CHAPTER TWENTY-FIVE

"So, do you want to tell me what you were doing in the woods by my house last weekend?" I cornered Colton when I saw him at school two days later.

He gave me a bewildered look. "I have no idea what you're talking about."

"Don't you?"

He ran a hand through his hair. "I was at a basketball tournament all weekend. You can ask anyone on my team."

Embarrassed, I glanced away. Okay, so what exactly was I accusing him of? "I know what I saw."

"Or what you think you saw." He shut his locker. Did I dare believe him? He and I hadn't exactly been on speaking terms lately. However, I reminded myself how easy it'd been for the creature to make me think my mom had been in the woods. It'd be just as easy for her to pretend to be Colton. Unless, of course, he lied to me and was the one in the woods.

Colton glared at something behind me, and I turned to see Gareth sauntering down the hall. "Next time, tell Gareth he can do his dirty work himself, he doesn't have to send you to try and get information from me."

"What? This has nothing to do with him."

"For some reason, I don't buy that. Later." He pushed by me, his shoulder nudging mine.

"Everything okay?" Gareth joined me.

"Yeah. So he claims it wasn't him I saw in the woods kneeling in front of some rock."

Gareth grabbed my books from me while I shoved my bag into my locker. "I don't trust him. He's been acting stranger since winter began. I think it's best if you stay as far away from him as possible. And make sure you keep that bracelet on."

$\mathcal{T}$he month following Christmas flew by in a predictable routine. Since Kadie had gotten a new car, my days consisted of riding with her to and from school. Lunch was dominated by Gareth. After school, I was off to Grandma's for chores and Nevin. A few times, I'd thought about asking Gareth to join me, but something about having Gareth and Nevin together didn't feel right.

It was a comfortable routine — except I knew nothing more about the curse. Somehow, it tied Nevin, the creature in the woods, and possibly Colton and Gareth, to me.

I had begun to spend all of my free time in the hidden room at Grandma's. I determined rowan wood kept people safe from malevolent spirits, although it only protected against a magical attack, not a physical attack. In hindsight, I probably would've kept it on me more if Grandma had just told me its use. Now I made sure I always had a piece with me, along with wearing Gareth's bracelet. I also learned that certain creatures, like faeries and such, didn't like iron. I tucked these tidbits in the back of my mind. On top of that, I had found many fantastical stories in the room. I read all about faerie magic and curses. I was beginning to formulate a plan to break the curse, nothing concrete, but a plan was better than nothing.

One disappointing part of my life was my mom. I never saw her anymore. With Dad gone, she'd been forced to get a full-time job. She needed the hours in order to cover the bills, which meant she was gone more often than she was home. It wasn't like she had a choice, but I missed seeing her. And Dad, I hadn't heard from him since that horrible night he'd thrown me outside. No calls. No letters. Nothing. It was like he'd disappeared off the face of the earth.

"So Valentine's Day is coming up," Kadie chimed as we made our way to first period with Gareth.

"Oh yes, the holiday of love." I snorted.

She laughed. "Don't be so cynical. You have to go to Snowcoming. Gareth, tell her she should go and have fun."

"How about you let Salome decide. Besides, high school dances are lame." He winked at me.

Oh great, he was baiting her. "Why don't we talk about something else," I interrupted.

"What do you mean they're lame? Have you actually ever been to one?"

He ran a hand through his blond hair. "No."

"Well then maybe you should take Salome so she has a date. We could double." She glanced between us. "You guys hang out all the time now, anyway."

He shot me a quick look.

My heart thundered like a bass drum.

"Actually, I'm gonna be busy," he said at last.

"Yeah, me, too." I ignored the disappointment. Had I really wanted him to ask me?

"What are *you* doing instead?" Kadie caught my arm,

trying to make me face her.

Damn. She knew I'd lied. "Um, stuff."

"Really? That's your excuse?"

"Actually, Salome and I were planning an anti-Valentine's Day movie marathon. Bunch of action flicks."

"Oh." She grinned. "Well as long as she's not alone."

Kadie sashayed down the hall smiling.

"Thanks. She's kind of crazy about the dances and stuff," I said.

"No problem. If you want, we really can hang out that night. Grab some pizza."

"Seriously?"

"Yeah. I need to keep you out of trouble." He laughed.

Butterflies tickled my stomach as he turned his chocolate brown eyes on me. "Don't pretend that you don't like trouble."

"Never said I didn't." With that, he sauntered down the hall, leaving me staring after him.

*A*fter school, Nevin already had the feeders filled and was sitting in the gazebo staring toward the pond.

"Hey." I plopped down next to him.

He grinned. "Hey yourself. So what news do you bring from school?" He wrapped an arm around my shoulder.

"So I'm gonna hang out with one of my friends on Valentine's Day. This is the first person besides you, Kadie, and Colton, who's ever invited me to do something."

Nevin's jaw tightened. "You should go. Enjoy life, Salome." He stood like he couldn't get away fast enough and moved over to the railing. He rested his arms against it, not meeting my gaze. "It's good for you to be normal. Have fun, enjoy things outside of just spending time with me."

"I—I do, but I don't feel like you really mean what you say." Anger tightened my chest. I wouldn't let him make me feel guilty. "I only get riddles, arrogance, and half-truths from you. I've given you my trust. My friendship. I've told you things I've never told Kadie or my family. I never know what I'm going to get when I come here. The happy Nevin? The arrogant Nevin? The Nevin who acts like he cares then in the next second shoves me away?"

Nevin's eyes darkened with fury. "Because I have nothing to give you. This," he hissed, waving his hands in front of him. "This is all I've got."

"Did it ever occur to you maybe that's enough?" My breathing became more difficult as I attempted to calm. "Damn it, Nevin, I—"

The words were on the tip of my tongue. I what? Cared for him. Adored him? Loved him? I was so confused. He'd become closer to me than anyone. I cherished his opinions, his time. Maybe I did love him, but it wasn't in a romantic, I need to marry him kind of way. I felt safe with him. Like he understood me better than anyone else. Kadie had her boyfriends and Gareth always seemed busy. Nevin gave me the one thing I craved more than anything. Friendship—to be needed.

"Don't say it. Please, don't." His gaze scanned the woods. A look of terror came over him.

"Why not?"

"Salome." His words softened. "Go home." He turned his back on me.

"She cares for him."

"Then why does he send her away?"

"Because he wishes to forsake us all."

God, I had no idea what I wanted. I needed to get my head on straight.

Chapter Twenty-Six

*G*areth parked outside the pizza place then turned to me. "I'll leave the car running while I go in and grab our food. I'll only be a minute."

"That's fine." I smiled, watching him climb out of the vehicle and head inside. Mom and Nancy had gone out for a "single ladies only" dinner tonight. They'd invited me to go, too, but it didn't sound quite as fun as watching spaceships blow things up with Gareth.

I wrapped my arms around my chest, when a tap sounded on the passenger side window. Colton stood there, gesturing for me to come out. What the heck did he want?

My muscles tensed, but I opened the door and slid out. "Hey, what are you doing here?"

"Getting pizza." He shrugged. His eyes darkened like inky pools. "Thought you said our breaking up had nothing to do with Gareth."

"It didn't."

"Yet, he's the one you have lunch with every day. He sometimes drives you home from school. And it's Valentine's Day, but instead of being at the dance, you're here with him. Tell me, does my cousin know how close you two are?"

"It's none of yours or his business who I decide to spend my time with," I said. My knees quaked and I prayed Gareth hurried up.

"We could have had it all, Salome. Even the kingdom."

Kingdom? Holy crap. He'd lost it. My hand slid behind me and I reached for my door. Just then, I saw Gareth exit the pizza shop, his eyes narrowed.

"Hope you're not doing anything stupid, Colton. Rumor has it you've been hanging around people you're not supposed to lately," Gareth said then his gaze slid to me. "Salome, why don't you get back in the car now."

A growl erupted from Colton and he started toward him. "How about you don't tell her what to do. As a matter of fact, stay the hell away from her or you'll be sorry."

Gareth's gaze glittered. "Is that a threat?"

Colton went rigid. "Yes."

"What games do you play, Colton? Playing both sides will get you nowhere. In the end an innocent will pay."

An innocent would pay? Who said things like that?

"You have no idea what's really going on. And by the time you do, it'll be too late. Take that back to your king." Colton backed away from me, then disappeared behind the building.

My pulse pounded and I let out a sigh of relief. "Oh God, if you hadn't come out when you did…"

Gareth set the pizza box on the hood of the vehicle. "Are you okay? Did he hurt you?" He examined me, then lifted my sleeves as if to check for wounds.

"I'm fine."

His eyes rested on my newly healed arm. "Does it hurt?"

"No." I tried to tug my sleeve back down. "I wish this stupid scar would go away."

"You're beautiful even with it," he said softly. He shoved strands of hair behind my ears for me. "Let's get you home."

My skin prickled with goose bumps, but not from the cold or the fear. Not the weird way I'd felt with Nevin or Colton… Before I started wearing the rowan bracelet. No, my skin prickled…in a different way.

We drove in silence and when we pulled into my driveway, Gareth walked me to the door. "I hate to do this to you, but there's something I need to take care of. I promise, I'll make this up to you."

"But you haven't eaten yet," I said.

"I'll be fine. You go ahead and enjoy the pizza. And whatever you do, stay in the house tonight, okay?"

"I will."

"And Salome?" Gareth held out a bouquet of daisies. "Happy Valentine's Day."

"I—thank you." I took a step toward him and his hand touched my cheek.

"Good night." He let his fingers drop away and he headed back to the Hummer.

I had a feeling whatever he had to do concerned Colton. And there was no telling what might happen. After Gareth pulled out, I was just about to go inside, when I heard strange music coming from the direction of my grandma's house. The same music I'd heard the night I'd had that strange dream about Nevin.

To my surprise, before I could go anywhere, I found Nevin on my porch.

I took a deep breath and moved toward him. His gaze met mine, lingering as he stared me up and down. With a single step, he came up beside me, cupping my chin in his hands.

"I thought you were going out for Valentine's Day?" Nevin said.

"I was, but Colton showed up and we decided to just call it a night."

"He didn't hurt you did he?"

"No."

"Good." He let his hand fall back to his side, but he continued to stare at me. "You're breathtaking."

In the distance, the faint tinkling of music erupted over the woods and everything blurred. I looked at my wrist, only now realizing I wasn't wearing the bracelet, but I didn't care. I was outside, but I was safe with Nevin.

"I want my night to end with you," I said.

He pulled me close, guiding me across the snow-covered porch. His movements were graceful, each step carrying me away with him as we swayed to the tinkling chimes.

The chill in the night air didn't affect me, not while I lingered in his arms. His fingers caressed my back, each touch sending bolts of fiery lava through my blood. I traced his chiseled jawline, memorizing each perfect moment.

He dipped me back, then pulled me up again, until I was pressed against his chest like I was a piece of his clothing.

He bent down, hovering above me. I stood on my tiptoes leaning in. The music, his touch, and the closeness intoxicated me.

"No!" The voices screamed from somewhere nearby. *"You mustn't."*

Nevin snapped out of whatever daze he'd been in. He pushed me back. I raised my fingers to my lips where the kiss should've lingered, but I had been robbed again.

"Why?" I whispered.

"I told you I can't."

"Can't or won't?" I cried. The chimes faded and I shook my head.

"Can't. Do you think I enjoy pushing you away?"

"I don't know."

"Look at me." He demanded, forcing my face upward.

And I did. I stared long and hard, taking in his pale face, his ice-colored eyes. His eyes. Oh God, I knew him. I'd always known him. Why hadn't I seen it before?

"You. You're the one that saved me that night. The pond, you kept me from drowning."

"Yes."

I swallowed the rock-sized lump in my throat. "You warned me to stay away. Why?"

"To keep *her* from getting you and to keep this from happening."

"What from happening?"

He brought my hand to his chest, covering his heart. It thudded beneath my fingers like ancient drumbeats. "From falling in love with you. And losing my heart."

I went into his arms, letting him hold me. "Nevin, I don't know what to say," I whispered.

"Then say nothing. But know that by my uttering these words I've sealed your fate—put you in grave danger."

"Tell me what I need to do." I buried my face in his shirt.

"Stay away from me and from Colton."

I frowned. "I'm not leaving."

"I can't always be here."

"What do you mean?"

He opened his mouth to talk but no words came out as pain seemed to overtake him.

"Go, Salome, it's time for bed." He backed away.

But this time, I wasn't going to let him off so easily. "No. I'm not going inside, not until you answer my questions. I've been patient with you. Please."

"I can't say… The curse…" He bent once more, holding his head in his hands as if some invisible force had been set loose on him.

"Nevin, if you love me like you say you do, then give me something, anything that'll help me out."

"The snow," he whispered then fled into the night.

CHAPTER TWENTY-SEVEN

*A*s the weeks passed the weather warmed, signaling the approach of winter's end. And even though Nevin had told me to stay away from him, I hadn't listened. He could've very well not shown up every day, but he came as well. Maybe we were foolish or maybe we thought we could really beat the curse.

The sun blazed in the sky like a forgotten lover coming home. The snow melted. Ice turned to slushy remnants. And excitement for spring sang in my blood. I imagined the warmth and envisioned the blossoming flowers.

With each day that went by Nevin looked paler, almost sick. At first I was concerned, but he assured me he was well, just suffering from a round of flu.

"Tomorrow it's supposed to get up to fifty-six degrees," I told him, staring at the last piles of snow turning into tiny streams in the yard. "Winter will be gone."

He glanced away, backing into the shadows of the gazebo. "I know." He closed his eyes.

"What's wrong?" I hurried to his side.

"I have to go away."

"W—what do you mean?"

"I'm leaving."

Pain ripped through me like it would swallow me whole.

"You said you loved me. That I was the closest thing you had to a friend." I stared at him in disbelief. He was abandoning me?

"All good things must end."

"But—"

He touched my face, giving me a sad smile. "Forget about me. You've got Kadie and your family."

Forget about him? I'd only survived the winter because of him and Gareth. This was the first time in years I'd had the courage to brave the snow. To be out on my grandparents' property. He'd saved my life long ago, giving me the chance to grow up. To become the person I was. How could I possibly just let him go?

He sauntered down the steps, glancing back at me before disappearing in the woods.

It wasn't supposed to be like this. Nevin was supposed to stay with me. To always be here. I leaped from the gazebo and chased after him. "Nevin, wait."

The sun hit my eyes and I had to stop for a moment before I followed again.

But the only trace of him I found were footprints leading to the shore of the pond.

Spring

Music, when soft voices die,
Vibrates in the memory—
Odours, when sweet violets sicken,
Live within the sense they quicken.
Rose leaves, when the rose is dead,
Are heaped for the beloved's bed;
And so thy thoughts, when thou art gone,
Love itself shall slumber on.

—Percy Bysshe Shelley

CHAPTER TWENTY-EIGHT

*S*pring was finally here. I wanted to rejoice with the birds fluttering from tree to tree, to dance in the wind like the flowers blooming in Grandma's yard. But my sadness wouldn't go away. Every day for three weeks I'd waited for Nevin to come back. I'd get home from school, sprint to Grandma's, and sit and wait. Darkness would settle in and he wouldn't be there.

My friend was gone.

Kadie had Zac from Waterfall Lodge. I'd gotten into spending time with Gareth, but he'd disappeared shortly after Nevin. He'd said he'd be busy handling things for his family, but would be back soon.

I was so alone.

"Salome, we're home." Grandma hurried into the backyard.

A lump formed in my throat as she hugged me tight. "Missed you," I whispered against her robust chest.

"Oh honey, I'm sorry I left you alone to deal with this."

"There's my girl." Grandpa squeezed us, ruffling my hair like I was still six years old.

Maybe things would get back to normal now. With them home, maybe I could forget.

"I've got some stuff I need to unload, but wanted to come say hi," he said with a grin. "Oh and we got ourselves a new cat." He pointed to the black and white kitten peeking out the door. "Her name is Mittens."

"She's as spoiled rotten as they come," Grandma muttered under her breath.

"I heard that." Grandpa made his way back toward the house, leaving Grandma and me alone.

She led me to the gazebo and settled beside me, stroking my hair. "I told you to leave Nevin alone, honey. He can never stay."

I sniffed as I curled up in her arms. "I miss him, Gram. He was one of my few friends. Kadie's so busy, and I mean, I have another friend who'll be back, eventually, but Nevin could be gone for good."

"Letting people go is always hard."

"Will he ever come back?"

Grandma stared off into the distance. "You never can tell."

"I need him."

"Winter's gone. It's time for change, time for you to make new friends and have fun." She gave me a sad smile. "Sometimes caring for or even loving someone isn't enough, sweetie. No matter how much we want it to be."

She was right. Look at how much Mom had loved Dad. In the end, he still walked away. It was time to move on. I had Kadie. Grandma and Grandpa were home now. Maybe Gareth would only be a phone call away, soon. It had been a while since we'd been able to really hang out.

*A*fter a big welcome home dinner with my grandparents, I went back to our place and stared at the TV. I'd cradled my head in my hands just as the phone rang.

"Hey, get changed into something sexy, we're going out," Kadie said, music blaring in the background.

"You're not going to quit bugging me until I say yes, are you?"

"Nope. So go put on that slinky black dress. I'll be there in fifteen." She hung up, not letting me say another word.

The tight black dress she ordered me to wear clung to me, each curve evident through the thin fabric. Next, I slid on a pair of strappy black heels then managed to get my make-up done. As I waited for her to show, I put on the locket Nevin had given me, along with Gareth's bracelet.

A few minutes later Kadie pulled in, honking her horn like a wild woman. She rolled down her window and whistled at me.

"Why are we going to the club? I thought you and Zac were in love." I smoothed my dress as I plopped down in her vehicle.

"Zac and I are still good. I'm doing this to get you out of the house and have some fun. Besides, I've got a surprise for you."

It seemed like forever since we'd done anything together. And she was right, I needed some girl time. I decided to go, even though I worried about whatever "surprise" Kadie had cooked up, but excited to let loose.

"Well thanks." After everything with Colton and Nevin this year maybe it was time to just let it go.

"Here, just in case." Kadie handed me a piece of mint gum as she drove.

When we climbed out of the car, the beat of the music shook the ground. Several guys shoved each other as they headed toward the entrance. I could almost smell their horny hopes as they chatted about finding some *chicks* to hook up with.

One of the guys turned in our direction, a big grin plastered on his face.

"Hey." He waved. His buddies spun around in unison, like robotic monkey toys with cymbals and scary grins.

"I hope they don't think they're tapping this ass," Kadie muttered under her breath.

"Can't blame 'em for trying." I covered my mouth to stifle a giggle.

"You two have dates?" The guy slowed so we could catch up to him. His smile looked more like a sneer and his glassy eyes gave me the creeps. He acted too smooth, his spiked hair too perfect.

With a pretend smile, I nodded my head. "Yeah, sorry. Maybe we'll see you inside though."

"You can save me a dance."

"Or not." Kadie snorted. "My boyfriend doesn't like to share."

"Well in case you change your mind." He leaned into me. "My name's Jake."

My skin crawled like there were millions of ants marching beneath it. I pushed closer to Kadie, but he remained close.

At last, we came to the window where we paid our cover and got our red bracelets, indicating we were minors. Then we stumbled into the club. The lights pulsated, throbbing to the music as large silver disco balls spun, casting star-like sparkles on the ceiling and floor.

There, standing next to one of the tables was Gareth and Zac. "Wait, you planned this?" I glanced at Kadie.

"Yes, I did. And you're welcome." She rushed over to Zac, who hugged her and led her out onto the dance floor.

"Gareth! Why didn't you let me know you were here?"

"Kadie caught me at Perky Joe's today on my first shift back and she came up with this."

Relief flooded me as I turned and gave him a hug. Cheeks on fire, I pulled back. "Sorry. I'm kind of a basket case right now. I—I've missed you." And I had. More than I realized.

He winked. "Don't worry. I'm used to women throwing themselves at me."

With a snort, I glanced around. "So what are you really doing here? I mean, other than the fact that Kadie probably paid you." I tried to play it cool.

The song changed from a techno dance to a slow, sultry, *screw me now* piece. Some people left the dance floor, while other couples sauntered on, pressing themselves together.

He followed my gaze. "What do people normally do at dance clubs?"

"Um—dance." A grin played at my lips.

"There's your answer." He held out his hand to me. "And by the way, I wanted to be here."

I smiled at him. "Well, I'm glad you came." He continued to extend his hand.

I must be crazy. I laced my fingers through his, letting him lead me between the swaying bodies.

We found a spot in the middle of the crowd, right beneath one of the disco balls that glowed purple and blue.

Gareth's arms wound around my waist, drawing me to him. I locked my hands behind his neck, bombarded by thousands of thoughts. I'd been close to him often, but dancing was different...intimate.

Feeling shy, I tried to look anywhere except at him. I watched a couple kissing beside us then turned my attention to another guy groping his girlfriend. From across the room, Kadie gave me a big, dorky thumbs-up.

"I'm not going to bite you," Gareth said in a soft voice, making me glance up at him.

I laughed. "I know. God knows you've had plenty of opportunities before now."

His gaze seemed to see right through me. "You'd do well to get on with your life."

Nevin. He knew about him?

"She's destroying you, which means she'll win."

"She who?"

Gareth lowered his head, his lips lingering near my ear. "How quickly you forget the danger. Winter may be over, but she still seeks you."

The creature in the woods.

"How do you know all this?"

"By paying attention, which you'd be wise to do." Gareth's eyes narrowed and I followed his gaze to the door, where Colton came in with some friends from school. "I see he hasn't given up on you yet."

"Just because he's here doesn't mean he's here for me." But even as I said the words, I knew otherwise. Not that Colton had approached me since Valentine's Day, but on those few times I went out, he always showed.

"Oh, he's here for you, trust me. He'll do anything to win." Gareth eased me closer. "We need to be more wary of him. He's been making lots of trips into the woods lately."

"What do you mean?"

"Something doesn't feel right. I can't explain, I just want you to be more aware of things." He gazed down at me. The answer was vague, but he had been the only person so far to want me to be more aware of the situation. Just the fact that he was trying was worth more to me than any pinball game or ballroom dance.

Colton seemed to search the crowd, his eyes coming to rest

on me. We stared at one another for long seconds. I trembled, wondering why he wouldn't just leave me alone. Gareth, pressed me against him, swaying to a haunting love song. I held tight to him. I needed his strength. His friendship. I needed him. Period. And he felt so right.

Colton glowered at Gareth, and I glanced up to see my dance partner smiling as though he dared him to come get me. One of Colton's friends tugged his arm and he turned away, heading for a nearby booth.

The music changed to something faster, but Gareth and I still swayed back and forth together like we were stuck in the slow song.

"Why do you and Colton hate each other so much?" I asked.

"Old feuds die hard." Gareth touched my chin with his thumb. "Do me a favor?"

I chewed on my bottom lip, wondering if I wanted to know what the *favor* was. "Sure."

"Smile. Because *I* want you to be happy."

I managed a sorry excuse for a grin…okay; it was closer to a grimace. "There, better?"

Gareth chuckled. "Much. Now, for a word of advice. Make sure you know who or what you're choosing before you choose." He released my chin then spun me around until I was dizzy with laughter.

I contemplated his words for the rest of the night

CHAPTER TWENTY-NINE

*S*ince my grandparents had made plans, I found myself looking after their place for the weekend. I stood in the kitchen devouring my last bite of oatmeal, the scent of apple cinnamon clinging to the air. I'd spent the better half of the night buried in books and ledgers in the hidden room. I found more references to Kassandra, indicating she had some type of ability to heal people. There were also several witness accounts accusing her of witchcraft.

I turned the faucet on to rinse out my bowl and watched the water bubble up over the sides. Rippling water.

The pond. Maybe it was time to face my fear head on. To prove, I could beat this. The curse. My fear of winter. The pond.

But I couldn't do it alone. I slid my phone from my pocket and dialed Gareth.

"Hey, so I wondered if you could come to my grandma's?"

"Sure, is everything okay?"

"I think it will be. Oh, and bring a pair of swim trunks."

"Do I want to know what we're doing?"

"Probably not."

"I'll be right over." He hung up and I went to the door to wait for him.

When he pulled in, I hurried out to meet him. "Hi."

He chuckled. "Excited to see me?"

"Always. But when I'm done explaining what I want to do, you might not be happy to see me."

"I don't think that'd ever happen, but go on, what's your plan?"

"I want to get over my fear of everything," I said at last. "Everything started the winter I fell through the ice on the pond. So I thought, maybe if I just dove in and tried to swim in it, I could prove to myself that there was nothing to be afraid of."

He caught my hand in his. "Are you sure you want to do this? The water will still be cold."

"Yeah. I have to. And I want you there with me. That way if something doesn't go right, you can save me. Because I know how much you like doing that," I teased.

"Lead the way."

We went through the house and out into the backyard. Gareth followed me down to the dock, where he stripped down to a pair of blue swim trunks, his t-shirt stretched tight over his muscled chest. He definitely looked the part of a lifeguard.

"Okay, I'm gonna count to three, then run and jump in," I said. Nervous, I took a deep breath. Already, my hands and legs shook.

"Salome?" Gareth said from beside me.

"Hmm?"

"I'll be right here."

"I know." I squeezed his fingers. With one last breath, I counted aloud. Pockets of fog sat atop the water like a steaming bathtub, inviting me in.

"One. Two. Three." With a running leap, I splashed into the water. The frigid temperature stole my breath. I tried to open my eyes and get my bearings, but it was too murky. Too dark. My hands against my chest, I sank into the depths. Something brushed my leg. Something that felt a lot like seaweed, which was impossible in a freshwater pond. I kicked to propel myself to the surface for air. My legs scissored me upward, but the aquatic plants tangled and jerked me back down.

Oh shit. My strokes became frantic, which made the weeds wrap me up tighter. My lungs burned. Too much dark, too cold. More plants wound around me like snakes. Dragging me deep. I reached out, trying to grab something. Anything. No. I had to fight. I struggled again, trying to break free.

A splash next to me sent the water stirring and strong arms pulled me from the grip of the deadly pond. We bulleted to the surface, my arms flailed, lungs almost exploding as I sucked in deep breaths of air.

Gareth dragged me to the shore. "Shit, Salome, are you trying to kill yourself?"

I focused on him. He was sopping wet, green algae smeared across his cheek. His eyes were wild with fear. "There was magic at work. I never should've let you jump in. Damn it, you could've died."

"Magic? But it's not winter. I've never had a problem once it got warmer."

My body shook and I held tight to him.

"Please don't leave me." I clung to him for all I was worth.

"I never will, Salome." He wiped my wet hair from my eyes, clutching me close to him. His chest radiated warmth; I pressed myself into him, focusing on the heat of his body to keep me conscious.

Reality sunk in. My life had almost been taken again. What had I been thinking? Then I remembered Gareth's warning while we danced. *"She's destroying you, which means she'll win."*

I understood. I wouldn't be safe until this curse was broken. No matter what I did, she'd still be out there, winter or not. My hand found Gareth's and I knew he'd always be there for me.

He bent down, his lips a breath away.

"Gareth," I whispered his name. I craved his warmth, his nearness. I needed him.

His hand wound in my hair as he pulled me closer. My heart beat out of control.

He looked at me, his fingers trailing my jawline, sending tingling feelings swirling throughout my body. It was like I was on fire.

He gently leaned me back on the dock, his body propped up above me. So many things splayed across his face. His eyes stared into mine, irises swirling with emotion.

I tugged his head closer, but before our lips touched a shout reverberated around us.

Startled, we leaped apart.

Nevin.

My eyes scanned the property. But there was no one there—just shadows and woods.

"I trusted you, Gareth. What are you doing?" Nevin's voice sounded.

"Protecting her."

"By letting her almost die in the pond?"

"I had a momentary lapse."

"Someone used magic."

"I know."

"Then find them."

Gareth tensed next to me as he stood. He held out his hand

to help me up. "Go on home, I'll call you later."

"This wasn't you're fault, you know that, don't you?"

"I never should've let you go in. I put you in danger." He frowned.

"It was my choice. I can't keep living like this."

"Perhaps, but I never should've let my guard down." With a sigh, he said, "I have to trace the magic, find the source."

"It's *her*, isn't it?"

"Salome," Grandma hollered from the deck. "What's going on?"

"Go on up and explain things to her. I've got to track this, while the residue is still fresh. I'll call you later." He squeezed my shoulder, then hurried off.

"I-I thought you were going to be gone the whole weekend." I shivered, still dripping with pond scum.

"We were gonna be, but then I got this strange feeling that something was wrong. So we turned back around. And here you are covered with half the pond."

"I was trying to overcome my fear."

"You've got a lot of explaining to do then." She ushered me into the house, watching Gareth's retreating form.

"And so do you," I countered, stopping outside the bathroom door. "Why won't you tell me anything?"

Grandma appeared startled by my outburst. "Salome, I can't—"

I stomped my foot. "No, that is not good enough. You keep avoiding the question. I want to know what's going on and I want to know now."

With a sigh, Grandma stared at the floor before raising her eyes to me. "It's not that I don't want to tell you, child. I can't." She reached for my hand but I backed away. "It's part of the curse. Everything I learned I had to research."

"I don't understand how the curse can affect you."

"Not me, our bloodline," Grandma answered, her eyes weary. "And Nevin. Bad things happen to people who talk about it." She shivered. "The more I say, the more likely I won't be around to provide you any protection."

"Because something will happen to you?" I trembled. "So you can't help me?"

"No, you must figure this out on your own. The answers are all around you, pay attention."

CHAPTER THIRTY

When I got home, I grabbed a pop from the fridge and went onto the deck, plopping into the porch swing. It rocked back and forth. The chains squeaked with age. I pulled my knees to my chest, resting my chin on top of them. Was it too much to ask to have just one thing go right?

The cool breeze licked my skin as if a gentle caress feathered across my cheek. I sat straighter, closing my eyes.

"How much longer should I let you live?" a voice sounded. *"Eighteen comes soon."*

I jerked my head up then leaped to my feet. "Why can't you just leave me alone?" I backed up until I pressed against the house.

An eerie laugh floated in the air around me. *"It's not you I'm trying to hurt. It's him. He will grieve for you when you're gone. It's so much fun toying with you both. Never knowing which day I'll pick."*

My hands covered my ears to shut out the voice. Maybe I missed something, but my idea of not hurting and hers were two different things.

"You have to die, Salome. It's the only way…"

After school, I sat in my Jeep, head propped up on the steering wheel. I was supposed to go right home but I needed to make sure Gareth was okay. He wasn't in school, and I hadn't seen him since I'd almost drowned in the pond.

Suddenly I craved cookies and cocoa—with several questions for a certain tall, golden, badass guy. So I headed into town, pulling up in front of Perky Joe's.

The smell of freshly baked sweets and coffee swarmed me as I walked in. I was disappointed to find Gareth wasn't working.

"Can I help you?" a perky blond asked.

"Yeah, I need two chocolate chip cookies and a cup of hot chocolate." I took a few bills from my purse.

She put the cookies into a small brown bag and went to pour my cocoa.

"Do you know when Gareth's supposed to work next?" I asked.

The girl grinned, giving me a *you don't have a shot in hell* kind of look. "Sure, he'll be in on Thursday."

"Thanks." I wanted to smack that smirk from her face. What a bitch. Instead of leaving, I took a seat at one of the mosaic tables and ripped open the bag of cookies. The chocolate melted in my mouth. I closed my eyes to savor each bite.

The bell above the door jingled and my lids opened to find Gareth sauntering in, his mocha-colored eyes landing on me. The girl behind the counter gave him a flirty wave. He nodded and headed right for me.

Seeing her surprised glance made me grin.

Gareth sat down across from me, a look of concern on his face. "You all right?"

"Thank God you're okay. I've been worried. You left to follow that trail—I thought…" I fought back the tears. I took a sip of my cocoa, studying a paisley napkin. I glanced back up at him.

"I'm sorry I didn't call. Things just took longer than I expected."

"But you're okay?"

"Yeah."

"When both you and Colton were missing today from class, I thought the worst."

"Well, I doubt Colton's gonna come around you for a long time."

"W—what's that supposed to mean?"

"It means he's bad news and he's been warned to stay the hell away from you." Gareth stood, catching my hand. "Come on. Let's go somewhere we can talk in private."

"Wait, you had something to do with his leaving?" My eyes widened, not sure if I should be grateful or angry.

"Not fully, but I did pay him a visit. The magic trail I followed ended at his house." He led me outside to where his motorcycle was parked against the curb.

"I have my car."

"We'll drop it off at your place then you can go for a ride with me."

"My mom doesn't want me going anywhere after my recent swim in the pond."

"Do you always do everything you're told?"

"Yes," I snapped. "Believe it or not, I try to be a good girl."

"Being good is overrated." He grinned, starting his motorcycle. "And for the record, you don't always listen. Otherwise I wouldn't be here protecting you."

He put his helmet on and gestured for me to get in my Jeep. I prayed Mom wasn't there when I got home, or the bike ride would be out of the question—and I needed answers.

CHAPTER THIRTY-ONE

"A little luck would be nice here." I groaned, seeing my mom's car in the drive. "Of all the days to be home."

I watched Gareth in my rearview mirror as he parked behind me, taking his helmet off. For a moment I considered leaving without letting Mom know. But that would likely land me with a punishment.

He met me at the porch. "You ready?"

"I have to let my mom know I'm going. She'll freak if I don't."

He chuckled. "And you think she's going to just let you go?"

Right, hadn't thought of that. "I'm about to find out." I flagged him to follow me.

"Do you need me to make her forget you're on house arrest?"

Now that would be nice, except it didn't seem ethical. And I didn't want him screwing with her head. "No. Just behave."

Voices sounded from the living room. Great. Grandma was there, too.

"Hey, Mom," I called out. "I'm going to take off for a while."

"Oh no you're not." She stormed into the kitchen, hands on her hips. "I told you, I don't want you leaving the property except when you're at school."

Gareth shot me a *hey, I told you so* look and I glared. "Listen, I've really got to go."

"What's all the commotion about?" Grandma came in behind Mom. Her eyes went directly to Gareth. Her lips puckered into a frown and she turned to me. "Do you have no sense of danger at all? All the guys in the world and you have to gravitate toward *them*."

Gareth put a hand on my shoulder. "Hello to you too, Doris."

Okay, was there any guy she didn't know?

Grandma sighed. "At least he's the lesser of the three evils," she conceded, giving him a nod. "What are you doing here?"

"I'm here to protect her."

"The same way Colton did?" Grandma gave a snort, pushing past Mom.

Gareth shifted, still holding my shoulder. "Trust me, Colton won't be bothering her anytime soon. I've taken care of it. But right now, I need to talk to Salome. There are things she needs to know."

Taken care of it? That sounded a lot worse than just warning someone.

Grandma surprised me. "Let her go with him. Lord knows the girl is almost eighteen anyway."

Mom glanced between the three of us, a look of defeat on her face. "Fine. But this doesn't mean you're going to be running around all week. And you'll have chores to do when you get home."

"You bring her back unscathed, you hear me?" Grandma warned.

"I'll be nothing less than honorable." Gareth gave her a crooked grin then grabbed my hand, tugging me out the door.

When we were outside, I asked, "How do you know my grandma?"

"Mutual friend." He handed me the extra helmet. "Hop on."

Once it was strapped on, I climbed onto the bike behind him, wrapping my arms around his waist. He started the motorcycle, revving the engine before shifting into gear. We raced down the road, wind whipping around us, scenery flashing by like a movie on fast forward.

I felt so exhilarated, so alive. My skin tingled like it might float away from my body. It was like nothing in the world could catch us. It was just Gareth, the bike, me, and open road. The scent of spring tickled my nose, the crisp air reminding me summer was only two months away. It beat back any thoughts of winter.

Gareth signaled a right turn and drove up the dirt road to the state park entrance. The narrow road wound around, the ranger station still closed, no cars parked in the lot. It was early in the season so most people wouldn't venture out this way yet.

Birds chirped overhead, while squirrels teetered on high limbs. Gareth killed the engine and waited for me to hop off. Once he took care of our helmets, he led me around a wooden sign that indicated we'd just entered the Manistee National Forest. We found a worn trail and followed it up to a lookout point where several benches sat empty.

"It's beautiful up here." I took a whiff of the pine-scented air. Scotch Pines, white pines, spruce, as far as the eye could see. Wildflowers bloomed in the grassy areas, while a stream trickled over mossy rocks in the distance.

"That's because nature is unmarred here." Gareth gestured

to the wooden bench.

"So, are you going to tell me what's going on?"

His gaze caught mine. "Colton used glamour and magic on you."

"Glamour? Like fairytale stuff?"

"Yes. He can make people forget things. And can appear to you in whatever form he wishes you to see. Before you started wearing that rowan bracelet, which by the way you better put back on, he was using spells and glamour to try and seduce you."

That explained my sudden strange reaction to him. The out-of-control feelings and lust. Was that what'd happened with Nevin in the woods, too?

"When you say Colton used glamour, it seems impossible. I mean I've known him since we were kids." I wrung my hands together in my lap. "We went to elementary school together."

"He made himself appear younger so he could keep an eye on you."

"Then where is he now?"

Gareth shrugged. "No one knows. But he's probably hiding because he ticked off the wrong people. Playing both sides can do that."

"Playing both sides?"

"Colton has a tendency to throw in his lot with whoever he feels can be of most benefit to him." He sneered, hand clenching into a fist.

"If you know Colton, then you know his cousin, Nevin, too."

Gareth gave a slow smile. "Now you're catching on. Ask the right questions, Salome."

"You know about his curse?"

He nodded.

"Can you tell me what it is?"

"It's seasonal." He stood, pacing around the bench, his eyes intent on me.

Seasonal. Then I remembered Nevin whispering the word "snow" to me.

How dense could I have been, I mean, it'd been right in front of me all along. Not to mention when I'd found all the gravestones. "It has something to do with winter, doesn't it?"

"Yes." Gareth pulled me up next to him. A couple of hikers came into view and we headed further into the forest. "Nevin can only materialize in the winter," he said as we stopped next to a white oak.

Materialize. No wonder he wasn't around. Why hadn't I figured it out sooner? But I knew the answer to my question. Because despite the talk of curses, fairy tales, and bleeding trees, I hadn't wanted to believe magic was real. After years of therapy and pills it was easier to hide behind my craziness. I mean, why would I, of all people, be the only one who could see it?

"How did he end up cursed?"

"By being an arrogant fool. He screwed over the wrong person and suffered the consequences of his actions."

"Who?"

"A hedge witch in the woods. He underestimated her powers."

"Kassandra?" I squeaked.

"I don't recall her name. All I know is the aftermath of what happened."

"And I'm supposed to somehow break the curse?"

"That's the plan anyway."

My teeth grazed my bottom lip. I leaned down to pick up a pinecone, then tossed it deeper into the woods. "So how come you can talk about the curse and no one else can?"

"Because I wasn't with the troupe the night they were cursed. And it's your bloodline that keeps your grandma from disclosing anything."

"How did you figure it out then?"

He smiled. "By paying attention."

"So you know how to break the curse?"

"No. I just know what doesn't work."

I gulped in a lungful of air picturing the cemetery on Grandma's property. "If no one else has been able to figure it out, I don't know how I'm going to."

"Just think, Salome."

Easy for him to say.

Another thought occurred to me. "Can I trust him? Nevin, I mean?"

"That's a loaded question." His tone softened.

Pockets of sunshine radiated through the canopies, hitting Gareth's golden hair. And I wondered why he was helping me.

"Can I trust him?" I asked again.

"To try and protect you, yes. With your heart, no. We are a fickle people and I can't say Nevin will always have your best interest in mind. He wants the curse broken and you need to remember that."

"I don't understand how I'm supposed to do that."

"That's what you need to figure out. But make sure the payment is worth it."

"I'm going to get hurt, aren't I?" I leaned against rough bark.

Gareth frowned. "Not if I can help it." He snagged my hand in his, forcing me to look up at him. "The kingdom we come from is falling apart. Nevin got himself and many of our people cursed along with him. He is our leader and without him we'll be destroyed. His actions have threatened us all. But I have my directives to keep you safe until the curse is broken."

"You keep saying kingdom and your people and you're talking about glamour. What does that make you?"

"We're known by many names. The Fair Folk. Fae. Faeries."

I swallowed hard. "And what happens after the curse is broken?" I whispered.

"Then hopefully all my people will go home. Nevin will take back leadership and force the enemy from our land."

"The enemy?"

Gareth's jaw tightened. "The Winter Queen, Grisselle, has declared war on us."

Grisselle? Where had I heard that name before? Then I recalled the packages of my dad's. Shit. Could it be one and the same?

Gareth continued, "She knows we are weak with our most powerful people stuck here. We've managed for years to keep her at bay, but the magic around the boundaries falters more each day. But enough of this talk."

"What if I fail?"

"Then Nevin will likely be stuck in winter forever and our kingdom will be overrun by the cold and darkness."

A frightening thought pierced my heart. "And what happens to you?"

He shrugged. "Where goes Nevin…"

"No pressure then." I gave a forced laugh. "So are you helping me for any other reason than to see the curse broken?"

Gareth tugged me closer. "I'm helping you because we're friends and I want to protect you if you're foolish enough to go through with this. And I think it's best to know what it is you choose."

So what did I *really* want? Everything came at a price. Knowing Nevin hadn't left me by choice made me feel better. Which made me consider that perhaps everyone had been right about Colton. He'd only used me to hurt Nevin.

I toyed with the locket at my throat and caught Gareth's startled glance.

"What's wrong?" I dropped the silver chain.

"Where did you get that?"

"Nevin gave it to me."

A low growl sounded from deep in his throat. "He's not taking any chances. Is he?" he said more to himself than to me.

"Okay, what's that supposed to mean?"

"He's laying claim to you. Anyone who sees it is supposed to know you're his."

I frowned. "Nevin needs me to break the curse and gave me this." I held up the necklace. "So why tell me I should move on? Get away from him?"

Gareth chuckled. "Because he knows you always do the opposite of what you're told. He is a selfish creature. Don't get me wrong, he cares for you, but for himself more."

Chills nipped my skin. I'd seen glimpses of Nevin's arrogance, but I'd seen the tender side of him, too. I believed he cared for me, but I had no idea how much. My shoulders felt heavier with the burden of knowing what was at stake. A kingdom. My heart. My life.

A change of subject was in order. "So, do you use glamour, too?"

"Yes."

I grinned. "Okay, so let me see you without it."

"No, not a good idea."

"Why not? I thought you said we're friends."

"Because then you wouldn't be able to resist me," he teased. "Humans are more susceptible to our charms in our true form."

"Okay, that sounds totally arrogant. Come on, just let me see you. I'll give you anything you want."

His smile vanished, his eyes serious. "Never offer up *anything*, Salome. People have died after uttering those words."

I shivered at the way he looked at me, but I barreled on.

"Then how about a trade of some type? You let me see you without your glamour and I'll do something in return. Within reason of course."

"What are you doing, Gareth?" a voice tinkled in the distance.

"Why does he have her in the woods? Master won't be happy."

My eyes darted around the trees, but I didn't see anything.

Gareth seemed lost in thought, then waved his hand in the air. Suddenly, the trees surrounding us looked like they'd been cloaked by a glittering curtain. The sounds of nature disappeared. Like I'd stepped into a sealed-off room.

"Um—what was that?"

"I don't want everything in the woods listening."

He heard the voices, too.

"So, about that trade?" I asked after long moments of silence.

"Bind yourself to me."

"Excuse me?" My face went hot.

He chuckled. "Not that kind of binding. I mean, through blood."

My nose wrinkled. "Um, is that supposed to make me feel better?"

"If we are bound by blood then I can keep you safe. If you're ever in danger I'll be able to find you. I can call you back from anywhere." His fingers wrapped around my elbow.

"And why would you offer me this?"

"Because we're friends and I don't want to see you get hurt. You didn't ask for any of this to happen, nor is it your mistake to pay for." His eyes burned into me. "I swore to do everything in my power to keep you safe. And this is the best way I can think of to keep my oath."

My knees wobbled, wondering why he cared so much about

what happened to me. "It seems very serious."

He stepped closer and squeezed my arm. "It is serious. I am committed to you. I have been since the moment I saw you."

Somehow, the way he said "committed" had another, deeper meaning and I trembled.

"W—what do we do?" I whispered.

He pulled a dagger from his belt. "We need for our blood to blend. It will only take a cut on our palms for the exchange."

"And what happens after that?"

"Then I'll be able to hear your thoughts no matter where you are. You, in turn, will be able to hear me, too."

"Hear my thoughts? I don't think that's a good idea," I muttered.

"Not all the time. There are rules you know." He grinned.

My heart clattered. "What kinds of rules?"

"Like you can block me out," he said as if that explained everything. "Listen, I wouldn't do anything to hurt you. If we're going to do this, it has to be now."

With reluctance, I nodded. He drew the blade across his palm and blood bubbled up on his skin. My hand quivered, but still I held it out to him. This was completely insane.

"This will hurt a bit." The knife sliced my skin and I yelped.

Blood beaded at the wound's surface and Gareth took my hand in his. We rubbed our palms together like it was war paint. A warm sensation traveled up my arm that made me gasp.

"I bind you to me Salome Montgomery. Blood calls to blood and now you are bound. Nothing shall break this binding, not life, not love, not magic, not death," Gareth said in a low voice.

My body felt like it was on fire, each moment welcoming more of his blood to seep into my bloodstream. I felt intoxicated, excitement, awe. His blood sang to me. Ancient songs drumming in my ears.

Friends. We'd be friends forever.

"Yes, Salome. We will."

And then it was done. Gareth released my hand and wiped his knife on his pants before sheathing it and putting it away.

"How do you feel?" His lips didn't move.

"I'm fine." I stepped closer to him. "Are you inside my head?'

"I can hear your thoughts as you can hear mine."

"Oh my gosh, you won't be able to see into my dreams will you?" It was a valid question. I mean I didn't want him dropping in on any of my fantasies or anything.

"Only if you let me." He chuckled. "Like I said, there are rules."

"Can you expand on that for me?"

He sighed then smirked at me. "You can block me out. Just imagine a door slamming shut in your mind and it'll keep me out. However, I will always be able to sense your emotions and vice-versa."

My eyes widened. "So I'll know when you're ticked off or something?"

"Only if I let you. But most importantly, I'll always know where you are."

I gave him a critical look. "Can we test that?"

"Sure. Go into the woods, away from me. Then call to me with your mind."

"No peeking."

I hurried through the trees. I wound my way off the path and toward the creek. Once I was up stream, I sat on a downed log. *"Okay, I'm ready. Come find me."*

"Give me a picture of where you are. Call for me."

I gazed at the stream and the trees surrounding me and reached out with my mind. *"I'm here."*

Within moments, he was by my side without breaking a sweat. "Now, I'll always be there for you."

"Thank you." A shy smile touched my lips. "You didn't have to do this."

"Yes, I did."

"So do I get to see you without your glamour now?" I tugged on his arm.

"You're not going to leave me alone until I do, are you?"

"Nope."

"Well, don't say I didn't warn you." He inched back and closed his eyes. Within seconds, he stood before me in his true form.

His bronzed skin glowed, the tattoos on his arms looked as if they'd been made from gold shavings. The golden locks of hair shined, his features more chiseled, and celestial. He was beautiful. Perfect.

I stepped closer, catching sight of the scar running the length of his right cheek. My fingers touched his face, tracing the healed skin. Gareth's lids opened. He stared at me, catching my hand in his.

"You're beautiful."

"Except for the scar," he said.

"No—you're amazing."

"I'm known as the ugly one amongst my people."

My mouth dropped open in shock. How could they call him ugly? Good God, he was perfect. His shimmering corded muscles, his mahogany eyes.

"Your people are wrong."

Gareth seemed astounded by my words, like he didn't believe them. He gazed at me with such intensity, and I realized that no one had ever called him beautiful—he had probably always felt like the outcast in his world of perfect faeries. What I wouldn't give to wipe the pain from his face. How dare anyone make him feel inferior.

"That's because you haven't seen the others."

"I don't need to." My fingers left a bloody trail across his cheek, but he didn't seem to mind. *"Tell me what happened?"*

"Colton."

Seeing the fury in his eyes, I didn't press any further. "I'm sorry."

He smiled, putting the glamour back in place. I blinked several times, missing his true form already. "I should get you home, it's getting dark."

But I stood rooted in place. I tried several times to say it, then choked the words out. "Listen. Since we're friends and all I wondered if you might want to tag along to prom with me? Kadie won't leave me alone about it—she's trying to set me up with that guy from the lodge. I mean, I know you said high school dances were lame…"

"Prom?" Gareth gave me lopsided grin. "Never been to one."

"So go with me. We don't have to stay the whole time. Just make an appearance."

"On one condition." His eyes glittered. "We only stay for an hour, then after that you have to go someplace of my choosing. No questions asked."

"Deal," I said.

"Looks like you've got yourself a prom date."

Chapter Thirty-Two

"Oh honey, you look gorgeous." Mom gushed, hooking a diamond teardrop necklace around my neck.

Grandma already had her camera, the flash reflecting back off the mirror as she snapped pictures. "Go on, spin around for us to see." She clicked another picture.

The strapless white dress poufed out around my hips as I twirled. Taffeta and tulle swished like a ballerina dress. The overhead light reflected off the silver and white sequined bustier that interlaced through the lace. The dress was elegant, playful, and sexy. Perfect.

"Time for the icing." Mom slipped a rhinestone headband into my hair. The faux diamonds sparkled like a halo.

"So, how do I look?" I smiled, trying to ignore the kangaroos bouncing up and down in my gut. Nerves shouldn't have been an issue. I mean come on, this was Gareth. Someone who'd become a good friend in the past couple of months.

"Breathtaking." Grandpa pushed his way into the cramped bathroom. "Now, if I'm not mistaken, your prom is not taking place in the shitter."

My hand flew to my mouth to stifle a laugh and Grandma shot him a dirty look. "Really, Frank. You'd think you were a sailor."

"Wouldn't be caught dead in one of them white uniforms." Grandpa leaned over to whisper in my ear.

The doorbell echoed through the house and everyone but me hurried into the kitchen. I took a deep breath then stepped into the hallway, to peek around the corner. *Holy crap*. Gareth looked hot.

He had on Harley boots, black tux pants, a tailored black coat and shirt, with a black bow tie. His golden hair fell softly around his face, some escaped strands brushed his cheeks.

Not wanting to look too astounded, I plastered a smile on my face and swung around the corner and into the kitchen, catching Gareth's eye.

"You clean up nice," I teased.

"Yeah, you're not so bad yourself."

We stared at one another for a moment until Grandma cleared her throat.

"Wow," he said aloud this time, producing a wrist corsage. "You look good."

"Thanks. You, too."

Mom handed me his boutonnière, which was a light blue rose. My fingers trembled as I tried to pin it to his lapel.

"Don't stick me." His breath warm as it fanned across my cheek.

"Then don't move."

Next, he slipped the white rose corsage around my wrist. Then the family wanted a million pictures, this being my first and last Prom.

"Why don't we get one out on the deck?" Grandma ushered us outside.

Gareth put an arm around my waist and pulled me closer.

"Okay, we've really got to get going." I caught Gareth's hand in mine before they could find more places for us to pose.

"Have fun." Mom stopped me so she could give me a hug. "No curfew tonight, but please don't do anything foolish."

"We won't Mrs. Montgomery," Gareth interjected. *"Do I really look like I'm out to corrupt you?"*

"A little." I grinned.

At last, we made it to the driveway, away from my crazy relatives and their blinding flashes of torture.

"I hope you don't mind, but I drove my bike." Gareth glanced at my long dress.

"I wouldn't have it any other way. I can tuck the skirt under me."

Removing his tux jacket, he wrapped it around my shoulders. "This will keep you warm. And I promise to use my magic to keep you from getting dirty or too windblown."

I hiked the skirt of my dress up around my thighs and bunched it underneath me, then fastened the helmet on, figuring I could fix my hair when I got there. Soon we were on the road heading for the country club. I leaned my head against Gareth's back, catching the scent of pine and spicy soap.

Before long, we drove up the winding road that led to the parking lot and main entrance. They actually had valet parking arranged, but Gareth wouldn't let anyone touch his bike, which made me laugh.

"Paranoid much?" I climbed from the cycle.

"It's my baby. Can't trust it with just anyone." He grinned, looping my arm through his. "Ready to make our grand entrance?"

"Yeah."

Music swept by as the doors swung open. I was overwhelmed by a wave of girls in formal dresses and guys in penguin suits.

Sipping punch from wine goblets that read—NIGHT OF DREAMS.

Cameras flashed like strobe lights as people rushed to take pictures of their friends and classmates they didn't even like.

"Let's find a table," I said. We bee-lined under the silver and blue balloon archway, only to be stopped by the photographer.

"Why don't you two come right this way?" He pointed to a cheesy beachscape background.

"Actually, I don't think we're ordering any," I said.

Gareth's lips tilted upward and he took an order form from the photographer. "Sure we are. Besides, someday you might want to look back and see how hot your date was."

Afterward Kadie waved us over to her table, where she sat on Zac's lap punked out in a black lacy gown, matching heels, and fishnet stockings like some dark princess.

"Oh my God! I can't believe you kept this from me." She glanced from me to Gareth then back again. "Are you guys going to dance right now?"

"Please say yes." I thought to Gareth. *"She's itching to get details here."*

His lips tugged up at the corners. "Yeah, that's where we're heading," he said, before leading me onto the floor.

"*I owe you,*" I said in my mind as he wrapped his arms around me. I dangled my hands over his shoulders, leaning against him.

"And I'm keeping track of all the times you say that." He chuckled.

The music changed to a romantic tune, filled with soft drumbeats, acoustic guitar, and a crooning male singer. The lyrics spoke of finding true love, holding onto destiny. The stuff dreams were made of.

Gareth's hand caressed my back as he spun me around, each movement a part of a story, some special memory I'd hold for the rest of my life. He was graceful, the way he glided across the floor, sweeping me along with him.

"So, is dancing a prerequisite for your kind?" My head lifted so I could see him better.

He laughed. "Of course. We have to be elegant, refined, strong, handsome, superior, and great dancers."

"Wow, that sounds like the qualifications for Miss America."

His eyes twinkled. I raised my hand to touch his cheek. Even though he used glamour, the scar made a ridge that I traced with my finger. I wondered if, once the curse was broken, he'd still come visit me, or if our friendship would end. I sure hoped he'd be around.

"Is this better than you thought it'd be?" He clutched my hand, bringing it back down to his chest.

"Yes," I said without hesitation. Tonight was my night. A chance to live.

"I want this night to be special for you." His cheek brushed against mine as he bent down. "You've had too many bad ones for someone so young."

I wet my lips with my tongue. "I'm not that young. I'll be eighteen next week."

His chest rumbled beneath me. "You are compared to me."

The song ended and another slow song belted to life. We danced, pressed closer together, and his heart pounded beneath my hand. I peered over his shoulder and saw Kadie and Zac weaving their way over to us.

"Kadie has that determined look on her face. I think she wants to talk."

"Do you want me to get you out of here or something?"

"So you two are really going out?" Kadie danced up next to us.

"Well, not—"

"For a couple of months. We were trying to keep it on the down low." Gareth gave me a wink.

"Holy shit, so you two *were* dating when we were up at the lodge. I knew it." Kadie giggled. "And here you told me I'd imagined him in our room."

Dang it, why hadn't he taken that memory from her?

"Listen, I think I'm going to go get us some punch." Gareth excused himself, giving me a sly look over his shoulder.

"You can't leave me here to explain all this." But that only made his grin wider.

"Make it juicy."

"I should tell her you can't get it up."

He was by the punch bowl, watching me intently. *"Do you think she'd believe that?"*

"So, details." Kadie tugged me toward the wall. "How is he?"

"We haven't done it." I was crazy for even having this conversation.

"Not yet, you mean. What kinds of dates have you two been on?"

"Hikes, bike rides, that kind of thing." Which wasn't a total lie. I mean we had gone to the state park and we did ride on his motorcycle.

"This is so awesome. I mean you finally have a serious boyfriend."

Her glance drifted to Zac, who was trying to talk to Gareth. "What are you guys doing after prom?"

"Please come save me." I begged.

"Not until you tell her what we're doing tonight—I want to hear our hot plans."

"Gareth, come on, please."

He sauntered toward us, handing me a cup of red punch.

"If you guys don't have plans, Zac and I are going to head over to Morgan's for a party then go out to breakfast in the morning," Kadie said.

"Actually, we can't." Gareth bent down, kissing my forehead.

Shock waves ripped through my veins and down to my toes. My eyes went wide as his fingers glided down my spine. I gave him a quizzical look, trying not to seem caught off-guard by his sudden display of affection.

"Am I missing something?"

"Just play along or we'll never get out of here." His smile widened and I gave an inward groan.

"I rented a cabin in the woods for the weekend," Gareth said. "For Salome's birthday."

Punch sputtered out of my mouth and back into the cup. When he decided to lie, he went big.

Kadie gaped. "Does your mom know?"

"No, so if she calls your house will you tell her I'm asleep?" I shot Gareth a sideways glance.

Kadie smirked. "Finally, our roles are switched. And I'm repaying my debt for all the times you lied for me."

"See, you corrupted me."

"If you don't mind, I think we'll dance a few more songs before heading out. The cabin is about an hour drive and I don't want to get there too late." Gareth took my punch from me and set it on a nearby table.

"Sure. Do you guys have protection?" Kadie whispered in my ear. "If not, I've got extra."

"Er—I think we're all set."

Gareth ushered me back onto the dance floor. "You just made her night." He laughed, encasing me in his arms. "Her little Salome is all grown up."

"Yeah, thanks for that. Now I'll have to make up some

ridiculous story about losing my virginity."

"You can tell her how great I was, all my bronze skin— Or just say it was the most romantic, amazing night of your life." He rested his forehead against mine, eyes intent on me.

"Okay so now you're trying to dictate my fantasies?"

"Am I?"

His body moved against mine as we swayed to the music, each rhythm echoing in time with my heart. Senior prom was perfect. After the next set of songs ended, we headed into the parking lot, where Gareth slipped his jacket off again. He draped it over my shoulders before we hopped onto his motorcycle.

"So where are we really going?" I slipped my arms into the coat sleeves while he prepared to start the engine.

"Someplace special."

We sped down the highway, stars blinking against the dark sky. The wind was chilly, but I didn't mind, not tonight. I felt like a princess on a flying carpet, rushing through the night, hair blowing behind me.

We drove up a long, gravel drive into the tree line. And when we emerged, there was an ancient looking log cabin nestled between some pines.

"Oh my God, you actually rented a cabin?" My mouth went dry, heart colliding with my rib cage as my grip on his waist tightened. *"I thought you were bullshitting."*

"I didn't rent it. This is where I live."

"Oh." If he was serious about the cabin, I wondered what else he might be serious about.

"I wanted to show you something real about me. Without the glamour or the lies."

He turned off the ignition, propping the bike on its kickstand. He climbed off then held his hand out to help me.

"You really meant it when you said we were friends." I smiled.

"Yes. But remember not all of *my kind* share my sentiments. They require something in return."

"And why don't you?" I turned to stare up at him.

He opened his mouth to say something and stopped as if he thought better of it. "Does it matter?"

"I guess not."

"Good." I watched his glamour fizzle away, revealing his perfection. "Welcome to my humble home."

Where the motorcycle was parked, there now stood a large black stallion. Its shiny coat was sleek like oil. It turned toward me, lowering its head before trotting into a nearby pasture.

"Holy crap! Your motorcycle has been a glamoured horse this whole time?" I squeaked.

"Yes. You don't think I'd actually ride in cars or on bikes do you? The iron and metal would make me sick."

Right. Faerie 101, iron can kill them.

My fingers entwined with his. "This is amazing."

He pointed to an old hay wagon and, with a wave of his hand, it turned into the black Hummer he'd used to drive me back and forth to school.

"And here I thought your dad was a car salesman or something." I rolled my eyes.

"Not quite."

We wound our way down a stone path to his cabin. The inside was like nothing I'd ever seen before. The outside was small, weathered, and oozed of hunting. But the inside: marble floors and wooden archways. Tapestries decorated the walls, while a fire blazed in a mammoth-sized stone fireplace. Like a mansion.

"What do you think?" he asked.

"This is beyond belief." My mouth gaped open as I noticed the antique mahogany furniture, jeweled dishes, rare paintings, and candlelit hallways. "So this is how everything really looks without magic?"

"Yes. But I didn't bring you here to admire my home. There are other things you *need* to see."

He opened a door to the backyard, which led into the woods where a white horse waited for us. Gareth boosted me up then slid into the saddle behind me; his arms circled my waist.

"Where are we going?"

"To let you see both the light and dark sides of my kind. You need to know what you choose."

The horse trotted down a path and I watched as tiny lights bobbed behind trees, while twinkling laughter filled the silence. Gareth tugged on the reins, bringing us to a stop outside a clearing. A troupe of beautiful faeries sipped wine and danced. There were fauns with wreaths of flowers hanging around their necks and tall, willowy, half-naked women with only leaves and long hair covering their bodies. Tiny men with pipes sat on stools smoking and laughing when two humans stumbled forward.

The humans looked drunk, but seemed happy to be near the faeries. I watched in horror as one of the willowy women cut the human man across his arm. He laughed and started to dance like he didn't feel the blood.

"What are they doing?"

"The humans are offering themselves as sacrifices. They're so drunk on pomegranate wine that they don't realize they're dying."

I covered my mouth with my hand. It was terrible; how could they do that?

Sensing my unease, Gareth kicked the sides of the horse and sent us galloping farther into the woods. This time we came to a place where a dozen humans, wearing garlands of flowers and chanting in a foreign language, surrounded a blazing bonfire.

Behind them the Fair Folk waited around the edges, watching their every move.

"What's happening?"

"The faeries will steal one of them away for a year in Faerie. But when they bring them back fifty years will have passed here."

"Why do they do stuff like this?"

"My kind like games. You need to understand this. Not everything is about dancing, love, and happiness. Not here."

A knot formed in my stomach. *"And Nevin? He's done stuff like this?"*

"Worse."

How could people so beautiful be so dark? Maybe the curse had been placed for a good reason. And maybe I tempted fate by trying to break it. However, I didn't see why Grandma would be so agreeable if she thought Nevin was so bad.

"Gareth, fancy seeing you here," a feminine voice called from behind us.

I spun around on the horse. One of the most beautiful women I'd ever seen stepped out. She had long golden hair that hung to her waist and skin that almost sparkled in the dark. A diadem hung on her forehead, her blue gown laced with sapphires and diamonds.

"Brigid." A hint of acid crept into his tone.

"Is this the human you're championing? She's a pretty little thing. No wonder Nevin has his sights set on her."

"What do you want? This is my territory." His grip on me tightened.

"The queen sent me to remind Nevin and you the longer you play around in the human world, the more the kingdom will suffer. It's only a matter of time before we break the barriers, friend."

"You will not succeed," Gareth answered. "Soon we'll have our forces back."

"She seems weak. I doubt she has it in her to break the curse. Then Nevin will be doomed and so will the rest of you." When she glided closer to the horse it gave a high-pitched whinny. She reached up and grabbed my arm, her grip like a vice. "So much fuss over someone who is hardly worth it."

Fury clutched hold of me like a cyclone forming on the plains. "Then I'm surprised you'd waste your precious time to come all this way to see me." I jerked my arm from her.

"So the kitten has teeth." Her smile sent chills charging up my back, but I held her gaze.

"And claws," I spat at her from my perch.

She opened her mouth to say something else, but Gareth raised his voice and cut her off. "Get out of my woods, Brigid, and tell the queen we will not lose the battle."

The woman waved a hand and disappeared. I let out a rush of breath I didn't realize I'd held.

"Well, she was friendly." A nervous laugh escaped my lips.

"Like I said, not everyone here has your best interest in mind."

"Why put yourself on the line to show me these things?"

"Because this isn't your war—and I think you're a nice girl."

But there was more to it than that. He kept bringing up the fact I needed to know what I chose.

Over and over, I considered what those choices might be. The most obvious was whether or not to break the curse. And, of course, choosing Nevin.

Of course, I had to figure out *how* to break the curse, first.

Thoughts continued to storm through me until they were interrupted by the lapping of water and scent of the lake. Gareth rode the horse right onto the beach. Moonlight glimmered on the cresting waves, sloshing and foaming over the rocks.

Sand sprayed up from beneath the horse's hooves and I smiled. It was like I was on the cover of a romance novel. Gareth pulled on the reins and the horse slowed, then stopped. He swung his leg over then reached up, catching my waist and lowering me to the ground.

"What do you think?" He smiled, guiding me toward the water's edge.

"It's awesome." I kicked off my shoes and held my dress up to let the waves lick my feet. "So this lake is yours, too?"

"Yes." He looked sad as he stared out over the water. "For now." When he noticed me watching him, he touched my shoulder. "But enough of that, I brought you here to enjoy yourself not to be burdened."

"Gareth, I promise things will work out, you'll see." With that, I dropped the bottom of my dress and waded farther in. The waves caressed my legs. I didn't care about the dress any longer; I'd only wear it once.

He paced the shoreline with his eyes focused on me. "Is it warm?"

"Yeah, you should come in." My dress clung to me.

"No, I think I'll stay here."

"Come on. Or are you chicken?" I splashed around up to my waist.

His gaze darkened and grin encompassed his face. "Is that a dare, Salome?"

"Well that depends on whether you want to prove your masculinity or not." I dove under water, the heavy material weighing me down when I attempted to propel myself farther out. At last I gave up trying to swim, not wanting to drown myself. When I broke the surface and looked back toward the shore, Gareth wasn't there. But his boots, jacket, and shirt were.

Panic rose in my chest. I thought something happened to him until he emerged beside me, droplets of water cascading down his bare chest and loose hair.

Perfect white teeth shone in the dusk as he smiled. His hands caught my shoulders, tugging me toward him. "What was that about me being a chicken?"

"Did I say chicken?" I laughed. "I meant brave warrior."

He hefted me up in his arms. "Better hold your breath," he whispered, then tossed me into the water.

I sank with a splash. When I burst back up again, he swam away.

My dress was heavy, but I didn't care. For the first time in a long time, I was having fun. Living. I ran in slow motion as I gave chase through the shallows of the lake. Gareth dove under water when I got closer and I plunged under, my fingers brushing his leg.

We bobbed next to one another and I threw my arms around his neck, taking him under with me. His hands curled around my waist, tugging me closer and we splashed to the surface again, where he pressed me against his chest.

We stood close, laughing. His fingers were gentle as he pushed strands of my hair from my face. As if on cue, music sounded from down the beach. Not the music box notes or wind chimes I'd heard with Nevin and Colton. This was like the ringing of tiny bells. The lake swelled with each note of the melody.

"Gareth?" My voice cracked as I panicked. What was wrong with me?

"Relax, Salome. It's not what you think. Music can be used by us to sway humans." *But you have to believe I'd never do that to you,* he thought to me.

I looked into his eyes. And I believed him. His music was

different. It was shiny and sweet like the sound of laughter and angel voices wrapped into song. I felt excited and happy—like I could take on the world. This was something new. Something wonderful. It made me feel clear, where Nevin and Colton's had made me feel fuzzy.

I realized then that the other two had been charming me, as was the nature of faeries. I should have been enraged, but I think that I had suspected it all along. Between all of the books that I had read in Grandma's room, and the unnatural pull I felt toward each of them when we were together, I had known that something was amiss. But I had never felt that way about Gareth, the attraction was not as instantaneous as it had been with Nevin, but it was much more genuine. Gareth had not used glamour on me, he had only been himself and I had fallen for him anyways.

"Shh…just take in the moment." He guided my head to his chest. And we swayed to the music, water surging all around us. Just him and me. The perfect night. We stood like that, long into the night, until the bright pastels of the sunrise streaked against the sky. Prom was over.

Summer

Dim vales— and shadowy floods—
And cloudy-looking woods,
Whose forms we can't discover
For the tears that drip all over—
Huge moons there wax and wane—
Again—again—again—
Every moment of the night—
Forever changing places—
And they put out the star-light
With the breath from their pale faces.

—Edgar Allen Poe

CHAPTER THIRTY-THREE

The summer heat was stifling, not that I was complaining. It was a hell of a lot better than snow, ice, and frigid temps. But the non-stop scorching took its toll.

"I can't believe you and Dad have been married for fifty years." Mom smiled. "And you're still in love."

Grandma laughed. "That depends on the day."

I sat on the couch next to them, tracing my finger over the embossed couple in fifties clothes. "So is it okay if I invite Kadie, Zac, and Gareth?"

Grandma handed me the invitations and a pen, and I filled the envelopes out. I wondered if Gareth was parked down the road again. Since prom, I hadn't seen him much. But I had found him keeping an eye on my house on several occasions. Each time he'd glamored himself up a different vehicle to humor me, I was sure.

I threw on a pair of clean shorts and a light blue tank-top, then slid into some flip-flops. The sun beat down as I made my way outside and down the driveway. I peered down the road, spotting Gareth sitting in a yellow mustang. I hurried down the shoulder until I stood outside his car.

"Hey." I smiled. "I haven't seen you much lately."

"Things have been kind of busy on the other side. I'm just hoping we can hold out until winter." He sounded tired. "But if this keeps up, I'm not sure what will happen."

"Is there anything I can do?"

"Just keep studying the curse."

With a faint smile, I shifted nervously. "Listen, I wondered if you might want to come to my grandparents' fiftieth anniversary party with me. There are going to be, like, a lot of old people there and dancing and stuff." I handed him the white envelope.

He slid his fingers between the paper flaps and ripped it open. Invitation in hand he read through it, setting it on his dashboard when he was done. "I don't think that's a good idea."

"Oh, um, okay." Disappointment laced my words. "You probably would've been bored anyway."

I scuffed the ground with my feet, staring at the bees flying around the dandelions on the side of the road. Man, I was stupid. Just because we'd gone to prom together didn't mean he wanted to hang out with me all the time. But why did his rejection bother me so much?

Gareth opened his car door and got out. He leaned against his hood and patted the spot next to him. "It's not that I don't want to go with you. With the summer solstice coming up, the veil between the worlds will be thinner, which means more possibilities for attacks. I've got to be on my toes or I won't be able to keep you safe."

"We're still friends though, right?" I held my breath while I waited for him to answer.

He wrapped an arm around my shoulders. "Yes. Always."

I smiled in relief. "I suppose I'll let you get back to guarding or whatever it is you're doing."

He caught my elbow before I could scramble away. "I tell you what. I'll make an appearance, just so you're not stuck dancing with a bunch of wrinkled-up prunes."

"You're the best." Before he could react, I gave him a hug. "See you on the twenty-first. Oh and, by the way, it's a forties-fifties theme, so dress up."

He groaned. "You know, I do a lot of crazy shit for you."

"Yep, and you like it." With one last wave, I hurried back to the house.

$\mathcal{M}$om and I carried the punch bowls and plates outside to the tables. Paper lanterns glowed against the evening landscape. Big band music blared from the deck. Grandma and Grandpa danced on the parquet floor they'd had installed for the party, their friends joining them.

"I think we're going to need more ice for the cooler." Mom wiped her brow with the back of her hand.

"I'll get it. Why don't you go dance with Daryl?" I gestured to her date, who sat by himself at a picnic table. He was good looking for an older guy, shaggy brown hair, nice build. Best part, he treated her well.

"Hey, we're going to go dance if you want to come along," Kadie said, holding Zac's hand.

"Nah, I'll wait a little while." I emptied the ice into the coolers.

"Worried about shaking the poodle off your skirt?" she teased.

I spun around and the skirt billowed out around me. "More like getting blisters." I nodded toward my saddle shoes, which killed my feet.

Her red and white flowered dress swished back and forth as she rushed off. It looked like something my grandma would've worn to her graduation.

After the next song, Grandma made her way toward me. "Honey, why aren't you dancing? There are lots of men to choose from."

Right, if I wanted some old fart holding me too close. "I'll dance soon."

She gave me a wistful glance. "The first night of summer is always magical. Anything can happen if you know where to look." She nodded toward the dock. The pond water glittered as the yard lanterns reflected off it.

Grandma ambled away and as I wove my way through the partygoers toward the dock, several shadows caught my eye. They hung on the outskirts of the wood line as if watching the festivities.

"*Salome.*" One of the shadowy figures stepped forward, taking on a form. Nevin. My breath caught in my throat, hardly believing it possible.

"Nevin—but how?" I clenched my skirt in my hands.

"It'll only last for a few minutes—but your grandma is right. The first day of summer is magical. It allows me to take form."

Within seconds he stood before me. My fingers traced his face.

"I've missed not being able to talk to you. Kadie and Gareth are probably sick of me by now."

"I'm sorry I wasn't able to save you when you jumped into the pond...." He swallowed. "Have you figured anything else out about the curse?"

"Just that you were cursed to winter. I'm trying to figure out how to break it."

He frowned, icy blue eyes staring beyond me. "I have faith

in you. But let's not dwell on curses, not tonight. I've only got a few moments and I want to spend them with you."

Music carried on the breeze and he pressed my head against his chest, swaying back and forth with him. "Did you send Gareth to watch after me?"

"Yes. I had no choice. You needed to be kept safe."

"Thanks, I mean he's been a great friend. He takes care of me."

"That better be all he's doing." He sounded jealous.

"It is," I added a little too quickly. "He and I are b—"

"Don't mention the bonding, Salome." Gareth's voice burst into my mind. *"Not everyone has your best interest in mind. The element of surprise is our best weapon right now."*

Nevin looked like he was waiting for me to finish my thought and I smiled. "Gareth and I are both avid chocolate eaters. He sometimes lets me get free cookies from Perky Joe's."

Although Nevin seemed suspicious, he let it go as he twirled me around. Over his shoulder, I caught sight of Gareth near the gazebo dressed like a greaser from the fifties. He seemed to emit the bad boy vibe like it was a style.

"Promise me you'll keep working to figure out the curse, Salome? I can't handle too many more winters. I want to be with you and not disappear every time you need me," Nevin said. He ran his hands through my hair and I sighed. I don't know what had happened to us, but he didn't feel genuine anymore. In fact, my relationship with Gareth made me wonder if he ever had been.

"I promise."

A sudden rush of anger swirled in my mind. I stopped dancing. It took me a moment to realize it hadn't come from me, but Gareth. But he wasn't standing by the gazebo any longer.

When the song ended, Nevin slipped away. His form became

wispy and transparent. Like a ghost, he turned into smoky tendrils and disappeared. My chest tightened like someone had gripped hold and squeezed the life out of me.

Grandma gave me a sympathetic glance and blew me a kiss. I pretended to catch it in my hand and touch it to my face. But Gareth's burst of anger consumed my mind. I searched for him amongst the dancers and people sitting at the tables. I couldn't find him anywhere.

"Gareth? Where are you?"

He didn't answer.

I rushed through the house, out the front door, and into the front yard.

"Gareth, please answer."

"I'm here."

I turned to see him leaning against his motorcycle in the driveway. "What's wrong?"

"I'm tired of the lies and the deceit. Of Nevin asking you to put yourself on the line for him when he doesn't know what is necessary to break the curse."

"I'm doing it because I want to. No one is forcing me."

He frowned, grabbing my shoulders and giving them a shake. "But it could harm you. Have you ever considered that?"

"Yes," I whispered. "But you said it yourself. If the curse isn't broken your whole kingdom will fall. *Yourself* included."

"Did you ever consider maybe it's our time to fade away into myth? That this is how things are supposed to happen!" He was angry, I knew he was thinking logically, but he was still scaring me. The thought of him fading away forever hurt me more than I could ever have suspected.

"Why do you care so much about what happens to me?"

"Because. You're the first human I've ever wanted to get to know. The first person I didn't use for my own benefit. You make me see my faults, but also see my goodness. No one has ever done that for me before."

"You're on the verge of going soft." I hugged him. "Just trust me, okay? I know what I'm doing." Or at least I hoped I did.

"No matter what happens, promise me you won't quit fighting." Gareth stepped back.

"You have my word."

He glanced around the driveway then back at me. "Do you want to get out of here for a while?"

"With you?"

He chuckled. "Yeah, that was the plan."

My gaze met his. "Okay."

He held out his hand to me and I hopped on the back of his bike.

CHAPTER THIRTY-FOUR

*S*tars twinkled above as Gareth sped down the darkened highway. The summer breeze licked at my skin and I nestled closer to him. I lived for taking rides with him. There was something almost magical about the wind rushing past or the way you could see the sky without having a windshield in the way. But mostly I liked how I felt. How freeing it was. Almost like an out of body experience without really going anywhere.

We traveled several miles before he pulled into a parking lot. He cut the engine and we climbed off. Already, I heard the waves crashing in the distance.

"Oh my gosh, I haven't been to the beach since prom," I said. When I'd spent an entire night dancing in his arms. A moment that'd be etched in my mind forever. For the rest of my life, the beach would hold a huge significance. It'd be the place I always associated with Gareth. And dancing. Stuff that dreams were made of.

Once we had our shoes off, he offered me his hand. We followed a path through waist-high grass, until we reached the beach. Cool sand squished between my toes.

Moonlight glittered off the cresting waves of Lake Michigan.

"It's so beautiful out here." I sighed.

"C'mon, let's go on the pier."

"Seriously?"

He chuckled. "Yes. Don't worry, I'll keep you safe." He tugged me closer.

We walked onto the cement pier, the water splashing below. We went out a ways, moving closer to the lighthouse at the end of the cement structure. Gareth sat on the edge and pulled me down next to him.

A campfire glowed on one of the beaches. This is what summer was supposed to be about. Friends. The beach. Having fun. A buoy clanged from somewhere on the water. I closed my eyes, letting the wind caress my skin.

"This is one of the places I like coming to in the human world. The water reminds me of home."

"Do you miss it there?"

His thumb brushed over my palm. "Sometimes, but it's not like I can't go back there. I take short trips when I can."

I glanced at his profile. Strong cheekbones, shaggy hair. He was so perfect. So kind. "I'm sorry."

He turned to look at me. "Why?"

"Because you're stuck here watching after me."

He swiped a strand of hair from my face. "Trust me, if I didn't want to be here with you, I wouldn't be."

My skin warmed. "Most days I don't know what I'd do without you. Not just because you look out for me, but because you get me. It's like I can be myself around you. There are no lies."

He shifted his gaze toward the shoreline. "I care about what happens to you. In the end, I just want you to be okay."

I scooted closer until my leg pressed against his. My head rested on his shoulder. This was how things should be. No worries. No frightening things happening.

Clouds drifted across the sky, blotting out the moon. Thunder rumbled in the distance.

Gareth climbed to his feet. "We need to get off the pier. There's a storm blowing in."

We hurried along the break-way. As soon as we hit the sand, the sky opened up. Large raindrops splattered on the side of my face.

"Holy crap, it's cold." I laughed.

"Quick, we can take cover over there." He pointed to the small pavilion.

My dress clung to me as the downpour soaked my clothing. Water dripped off my hair and down my face. Wet sand stuck to my feet, spraying across the back of my legs as I ran. At last we made it to the roofed picnic area.

"Maybe the beach wasn't the best idea," Gareth teased, shaking his hair out.

"You think?" I giggled, trying to ring out my skirt.

He grinned, grabbing me around the waist and tugging me closer. "Are you mocking me?"

I wrapped my arms around his neck as he spun me around. "No. I swear."

We laughed as he twirled us. When he stopped, we didn't move apart. Instead, we stood, staring at one another. His fingers touched my face with gentle strokes. My heart pounded.

He leaned down and, for a brief second, I thought he might kiss me. But he stopped and cleared his throat. "You should probably call your mom and let her know we're gonna wait for the rain to let up. I don't want her to worry."

I swallowed hard. "I—um don't have my phone."

He reached into his pocket and handed me his then sat on a picnic table. He patted the spot next to him.

I climbed up beside him then called Mom. After I hung up, Gareth wrapped an arm around my shoulders and we watched the storm move across the lake. Lightning illuminated the darkened sky. The constant rhythm of rain pounded against the metal roof.

"I wish everyday could be like this," I said.

"Like what?"

"Perfect." I glanced at his mahogany eyes.

He raised an eyebrow. "Hmmm...if this is your idea of perfect, it won't take much more to really impress you."

I smiled, nudging his leg with mine. "I'm serious. It's nice not having to worry about anything. To just be here, you know."

"Yeah. I think I do." He squeezed my arm.

When the rain stopped, Gareth led me to his motorcycle. He grabbed a towel from one of the side pouches and dried off the seat.

"Are you going to be warm enough?" He eyed my short skirt.

"I'll be fine."

He climbed on the bike and I slid in behind him. The breeze was cool, but not unbearable. Already, I felt the heat from his body and it instantly warmed me. The trip home seemed to go much faster than I wanted it to. The truth was, I wouldn't have minded spending a little more time with him.

When we got to my house all the lights were blazing. He parked next to my Jeep then cut the engine.

"Thank you for tonight," I said as we stood in the driveway.

He smiled. "You're welcome."

"So, I'll see you around?" My voice sounded way more hopeful than I meant it to.

He was quiet for a long moment then glanced down at me.

"Yeah, how about tomorrow? I heard there's a carnival in town—"

"Yes. I want to go with you."

"Then I'll pick you up around seven." He caught my hand in his and pulled me into a brief hug.

When I got to my room, I fell back on my bed smiling. Gareth made me so happy. Was it stupid for me to wish that my life could just stay like this? When I was with him I forgot about everything else. I pictured him standing beneath the pavilion, white T-shirt clinging to his muscular chest.

Okay, so he was way hot. And he'd totally grown on me more than I imagined he would.

"Looks like you'll have sweet dreams tonight." Gareth's words wrapped around my mind.

"Oh my gosh. What are you doing in my thoughts?"

He chuckled. *"You're the one who didn't close off your mind. You're broadcasting your thoughts like a satellite, sweetheart."*

"And of course you couldn't just quit listening?"

"Nope."

"You—you're impossible."

"So I'll still see you tomorrow?" Even in my mind I heard his teasing undertone.

"Maybe."

"I'll take that as a yes."

"I never said—"

"You didn't have to." I felt him smile. *"Night, Salome."*

He shot me an image of him holding my hand on the pier.

CHAPTER THIRTY-FIVE

I scoured my closet for something to wear. So far I'd tried on like five outfits. Why was I freaking out? It wasn't like I had to impress Gareth. I settled on jean shorts, a black tank top, and pair of sandals.

Mom eyed me when I stood at the window, watching for him. "You must really like Gareth."

"Why do you say that?"

She laughed. "Because you're antsy as ever. And I've never seen you spend so much time trying to get ready."

The black Hummer came up the driveway.

"Hey, you ready to go?" He smiled when I came out onto the porch.

I swallowed hard. He looked way hot in his baggy cargo shorts and sleeveless shirt, which gave me a good view of the tattoo that wound its way around his arm. Today, he had his hair tied back at the nape of his neck, his sunglasses propped on top of his head.

"Yeah."

He grinned at me. "So did you sleep well last night?"

"You should know." My cheeks went hot, trying not to think about the dream I'd had the night before. And the someone who'd been on the receiving end of the imagined kiss.

Mom stepped outside carrying a pitcher of lemonade. She smiled at us. "I hope you two lovebirds have fun today."

When we got into the Hummer, he chuckled. "Lovebirds, huh?"

"Don't you dare start."

"Why? I think it's cute." He playfully tapped my bare leg.

I spent the rest of the car ride pretending to be interested in the scenery flashing by my window.

Gareth managed to find a parking spot across from the fairgrounds, where the carnival was set up.

"Are you going to be okay on the rides?" I eyed the metal contraptions.

Gareth nodded. "Yeah, I can be around the iron in small doses."

"You know, we don't have to do this. I—I don't want you to get hurt."

He grinned, entwining his fingers through mine. "I'll be fine."

The scent of popcorn filled the summer air. Kids and adults screamed and laughed from the rides. Colorful lights pulsated, while the music blasted.

We made our way to the Ferris wheel, where we were loaded into one of the small cars. Gareth climbed in first, then pulled me next to him. He rested his arm across the back of my shoulders, his fingers brushing against my bare skin. The ride jerked, moving us up in the air.

"Wow, the view up here is beautiful."

"Yeah—it is." His voice sounded hoarse as he stared at me.

I leaned against him as the Ferris wheel twirled us around. I let myself believe that things would finally be normal for me. That I'd have no more bad days. Winter or otherwise. Because the more I hung out with Gareth the more I realized there were so many things I'd been too scared to do over the years. He was opening my eyes to so many things. And I never wanted it to end.

When we got off the ride, Kadie, standing next to Zac, called to us from the Tilt-a-Whirl line.

"Want to go over?" I glanced at Gareth.

His lips turned up at the corners. "It's always entertaining to see what she's gonna ask you."

So we made our way over and Kadie gave me a big hug. "Hey, what are you up to?"

"Just hanging out," I said.

"And kissing?" She bumped me with her hip.

"A lady never tells."

"Aw, you're no fun. You never tell me anything."

"Because it's private." I met Gareth's amused glance over my shoulder and couldn't look away.

"Salome and I are going to head over to the Haunted Hell Hound ride." Gareth's thumb stroked mine.

"Oh, we've already been on that one." Kadie frowned. "Maybe we can meet up later for fireworks."

We waved good-bye then headed toward the haunted ride. While we stood in line, Gareth came up behind me and wrapped his arms around me. I leaned into his chest, my back pressed against him. I loved the feel of him. Of being with him. I ignored the fleeting guilty thoughts about Nevin, the one I was supposed to save.

"Are you having a good time?" he whispered, as if he sensed my conflicted emotions.

"Yes. This is most fun I've had in forever." And it was.

"Good."

The attendant helped us into one of the red mining-type cars.

The cart clanged forward, jerking along the makeshift track. When we got inside, we were plunged into darkness. The air felt much colder. Strobe lights flashed as a werewolf creature popped up next to me.

I screamed. "Holy shit."

Gareth chuckled, tugging me closer to him. I buried my head in his chest, trying to get my heart rate back under control. Goose bumps puckered across my arms. An icy chill raced over me. Something felt wrong. I lifted my head.

"Salooooome," someone whispered my name.

The strobes pulsed faster and within the flashes of light I saw the gauzy lady who'd been on the bus. Oh God. The lights went out. Darkness strangled me. And when the lights flashed on again, she stood next to our car.

"Salome, you won't get away from me. Ever." The creature reached out and her nails scratched my arm. "This winter will be your last."

Gareth ripped off our seat belt and jerked me out of the moving car. He rushed me toward the exit. I struggled not to run into animatronic monsters or trip over fake rocks.

"Hey, get back in your cart," a man by one of the exit doors yelled. A security guard. But when the guard got close, Gareth shoved him out of our way.

In the background, I heard the creature's high-pitched laugh.

"No. This isn't happening," I cried.

In one swift motion, Gareth scooped me into his arms and we burst outside. He carried me to the parking lot, stopping only when we reached the vehicle.

He sat me on the seat and examined my bloody arm where I'd been scratched.

"Damn it!" Gareth's eyes blazed. "This happened because I let my guard down. You got hurt because of me."

"No. This isn't your fault."

He opened his glove box, pulled out a cloth and bottle. He dumped some water on my wound and then cleaned it with the cloth. It stung, making my eyes water.

"I knew this wasn't within a safe circle, but I was sure I could protect you."

"Gareth." I touched his face with trembling hands. "I'm okay. See? It's not your job to protect me."

"Yes, it is."

My throat tightened. "So is that all I am to you? A job?"

Gareth pulled back. "Come on, let's get you home."

"You didn't answer me," I whispered.

"No, you're not just a job." He whipped around so his back faced me; I wanted to see his face.

I slid from the seat and walked around the Hummer until I stood in front of him. "Listen to me. You couldn't have known she'd attack me on a damn carnival ride. I mean, look how many times we've been farther away than this and she's done nothing." I rested my hand on his cheek. "I'm not gonna let you take the blame for this."

Dusk settled around us, the carnival ride lights blinking against the black sky like fireworks. He closed his eyes, his fingers closing over mine. When he opened his lids, he embraced me, wrapping me in his warmth.

"I will keep you safe, I promise."

"I know. Whether I want you to or not."

"Come on—let's get you home."

When we got to my house, Gareth followed me to the deck where we slumped into the porch swing. I curled against him, my heart thudding in my ears. We listened to the fireworks going off in the distance.

"I wish we could've met under different circumstances," he whispered, twirling a lock of my hair around his finger.

My arms wrapped around him. "Me, too."

I had no idea what the future would bring. But there were two things that scared me. One, that I wouldn't be able to break the curse. And two, that if I did, I'd never see Gareth again.

Autumn

The dearest hands that clasp our hands,—
Their presence may be o'er;
The dearest voice that meets our ear,
That tone may come no more!
Youth fades; and then, the joys of youth,
Which once refresh'd our mind,
Shall come—as, on those sighing woods,
The chilling autumn wind.
Hear not the wind—view not the woods;
Look out o'er vale and hill—
In spring, the sky encircled them—
The sky is round them still.
Come autumn's scathe—come winter's cold—
Come change—and human fate!
Whatever prospect Heaven doth bound,
Can ne'er be desolate.

—Elizabeth Barrett Browning

Chapter Thirty-Six

My hands blistered, sore from raking all day at my grand-parents', and my clothes smelled like smoke from the burn piles. Mom went out with Daryl and I was alone. For once I couldn't call Kadie to drop in and cheer me up because she'd gone to Texas for school, along with Zac. I missed her tons, but always knew that eventually we'd go our own ways. And with winter fast approaching, I realized just how much I counted on her.

The air grew crisper every day, more frost needing to be scraped from the windows. The reckoning was coming; I could feel its wintry chill in my bones. This would be my last winter like this. Either I'd break the curse and be able to move on with my life, or it would claim another soul.

With a sigh, I hung my new work schedule up on the fridge. Lucky for me a position at the library had opened up at the end of the summer. And since I decided to wait another year for college, I needed the income. Although, remembering the attack at the library, maybe I should've taken a job at the gas station instead.

Turning from the fridge, I glared at the pile of fairytale books on the table. God, why couldn't I figure it out? It'd be nice to have some type of step-by-step "break the curse" form or at least a multiple choice story problem. I'd spent almost all summer trying to figure this out. But I kept coming up empty. And now that autumn was here, I was running out of time to find answers.

A knock resonated through the house. I scampered to the door to find Gareth standing there.

"Hey, what are you doing here?" I moved aside to let him in.

He caught my gaze, eyes full of worry. "Listen, I stopped by to let you know I have to go away for a while. Things aren't going well in Faerie right now."

"You'll be okay though, right?" My hangnails suddenly became intriguing.

"Yeah," he answered. "If you need anything, call to me and make sure you carry that rowan wood on you at all times."

I didn't want him to go, yet I knew he had an obligation to his people.

I rushed forward, flinging myself into his arms. "Be careful."

"You, too. And, Salome." Gareth touched my cheek like I was fragile glass. "No matter what happens know you can trust me. In the end, I'll be there." He bent forward, his lips brushing my forehead.

Above everyone else, I trusted him. Truth be told, I trusted him more than Nevin. I clung tight to him. Somehow I knew when we saw each other again things would be different.

When he finally left that night, I sat on the deck contemplating how to end the curse once and for all. I had two ideas. One seemed almost too easy and the other one meant making the ultimate sacrifice. Because looking back over the last year,

I realized one very important thing. Nevin wouldn't kiss me, which meant there was a reason for it. And this had to be the key.

As darkness set in, I headed toward the door.

"Your time draws close, Salome. I tire of taunting you both. Soon, I will add another headstone to the cemetery and Nevin will be destroyed, stuck in winter forever."

Panic raked greedy claws down my spine, a cold sweat breaking out on my brow. Oh God, what if I failed? *She* had already proven the human soul was no match for her. How was I any different? In a few months the first flakes of snow would fall. And I was eighteen.

Winter

Fond lovers' parting is sweet painful pleasure,
Hope beaming mild on the soft parting hour;
But the dire feeling, O farewell for ever,
Is anguish unmingl'd and agony pure!
Wild as the winter now tearing the forest,
'Till the last leaf o' the summer is flown;
Such is the tempest has shaken my bosom,
Till my last hope and last comfort is gone.

—Robert Burns

Chapter Thirty-Seven

*G*randma and Grandpa had their suitcases in the living room, even though they weren't leaving for another week. The weatherman popped up on the screen.

"Looks like we'll get our first taste of winter tomorrow," the TV echoed the weatherman's prediction. "Several inches will fall before noon and by tomorrow night we're looking at a total of eight inches."

"Guess I better get the shovel and salt out," Grandpa muttered. "Damn cold weather anyway."

Snow. I'd been both dreading it and looking forward to it over the past months. My mind conjured visions of icy cold graves, blustery winds, and *her*. Everything I feared came to be when the snow flew. The pond, the woods, the voices—they would soon be my constant companions.

I shivered, hugging my arms across my chest. But winter also meant Nevin was coming back. My savior who had rescued me from *her* when I was six. I missed him, but I also dreaded his reappearance. He had lied to me and used his magic to charm me;

forcing my love for him. But he had succeeded—I had loved him—and old feelings die hard. This was going to be a rough winter.

"You okay, Salome?" Grandma sat next to me, worry lines etched deep into her forehead.

"Yeah, a little nervous is all."

"You can still choose to walk away and go with us to Arizona."

I clasped her hand in mine. "I gave my word I would try to break it, I have to make the attempt."

"Of course you do, and I'll be here when you face it down."

"I suppose I should head home. I'll be back tomorrow." I gave them hugs good-bye.

Tomorrow. The day that'd change my life forever. I took a deep breath. There was so much more at stake than just Nevin and me. There was my family to consider. Nevin and Gareth's kingdom. In that moment, I realized I'd be willing to do whatever it took to make things right.

When I woke up the next morning, I rolled from bed, wiping the sleep from my eyes. I hadn't slept well, too many nightmares and worries played through my mind.

White flakes hit my window like pellets. The wind howled like monsters in a horror flick.

It was happening.

Throwing my closet open, I grabbed a pair of jeans, a sweatshirt, and my winter coat. Mom glanced up from her cup of coffee as I raced past.

"Where are you going?" she asked as I tugged on my boots and hat.

"To Grandma's." I tried to ignore the thrashing of my heart against my insides.

"You haven't eaten yet." She pointed to the stack of pancakes on the table.

"I'll eat later." The door slammed behind me and I ran like I was in a marathon, across the yard and up the driveway. I bypassed the house and dashed down the path next to the garage, skidding to a stop when I reached my grandparents' backyard.

There, leaning against the gazebo, was Nevin. Dark hair fell across his forehead. His ice-touched features just as I remembered them. His glacial eyes met mine.

"Nevin." I flung myself at him.

He caught me in his arms and swung me around. When he set me down, his fingers traced my cheeks.

"I've missed you." He pulled me against his chest once more.

"I didn't think I'd see you again."

"And yet here I am," he teased. Taking a deep breath, he rested his chin on my forehead. "You don't know how long I've waited to hold you. To feel your warmth."

"Eight months. Well unless you count the dance we got this summer."

He chuckled. "I forgot how funny you think you are."

"And I forgot how arrogant you are." I pulled back to stare up at him.

"Have you had any more thoughts on the curse?" He ventured to bring up the one subject I'd avoided.

"I—I think I do." My teeth grazed my bottom lip.

Wind whipped across the yard, carrying snow with it. It sprayed the side of my face and I closed my eyes until it stopped, then wiped my cheek off. It was so cold.

"Please try, Salome. Even if they don't work, I'm no worse

off than I was," he whispered.

With shaking hands, I touched his face. God help me. Just then, the gate squeaked behind me. I went still. The hairs on the back of my neck bristled. It was supposed to be locked.

Very slowly, I turned to find Colton leaning against it, clapping his hands.

"Together again, but not for long." A sardonic grin splayed across his lips.

"Colton, what are you doing? The gate is supposed to be shut." My eyes widened with fear. I jerked away from Nevin, terror washing over me. Colton's gaze looked cold.

"I thought you might like to meet Kassandra. The woman my cousin destroyed. The one who cursed our people because of him."

A gauzy figure made its way through the gate. Red eyes glittered, dark hair snarled, with nature's litter clinging to her. There were sticks, leaves, and thorns all stuck in her hair and to her skin. Long fingers looked more like bark than flesh. She smiled at me, teeth sharpened to thorny points.

"We meet at last, Salome," she hissed.

"Kassandra? From the letters?" My voice squeaked as I turned on Nevin. "The woman you deceived with Aidrianna?" I couldn't breathe. He'd hurt this woman—this creature—and she'd cursed him. And he deserved it—at least some of it. Now, he wanted me to free him.

Nevin stared at the ground, then back up at me. "Yes," he lowered his voice. "I made a mistake. I am a selfish person, but I did not deserve this." He flung his arms wide, gesturing to the wintry landscape. "Year after year of cold. I can't build a fire, go indoors, or enjoy the seasons. I can't even enter my homeland. I have been stuck in a place worse than death."

The creature hissed. *"You deserved it, Summer King. To feel the same coldness that clung to me after I found you and Aidrianna together. And hearing from the servants that I was just a tool in your sick games."* Kassandra's thin lips twisted into a sneer.

"And don't forget what you cursed the rest of us to, dear cousin," Colton said. "I had no part in your games, but because I was in the human world that night I ended up stuck here. I might not have had to face the winter, but I couldn't return home. I was exiled with the rest of you. Not able to use the portals or see Faerie."

"So that's why you betrayed me, cousin? Handing over our people's lives for your own?" Nevin snarled. "You told me you would help to keep Salome safe."

"My lies are no worse than yours. And Kassandra promised if I helped destroy you by aiding in the capture of Salome, she would lift my curse, which is more than what you offered me."

"But I never did anything to you, Colton." My stomach knotted as tears pricked at my eyes.

"It was more fun to make Nevin mad and see just what he had to lose," Colton sneered.

How could I have been so stupid? My throat went dry, legs quaking beneath me. "That day on the bus, you meant for me to be on it. You practically pushed me onto it after the fight at school." My words barely registered above a whisper.

"Yes, but I didn't count on Nevin going behind my back and talking to Gareth. It didn't take me long to realize they didn't trust me any longer." He stepped closer.

I backed away, bumping into Nevin. "But you didn't kill me when you had the chance. You could've used your magic at any point to do so."

"Because we wanted Nevin to be here when you died. For him to watch his last chance at freedom disappear." Kassandra's eyes blazed brighter than hot coals. *"He will suffer as I did."*

"That makes you no better than him," I whispered. "I know he hurt you, but you've had your revenge. You've killed most of the females in my family for generations."

"You were all of Aidrianna's bloodline. Her curse tied into Nevin's. None of you deserved to live, but I was merciful. You should have thanked me, really, for I left a few of you alive — your mother, her mother, and hers. I left one of Aidrianna's bloodline alive each generation, so that you would continue to have daughters, continue to fight the curse, and continue to fail. I have enjoyed toying with you." She added the last line with a sickening laugh.

The back door opened and Grandma rushed out, her walking stick in hand. "You cannot be here," she hollered.

"The gate was opened, old woman. I've come to collect the final price." Kassandra raised her arms and a whoosh of magic flew from her hands, slamming Grandma backward, pinning her to the ground. The air stirred with currents of glowing fiery orbs, sizzling and crackling like flames.

"Let her go!" I screeched.

"Gareth, I need you." The thoughts rushed from my mind and I watched as more forms fell in behind us. The winter people, Nevin's cursed troupe. Icy features touched with the blues and whites of winter: tiny beings, tall beings, and incredible beauty. All cursed.

"Salome, please, if you know how to break the curse — do it now," Nevin urged, his hand brushing mine.

I'd read enough fairytales — I just had to try.

Spinning around, I clutched Nevin, taking his face in my hands. I pressed my lips to his. At first he tried to pull away, then his lips parted, kissing me back.

"No, Master…Salome, no…You have to stop," the voices called out around us.

All of a sudden, Nevin shoved me back, his eyes wide. "What have I done?"

My stomach clenched at the light-headedness. I didn't feel so well. Dizziness gripped hold of me.

The creature laughed, sounding like nails on a chalkboard. *"Foolish girl. Do you think I would've made it that easy? Quite the opposite. His kiss is poison and you've taken a big sip."*

"I know," I whispered, staring right at her.

The air changed. I glanced up to see Gareth rushing into the yard.

"What did you do?"

"Kissed him."

His face paled, eyes widening with horror. Grandma wailed from her place on the ground and the winter people receded toward the trees.

The fairytales always had quests, or someone being rescued, or kissed, or…*a sacrifice.* The ultimate price, which most people weren't willing to pay. But I wasn't most people. I knew what I was doing. I just needed to say the words aloud.

Kassandra stepped closer to me, Colton on her heels.

"Soon you will perish, Salome. I hope the price of a kiss was worth it. This will be the end of Nevin because your bloodline will not continue, which means there is no other hope."

I glanced at Grandma, at Nevin, at his people, then finally to Gareth. I fell to my knees. Wet snow seeped through my jeans. Everything went still. The wind calmed. The voices hushed, there was just the occasional flake sputtering from the sky above.

Winter would be the death of me. I always knew it. But at least now, I could go knowing I'd made a difference.

"It was my choice to make. I knew what his kiss would do to me. I offered my life in exchange for Nevin's. The ultimate sacrifice." I looked at Gareth as I said the words and his eyes widened. I wanted him to know that I had not only sacrificed myself for Nevin, but for all of the winter people; so that they could go home, back to the summer. And maybe, just maybe, they would remember my sacrifice and stop tormenting *my* people.

Kassandra shrieked. *"No, what have you done you foolish girl? This can't be. Why would you give your life for one who wouldn't have done the same for you?"*

"Because, I'm different than you. I'm different than Aidrianna. I care…"

A bright light flared. I watched in awe as the winter people began to glow. Their features thawed and they had golden and bronze skin, flowers bloomed at their feet, chasing away the remnants of snow piling on the ground around them.

And Nevin looked celestial—a crown made of sunshine shone bright on his head. His smile widened as he tipped his face toward the sky, welcoming in the warmth.

"You broke the curse, Salome, now the price must be collected," Kassandra hissed.

Then all hell broke loose. Colton rushed forward and Gareth unsheathed his sword. I watched the two of them circle one another. Metal clanged against metal after Colton produced his own sword.

Nevin shouted orders to his followers while I knelt where I'd fallen.

Kassandra rushed toward me, dagger glinting in her hand. But I couldn't move.

"Salome," Gareth shouted in my mind. *"The rowan, use the rowan."* In the midst of his own battle, he tossed a piece of the wood to me. It fell in the snow several feet away.

Dizzy, I tried to reach for it right as she plunged the blade into my chest. A scream tore through me, but all I heard was silence ringing in my ears.

But before she backed away, I saw Grandma charging at her from behind. In one swift strike, she plunged her rowan walking stick through the witch's back. Kassandra screamed. Writhing in pain, she fell to the ground beside me.

Her body twitched then exploded into dark, shadowy plumes of dust that showered the snow and thawed areas of ground.

The last thing she shouted was, *"You will still perish, and Adirianna's bloodline shall live no more!"*

Coldness gripped me and I teetered the rest of the way to the ground. Pain shot through my body as I sputtered, gasping for breath.

The muted smell of pine wafted to my nose.

The clash of swords, the grunts and cries of battle swirled, then ebbed.

The chill breeze brushed tufts of my hair across my forehead.

The scents, the sounds, the touches of my world faded as I fought to fill my lungs.

My fingers scratched the ground, as if I could hold on to my life, but I was fading. Fast.

"Salome." Grandma staggered to my side. She fell to her knees, hands touching my chest and coming away with blood. "No. No, not my baby." She sobbed. "Nevin! Do something. She gave her life for you."

As my eyes blurred, Gareth shoved his sword through Colton's chest. Colton slumped to the ground, blood seeping into the snow around him. In a way I felt sorry for him. All he'd wanted was to go home.

Then the darkness beckoned, chilled fingers trying to pry my soul from my body.

"Please, do something," Grandma said again.

Nevin glanced at me, his face stricken. "There is nothing

I can do for her. The curse called for a sacrifice. That kind of power cannot succumb to my own."

"Will you not try? It's your fault she's dying."

"Doris, I never meant for this to happen," he said. "I will do what I can." He knelt beside me, cradling my head in his lap. The warmth radiated from his fingers, but it wasn't enough. He released me, peering around at the others.

"Nevin, you have to do more." Gareth dropped down beside him and grabbed my hand. The song of his blood called to mine, but even the ringing of the bells diminished, then died. "I am bound to her."

I heard several gasps fan out. "You're what?"

"She is bound to me. By blood."

Tears leaked from the corners of my eyes, my heartbeat slowed. So tired. The pain felt so far away. Shadows reached out for me, tugging me along, and I drifted after them. So cold.

"Use your power, Nevin, and I will call to her," Gareth said.

A glistening river flowed before me, ghostly figures floating by. I lay in a wooden boat, bobbing back and forth as the currents carried me. Sun touched my cheek. I smiled. I was going home. No more pain. No more tears.

"Salome, don't you give up. Come back to me," Gareth said.

"I don't know how."

"Yes you do."

"But I'm almost there." I stared at the glowing white lights up ahead and the soft music playing me home.

"No. Salome, you cannot leave me. Not today."

The sun disappeared and the boat moved faster. As I sat up, Colton drifted past; his dark gaze met mine. His hand reached over, grabbing hold of my boat. He pulled himself up, rocking me back and forth.

"You cannot escape me. I won't let you go back," he said.

"You chose death. You chose me."

His eyes burned like embers. I screeched, scooting away from him, but he leaned over, and the cold fingers of his anger almost strangled me with fear.

"Salome. You have to come back now."

"I don't know the way. Please, Gareth, I'm scared. Colton's here."

"Remember the first place I found you? When we were in the woods?"

"Yes."

"Go there and I'll find you. I promise I won't let you go."

Colton rocked my boat when he tried to climb in. I struggled to shove him out, the sides swaying and pitching as he grabbed for me.

Out of the corner of my eye I noticed the shore come close and I leaped from the boat. Colton's fingers grazed my leg. Tall pines and spruces littered the banks, a well-worn path beckoning to me. Then a hand tugged me toward the river.

"No, let me go."

"You can't win, Salome." Colton jerked me down.

"Fight, Salome. Get to the place in the woods. You've got to trust me—you've got to try."

With all my strength, I kicked Colton in the chest. He flailed backward, landing in the river. Several figures drifted toward him. Most wore old-fashioned clothing, but there was one I recognized from pictures I'd seen. Grandma's sister, Maude. My eyes welled.

They were helping me, my ancestors who'd died at Kassandra's hand.

"Go, we'll take care of him," she said.

Colton gasped for air, but several hands reached up, tugging him down. Screams vibrated all around me. I clapped a hand over my mouth as he disappeared beneath the currents.

"Tell Doris, I love her," my great aunt said, fading into the river.

Scooting back, I jumped to my feet and dashed into the woods. Death hot on my heels. Branches snagged at my clothing, holes and stumps tried to keep me from going on. But soon I came to familiar territory.

"Gareth?" I shouted.

"Here. Follow my voice. You're almost there."

At last, I stood beside the stream and Gareth stepped forward from the trees. He scooped me up into his arms.

"I've got you, we're going back. Just hold on tight."

"Salome." Grandma and Nevin called my name.

Then a rush of air entered my lungs. I gulped it down like a fish on dry land.

"Gareth?" My eyelids fluttered open, and I was in Grandma's backyard surrounded by the fae.

"I'm right here." He held my hand on one side, while Nevin held the other.

Grandma wiped my hair from my face, bending down to kiss my forehead. "Oh, thank God. I thought we lost you."

I was still alive. Winter hadn't destroyed me. The sky somehow seemed brighter. The wind more musical and gentle.

"I owe you more than words can say, Salome Montgomery. You've done something no one has been able to do for centuries. We will no longer have to look upon winter or ice or feel the cold bite of snow," Nevin said. "A life for a life. I pulled you from the pond as a child, and you've rescued me from my curse. We're now even." Nevin touched my face then stood. "Your friendship has meant a lot to me." He smiled at me and turned to the others. "Now it is time we returned home," he said to his people.

Some of the tiny elves, gnomes, and fauns came forward

and bowed to me. Several said thank you before circling around Nevin.

"I wish you the best, Salome—you too, Doris," Nevin said. "We will not forget your kindness or sacrifice through the years. For the sacrifice you were willing to make in order to save us."

"You're leaving me, too?" I turned toward Gareth, as I fought the rock-sized lump in my throat. I didn't want Nevin to go, but I wasn't sure I could survive without Gareth.

Nevin glanced at me then back to his troupe. "We *all* have to get back. I've spent too much time away from my kingdom. They need us to return. To restore our borders and protect our lands. I will never forget you."

Grandma clutched me to her chest.

"Gareth? No!" I turned to stare at him. Please, oh please let him stay.

He nodded his head, but his eyes shone with sorrow. *"I have to, I'm sorry. I told you that you might get hurt."*

"Yeah, you did."

And so I watched the winter people disappear into the woods, heading for their kingdom of summer.

Grandma sat on the snowy ground and let me cry, until no more tears would come. I'd lost everything. Gareth. My love. My heart.

CHAPTER THIRTY-EIGHT

I sat around the campfire with Grandma, Grandpa, Mom, and her boyfriend Daryl as the downy white flakes came down harder. I checked my marshmallow at the end of my stick.

"I don't think people know what they're missing with these winter bonfires." I grinned. "I mean where else can you get frostbitten while roasting marshmallows?"

Grandpa snorted. "That's because summer campouts have more advertisements and media hype."

Grandma moved her chair closer to mine and reached over to give my hand a squeeze. "Now that everything is behind you, have you decided what you want to do with your life?"

"I thought about pole dancing," I said with a straight face. Mom and Grandma shrieked and I started laughing. "I'm kidding. But seriously, I don't know. Maybe school next term."

"Leave the girl alone, she's got plenty of time to figure it out." Grandpa caught my glance. "Besides, this here fire is for the roasting of food, not the determining of futures."

I rolled my eyes, shifting in my chair. Just then a strong gust of wind blew through the trees and an envelope landed in my lap. My eyes scanned the surroundings, but I didn't see anyone. I propped my stick up on the arm of my chair and ripped open the envelope.

You are cordially invited to the Summer Estate this evening for celebration.

My heart raced out of control. An invitation to join the world of the fair folk. I had read that these were possible, but I thought that was only in books. I looked at Grandma. She smiled and my mom stood and came to my side. I showed them the invitation.

"What are you going to do?" Mom rubbed my shoulder.

"I—I don't know."

"You've got to do what your heart tells you," Grandma said.

My gaze moved from one person to the next. For so long I hadn't been able to do anything without them. They protected me, counseled me, and coddled me. Yet, over the last year I'd learned what freedom was and I realized I needed a life outside of them.

"I love you all." A lump formed in my throat.

Mom squeezed my hand. "And maybe they'll let you come back so we can still see you." She already knew my choice.

I smiled. "What am I going to wear?" I hopped up from the chair.

"Come with me. I've got just the thing." Grandma and Mom ushered me into the house where we went into the faerie room and they scavenged the old dress-up closet.

"This should do." Mom held up a long, light blue, silky gown with an empire waist. The sewn green and blue vines sparkled at the hem of the skirt. She also produced a garland of blue flowers and white slippers.

My heart beat out of control as they helped me change.

My hair hung down my back as they wove the flowers into it. After long minutes, I stood before them, like a bride on her wedding day. Butterflies fluttered in my stomach. My chest ached, hoping I was making the right choice.

"I love you," Mom whispered. "Remember that you are your own person—and you *are* strong."

"Whatever choice you make, child, we will always be here." Grandma hugged me tight.

Grandpa knocked on the door and came in holding a shawl. "Don't want you catching your death out there. Just you be careful, you hear?"

"Thank you."

With one last round of hugs, I raced outside and into the woods. All around me I heard whispers, but this time they didn't scare me. Music tinkled in the air like wind chimes and flutes. I followed the noise, knowing it would lead me where I needed and wanted to be. Bright light encompassed the forest. As I rounded the bend, there was a grand estate where the ruins had once stood.

My footfalls slowed. I gaped at the marble columns and running fountains. Roses grew up the side of the stone exterior, while great white oaks seemed to wall it in.

"She's here," a tiny voice said from beside me.

"She's as beautiful as I remember."

"Come in, we're all waiting for you." I looked down to see a small faerie fluttering by my waist. Her iridescent wings beat like a hummingbird. She reached up and tugged on some strands of my hair, urging me forward.

We stepped down a long corridor of knotted wood. Rose petals blew over the floor tiles. The scent of honey and pine gave me a heady sensation. I inhaled deeply. My palms grew sweaty and no matter how many times I tried to dry them on my gown, they still felt slimy.

At last, we came into the great hall where fantastic creatures lined both sides of the room. There were fauns, with their hairy goat legs and human faces; beautiful elves, with their pointed ears and woodsy appearances. The royal fae, with their blinding looks and statuesque features. And every one of them watched me walk up the path toward a dais, where Nevin sat upon a throne. A crown sat atop his head, made of wood, vines, jewels, and gold. His skin no longer held the winter pallor it once did. Instead, his skin looked as if it'd been dipped in bronze. His once glacial eyes bespoke more of sapphires than ice, his tall frame more filled out, more authoritative.

He smiled, waving me forward.

"Salome Montgomery, we welcome you to the Summer Estate," he said. "We have called you here this night to not only give you thanks for breaking the curse, but to offer you a boon of your choosing."

"A boon?"

Nevin nodded. "We want to gift you. But remember to choose wisely, for you only get one."

Just breathe. I know what I want; it's what I've wanted forever. My heart's desire, the only thing that mattered in life. *Love.* It made me whole, it made me happy, and it called me back from death. And my love had a name.

Someone wise once told me to know what I was choosing.

My eyes flickered to Gareth, who stood beside Nevin. He looked like a bronzed warrior, his sword strapped at his waist. My friend.

"Go on, Salome. Make your choice," he said.

"And what if I choose wrong?"

A smile tugged at his lips. *"You won't. You already know what you want and I guarantee you won't be disappointed."*

"Arrogant much?"

"You like it."

"Have you made your decision, Salome?" Nevin asked, hands crossed at his chest.

"Yes. I choose love. I choose Gareth." My voice quivered as I said his name, but I knew it was true. He'd been my friend first. He never once asked me to do anything other than be safe and know what I was choosing. He'd rescued me when the others would've let me die. He gave me the truth when everyone else around me had lied.

Gareth stepped forward while everyone behind me whispered amongst themselves. In seconds, he had me in his arms.

"Finally," he whispered. He bent down to kiss me when Nevin interrupted.

"In choosing Gareth, Salome, you must realize you give up all rights to your human life and form. By joining with him, you will be like us. Immortal. Do you accept these terms?"

"Yes."

"Then so be it," his voice boomed. "From this day on, Salome will make her home here. She is bound to Gareth by blood and love. We welcome you into our family." Nevin stood and embraced me. "I am happy for you both. And I'm indebted to you for all you have done. You should know that if you'd chosen me, I would have accepted. I owe you my life and my kingdom."

I smiled, touching his cheek. "But I didn't want you to care for me because of a debt."

Nevin leaned down and kissed my forehead. "I know. I wish I could have loved you like you deserved." He released me. "You will always have a place here." He gestured to his home.

Next, he embraced Gareth, who smiled when he whispered in his ear. "Of course, milord," Gareth answered.

"You are free to go now," Nevin said.

Gareth took me by the hand and led me from the estate. Once outside, he clutched me to his chest and bent down. His lips captured mine.

"I love you." His words enveloped my mind. *"Your blood sings to my blood and always has."*

"Not death or life, or pain or love can ever keep us apart," I said. *"I'm yours—forever."*

When he pulled back, I noticed his motorcycle parked off the path.

"Ready to go home?" He brushed my hair from my face.

I laughed. "You knew I would choose you?"

He shook his head. "No, but I damn sure wanted to be prepared in case you did."

"And here I thought you'd bring the Hummer."

He kissed me again, until I was dizzy, then he scooped me in his arms, setting me on the back of the bike. "Nope, I know what you like. A bike under you, the wind in your hair, endless roads, and me in your arms."

"Three out of four ain't bad," I teased, clinging tight to him.

The engine revved to life and we rode away.

"I hope you're ready for forever," he said.

"As long as you're there."

"Always."

And my blood sang, humming a song only we could hear.

ACKNOWLEDGMENTS

First of all I have to thank my editor, Liz Pelletier, for loving this story and the characters and helping bring my world to life. I promise I won't write anymore love "quadrangles." You had to read so many versions of this story and I thank you for pushing me to make it better. And I have to give you squishy hugs for keeping me caffeinated during my big deadline. Thank you for believing in me and in *The Winter People*. I also want to thank Robin Haseltine and Stacy Abrams for your editorial comments and insight. You are fabulous and brilliant. Huge thanks also goes out to Jaime Arnold and to Liz's daughter, Madison, who both read this story in the slush pile and loved it enough to talk about it and help get it in the right hands.

And where would I be without my fabulous critique group YA Fiction Fanatics (YAFF)? You ladies see my stories at their worst and help me to mold them into something so much more. Thank you for being my cheerleaders, my character T-shirt wearing fans, and, above all else, my friends. So here's to you Penny, Barb, Traci, Rachel, Min, Vanessa, Jen, Kelbian, Samantha, Amy, Kelley, Karen, and Carly. Seriously, we all have way too many book boyfriends.

To my day job besties who get to listen to me talk about my stories probably way more than they want to hear about them: Heather, Cholle, Tricia, and Danie. Work would not be nearly as much fun without you. And a big, ginormous shout-out to my day job boss Wendy, who lets me take days off work when deadlines come in, and who also shares in my love for all things vampires, werewolves, and love triangles (I swear we were separated at birth).

And where would I be without my lovely agent, Jenn Mishler, who undoubtedly answers more crazy emails from me than anyone else. Thank you for being there for me and for being the champion of all my stories. You truly do wield a lightsaber and are strong with the Force!

To Mom and Dad for nurturing my love for the written word by buying me books growing up.

To Rachel and Phil, the best siblings a girl could have. Love you. And to my hubby Tim for all your love and support over the years. Thank you for not letting me give up and for always encouraging me along the way.

And to my dear friend, Pam Powers, who believed in me enough to pay for the mailing of my first ever full manuscript request after my husband's plant had closed down, and we were down to our last $10.00. That is something I will NEVER forget.

Finally, I want to thank my Lord and Savior for blessing me and giving me this amazing gift that I can share with others.

LUX BEGINNINGS, COLLECTOR'S EDITION

Featuring Obsidian and Onyx by Jennifer L. Armentrout

OBSIDIAN

There's an alien next door. And with his looming height and eerie green eyes, he's hot...until he opens his mouth. He's infuriating. Arrogant. Stab-worthy. But when a stranger attacks me and Daemon literally freezes time with a wave of his hand, he lights me up with a big fat bulls-eye. Turns out he has a galaxy of enemies wanting to steal his abilities and the only way I'm getting out of this alive is by sticking close to him until my alien mojo fades. If I don't kill him first, that is.

ONYX

Daemon's determined to prove what he feels for me is more than a product of our bizarro alien connection. So I've sworn him off, even though he's running more hot than cold these days. But we've got bigger problems. I've seen someone who shouldn't be alive. And I have to tell Daemon, even though I know he's never going to stop searching until he gets the truth. What happened to his brother? Who betrayed him? And what does the DOD want from them—from me?

LUX CONSEQUENCES, COLLECTOR'S EDITION

Featuring Opal and Origin by Jennifer L. Armentrout

OPAL

After everything, I'm no longer the same Katy. I'm different... And I'm not sure what that will mean in the end. When each step we take in discovering the truth puts us in the path of the secret organization responsible for torturing and testing alien hybrids, the more I realize there is no end to what I'm capable. The death of someone close still lingers, help comes from the most unlikely source, and friends will become the deadliest of enemies, but we won't turn back. Even if the outcome will shatter our worlds forever.

ORIGIN

Daemon will do anything to get Katy back. After the successful but disastrous raid on Mount Weather, he's facing the impossible. Katy is gone. Taken. Everything becomes about finding her. But the most dangerous foe has been there all along, and when the truths are exposed and the lies come crumbling down, which side will Daemon and Katy be standing on? And will they even be together?

THE SOCIAL MEDIA EXPERIMENT

By Cole Gibsen

September 2014

Seventeen-year-old Reagan Fray is popular, Ivy League bound, and her parents are rich enough to buy her whatever she wants. But behind the scenes, Reagan is struggling to hold the fraying threads of her life together. When she's suddenly ostracized from her friends and on the receiving end of the bullying she used to dish out, Reagan fights to reclaim her social status by teaming up with outcast Nolan Letner. But the closer Reagan gets to Nolan, the more she realizes all of her actions have consequences, and her future might be the biggest casualty of all.

THE WARRIOR

A Dante Walker novel by Victoria Scott

Dante is built for battle, Dante's girlfriend, Charlie, is fated to save the world, and Aspen, the girl who feels like a sister, is an ordained soldier. In order to help Charlie and Aspen fulfill their destiny and win the war, Dante must complete liberator training at the Hive, rescue Aspen from hell, and uncover a message hidden on an ancient scroll. The day of reckoning is fast approaching, and to stand victorious, Dante will have to embrace something inside himself he never has before—faith.

PERFECTED

by Kate Jarvik Birch

Ever since the government passed legislation allowing people to be genetically engineered and raised as pets, the rich and powerful can own beautiful girls like sixteen-year-old Ella as companions. But when Ella moves in with her new masters and discovers the glamorous life she's been promised isn't at all what it seems, she's forced to choose between a pampered existence full of gorgeous gowns and veiled threats, or seizing her chance at freedom with the boy she's come to love, risking both of their lives in a daring escape no one will ever forget.

ANOMALY

by Tonya Kuper
November 2014

What if the world isn't what we think?

What if reality is only an illusion?

What if you were one of the few who could control it?

Yeah, Josie Harper didn't believe it, either, until strange things started happening. And when this hot guy tried to kidnap her… Well, that's when things got real. Now Josie's got it bad for a boy who weakens her every time he's near and a world of enemies want to control her gift. She's going to need more than just her wits if she hopes to survive much longer.

PSI ANOTHER DAY

By D.R. Rosensteel

By day, I'm just another high school girl who likes lip gloss. But by night I'm a Psi Fighter—a secret guardian with a decade of training in the Mental Arts. And I go to your school. And I'm about to test those skills in my first battle against evil. Unfortunately, so do the bad guys. My parents' killer has sent his apprentice to infiltrate the school to find me. And everyone is a potential suspect, even irresistible new kid, Egon, and my old nemesis-turned-nice-guy, Mason. Fingers crossed I find the Knight before he finds me…

SCINTILLATE

By Tracy Clark

Cora Sandoval sees colorful light around everyone—except herself. Instead, she glows a brilliant, sparkling silver. As she realizes the danger associated with these strange auras, she is inexplicably drawn to Finn, a gorgeous Irish exchange student who makes her feel safe. Their attraction is instant, magnetic, and primal—but her father disapproves. After Finn is forced to return home to Ireland, Cora follows him. There she meets another silver-haloed person and discovers the meaning of her newfound powers and their role in a conspiracy spanning centuries—one that could change mankind forever…and end her life.

LOVE AND OTHER UNKNOWN VARIABLES

By Shannon Lee Alexander

October 2014

Charlie Hanson has a clear vision of his future. A senior at Brighton School of Mathematics and Science, he knows he'll graduate, go to MIT, and inevitably discover the solutions to the universe's greatest unanswerable problems. But for Charlotte Finch, the future has never seemed very kind. Charlie's future blurs the moment he meets Charlotte, but by the time he learns Charlotte is ill, her gravitational pull on him is too great to overcome. Soon he must choose between the familiar formulas he's always relied on or the girl he's falling for.

THE BOOK OF IVY

By Amy Engel

November 2014

After a brutal nuclear war, the United States was left decimated. A small group of survivors eventually banded together, but fifty years later, peace and control are only maintained by marrying the daughters of the losing side to the sons of the winning group in a yearly ritual. This year, it is Ivy Westfall's turn. Only her bridegroom is no average boy. He is Bishop Lattimer, the president's son. And Ivy's mission is not simply to marry him. Her mission, one she's been preparing for all her life, is to restore the Westfall family to power by killing him.